THE GOLDEN SPHINX

LEX FAULKNER

Boldwood

First published in Great Britain in 2026 by Boldwood Books Ltd.

Cover Design by Colin Thomas

Cover Images: Colin Thomas, Dreamstime and iStock

A CIP catalogue record for this book is available from the British Library.

Paperback ISBN 978-1-80557-911-3

Large Print ISBN 978-1-80557-912-0

Hardback ISBN 978-1-80557-910-6

Trade Paperback ISBN 978-1-80656-172-8

Ebook ISBN 978-1-80557-913-7

Kindle ISBN 978-1-80557-914-4

Audio CD ISBN 978-1-80557-905-2

MP3 CD ISBN 978-1-80557-906-9

Digital audio download ISBN 978-1-80557-909-0

This book is printed on certified sustainable paper. Boldwood Books is dedicated to putting sustainability at the heart of our business. For more information please visit https://www.boldwoodbooks.com/about-us/sustainability/

Boldwood Books Ltd, 23 Bowerdean Street, London, SW6 3TN

www.boldwoodbooks.com

PROLOGUE

KHARGA OASIS, EGYPT – 1906

The gentle evening breeze rustled the cream-coloured tent's canvas as the elderly American readied himself for departure. Inside the tent, it was still warm after a long day of unbroken sunshine, but outside, the temperature was finally beginning to drop now that the sun had gone down and the western skies were changing from bright orange to pale blue. Stroking his short, grey beard, he adjusted his round glasses and surveyed the equipment he was about to pack into a large leather saddlebag to be mounted on his camel. Aside from food, water and a few tools, there was a compass and a sextant, as well as his journal. As had been the case on his previous expedition to these ancient lands, he had written down his thoughts and observations throughout his travels. And upon his return home in a few weeks, he was hoping to collate them all into a thesis that would finally prove all of his doubters wrong. He had spent years on this project and had been met with nothing but derision and ridicule along the way. But that wasn't going to stop him. There was once a time when everyone would have sworn that the Earth was flat and that the Sun moved around the Earth. Everyone had known these things for a fact, right up until hard evidence had proven otherwise. And so it would be with his own theories. All he needed was the evidence.

'Mustafa,' he called over his shoulder.

A few seconds later, his young, eager Bedouin helper appeared through the tent flap.

'Sir?' he said with a heavy accent.

'Is my camel ready?' said the American, still with his back to the tent entrance.

'Yes, sir,' said Mustafa warily. 'But...'

The young man hesitated, unsure if he was about to speak out of turn.

'Speak your mind,' the American said curtly.

'Sir, it's just that...' Mustafa began uncertainly. 'There is a sandstorm approaching. All of the elders say so. You will not survive. Especially not by yourself.'

The American nodded solemnly, standing immobile for a moment before speaking again, this time with a noticeably softer, contemplative tone of voice.

'It matters not,' he said. 'Whatever happens now, my fate is in the hands of the old gods.'

Then he packed up his bag and stepped outside the tent. He strode purposefully towards his recumbent camel, where he attached the saddlebag. Donning his colonial-style tropical hat, he mounted the camel and flicked the reins to make it stand. The creature got to its feet and snorted, and then the American turned to look at Mustafa from his high perch in the saddle.

'Thank you for all you've done to help me get this far,' he said earnestly. 'Perhaps one day, we will meet again.'

Then he spurred the lumbering beast of burden on and, as the moon slowly rose over the open desert, he began his long journey south-west, where he hoped to finally locate what he knew in his heart was out there just waiting for him to find. And when he did, everything would change.

* * *

Cairo, Egypt – Ten days ago

It was a hot, sunny afternoon when the white van drove off the main road and into the parking lot of the huge shopping centre. The centre had been built in a relatively affluent suburb of Cairo five years ago, and since then, it had established itself as the go-to place for not just the immediate area but also for large parts of the Egyptian capital city. With hundreds of shops selling everything from clothing to electronics and homewares, and also serving as a venue for several popular restaurants, it was heaving with people every day of the week, and today was no different.

The van parked near one of the entrances, but for several minutes, nobody stepped out. The vehicle's windows were heavily tinted, making it impossible to see who was inside, but anyone watching closely would have noticed the van rocking gently a number of times, betraying the fact that someone was moving around inside it. When the driver's side door eventually opened, a large, bearded man wearing sunglasses and a baseball cap pulled low in front of his face stepped out. He took a moment to look around, making sure that the van was in full view of the nearest CCTV cameras mounted on the shopping centre's exterior walls. He needed what was about to happen to be captured and broadcast as widely as possible.

Adjusting his baseball cap, he then started walking away from the van and away from the entrance, lighting a cigarette as he went. When he had reached the road on the opposite side of the parking lot, he stopped and reached inside one of his trouser pockets for a small, black electronic device. At that moment, a silver sedan pulled up next to him, its engine idling as the man turned to face the shopping centre with the device in his hands. Taking a moment to savour the significance and the inevitable consequences of what was about to happen, he then pressed a button on the device, and in that same instant, the white van was engulfed in a massive explosion that ripped through the crowds and flung shredded pieces of the van in all directions as the boom of the detonation reverberated across the entire suburb, and a black, menacing cloud of smoke rose from the scene. Amid screams of horror and hundreds of car alarms going off at the same time, the man turned around, calmly opened the door to the waiting sedan and got into the passenger seat. Moments later, the car sped off and disappeared into the heavy traffic.

1

THE CATSKILL MOUNTAINS, NEW YORK STATE

It was just before noon on a bright and beautiful day in the sparsely populated, forest-covered Catskills when Ethan Frost finished his meal at the local diner in Tannersville, where he had decided to stop in about an hour earlier. In his mid-thirties with an athletic, muscular build and an easy confidence, his facial features were sharp and defined with a square jawline, piercing blue eyes, and dark hair that was styled in a tight and practical crew cut that he had kept since leaving the military. His skin was smooth but bore the signs of time spent outside under the sun, and he had stubble that had appeared since leaving New York City the night before. Wearing maroon cargo trousers, hiking boots, a dark green shirt with the sleeves rolled up, and a charcoal baseball cap, he was looking out of the window onto Main Street when the waitress swung by his table with the bill.

'Going hunting?' She smiled as she placed the bill on the table in front of him.

Ethan turned from the window and looked up at her. She was a pretty blonde in her early twenties, and she had one of those girl-next-door looks that somehow fit perfectly into the general vibe of the small town. She was wearing a uniform consisting of a sky blue, short-sleeved shirt and a dark navy skirt, and her mid-length hair was done up in a ponytail. Attached to the front of her shirt was a plastic name tag that read 'Holly'.

'How did you know?' Ethan said, giving her a casual smile.

'I don't know.' Holly shrugged. 'You have that look about you. You're from the city, right?'

'Right again.' Ethan nodded, now genuinely impressed with her powers of observation. 'But to tell you the truth, I'm mostly just here for the scenery. I love it up here.'

'I'd like to live in New York,' said Holly as she glanced somewhat wistfully out of the window. 'Maybe one day.'

'Don't rush it,' Ethan offered, gesturing out of the window. 'This is a really special place you folks have here.'

'I guess,' Holly said, tilting her head slightly to one side as if pondering it. 'I mean, nothing much ever happens here.'

A faint look of dejection moved across her face, and Ethan picked up the sense that here was a small-town girl dreaming of the big city.

'I know.' He smiled amicably. 'That's part of why I like this place so much. I reckon you might miss it if you moved away. But that's just me.'

'Maybe it's true what they say,' Holly said, brightening again. 'The grass isn't always greener on the other side, right?'

'Wise words,' Ethan said as he pulled his wallet from his back pocket and extracted a credit card. 'Hey, thanks for the meal. It was delicious.'

'I'll tell the chef,' Holly said with a nod and a smile as she scanned his card with her portable card reader. 'Have a good day.'

'Thanks a lot,' said Ethan. 'You too.'

Ethan exited the diner and climbed in behind the wheel of

his grey compact SUV. He turned to make sure that his hunting rifle was still in its leather slip bag on the back seat, and then he drove out of town for the wooded hills a couple of miles away towards the south-west. The warm midday sun now shone from a clear blue sky onto the rolling hills of Greene County, and the air was fresh and clean. Located in wooded upstate New York, some ten miles west of the Hudson River and four miles east of the main town of Hunter, Tannersville was sometimes called the Painted Village in the Sky on account of the many brightly coloured storefronts that lined Main Street, giving the place a cheerful and somewhat bohemian look. Sitting at an elevation of roughly two thousand feet, it was about a two-hour drive from Manhattan, and Ethan was a regular visitor to what was a quaint and laid-back destination for many New Yorkers looking to get away from the frenzied pace of the Big Apple. Most people came for the relaxed, wholesome atmosphere and the friendly vibe of the shops, or for the outdoor activities that included hiking, biking and kayaking, but Ethan's purpose was somewhat different.

As a subrange of the Appalachian Mountains that dominate the landscape throughout much of the north-eastern United States, the Catskills came into existence through a geological process that began some four hundred million years ago. However, unlike the Appalachians, the Catskills were not formed by the folding of tectonic plates. They came to be when an enormous prehistoric river delta deposited huge amounts of sand, silt and mud, which then compacted over millions of years to become sandstone. Due to tectonic uplift forces, the terrain was then slowly raised thousands of feet, after which rivers carved and sculpted the mountain range over the course of yet more eons. Finally, during the last ice age, massive glaciers several miles thick scoured the landscape, leaving their indelible mark on the mountain range. The result was an enormous area of natural beauty that was dominated by rounded peaks reaching close to four thousand feet. They were criss-crossed by valleys, rivers and streams, and they were dotted with waterfalls, lakes, cliffs, escarpments and caves. And all of it was covered in dense and mainly deciduous forest, making for a truly spectacular place to spend time.

Soon after setting out from Main Street and driving through the outskirts of the sleepy town, Ethan found himself on a familiar winding road through the forest. He could already sense the terrain beginning to rise ahead of him, and after a few minutes, he took a right onto Mink Hollow Drive, which wound its way deeper into the forest and up into a valley with a small river called Roaring Kill. Another couple of minutes later, he reached the end of the road, where a trailhead marked the beginning of a path leading up into the wilderness. The Catskills cover roughly six thousand square miles, and there was no one else around as Ethan parked the car, got out, slipped his hunting rifle from its case, and slung it over his shoulder.

The weight of the modified weapon on his back was a familiar and welcome feeling. He had spent most of his adult life handling a multitude of different types of firearms, ranging from pistols to assault rifles and other semi-automatic weapons to sniper rifles and grenade launchers. Aside from peak physical fitness, weapon-handling skills and marksmanship were at the core of any special forces soldier's skill set, and as a former elite Delta Force operator, Ethan had those in spades.

He performed a quick inspection of the hunting rifle and its modified scope, and then he locked the car, adjusted his baseball cap, and began making his way up the trail and into the woods. The sunlight was filtering down through the canopy above, and the only sounds were of birds chirping and a gentle rustling of the light breeze through the trees overhead. After about fifteen minutes, he left the trail and headed north-east up the side of a mountain and through a curving gorge towards the peak of Sugarloaf Mountain. Before long, he might as well have been a hundred miles from the nearest road or town. There were no signs of people anywhere, and if somebody had told him that no one else had set foot where he was walking for a couple of centuries, he would have believed it.

The leaf-covered forest floor crunched gently as he pushed forward through the gorge, and as he advanced, his eyes were scanning ahead for movement or shapes of animals through the low foliage. High and to his left was a rocky escarpment that could be glimpsed through the trees, and he began curving up towards it for a better view of the terrain. Soon, he was walking along just a few metres from the almost vertical cliff face, rarely taking his eyes off the forest floor below as he kept looking out for what he had come here to find.

Eventually, he reached a steep section where a tree had fallen over and was now partly blocking his way. As he was about to move along its trunk to get around the huge bundle of thick roots that were sticking up into the air, he suddenly spotted a deer some fifty metres away. It was a buck that looked like it might be three or four years old, and Ethan froze and then slowly brought up the hunting rifle to allow him to watch it through the scope. The male deer looked healthy and strong, and its antlers bore signs of having been rubbed vigorously against trees. They had now almost been cleared of their furry velvet, and their tips looked as sharp as knives as Ethan examined them through the high-powered rifle scope. He was about to draw back the bolt when the buck's head suddenly jerked up at the dry crack of a distant rifle shot echoing across the mountain range. Evidently, Ethan was not the only person out here looking for deer. The buck stood still like a statue for a few seconds, but then it moved skittishly away behind a couple of tree trunks where Ethan could no longer see it. He lowered his weapon and proceeded carefully past the fallen tree while making sure to be as quiet as possible and stay out of sight of his quarry.

Although he hardly ever spoke about it, and never to anyone who wasn't a fellow operator, there were deep and strange parallels between stalking deer in the Catskills and going after Taliban fighters in the barren mountains of northern Afghanistan, or hunting the deranged religious fundamentalists of Boko Haram in the deserts of Mali. The targets were both living, breathing creatures, and a single bullet could end them in an instant. However, unlike animals, the terrorists that he and his Delta buddies had been hunting when deployed on missions overseas were a clear and present danger to US national security, and he had never regretted being part of that organisation or eliminating those threats wherever and whenever it was required.

Ethan's military career had begun almost twenty years earlier, but it had not happened in the US. At least, not initially. Although he was born in New York City, he spent much of his childhood and adolescence in London. His American father, Robert Frost, was a wealthy industrialist and financier, and he was the founder and CEO of Frost Industries, which grew to become a global conglomerate of companies in the heavy industry, high-tech, and defence sectors. His English mother, Isabella, was an archaeologist and lecturer at King's College London, specialising in ancient Greek and Near Eastern studies.

Growing up, Ethan often felt pulled in two directions. Part of him wanted to please his father and eventually take over the family business, and his academic performance was more than strong enough for him to do so. Another part was irresistibly drawn to Isabella's passion for history and archaeology, and as a boy on their country estate in the South of England, he would often explore the outdoors and pretend to be on an adventure looking for buried treasure in some exotic and far-off land. When he became older, he had been allowed on several occasions to join his mother on archaeological digs in places like Jordan, Egypt and Turkey, and he would never forget those magical days with her under the baking sun, uncovering ancient artefacts from forgotten temples and mysterious burial sites in the desert.

He completed a bachelor's degree in history at University College London at the age of twenty-one, but then realised that he was not ready for a master's degree and a PhD, which would be required for him to undertake a serious academic career. Instead, his father, Robert, arranged for him to be shoehorned into a position at Frost Industries HQ in New York City. It was going to be a learning-on-the-job, fast-track to a management position, but shortly before he was due to start, Ethan got cold feet. Somehow, he felt that there was a lot more for him to experience before committing to a life in the corporate world, from which he would most likely struggle to extricate himself once he began.

Unable to decide on a career path, he decided to join the army. At twenty-two, much to his father's frustration, he signed up for the Potential Royal Marines Course alongside roughly sixty other recruits. The gruelling thirty-six-week selection course, among the longest in the world, took place at the Commando Training Centre Royal Marines near the town of Lympstone in Devon in the south of England. Completing the course, he felt for the first time that he was truly standing on his own two feet, and he had also discovered that he possessed a natural aptitude for soldiering. He was physically extremely fit, bright and sharp in his decision-making, even under extreme stress, and his weapon-handling abilities were at the very top of that year's recruit intake. Once he had received his Royal Marines green beret, he was sent to 40 Commando, where he served for almost three years, honing his skills as a war fighter in a number of hot zones across the globe.

Eventually, however, at the age of twenty-six, he decided to leave the UK behind and return to his country of birth. But he wasn't ready to leave military life behind, and on account of his dual US and UK citizenship, he was able to join the US military. After the obligatory selection course, he joined the 82nd Airborne at Fort Bragg in the rolling, wooded hills of central North Carolina. In many ways, this was a continuation of the types of roles he had filled in the Royal Marines, but it didn't take long for him to begin eyeing the somewhat reclusive, insular, and highly secretive facility inside the huge Fort Bragg complex where the very best special forces operators in the US Army were based. It was the compound of the elite 1st Special Forces Operational Detachment – Delta, commonly known as Delta Force but referred to by its members simply as 'the Unit'. Officially, it didn't exist, and its operators effectively disappeared from the world when they joined, training and working in absolute secrecy, which allowed the US government complete deniability.

Delta had been the brainchild of US Army Major Charlie Beckwith, a bear of a man with a square jaw, bushy eyebrows, a hot temper, and a good-natured glint in his eye. In 1962, after serving as an exchange officer with the Special Air Service in Hereford, England, he pushed for a similar unit to be created in the United States. After initially meeting resistance to the idea, in 1977, after several years of trying, and following a surge in international terrorism most often originating in the Middle East, he finally managed to convince the top brass that the US Army needed a similarly trained and equipped small direct-action counterterrorism force. Its sole purpose was to be deployed at a moment's notice to eliminate threats to civilians, either during hostage situations or as part of an ongoing effort to hit their training camps overseas before they could travel to the West and cause chaos and death.

The new unit was to be organised similarly to the SAS, with several squadrons, each with small troops of about sixteen men. Each of these was broken into flexible teams led by exceptionally talented non-commissioned officers in the same informal but highly professional fashion as was the case in the SAS. Beckwith also insisted that rather than having an armchair general come up with the details of how to execute a mission, the operators who would actually end up putting their own lives on the line were to be given the authority to plan their own missions. This was a crucial difference from how the regular army operated, but it would ultimately result in much higher success rates during direct-action operations. In 1978, the first batch of potential recruits was identified and brought in. From the original cohort of 163 applicants, only twelve made it through the gruelling selection process to become the first Delta Force operators. This equated to a seven per cent pass rate, which would later prove to be the highest in Delta's history.

At twenty-eight years old, after a couple of years in the 82nd, Ethan completed the Delta Force selection process at Fort Bragg, and then he spent six months on the Operator Training Course. By design, this was an extremely demanding program and included specialised training in marksmanship, CQB or close-quarters battle, hostage rescue, breaching operations, covert tradecraft and clandestine operations skills, as well as advanced medical training. Initially, being a young man with an impressive amount of experience already under his belt, Ethan had been somewhat cocky after completing the selection course and joining the Unit. However, on the first day of CQB, he had received a harsh but ultimately welcome reality check.

'Try to keep up,' the sergeant major had told him flatly as they stacked up on the door to the kill house.

'Yes, sir,' Ethan had replied, but in his mind, he had thought to himself. *Dude, do you know how good I am?*

When the live-fire explosive breach happened, the older team guys rushed inside in a tight, clean sweep and cleared the room so fast that Ethan barely had time to enter before they were gone and had pressed further through the smoke into the building's interior, where they fired short, rapid bursts at dummy targets without hitting a single one of the civilians. That was when it finally dawned on him just how good the existing members of the Unit really were. These guys, most of whom were quiet and unassuming, were on a whole different level of skill and experience from what he had seen before in his career.

He then spent the next several months simply attempting to follow the sergeant major's advice, just trying to keep up. As humbling as that day had been, it had also allowed him to get a glimpse of what was possible and to eventually raise his own game significantly. And soon enough, he became as skilled a warrior as he could be and one of the best in his squadron. Ethan spent the next six years as part of the Unit, ending up with the rank of master sergeant and being very happy to remain a non-commissioned officer. Leadership in itself had never attracted him beyond its basic usefulness during deployments, but unlike a lot of people in the army, he never had any ambition to be the one to shout at people and tell them what to do.

During his time with Delta, he was deployed in a dozen

different hotspots in countries like Libya, Mali, Iraq and Syria, where he and his fellow operators conducted countless raids against terrorist training camps and high-value targets, often in sprawling urban areas of those unstable and chaotic countries. And despite the violence and the carnage and the occasional loss of one of his brothers in arms, he cherished every minute of it. The camaraderie, the brotherhood, the constant striving for improvement in every aspect of his performance, and the clear and unambiguous purpose of it all.

Being a Tier 1 operator was like a drug, and there was no better natural high than being part of an elite team of the very best special forces soldiers in the world, sitting in a chopper, racing low over exotic terrains towards a target where a mission had to be carried out. Combat was the pinnacle of the sensation of being alive, probably because death was never more than a split second away. It was an exciting, intoxicating, and unrivalled rush that could not be found anywhere in civilian life, and Ethan now sometimes found himself missing those days.

However, the loss of team guys on missions was the nature of the beast, and there was a wall at Fort Bragg with the names of the many fallen Delta members since the Unit's inception. That wall now carried many names. Too many. And it was one of those losses that had eventually sown the seeds of Ethan's departure from the Unit. A top-notch operator from Utah by the name of Frank Olsen. He and Ethan had gone through selection together, and the two of them had become good friends. Frank had lost his life to an IED placed inside a Boko Haram safehouse in northern Niger near the border with Libya. Somehow, the terrorists had gotten wind of the hit on the compound, and as one of the assaulters, Frank had been first through the door. The only saving grace was that the blast had killed him instantly, but for the first time ever, Ethan had begun to think seriously about a future after Delta. Maybe there was more to life than being in the military. Deep down, he had always known this. Everybody at the Unit knew, but no one ever talked about it openly, despite it being a fact of life in the special operations community. However, the truth was that every time he strapped on his tactical gear and weapons and jumped into the back of a chopper, the chance of him one day not coming home alive went up by a few percentage points. On top of that, it was simply the case that there was an effective age limit for Tier 1 operators, so everyone needed to have an exit strategy at the back of their minds.

The decision had been a long time coming, and he had wrestled with it for weeks before finally making it. When it finally settled comfortably in his mind, the conclusion was clear. If he wanted more out of life than being a war fighter, he had to quit now. Nevertheless, walking into the squadron commander's office and declaring his desire not only to leave the Unit but the army altogether had been one of the hardest things he had ever done. As he stood to attention in front of Colonel Cooper's desk and announced his intention to hang up his weapons and leave, part of him wanted to turn around and run out of the building. But that part had been the immature Ethan who joined the Royal Marines more than a decade earlier. Delta had been everything he had ever wanted as a much younger man, but at the age of thirty-six, he knew that he probably only had a couple of years left of being at the top of his game. And as much as he hated to admit it, he could either watch himself gradually fade and eventually be replaced by new, younger and hungrier team guys, or he could leave on a high and have a shot at opening a new chapter of his life.

Colonel Cooper had eyed him silently for a long moment, but to his credit, he had then simply nodded and accepted the resignation. The colonel had no doubt seen this sort of thing before. Delta operators were some of the smartest, toughest, and most skilled soldiers the country had ever produced, and every day, they invested one hundred per cent of their time and energy into getting even better. For as long as they were in the Unit, it was their family and their entire focus, and they poured their whole lives into it. But once that fuel tank ran empty and it was time to leave, there was no point in arguing. When it was over, it was over. On his way out, Cooper gave him a sharp salute and a firm handshake, and then Ethan turned around, stepped out of the office and out of the army.

Immediately after leaving, Ethan had applied for a place at Yale University in New Haven, a couple of hours' drive north of New York City, where he then began his studies for a master's degree in history and archaeology. His mother's influence had never left him, and he had always devoured books about the history of the various countries he had been sent to during his time with Delta. There was usually plenty of downtime between missions at the various forward operating bases he had been deployed to, and he still vividly remembered celebrating his thirty-fifth birthday in an FOB in Mali and reading about the ancient city of Timbuktu just a few hundred kilometres away. He remembered feeling the pull of that place, as if it was calling for him to go there and start an archaeological dig. Maybe it was in his blood, or maybe his mother's fascination with ancient civilisations had simply rubbed off on him. Whatever it was, there was no doubt in his mind that he wanted to follow in her footsteps. He just had to find a way to do it.

Leveraging his bachelor's degree in history from University College London, he completed his master's at Yale in the standard two years, and during his time there, he struck up a friendship with one of his professors. A gregarious but somewhat

eccentric man by the name of Tobias Goodwin, whose enthusiasm for the ancient world was genuinely infectious. And it
rekindled the raw fascination with history that his mother had
first sparked in him. Every once in a while, Ethan would
approach Professor Goodwin after a lecture and ask him to
expand on something he had talked about, and the depth of the
professor's knowledge was simply astounding. There was very
little about ancient civilisations that Goodwin didn't know, and
like many in his field, he seemed to have a particular penchant
for ancient Egypt.

Graduation day should have been a happy occasion, and his
parents were flying over from their beach house in West
Hampton on Long Island. However, it soon turned into the
darkest day of Ethan's life. The investigators were never able to
identify precisely what had gone wrong, but their helicopter, one
of several belonging to Frost Industries, had gone down in Long
Island Sound roughly fifteen miles from New Haven. Robert and
Isabella Frost were both killed in the accident, along with the
pilot. Weather conditions had been good, and the accident
remained a mystery. Air accident investigators from the National
Transportation Safety Board concluded that the most likely
cause of the accident was a sudden and catastrophic failure of
the tail rotor assembly, but there was insufficient evidence to
determine precisely which components might have failed or
why. Despite an internal investigation personally overseen by
Frost Industries' CEO Victor Stanhope, no further clues were
ever uncovered. A few days after the tragic event, the bodies of
Ethan's parents were recovered from the cold waters of Long
Island Sound and laid to rest at the Sleepy Hollow Cemetery
near the Hudson River, not far from where his father grew up.
Ethan remembered that occasion as being dark, gloomy and

oppressive, yet when he saw some of the photos a while later, he could see that it had been a clear, sunny day.

The week that followed had been a foggy blur, and Ethan had felt numb with grief and shock at what had happened. Being an only child, he had struggled with the sudden realisation that he was now essentially alone in the world. As the only surviving member of the family, he was left with a huge inheritance, including fifty-one per cent of Frost Industries, in which he became a non-executive board member as stipulated in his father's will. The will had been presented to him and his attorney during a meeting with Victor Stanhope and a team of four corporate lawyers who had flanked the CEO as he laid out its terms and the various required legal papers. It had been a sombre and surreal affair, but the overriding memory of that day had been of him leaving the meeting and realising that he didn't care one bit about the money. It meant nothing to him. Life had to be about more than that.

Stepping out of Frost Tower in Midtown Manhattan after the meeting and walking through Central Park on what had been a beautiful, sunny day, Ethan had felt numb. After a couple of hours in the park, he realised that he had kept on walking because he simply didn't know where he needed to go. His life had been turned upside down, and he could see no clear direction in which to head. The next day, he had packed a holdall, booked a plane ticket to Nepal, grabbed his passport and wallet, and left the country. He spent the next four months travelling the world and visiting a laundry list of ancient sites that his mother had talked about and that he had always wanted to see for himself. And every time he arrived at a historic location and marvelled at the seemingly timeless structures, temples and monuments, he would think of her and her work as a historian and archaeologist, and it would be clear to him that his future lay there. He just wasn't sure how to make it happen yet.

When he arrived back in New York City, taking up residence in a large, newly refurbished penthouse at the top of Frost Tower, he felt very different from when he had left. It soon became obvious that his sojourn in those far-off and exotic places had been cathartic. He felt as if the dark clouds bearing down on him had finally begun to lift, and that he was now able to raise his gaze and look towards a future horizon that wasn't dominated by the events of the past. Within weeks, he had settled into a routine of strenuous exercise, healthy food that he cooked in his own kitchen, and regular trips up to the Catskills, where he would spend time out in the wilderness by himself. It was the best therapy he could have hoped for, and now, several months after returning to the US, he had found himself again. Physically, he was in the best shape he had been in since leaving Delta, and he felt focused, calm and confident in himself and his future, whatever it might bring.

Treading gently on the leaf-covered ground beneath his boots, Ethan moved cautiously along the fallen tree trunk and then leaned out from behind the huge bundle of dry roots. The deer appeared calm once again, and it was grazing on small bundles of white flowers that had sprouted up through the mossy forest floor. He brought up the hunting rifle once again and used one of the thick roots to stabilise his aim. The buck raised its head to look around, and it was now perfectly framed in Ethan's scope as he placed the cross hairs right where the animal's heart would be. He steadied his breathing, drew in a slow breath, exhaled half of it, held it, and squeezed the trigger. When it broke, there was no crack from a supersonic bullet leaving the muzzle. Neither was there any recoil from the rifle slamming into his shoulder nor a flash from the hot, combusted gases leaving the barrel. There was only a faint click as the modified scope took a high-definition picture of the elegant buck. At the sudden sound, the animal turned its head and looked straight at him. After a few seconds of indecision, it then suddenly turned and bounded into the trees, where it soon disappeared behind bushes and thick tree trunks.

Ethan lowered the weapon, reached for the phone in his back pocket, and opened the photo app. It was a perfect shot, and he felt good about being able to add it to his collection, knowing that with any luck, the buck would have many more days of life here in the tranquil and beautiful Catskills. He slipped the phone back into his pocket, slung the rifle over his shoulder, and glanced up at the sun. It was now mid-afternoon, and he knew that he was roughly half a mile north of the forest plot he had bought a couple of months earlier. It was a more or less square plot about six acres in size, or roughly 150 metres on all four sides. In the middle of it, he had cleared the trees and begun building a log cabin for himself. He had decided to only allow himself basic hand tools like a drawknife for debarking logs, winches, pulleys and timber tongs for moving them, hammers, chisels and mallets, as well as a large T-handle auger for drilling holes. No motorised equipment was allowed, even if that would have sped up the process by many weeks. This was going to be a project completed only by hand if at all possible.

Arriving at the sunlit clearing, he unlocked the door to the small wooden shed that had been brought in, and then he carried his various tools outside. He ate some of the food he had brought in his small backpack, and then he rolled up his sleeves and set to work. He cut up several of the straight, thirty-foot-long and almost three-foot-wide tree trunks that he had felled a few days earlier, and then he used the slightly curved dual-handle drawknife to strip off the bark to reveal the light-coloured wood underneath. It was hard work, and each trunk took almost an hour. Once that was done, he used a metal chain winch to lift the trunks up into position on top of a set of similar trunks that would eventually become a complete wall. It was slow going, and he was drenched in sweat by the end of it, but he felt good. Once this cabin was completed, it would be the product solely of his own efforts.

Wiping sweat from his brow with the back of his hand and unscrewing the cap on a bottle of water, he took a big gulp and allowed himself a moment to glance around the plot and imagine what it would look like once it was all finished. With a bit of luck, this would end up as a pretty idyllic little place, complete with a nice interior and a log fire. The sort of place he might even want to bring a girlfriend. But of course, he would need to find one first. As a good-looking, confident and athletic guy with a lot of money, he had never been short of options, and there had been plenty of fun along the way. But he had yet to find someone that he could picture himself spending the rest of his life with.

Perhaps someday, he thought to himself.

As he stood there contemplating what the forest clearing might end up looking like, he heard the distant and instantly recognisable sound of a helicopter approaching across the rolling hills. The thudding of rotor blades and the whine of the turbofan engines gradually grew louder, and by the time he could see the chopper through the foliage, he knew what he was looking at. Ethan's brow furrowed as he recognised the metallic navy blue livery of Frost Industries, and as the helicopter swung around and came down into the clearing, creating a whirlwind of leaves and dust as it did so, he could see that there was no one inside the passenger cabin. The only person in the aircraft was the pilot, and Ethan recognised him immediately. His name was

Mitch Kazinsky, and he was a former army pilot. Originally from Florida, he had served with the elite 160th Special Operations Aviation Regiment out of Fort Campbell, Kentucky. This helicopter aviation unit, often referred to simply as 'SOAR', specialised in covert, high-risk missions such as direct-action raids, counterterrorism, and infiltration and exfiltration of special forces from active combat zones. They call themselves 'The Night Stalkers', since they most often conduct operations during night-time, and Ethan knew them to be some of the best pilots in the world. When they weren't on active missions, they spent all day practising their flying skills, and they could manoeuvre their aircraft in ways that seemed almost unnatural, even in pitch-black and using only night-vision goggles.

Ethan had seen the extraordinary skills first-hand on numerous occasions during dicey insertions and extractions in dense urban areas, often under fire, onboard either the MH-60M Black Hawk or the much smaller and more nimble MH-6M Little Bird, which pilots like Chief Warrant Officer Kazinsky could land on a dime with his eyes closed. People like him could fly under a bridge at full speed with mere inches to spare above the rotor dome or put a bird down in a courtyard so small that the tips of the rotor blades almost touched the walls. They seemed to have a sixth sense for the position and orientation of their aircraft, and they didn't so much climb up into the cockpit of a chopper. Rather, they strapped the aircraft on like they did their flight suits. To Kazinsky, the helicopter was an extension of his body, and he was able to move, turn and twist it with incredible speed and control, and practically everything he did in that cockpit was instinctive.

Ethan had rated Kazinsky as one of the very best of the Night Stalker regiment, and he had been glad to help him get a job with Frost Industries after Mitch had decided to transition into civilian life several months ago. There had been an opening for a pilot to fly the corporate executives to and from meetings all over the country, and after Ethan had set up an interview for him, Kazinsky had got the job.

The former SOAR pilot swung the chopper around and came down fast towards the floor of the clearing. To anyone not familiar with what a helicopter could do in the hands of a true expert aviator, it might have looked risky and even unsafe. However, Ethan watched calmly as Mitch twisted the control stick to increase the collective, which then caused the chopper to slow down rapidly in the middle of its descent, after which it touched down on the grass as gently as a feather falling to the ground. Mitch killed the turbofan engines, and within seconds, their whine began to abate as the rotors slowly spun down.

Ethan waited a few seconds, after which he emptied his water bottle and approached the chopper. When Mitch opened the door to the cockpit, he shot Ethan a grin and gave a quick wave. He then jumped down onto the mossy ground and walked towards Ethan. Mitch was of medium height and build with short mid-brown hair and a neat side parting. He was wearing dark navy trousers and a white shirt carrying the Frost Industries logo, and he moved with an easy swagger that some might mistake for arrogance, but which Ethan knew simply to be natural self-confidence.

'Hey, Mitch!' Ethan called out as the two men approached each other. 'What's going on?'

'I've been asked to come and get you,' Mitch replied. 'Mr Stanhope needs you back in the city ASAP. They tried to call, but you didn't pick up.'

'I left my phone in the car,' said Ethan. 'I don't want to be plugged in to the rest of the world out here.'

'I understand, sir,' said Mitch. 'I wish I could do that.'

'And Mitch,' said Ethan, placing a friendly hand on the pilot's shoulder. 'Stop it with the "sir", alright? We're old buddies. No need for that stuff.'

'Right,' Mitch said with a self-conscious grin. 'Sorry. I guess old habits die hard.'

'What's this all about anyway?' said Ethan.

'That's way above my pay grade.' Mitch shrugged and smiled. 'I'm just here to bring you back. But it sounded kind of urgent.'

'My car's still back at the trailhead,' Ethan said.

'No problem,' said Mitch. 'We'll have it brought back to New York for you. Ready to go?'

'Sure,' Ethan said somewhat reluctantly as he glanced back at the portable shed. 'Just let me lock up here.'

A couple of minutes later, the gleaming corporate helicopter was racing south-east over wooded hills towards the Big Apple. Sitting in the chopper and feeling the vibrations while listening to the engine noise and the faint thudding of the rotor blades slicing through the air outside, all Ethan had to do was close his eyes, and he was immediately transported back in time to the days when he and fellow team members from the Unit were flying towards a target in the back of one of the modified Black Hawk helicopters whose rotors were virtually silent. There was probably never going to come a time when part of him wouldn't still miss those days.

'Never gets old, does it?' said Mitch, glancing at Ethan from the pilot's seat with a knowing grin.

'Nope,' said Ethan, looking over at him with a wry smile. 'Never does.'

By the time the chopper approached Manhattan, the sun was setting behind a dark weather front to the west. He looked out over the city, the skyscrapers of Midtown and Lower Manhattan rising up like two forests made of steel and glass. New York was a brash, loud and frantic place full of irrepressible energy. To visitors, it was a crazy and often overwhelming place full of extremes. To Ethan, it was now home, and returning here was like slipping into a set of comfortable clothes. The vibe and variety of the city that never sleeps suited him well despite his appreciation for time alone in the woods. New York always had something new to offer, and there was a unique feel to the place that he had felt nowhere else on his travels. He would often head down to his private vehicle garage on the lower of the two basement levels under Frost Tower, where he would then fire up his motorcycle and go for a drive through the city. No two rides were ever the same, and there was always something new to look at.

When the chopper's wheels finally touched down on the large helipad on top of Frost Tower, the sun was setting. Ethan thanked Mitch for the ride with a quick salute and jogged to a small glass structure by the helipad's edge, which housed two elevators going down into the building below. One was for the executives of Frost Industries, and the other was for his private use. He placed his hand on the sensor plate, and the security system instantly recognised his fingerprints and opened the elevator doors. He stepped inside, and the doors slid shut behind him. The control panel had only four buttons. One for the rooftop, one for his penthouse on the thirty-second floor, one for the executive level two floors down on thirty, and one for the lobby on the ground floor. He pressed the button for his own floor, and seconds later, he stepped inside the huge, luxurious penthouse that took up half of the thirty-second floor and overlooked Central Park towards the north and Midtown and Queens in the distance towards the east.

The penthouse had large floor-to-ceiling windows, dark wood flooring and off-white walls. It had been configured exactly according to Ethan's specifications when it had been refurbished, and its central hub was a large open-plan kitchen and dining area with spectacular wrap-around views out over the city. It also contained a fifty-foot swimming pool, a private gym and a big living room adjacent to the dining area next to the master bedroom. The other half of the thirty-second floor was currently unoccupied, but he had toyed with the idea of having a shooting range built there. So far, he hadn't come up with any better ideas for what to do with all that space, but he liked the idea of maintaining the weapons skills that had been at the centre of such a large and important part of his life.

Fifteen minutes later, he had showered and changed into a sharp navy suit and a white shirt. He decided to dispense with the tie and headed back to the elevator. Hitting the button for the executive level, he waited a few seconds as it descended, and he soon found himself walking along the corridor to the board-room where, several months ago now, an ashen-faced Victor Stanhope had explained the details of his father's will.

When he opened the door and stepped inside now, Ethan saw that the long boardroom table was flanked on both sides by company executives, many of whom he had never seen before. Outside the windows, darkness had fallen, and the sea of city lights stretched away towards the east. Sitting at the head of the table at the far end of the room was Victor Stanhope. A tall and remarkably fit man for his age, he was now in his early seventies with thinning grey hair and a strong jawline that was turning faintly jowly, giving him a somewhat stern appearance. Although he had slight bags under his eyes after too many nights working late at Frost Tower, his eyes were clear and blue underneath thick, greying eyebrows, and his somewhat severe face combined with his sharp pinstriped suit and silver tie gave him an air of natural authority that had no doubt helped him remain the unquestioned man at the helm of Frost Industries for close to three decades now. When he spotted Ethan enter, he immediately got to his feet and came to greet him with a smile while everyone else in the room remained silent.

'Ethan,' he said in his usual calm rumble as he shook Ethan's hand warmly. 'Thank you for coming. I'm sorry to have cut your trip to the mountains short. I know how much you enjoy your time up there.'

'Not a problem,' said Ethan. 'What's going on?'

'Please,' said Stanhope affably, gesturing to the only empty chair in the room, placed next to his own. 'Take a seat, son. I'll explain.'

As Ethan sat down, he realised that he had never taken part in what appeared to be a full board meeting before, and he felt decidedly self-conscious and out of place among the perfectly groomed, middle-aged career types who all sat upright with their attention firmly directed towards Stanhope and himself.

'Let me get straight to it,' said Stanhope, flipping open an expensive-looking black leather folder lying on the table in front of him, containing a single sheet of paper with a few typed-up notes. 'As everyone here knows, Frost Industries, thanks to the tireless work and frankly unsurpassed business acumen of Robert Frost, God rest his soul, has grown into one of the foremost high-tech and heavy-industry conglomerates this great country of ours has ever seen. Our subsidiaries represent the cutting edge in everything from satellite communications, weapons, defence technology and hardware, aviation, computing and artificial intelligence. We play a crucial role in the military-industrial complex and, therefore, also in our nation's security. For this reason, any threat to our technological lead or to our intellectual property rights represents a threat not only to us as a company but to the national security of the United States.'

Stanhope looked around the room, and Ethan watched the serious faces of the executives nod sombrely as they sat around the boardroom table.

'Now, as I know some of you are already aware,' he continued, 'over the past few weeks, we have observed indications in the stock market that certain Chinese corporate entities have attempted to use various shell companies to acquire stock in some of our publicly traded subsidiaries, particularly in the defence industry. More specifically, I'm talking about Frost Drone Technologies, Frost Cyber, and Frost Space Launch Systems, where we currently maintain a minority stake while the rest of the stock is traded on the markets. And as you all know, these companies control dozens of patents for a whole host of advanced future technologies that have yet to make it into this nation's military hardware arsenal. Patents that are worth tens of billions of dollars. As far as we can tell, this clandestine effort to acquire our intellectual property has been slow and methodical, but we believe that Chinese ownership is now approaching fifty per cent in at least one of those three subsidiaries.'

Several of the executives exchanged concerned glances as Stanhope went on.

'Now,' he said gravely. 'I don't need to tell anyone here how serious this could turn out to be. If the Chinese end up acquiring a majority stake in one or more of our companies, we can pretty much take it for granted that all of that technology will eventually make its way to China's defence industry. For obvious reasons, this would be a major problem for us as a company and for US national security, which is why I, along with a handful of you here today, have put together a plan of action to eliminate this threat. What I propose is that we use Frost Industries' capital, of which there is plenty, to buy back enough stock in those subsidiaries to prevent the Chinese from ever acquiring a majority stake. This will obviously be costly and require a restructuring of our balance sheet, but it will secure our company against what is frankly ill-disguised theft on the part of the Chinese Communist Party.'

The executives nodded sagely as they signalled their agreement to Stanhope's plan, and then the CEO turned to Ethan.

'Now, Ethan,' he said. 'Since you own fifty-one per cent of Frost Industries, it goes without saying that we will need your agreement for this plan to go ahead. I can't emphasise enough how important this could turn out to be. If we don't act now, your father's life's work could be under threat.'

'Right.' Ethan nodded, leaning forward in his chair, folding his hands and placing them on the table in front of him as he considered the proposal. 'I understand. It sounds like we don't have much of a choice.'

'That's right,' said Stanhope. 'So, what do you say?'

'It sounds like the right thing to do,' said Ethan with a faint nod. 'My father would never have allowed this company's technology to fall into the hands of the Chinese. We need to protect what we have here. Let's make it happen.'

'Great,' said Stanhope, and as Ethan glanced at him, he saw a hint of relief move briefly across the CEO's face. 'I'm glad to hear it. I'll arrange for the paperwork to be produced as soon as this meeting is over. It'll be with you later this evening.'

'Alright,' said Ethan. 'I'll sign it and get it back to you ASAP.'

'Perfect.' Stanhope smiled, placing a hand on Ethan's shoulder. 'I knew I could count on you. Your father would be proud.'

Stanhope sat up straight and turned to face the rest of the board, whose members were all looking right at him.

'Right,' he said. 'That concludes this meeting. Thank you all for coming. Now, I want you to go back to your departments and prepare for what we need to do here. There is still a lot of groundwork in legal and finance that needs to happen before we can go ahead with this, so let's get moving.'

Realising that another late night at the office awaited them, the executives immediately picked up their folders and stacks of paper and moved towards the door. As they left, Ethan reflected on how the machinations of the boardroom were a world away from his log cabin project in the Catskills, and it was clearer to him than ever where he would rather spend his time. Once the log cabin was completed, he would pick an evening in front of a roaring fireplace with a bottle of wine and a good history book over this place any day of the week. He pushed out his chair and stood when Stanhope gripped his elbow gently and leaned closer.

'I'd like a quick word, if that's alright,' said the CEO.

'Sure,' Ethan said, stopping and letting the last executives file out of the room.

'Tell me,' said Stanhope, once the door had been closed. 'How's it going up there in the Catskills? Making progress with that cabin of yours?'

'I'm getting there,' said Ethan. 'I'm not in a rush. It's about the journey, not the destination.'

'You sound exactly like your mother.' Stanhope smiled with a hint of melancholy. 'She was an amazing woman. And your father was an incredible man. Not a day goes by that I don't think about him. But this great company is his legacy, and every day it keeps his memory alive. Anyway, tell me, how are you doing, son?'

'I'm good,' said Ethan. 'Finally got my head straight after what happened. I'm looking for a way to put my degree from Yale to some use. It feels like the right thing to do.'

'Well, listen,' said Stanhope, his voice dropping another octave. 'I can see that academic pursuits have gotten their claws into you, but just remember this. There's always going to be a place here for you at the company. Anything you want. Just say the word. We'd be happy to have you.'

'Thanks,' said Ethan. 'I'll remember that.'

* * *

After the board meeting, Ethan returned to his penthouse, stripped out of his business suit, donned his dark navy running kit, and strapped his phone into the tight pouch on his left bicep so that he could listen to some music through his earbuds as he ran. He devoured an energy bar, downed half a glass of orange juice, and left the apartment. After taking the elevator down to the lobby, he exited Frost Tower onto 6th Avenue and walked north. It was now close to 9 p.m., but the city seemed just as busy now as it did during the day. Yellow cabs were moving swiftly along the streets, distant police sirens wailed and horns honked occasionally, and throngs of people were walking along the side-walks, either making their way home after working late at the office or heading out for dinner at the city's countless eateries.

Reaching the end of 6th Avenue, he crossed over West 59th Street and entered Central Park along Center Drive, where he began his run. Despite the many streetlights inside the park, most of it was murky at this time of night, and with the dark clouds overhead now looking like they might be threatening a downpour, there were only a few people around on the smaller footpaths. Most runners in Central Park picked either the six-mile road loop around the entire park or the shorter four-mile bridleway loop, but with some fifty-eight miles of footpaths, Central Park offered an almost unlimited number of different route permutations. Ethan set off past The Pond and immedi-ately peeled off to the right along a small footpath leading past a massive, grey piece of bedrock that protruded up through the ground.

Many New Yorkers imagine that Central Park is the result of a large, open natural area that was eventually surrounded by the urban sprawl of Manhattan. But that is not the case. The entire park used to be built up with roads and houses covering almost all of it until the park was created. The whole area was expropriated, and all existing housing was torn down to make way for the new communal area for the city's residents. When the park's design was first commissioned in the mid-1800s, most of the proposals included many large and intricately designed spaces with hundreds of flower beds, neat rows of exotic trees, narrow footpaths, and a plethora of pavilions akin to Greek and Roman temples, making the whole thing reminiscent of a botanical garden or European royal gardens. Some of the proposed designs even included parade grounds for soldiers to march on.

However, when the final design was chosen in 1856, the planners settled on a much more natural layout that was more akin to wild forests, ponds and open meadows. Another important part of the design was that it included wide avenues, mid-sized bridleways and smaller footpaths curving and weaving their way through the park. Importantly, the network of paths was designed to minimise congestion by routing each path either over or under other paths. For this reason, there are dozens of bridges and underpasses in the undulating and heavily wooded park, and this design feature resulted in some unfortunate and unintended consequences, namely crime. Late at night, bridge underpasses in relatively secluded areas of the park are prime spots for muggings, and as it turned out, Ethan was about to become part of such an incident.

He had made his way up past Sheep Meadow and The Lake and then around The Reservoir in the northern half of the park before looping back down south past the Metropolitan Museum, which sits inside the park grounds. He then swung past the iconic Bethesda Terrace and picked a small path south, which would take him back down to West 59th Street. At that point, he had been running for about thirty-five minutes, and he was planning to go for another lap when the footpath curved left and down through Willowdell Arch, which was surrounded by bedrock and bushes. During the day, the arch appeared as a quaint and attractive Victorian brick structure that allowed for pedestrians and runners to move under the busy East Drive thoroughfare above. However, during the night, it was a narrow, barely lit tunnel that was practically begging for criminals to use as a launchpad for their nefarious activities.

When Ethan saw the two men in their twenties leaning against one of the walls down in the underpass, his sixth sense immediately began to tingle. There was something about the way they carried themselves that told him they weren't just hanging out down there for the fun of it. The taller of the two was slightly lanky and smoking a cigarette. His mid-length, blond hair was swept back, and he was wearing white trainers, jeans and a brown leather jacket. The other, who wore black jeans and a dark hoodie, was shorter and stockier, and his hair was shaved down to a buzz cut.

As soon as they saw Ethan approaching in his running gear, it was clear that they thought they had identified an easy target, because they both pushed off the wall and began moving lazily out to stand in the middle of the underpass, effectively blocking Ethan's way. The lanky blond man took a final pull on his cigarette and tossed it aside as his companion squared up next to him with his feet slightly apart and his chest pushed out. Ethan could read their body language a mile away, and he almost turned around to avoid trouble before deciding that he simply wasn't in the mood for backing down today. And besides, if he turned tail and left, these two guys would almost certainly attempt the same manoeuvre on someone else a few minutes later. Someone who might not be as capable of defending themselves the way he was.

As he entered the underpass, he gradually slowed down and came to a stop about three metres from the two men. They eyed him for a moment before the lanky one grinned and spoke up with practised confidence in his voice.

'Alright, dude,' he said calmly in what sounded to Ethan like a Queens accent. 'You know the drill. Hand over that phone and your money.'

Ethan stood with his hands on his hips, panting slightly from his run, while he looked the two men up and down. Then he gave a slight shake of the head and pressed his lips together before looking the blond man straight in the eye.

'You don't want to do this,' he said evenly. 'Trust me. You've got the wrong guy.'

'Oh, I don't think so,' said the stocky companion, taking a step forward and reaching into his hoodie's large front pocket for a switchblade, which he unfolded with a flourish.

Ethan shifted his gaze to him and tilted his head slightly to one side.

'I'm telling you, buddy,' he said. 'You're making a mistake. Walk away now.'

'Hey, I ain't your buddy,' replied the stocky one with a sudden flash of anger. 'Now hand over the goddamn phone. We ain't got all night.'

'Alright, fine,' Ethan sighed, taking a slow step forward, rolling his shoulders once, and flexing his fingers while he calmly placed his feet slightly apart. 'But you're gonna have to come and take it from me yourself.'

The two young men glanced briefly at each other and exchanged bemused grins.

'Dude, is this guy for real?' said the stocky one before returning his cold gaze to Ethan. 'There are two of us and one of you. Are you stupid or something?'

'Let's just get this over with and get the hell out of here,' said the lanky blond, clenching his right fist and glancing over his shoulder towards the other end of the underpass. 'That phone's worth about a grand.'

'Closer to two grand, actually,' said Ethan as he stood immobile and watched the two men whose body movements exuded overconfidence.

'Alright, enough of this shit,' said the stocky one, moving forward decisively while holding the knife in his right hand and reaching for Ethan's phone with his left.

Ethan waited until the man had gripped the phone with his fingertips and was in the process of pulling it out of the fabric sleeve holding it in place on his left bicep. Then he made his move. As fast as a viper strike, he reached up with his right hand, gripped the man's wrist, and twisted it violently over and down while pulling it towards himself. The man cried out in pain, and a split second later, Ethan slammed the heel of his left hand up under his jaw as hard as he could. The man's knees buckled immediately, and as he slumped to the ground and the knife clattered away from him, the back of his head smacked into the asphalt with a nasty crack. Then he lay still.

To his credit, the lanky blond man didn't run away despite his friend being neutralised with such speed and ferocity. Seeing his partner in crime fall to the ground, he produced his own switchblade and threw himself forward, lunging at Ethan's head with a wide, scything swipe. However, as soon as Ethan saw the man reach into the pocket of his leather jacket, he moved inside his reach, gripped the front of his jacket with his left hand, and pulled him hard towards himself. Then he brought up his right elbow in a quick, short strike across his chest that found its mark perfectly. It connected cleanly with the blond man's jaw, instantly knocking him out and sending his blond hair flailing out into the air as his body went limp and folded onto the ground like a bag of wet laundry. The switchblade spun away through the air and bounced off the brick wall before falling onto the ground with a metallic clank. Ethan stood over the two unconscious men for a moment. Then he shook his head.

'I tried to tell you,' he sighed, barely out of breath.

He dragged the two limp bodies out of the underpass to the nearest lamp post, where he then pulled the belts from their jeans. He used them to tie up their hands while they lay passed out on the grass, and he briefly considered calling the NYPD to come and pick them up. However, the last thing he felt like doing right now was waiting fifteen minutes for a squad car to show up and then spending the next half hour explaining what had happened and possibly being charged with vigilantism. Instead, he went for a simpler option. He used one of the switchblades to slice open and yank off the dim-witted duo's jeans. He threw the lacerated remains deep into some bushes nearby, leaving the two trouserless men to somehow make it back to Queens once they woke up. With any luck, the experience would deter them from ever coming back to this spot. Then he left the underpass, broke into a jog and returned to Frost Tower.

2

The next morning, Ethan awoke to the faint tapping of raindrops on his thirty-second-floor bedroom windows. By the time he had showered, shaved, and had breakfast, the rain had stopped, and shafts of sunlight were piercing the thick, grey cloud layer hanging low over the Big Apple. He made himself another cup of strong black coffee and crossed from the open-plan kitchen to the living area, where a large, comfortable, cream-coloured sofa sat in front of a huge flatscreen TV hanging on a wall. On the adjacent wall were two large, framed black-and-white prints of photographs. One was a shot from a drone hovering about fifty metres above his Catskills plot. The other was of a prize male deer with near-perfect antlers looking straight into the camera from about fifty metres away. Ethan slumped down onto the sofa, leaned back, and took a sip of his coffee.

'Eve,' he said. 'Please turn on the TV.'

'TV on,' said a smooth and pleasant female voice.

The voice belonged to the advanced artificial general intelligence unit developed by Frost Industries' AGI subsidiary, Frost Neural Networks. Eve's name was an acronym for 'Enhanced

Virtual Entity', and it had been incorporated into the AV, security, power and lighting systems of the entire penthouse. The TV came on and began displaying a sports channel showing a baseball game.

'NY-News 24,' he said.

'Certainly,' said Eve, and the TV immediately switched to the local New York news channel, where an attractive female news anchor was reading today's top stories off the teleprompter.

The platinum blonde, whose name was Courtney Reed, was talking about the upcoming race for New York mayor, which had turned into an unseemly and fairly embarrassing mud-slinging contest between two middle-aged former local lawmakers who seemed to spend their time attacking the other candidate's character rather than presenting their vision for the city's future. Ethan took another sip of coffee as the blonde anchor gave an almost imperceptible shake of the head and proceeded to the next segment.

'In global news,' said Reed, 'Egyptian authorities now say that the shopping centre blast that killed dozens of people, including two New Yorkers, just over a week ago, was likely carried out by a separatist movement from the Sinai Peninsula. Militant groups in that part of the country have sought independence from Cairo for many decades. According to Egyptian military intelligence, based on evidence found at the site of the blast, one of these groups was behind the recent terrorist attack, although no one has yet claimed responsibility.'

Ethan was familiar with several of the groups being referred to, and they had carried out a number of bombings in the past, although it had now been years since the last attack. Up on the TV, the camera angle changed, and Reed swivelled slightly in her chair to once again face her audience.

'And finally,' she said with a well-practised, troubled expression on her face, 'we're just now getting shocking news that a murder has been committed on the campus of Yale University in New Haven, Connecticut.'

Ethan lowered his coffee cup and furrowed his brow, astounded by the news of a murder having taken place at his alma mater.

'Eve,' he said. 'Volume up 5.'

'Volume up 5,' Eve repeated, and the anchor's voice now filled the living space of the penthouse.

'The victim,' continued Reed, 'has been identified as Tobias Goodwin.'

Ethan instantly felt an icy chill run down his spine, and his mouth fell slightly open as he placed the coffee cup on the marble and brass coffee table in front of him.

'What the hell,' he breathed as he stared up at the TV.

'A former professor at the university,' the anchor went on, 'Professor Goodwin had recently retired from teaching at the university's Near Eastern Languages and Civilizations department. He had then been appointed to a position at the Yale Peabody Natural History Museum, which is located on the university campus. Our reporter, Claire Rodriguez, is there now. Claire, what more can you tell us?'

The image switched to a split-screen view with the anchor on the left and Rodriguez on the right, standing in front of a large building that looked more like a red-brick cathedral than anything else, but which Ethan immediately recognised as the Peabody Museum.

'Yes, I am here on the Yale campus,' said the slightly built Rodriguez, 'where it's fair to say that the university and the museum have been shaken to the core by this tragic event. We have very little information to go on at this time, but just a few minutes ago, I spoke to Detective Jim Callahan from New Haven

PD's Major Crimes Unit. He has been assigned as the lead investigator, and here's what he had to say.'

The anchor and the reporter disappeared to be replaced by a full-screen view of Detective Callahan speaking to Rodriguez just out of shot on the right. The stocky, serious-looking detective appeared to be in his late forties. His hair was short and dark with streaks of grey at the sides, and it had thinned and receded significantly at his temples. He had a round face with a broad, lined forehead, and his slightly narrowed eyes were dark brown and framed by black eyebrows, giving him a focused and somewhat stern demeanour. There were faint bags under his eyes that looked like they were a permanent feature, and he was wearing a white shirt and a dark navy suit and tie.

'What can you tell us about what happened here?' Rodriguez's voice could be heard off camera, her voice rich with intrigue and expectation.

As she spoke, a small image was overlaid in the corner of the screen. It showed a photo that had been lifted from the Peabody Museum's website, and which Ethan was more than familiar with. It showed Tobias Goodwin standing in some sort of desert environment with an active archaeological dig site in the background. He was tall, lean and wearing khaki linen trousers and a white shirt with the sleeves rolled up. On his head was a beige, wide-brimmed hat, and on his lips was the same quiet, lopsided smile that Ethan had come to know so well. When he saw the professor's face, his heart sank into his stomach. It was really true. Tobias was dead. Putting his head in his hands, Ethan rubbed his face and shook his head. Then he looked back up at the TV.

'Well, Claire,' said Detective Callahan gravely, shifting uncomfortably on his feet as if he wasn't used to being in front of a camera, 'we received a call from the Peabody director's office at around 7 a.m. this morning and dispatched a unit immediately. I arrived a couple of hours ago and took over from the Yale campus police, who had been handling the situation up until then. We believe the victim was killed with a knife somewhere around 1 a.m. last night, but his body was only discovered by staff early this morning.'

'Any idea who might have perpetrated this terrible crime?' said Rodriguez.

'Not at this time,' said Callahan, looking mildly distracted by someone seemingly talking to him off to his left, 'but we'll obviously be going over all the available footage from the security cameras both in the building and in the wider campus area. We're hopeful this will help us in our investigation.'

'I certainly hope so,' said Rodriguez. 'Thank you for your time. Back to you, Courtney.'

Ethan continued staring at the big screen on the wall in front of him as the news transitioned to business and weather, but he heard nothing. His mind was a jumble of confusion and sadness. Who in the world would want to kill Tobias Goodwin, and why? Ethan knew him as a gentle soul with an insatiable appetite for his subject matter of ancient civilisations, and for teaching young students everything he knew. Ethan had never seen him become even mildly irritated with anyone, despite regularly being asked very basic questions by students who really should know better. But it was as if he took every opportunity to impart his knowledge to anyone who would listen, and he had been an important resource for Ethan when he had been writing his final dissertation for his master's degree. But Goodwin had been more than that. He had been a friend, and now he was gone. Murdered.

Ethan sat immobile for several minutes, images of his past interactions with the professor flashing through his mind.

Countless fascinating lectures as well as many private conversations between the two of them, during which time Goodwin had been more than happy to offer guidance and ideas to Ethan. He clenched his jaw as the familiar and unwelcome feeling of loss welled up in his mind, but it was mixed with an urge not to simply sit by and watch it unfold on TV. He felt the need to do something about it. He put down his coffee cup and got up from the sofa. Then he went to his bedroom and put on a pair of dark blue jeans, a white T-shirt and a black leather jacket. As he did so, he addressed the AI again.

'Eve,' he said. 'I'm going to New Haven right now. What's the traffic situation?'

'There are currently no incidents reported on that route,' replied Eve instantly. 'Expected travel time should be less than ninety minutes.'

Ethan left the penthouse and took the elevator down to the basement level. Once there, he used a biometric access system to enter his private garage, where he walked up to one of his motorbikes. It was a thirty-year-old Harley-Davidson with gleaming chrome and thick tyres that he had bought a couple of years earlier, and when he swung his leg over the bike, sat down, and pushed the starter button, its 121-horsepower Milwaukee-Eight engine immediately sprang to life and settled into a throaty rumble. Driving up the long ramp, he proceeded past the security station and out onto 6th Avenue. He then headed west to the Hudson River, where he made a right turn. A few minutes later, he had left Manhattan and was racing north along Interstate 95 towards New Haven.

* * *

When Ethan arrived in New Haven, the sun was climbing higher in the sky and shining down through patchy clouds onto the coastal city. Its tree-lined streets, characterful buildings, and numerous small, independent boutiques and cafés gave it a unique vibe that was a world away from the frenetic pace of Manhattan. Ethan drove from the city centre up into the sprawling Yale University campus and parked his bike on Whitney Avenue directly across from the Peabody Museum. As he did so, he glanced over to the corner of Sachem Street and the Yale Council on Archaeological Studies building, where Goodwin had his office. Ethan had visited on a number of occasions to quiz the professor about this or that topic over cups of strong, black coffee, and he had enjoyed every minute of it. Now, he was struck by how pleasant and peaceful it all looked, despite the fact that this was now a murder scene.

When he took off his black helmet, he could see that there were two New Haven Police Department cruisers parked across the sidewalk in front of the main entrance, and several groups of people were huddled in small groups outside. Two of them wore the distinctive blue trousers and white shirts of the Yale University Police Department, while others wore the dark all-navy uniform of the NHPD. Another group included a sturdily built middle-aged man whom Ethan instantly recognised from the news report as Detective Jim Callahan. He placed his helmet on the seat of the motorbike, unzipped his leather jacket, and ran his fingers through his short hair. Then he crossed the street and headed for the detective.

When Ethan reached Callahan, he appeared to have just finished speaking to two uniformed officers who turned and left, and the detective was now in the process of typing something on his phone when Ethan called out to him.

'Detective Callahan?' he said as he approached, and Callahan turned to face him while lowering the phone slightly.

'Yeah,' said Callahan, looking mildly distracted. 'Who are you? Can I help you?'

'My name is Ethan,' said Ethan, putting out a hand in greeting. 'I knew Tobias Goodwin. I saw the news, and I wanted to come up here from New York to see if I could offer any assistance.'

'Right,' said Callahan dubiously, giving Ethan's hand a quick, firm squeeze. 'And how would you do that?'

'Well,' said Ethan. 'I figured that if you could tell me exactly what you think happened here, then maybe I could help provide some information about Goodwin that might prove useful somehow.'

Callahan glanced back down at his phone, typed a quick message, and looked back up at Ethan.

'Look, buddy,' he said. 'We don't tend to share any details of our investigations with people, even if they are just trying to help.'

'I understand,' said Ethan. 'But I felt like I knew him pretty well, so maybe there's something I can assist with.'

'I'm sorry, who are you again?' said Callahan, now looking somewhat harangued.

'My name is Ethan Frost,' said Ethan. 'I was a student of Goodwin's until a few months ago.'

'Wait,' said Callahan, seemingly taking a moment to study Ethan's face. 'Frost? As in, Frost Industries? Your father was Robert Frost?'

'That's right,' said Ethan, giving a small nod.

'Shit, I'm sorry,' said Callahan, giving a faint shake of the head as his demeanour appeared to change completely. 'I'm from New Haven PD's Major Crimes Unit, and I was involved in the initial investigation of the crash that killed your parents. And I am real sorry for your loss.'

'Thanks,' said Ethan, unprepared for the sudden reminder of the death of his parents.

'We were brought in early,' continued Callahan, 'to try to determine if there was any evidence of foul play. But as I'm sure you know, we never found any. Most of it was handled by Frost Industries.'

'I know,' said Ethan. 'A one-in-a-million fault in the tail rotor assembly, apparently.'

'I can only imagine,' said Callahan, shaking his head. 'It must have been awful for you.'

'Yeah,' Ethan sighed. 'It was tough. Real tough.'

'Alright, listen,' said Callahan, lowering his head slightly as he looked intently at Ethan. 'I'm gonna cut you a break here. I really respected your dad for his charity work. My son Benjamin suffered from leukaemia when he was about five, and one of your father's charities partly funds the hospital where he got his treatment. It made a huge difference to us as a family. Benji might not be alive if it wasn't for that funding.'

'Well, I'm glad to hear the money was well spent,' said Ethan. 'How's he doing now?'

'Benji?' said Callahan. 'He's doing good. It's been tough for him, but we think we've beaten this thing. The doctors say he will make a full recovery. So we'll always be grateful to your father.'

'I'm very happy for you,' said Ethan, an empathetic smile spreading across his lips. 'That's really amazing.'

'Wouldn't have happened without your dad,' said Callahan. 'Anyway, I'll tell you what I know about what happened here. Just keep it to yourself, alright?'

'Thank you, sir,' said Ethan. 'I really appreciate it.'

'Call me Jim,' said Callahan. 'Right, so here's what we know so far. Professor Goodwin was found by one of the caretakers early this morning. Apparently, he had been working late in his office last night, but he was found dead down on the basement level, where I understand the museum keeps its collections of artefacts. Severe wounds. It was pretty bad, I'm sorry to say.'

Ethan clenched his jaw as his imagination produced the image of Goodwin lying dead in a pool of his own blood in the basement storerooms that he knew so well. They contained collections of thousands of items from the ancient civilisations of the Middle East, particularly from ancient Egypt and Mesopotamia, and Ethan had joined Goodwin down there a few times for a walk and talk when the professor was retrieving or returning an artefact he was writing about.

'Any idea when it happened?' said Ethan, having to make an effort to stay level-headed.

'Preliminary forensics results point to somewhere between midnight and 2 a.m.,' said Callahan. 'But we should be able to pin it down more precisely soon.'

'What about motive?' said Ethan. 'Why the hell would anyone kill Tobias?'

'We've got nothing yet,' said Callahan. 'It might take a while to establish one. We first need to collate all the information we've gathered from interviews. But you're right. It's difficult to see why anybody would want him dead.'

'How about security cameras?' said Ethan, glancing over at the Peabody Museum building. 'There must be a whole bunch of them in there.'

'One of our officers is retrieving the recordings as we speak,' said Callahan. 'With a bit of luck, one of those cameras will have caught the murder.'

Ethan grimaced at the thought and gave a small shake of the head.

'Sorry,' said Callahan. 'I know how that sounds, but I just want to get the bastard who did this.'

'I'm right there with you,' said Ethan. 'Trust me. That's why I'm here. Would you be able to share the security camera footage with me when you've gone over it?'

'Well,' said Callahan reluctantly. 'I pride myself on being a by-the-book kinda guy, but in this case, I'll make an exception. If you give me your email address, I'll send them to you in an encrypted format once we've finished with them.'

Ethan reached into the inside pocket of his leather jacket and extracted one of his Frost Industries business cards. He handed it to Callahan, who pocketed it and gave a brief nod.

'Alright,' he said. 'I should be able to get them to you in a few hours. How does that sound?'

'That would be great,' said Ethan. 'Thanks a lot.'

As Ethan spoke, his gaze drifted over to the corner of Whitney Avenue and Sachem Street, beyond which lay the elegant, three-storey Edwardian dual-purpose building that housed the Yale Council on Archaeological Studies. Standing on the sidewalk in front of it was a young, petite woman wearing a pair of dark blue jeans and a plain beige jumper with sleeves reaching down over her hands. Her slightly wavy, auburn hair reached down below her shoulders, and she had an attractive face with high cheekbones, full lips, and what from a distance appeared to be intense blue eyes. Standing there in conversation with a female officer from the NHPD, she was hugging herself with her shoulders slightly raised as if she was feeling cold. As Ethan took a moment to study her, he felt vaguely as if he might have seen her before, but he couldn't put his finger on exactly when or where.

'Who's she?' he said, jerking his head in the direction of the woman.

'She's Goodwin's assistant,' said Callahan, following Ethan's gaze. 'Sophia Lockwood. She arrived just after the caretaker had found the body. She was in a bit of a state. Obviously very shocked and disturbed, as anyone would be in her shoes.'

'Right,' said Ethan. 'I think I might have met her briefly a long time ago. Did you speak to her yet?'

'Yes.' Callahan nodded. 'She wasn't able to provide any useful information at this time, but we'll want to interview her in more detail at some point over the next few days.'

'Do you mind if I talk to her?' said Ethan. 'I think she might remember me.'

'Sure.' Callahan shrugged. 'Of course. It's a free country. My colleague is just taking her details.'

'Right,' said Ethan, turning back to face Callahan and presenting his hand once more. 'Thank you very much for your time, detective. I know you're busy here, so I really appreciate it.'

'Don't worry about it,' said Callahan, taking Ethan's hand and giving it another firm squeeze. 'It's the least I could do. I'll send over those recordings later today.'

'Great,' said Ethan. 'Thanks again.'

'You take care now,' said Callahan, and then he began walking back towards one of the civilian cars parked near the entrance to the museum while holding his phone up to his right ear.

* * *

When Ethan caught up with Sophia Lockwood, she had ended her talk to the female officer, turned back towards the building housing the Council on Archaeological Studies, and was walking swiftly along the footpath towards the front door.

'Sophia?' he called as he jogged across the street towards her.

At the sound of her name being called, Sophia stopped and turned around to see him coming towards her. Her face looked puzzled and slightly anxious for a moment, but then it suddenly changed as she realised who he was. As he slowed down and walked up to her, a faint, cautious smile spread across her lips.

'Sophia,' he said as he approached her and held out his hand. 'I'm Ethan. I think we met about a year ago.'

'Oh, hi,' she said, tilting her head slightly to one side. 'Ethan Frost, right? Professor Goodwin mentioned you a few times, too.'

'Right,' said Ethan. 'Sorry to bother you. I was wondering if we could talk.'

Studying her otherwise pretty face more closely, he noticed her slightly bloodshot and sunken eyes, and it was clear that she had been crying.

'Well, sure,' said Sophia cheerlessly after a brief moment of hesitation. 'I've been speaking to the police all morning, so it's nice to see a familiar face. Do you want to come inside for some coffee?'

'That sounds really good,' said Ethan, glancing up at the handsome building next to them and gesturing towards the entrance at the top of a set of steps. 'Lead the way.'

He followed Sophia inside and up the stairs to the second floor, where she showed him into her office. It was modest and styled in a traditional and functional manner with a varnished wooden desk and shelving behind it. The single window looked out over the street towards the Peabody Museum, and there was a small green plant with a white flower on the windowsill.

'This is me,' she said with a shrug and a wan smile that failed to conquer the sadness that had etched itself into her face.

'It's small, but it's mine,' she went on as the two of them stepped inside. 'And I get to spend my time in here with no one bothering me. Although right now, I wish Professor Goodwin would walk through that door.'

She glanced towards the door to the corridor outside with a forlorn and wistful look, and Ethan could see that she was about to choke up again.

'I'm sure it must have been awful for you to come to work today,' said Ethan. 'I was pretty shocked myself. I saw it on the news this morning and came straight up here from New York.'

'You live there?' said Sophia.

'Yeah,' said Ethan. 'Midtown.'

'Nice,' said Sophia bleakly, gazing vacantly out of the window. 'I like New York. Anyway, please, sit down.'

She gestured to a chair opposite her desk, and as he took a seat, she walked to her office chair and sat down.

'Listen,' said Ethan, leaning forward with his hands clasped together as he looked across the desk at her. 'I want to do whatever I can to help find out exactly what happened here. I got to know Tobias pretty well over the past few years, although I haven't spoken to him for about four months. But this whole thing is a mystery to me. Did someone come here to kill him, or was he just in the wrong place at the wrong time? It just doesn't make any sense. Is there anything you can tell me that might explain what happened here?'

'No,' said Sophia, shaking her head with a pained expression on her face. 'I can't imagine why anyone would want to hurt him. I feel like the world is going crazy.'

'Did he say or do anything unusual over the past few weeks or months?' asked Ethan.

'I don't think so,' said Sophia, looking up and to one side as she appeared to try to remember, before returning her gaze to

Ethan. 'I'm not sure if you know, but he retired from teaching about two months ago, and he was then given the job of Keeper Emeritus at the museum. It's basically kind of an honorary title for someone who still wants to be involved. He had a few official responsibilities, but with free access to the artefact collections, he could devote most of his time to his research.'

'And the collection is pretty huge, if I remember correctly, right?' said Ethan.

'Yeah, you can say that again,' Sophia said, her eyebrows rising as she spoke. 'I'm pretty sure that the Babylonian and the Egyptian collections alone contain at least fifty thousand individual artefacts. It's enormous. So, Professor Goodwin was never short on things to look into. He was like a kid in a candy store.'

'I know,' said Ethan, giving a faint nod and pressing his lips together as he recollected some of his memories with the professor. 'I joined him down in the storage rooms under the museum a few times. Do you know what he has been working on lately?'

'Kind of,' said Sophia. 'As I am sure you know, his area of expertise was the ancient Near East, but he always had a special place in his heart for ancient Egypt, or to be more precise, predynastic Egypt.'

'Predynastic.' Ethan nodded. 'So, before the ancient dynasties, right?'

'That's right,' said Sophia. 'From the time around 6000 BCE to 3100 BCE. When most people think of ancient Egypt, they think of the Pyramids of Giza and the Sphinx and the tomb of Tutankhamun, but the Egyptian civilisation stretches back much, much further than that. Goodwin always said that the famous Pyramids, which are only about 4,500 years old, get all the attention because they are bigger than anything else. And it's true. The Egyptian civilisation is so much older than the Pyramids. They were built thousands of years after the first advanced civilisations emerged there. Now, sure, the Pyramids are pretty old. They date back to some of the first Old Kingdom dynasties, around 2600 to 2100 BCE. But like I said, the history of Egypt goes back so much further than that. And I think Professor Goodwin was becoming convinced that the first Egyptian civilisations existed much earlier than most historians and Egyptologists are prepared to even consider.'

'What do you mean?' said Ethan.

'Well, he was a bit cagey about it,' said Sophia, 'but he mentioned something about Yale's first expeditions to Egypt in the early twentieth century. Around 1911, if I remember correctly. But then he also mentioned an Egyptologist by the name of Howard Templeton, who was affiliated with Yale's Council on Archaeological Studies, and who travelled to Abydos several years before that. In fact, I think it's fair to say that Professor Goodwin became somewhat obsessed with Templeton, and I believe he was planning a trip to Abydos himself.'

'Abydos,' said Ethan pensively. 'That's pretty far to the south along the Nile, right?'

'That's right,' said Sophia. 'Not quite as far south as Luxor, but it was definitely part of what later became Upper Egypt.'

'The southern part of Egypt,' said Ethan, referencing a mental map of the ancient country where Upper Egypt was the area along the southern half of the Nile, and Lower Egypt was the northern half where the massive river meets the Nile Delta and the Mediterranean.

'That's right,' said Sophia. 'For several thousand years, Abydos was one of the most important religious sites in ancient Egypt, and it served as the centre for worship of the god Osiris, the god of the underworld. But the interesting thing about this is that some of the finds from Abydos actually predate the ancient Egyptian dynasties. And not just by a little. The first Egyptian dynasty began around 3100 BCE, but the Abydos artefacts were created by what is known as the Naqada culture, and they date back to around 4000 BCE. That's more than six thousand years ago, and almost a millennium before the first dynasties.'

'Wow,' said Ethan. 'That's around 1,500 years before the Pyramids of Giza were built. That's amazing. But what was the deal with this Howard Templeton character? Why was Professor Goodwin so interested in him?'

'Well,' said Sophia, 'Goodwin was always slightly guarded when he spoke about him. But apparently, Templeton undertook an expedition to Abydos in 1906, about four years after it had been discovered, and Goodwin once told me something about Templeton having found artefacts there that simply didn't fit into the standard narrative about the history of ancient Egypt.'

'What sort of artefacts?' said Ethan.

'He never told me,' said Sophia. 'In fact, I don't think he told anyone. It felt like he was worried that people would ridicule him for buying into Templeton's wild theories. And to be honest, those were pretty far out. It's a lot like when serious scientists suddenly start talking about little green men from outer space. It's as if their credibility suddenly plummets through the floor, and no one will ever want to have anything to do with them again. Obviously, that doesn't mean that there isn't alien life out there in the universe. In fact, it's perfectly possible, but until there is proof, scientific dogma can prevent an honest inquiry. Anyway, that's what I think Goodwin was afraid of.'

'What do you mean by wild theories?' said Ethan.

'I don't know all the details,' said Sophia, 'but it seems that Templeton had managed to convince himself that a long time ago, long before the ancient Egyptian dynasties and even before the Naqada culture, there once existed some sort of advanced ancient precursor civilisation, from which everything else evolved.'

'And Goodwin believed this too?' said Ethan sceptically.

'I think so,' said Sophia. 'He was certainly interested enough to research it. And like I said, he was careful not to say too much about it. I know he spent hours down in the storage vaults, and he hoovered up all the books and papers on the subject he could find.'

'Well,' said Ethan. 'It's certainly a fascinating idea.'

'Of course it is.' Sophia nodded. 'Just think about how much traction Plato's description of Atlantis has gotten over the past 2,500 years. But the Atlantis story is widely accepted as being an allegory designed to warn of the hubris of man and about the consequences of moral and political corruption. There's no actual evidence that it ever existed.'

'I know,' said Ethan. 'But what about Templeton's theory? Could that still be true? Could there have been some sort of advanced civilisation somewhere in Egypt long before the pharaohs?'

'It's possible, I guess—' Sophia shrugged '—but as far as I know, no physical evidence has ever been found.'

'So, why did Professor Goodwin end up believing that Templeton was onto something?' said Ethan. 'I couldn't imagine him being led on some wild goose chase without any proof at all. He just wasn't that kind of person.'

'I know,' said Sophia. 'That's what's so weird. I know that Goodwin was spending a lot of time poring over the journal that Templeton wrote during his expedition in 1906, but he never told me what it contained.'

'A journal?' said Ethan. 'That's interesting. Do you know where he kept it?'

'In his office,' said Sophia. 'Just down the hall.'

'I would like to see it,' said Ethan. 'Is that possible?'

'Yeah, sure.' Sophia shrugged. 'If you know how to break into a safe. He always kept it in there along with some of his research notes. I saw him put it in there a couple of times, but I don't know the access code.'

'Right,' said Ethan with a dejected look. 'That's not going to be easy. Still, do you mind if we have a look?'

'No, of course not,' said Sophia. 'Follow me.'

The two of them exited Sophia's office and walked about ten metres along the carpeted corridor to a closed door. On the wall next to it was an attached brass nameplate with Goodwin's name and title engraved into it. Ethan had been there a couple of times before, but it suddenly felt very different now. Sophia gripped the door handle, opened the door, and then they stepped inside. The office was as Ethan remembered it, with bookcases bursting with books on Goodwin's favourite topics and a wide and substantial wooden desk placed on the left side of the room near one of two large windows that looked out over the leafy street below. It looked and felt more like a small library than an office, and it smelled like tobacco and old books. Ethan glanced across to Goodwin's leather armchair behind the desk, and he felt a stab of sadness at the realisation that Goodwin would never sit in that chair again.

'It's weird being in here now,' said Sophia. 'I don't like it.'

'I know what you mean,' said Ethan.

'The safe is over here,' said Sophia, stepping over next to a painting hanging on the wall directly behind the armchair. 'It's hidden behind this.'

She gripped the gilded frame and pulled it out from the wall, and it came away smoothly on hinges mounted on its right side. Behind it was the steel door of a small safe, but as soon as they laid eyes on it, they both realised that something wasn't right.

'It's open,' said Sophia, turning her head to look at Ethan before returning her gaze to the safe whose small door was slightly ajar. 'He would never have left it like this.'

Ethan stepped over next to her and pulled a leather glove from a jacket pocket. Putting it on, he then used the tips of his fingers to swing the safe door open. Inside was a compartment that was roughly the size of two shoeboxes, separated by a shelf in the middle. But the safe was completely empty.

'Where is the journal?' said Ethan with a frown.

'What the hell?' Sophia whispered as she looked again at Ethan. 'It's gone. Templeton's journal is gone.'

Ethan had never found himself having to piece together evidence from a murder, but he now had the distinct and uncomfortable feeling that what he was looking at was no coincidence. Somehow, Tobias Goodwin's violent death and the disappearance of the Templeton journal had to be connected. But how?

'Did you tell the police about this safe?' said Ethan.

'No,' Sophia said, giving a quick shake of the head. 'It never occurred to me. Ethan, what's going on here?'

Her voice was now suddenly tense, and as she looked at him and he returned her gaze, he could see fear and confusion in her blue eyes.

'I don't know,' said Ethan, 'but I intend to find out. I'm going to be getting the footage from the security cameras later today. Detective Callahan did me a solid and promised he would send it over. Hopefully, that will answer some of our questions.'

Then an idea occurred to him.

'Listen,' he said. 'I could really use your help here. You probably knew Tobias better than most people. Would you be willing to look at the footage with me? You might spot something that I would miss.'

'I don't know about that,' said Sophia hesitantly, clearly worried about the prospect of what the footage might show. 'I'm not sure I'm up for it.'

'Alright,' said Ethan. 'I understand. What if I watch it first, and then I can show it to you afterwards? If there's anything there I think you won't want to see, I'll just make sure not to replay that for you.'

'I guess,' said Sophia, although she still sounded unconvinced. 'When will you have it?'

'I'm not sure,' said Ethan. 'Sometime this afternoon or evening, I imagine.'

Sophia pulled up the left sleeve of her jumper and glanced at her wristwatch. It was a petite and elegant rose gold watch with a light brown leather strap, which Ethan thought suited her perfectly.

'That could be hours from now,' she said, clearly still wavering.

'OK,' said Ethan. 'How about this? If you come with me down to Manhattan, then I'll fix us up some lunch, and we can talk some more until Callahan gets in touch. I would really like to understand more about what Goodwin was working on.'

Sophia appeared to hesitate for a long moment, but then she glanced around the professor's office with a furrowed brow, after which she seemed to conclude that maybe she didn't feel like spending the rest of the day in that building anyway.

'Fine.' She finally nodded. 'I'll come with you.'

'Great,' said Ethan. 'Thanks. I'm parked over on Whitney Avenue.'

The two of them left the building, crossed the road, and walked side by side back past the Peabody Museum's entrance to where Ethan had parked his Harley-Davidson.

'You came on a motorbike?' Sophia said as she glared briefly at the bike with her mouth open before looking at Ethan.

'Sorry,' he said. 'I should probably have told you. I prefer this to a car. I like the freedom, and I never get stuck in traffic. I have a spare helmet for you right here.'

'Right,' said Sophia, swallowing as Ethan grabbed the red helmet that was attached to the back of the seat and handed it to her. 'OK. Fine.'

'Alright,' said Ethan, donning his own helmet before mounting the bike and starting the engine. 'Hop on. Let's get going.'

3

When Ethan and Sophia arrived at the soaring Frost Tower on 6th Avenue, its angular and virtually black glass façade gleaming in the sunlight, Ethan decided to park the bike near a wall on the small, open square directly in front of the building's main entrance rather than driving them both down into the parking basement. He rolled the bike to a stop and killed the engine, and Sophia hopped off and took off her helmet, releasing her auburn hair. As Ethan took off his own helmet and dismounted, one of the uniformed doormen came over to greet him.

'Afternoon, Mr Frost,' he said.

'Hey, Tom,' said Ethan, exchanging a quick fist bump with the man. 'I'm just parking here for now.'

'No problem,' said Tom. 'Want me to have it brought downstairs?'

'No thanks,' said Ethan. 'I'll do it myself later. Thanks anyway.'

'Sure thing,' said Tom, turning to head back towards the main entrance. 'Enjoy your day.'

'You too,' said Ethan, giving the doorman a quick salute.

He then turned to Sophia, who had a vaguely perplexed look on her face as she held on to the helmet and looked up and around her.

'Well,' said Ethan, lifting his hands out to his sides. 'This is me.'

'You live here?' said Sophia, sounding puzzled. 'In this building?'

'Well, yeah,' said Ethan. 'I sort of own it.'

'What?' said Sophia, an incredulous smile spreading across her face. 'You're kidding, right?'

'Nope,' said Ethan. 'This is where I live.'

'Wait,' she said, her brow furrowing. 'You're part of the Frost family? As in, *the* Frost family.'

'Yes.' Ethan nodded.

'And this thing is yours?' said Sophia as she looked up towards the top of the building, which had the words 'Frost Tower' emblazoned in white lettering on all four sides.

Ethan took a couple of steps towards her and then stopped and followed her gaze to the top of the tower.

'Well, technically it belongs to Frost Industries,' he said. 'But since I own fifty-one per cent of the company, then I guess you're right. To be honest, I never really thought of it that way.'

'So, you own a gigantic high-rise smack in the middle of Midtown—' she smiled with a playful glint in her eye '—and you never really thought about it? What kind of weirdo are you?'

'What can I say?' He shrugged, slightly self-consciously. 'I was just never that interested in the money.'

'Yup,' she said, her eyebrows shooting up briefly as she gave him a good-natured smile and wink. 'Definitely weird.'

'Look, there's got to be more to life than money, right?' he said.

'Sure.' Sophia grinned. 'Easy for you to say. You've never had to worry about not having enough of the stuff.'

'Point taken.' Ethan smiled, finding himself really liking her spunk. 'You got me there. Anyway, let me take you up to my place.'

They entered the cavernous lobby, and Ethan led them to the private elevator that would take them up to his penthouse. Once again, the building's security systems verified his identity using a fingerprint scanner, and the doors slid open.

'After you,' he said with a small bow, and Sophia then entered the cab.

He followed her inside and hit the button for Level 32, and about a minute later, the doors slid aside to reveal the penthouse foyer. At the sight of the large, marble-floored, and wood-panelled space that could have fit Sophia's entire apartment in New Haven, beyond which she could see the tall floor-to-ceiling windows of the main living space that looked out over New York City, her mouth fell slightly open.

'Holy crap,' she said as they stepped out of the elevator. 'This place is amazing. How long have you lived here?'

'A few years,' said Ethan. 'Ever since I left the military.'

'Really? You were in the army?' she said as they walked through to the open-plan kitchen and the expansive view from the living area out over the city. 'My dad was in the army a long time ago. Logistics, I think. What did you do there?'

'Special forces,' said Ethan. 'Fort Bragg.'

'Isn't that where the Green Berets are based?' she said. 'Were you one of those?'

'Delta,' said Ethan.

'Really?' she said, turning to look at him, and her eyes appeared as if she was now seeing him in a new light. 'That's pretty hardcore. Why did you leave? Isn't that like every little boy's dream job?'

'Yeah, I guess.' Ethan shrugged as he dropped his motorbike keys on the kitchen island and flung his leather jacket over a bar stool next to it. 'But it's not something you can do forever, you know? So I decided to get out while the going was good and do a degree in history at Yale. I always loved history. And that's how I met Tobias.'

'Can I ask you a question?' said Sophia, her head tilted slightly to one side as she looked at him with a faint smile.

'Sure,' he said, realising that he was really enjoying her company. 'Ask away.'

'Your accent,' she said. 'What is that?'

'Right.' Ethan smiled, slightly self-consciously. 'I was born here in New York, but I spent a long time in the UK.'

'What were you doing over there?' she said, taking a couple of steps towards one of the windows and looking out towards Central Park.

'Normal stuff,' said Ethan as he opened the fridge to grab two cans of soft drink. 'Growing up. Going to school. And I also joined the Royal Marines there. Thirsty?'

'Sure,' she said, glancing back at him with a smile.

Taking the can and popping it open, Sophia continued her slow meander around the living room as she took the whole place in. She stopped by a console table where she spotted a silver frame with a photo of two people. One was a handsome man wearing a suit and tie, and the other was a tall, blonde woman with classically beautiful features and a perfect smile. Between them stood a small boy of perhaps twelve years of age.

'Who is this?' she said, picking up the frame and studying the photo.

'My parents and I,' said Ethan. 'They're dead now.'

'I'm so sorry,' said Sophia, turning her head to look at him with a pained look in her eyes. 'I didn't mean to pry.'

'It's OK,' said Ethan. 'It happened last year. It was a helicopter crash.'

'Wait,' said Sophia. 'I read about that. It was that Frost chopper that went down in the Sound. Those were your parents? Oh God, I'm so stupid. I don't know why I didn't put two and two together before now. I feel terrible.'

'Hey, don't,' said Ethan with a faint shake of the head and a reassuring smile. 'Honestly. It's OK. I've worked through it, more or less. It happened, and there's nothing anyone can do to change it now. Life has to go on. How about you? Are your parents still around?'

'Yes,' she said, rejoining him near the kitchen island. 'They live out in California. My dad teaches molecular chemistry at Berkeley. He's just about to retire. And my mom is a journalist. I don't see them as much as I want to these days, but they're happy and healthy.'

'That's all that matters,' said Ethan, taking a quick swig from his drink. 'Anyway, let's grab some lunch. Are you hungry?'

'Sure,' she said. 'Let's eat.'

Ethan got out some bread, cheese and fruit from his fridge and opened a bottle of white wine. The two of them then sat on bar stools by the kitchen island and tucked in. Sophia appeared to have worked up a serious appetite, and she didn't hold back on the wine either.

'This is delicious.' She smiled, seeming now like a different person from when Ethan had first seen her on the Yale campus.

'Tell me something,' said Ethan between bites. 'This Howard Templeton character. What do you know about him? Have you ever looked into his theories?'

'Not very seriously,' she replied. 'And there's very little to look into for various reasons. The main source has always been that journal of his.'

'What do you know about it?' said Ethan.

'Well,' began Sophia. 'The journal has been kept in the collection here at Yale since 1906, when Templeton returned from his first expedition. And ever since then, it has basically been seen as toxic for any researcher. Imagine being a jet engine designer and showing up to some propulsion conference, and then you start talking about "Roswell" and "Area 51". Pretty soon, everyone in the room will come up with some excuse to leave for fear of being associated with you and your crazy talk. That's what it was like with Templeton's journal in Egyptology circles. That's why Goodwin kept it all quiet and really only began working on it after he retired.'

'But why?' said Ethan. 'It seems Templeton spent a lot of time in Egypt. He must have found something.'

'Like I said,' Sophia continued. 'I don't know exactly what was in it. But apparently, it contained all sorts of stuff that really didn't fit with the accepted view of Egyptian history, and the mainstream Egyptologists at that time wouldn't touch it with a bargepole. On top of that, Professor Goodwin once told me that it was pretty rambling and fairly incomprehensible at times. Almost as if Templeton had written it in a kind of private code or shorthand that wasn't meant for anyone else.'

'So Templeton went on his expedition to Abydos in 1906?' said Ethan.

'That's right,' said Sophia.

'OK.' Ethan nodded. 'So, what do we know about that?'

'Well,' said Sophia, 'Abydos was a major centre for religious and political power in Egypt in predynastic times. And we know that it was probably the main capital for the Naqada culture for many centuries from about 3200 BCE. That culture, which began around 4000 BCE, was highly advanced for its time, and there is evidence of the use of metalworking, specifically copper. We also know from various finds around Abydos that it had extensive and sophisticated trading networks that connected it with the remote oases in the western deserts of Egypt, several hundred kilometres away across a sea of sand dunes. They even reached as far as Nubia to the south, some 750 kilometres along the Nile, and even to the Levant, far to the north-east. These were huge distances, especially more than five thousand years ago.'

'Yes, that's incredible,' said Ethan. 'I always thought of predynastic times as fairly primitive, at least relatively speaking, but they clearly weren't.'

'Hell no,' said Sophia. 'Not by a long shot. Now, interestingly, it was also from Abydos that Upper and Lower Egypt were first united and ruled over by one king. A man called Narmer, who is generally accepted as being the founder of the first ancient Egyptian dynasty. For that reason, Abydos is regarded as the cradle of the main pharaonic dynasties, and a number of royal tombs dating back to that period have been discovered around that area. Archaeologists have also found some amazingly sophisticated art and early hieroglyphic inscriptions from that period. Much later, during the New Kingdom around the thirteenth century BCE, Pharaoh Seti I built a massive complex there, which was discovered in 1818. And it quickly became apparent that its purpose was to commemorate and honour the long line of earlier pharaohs of Egypt.'

'Why was that so obvious?' asked Ethan, taking a sip of his wine.

'Because,' said Sophia, seemingly now getting into her stride, 'one of the main finds was the so-called King List, which is an incredible elongated stone hallway in which the walls are covered in cartouche reliefs, one for each of the kings of the many previous dynasties going all the way back to Narmer.'

'Right,' said Ethan, glancing towards the picture of his parents, and suddenly unable to shake the feeling that his mother had told him about that temple many years ago. 'I think I remember now. A real treasure trove for archaeologists.'

'Exactly,' said Sophia. 'And it is really interesting because it tells us that these people had a real sense of their identity and history stretching back thousands of years as one continuous civilisation. It also helped cement the history of the ancient dynasties for modern historians and Egyptologists. But then, in 1902, almost a century later, something else was discovered right next to the Temple of Seti complex. Something that was very different and which has created a fair amount of controversy.'

'What was it?' said Ethan.

'It is known as the Osireion,' said Sophia, 'and the clue is in the name. It is a large complex designed for the worship of Osiris, the god of the underworld. It was immediately behind and below the Temple of Seti, and it was buried deep underground, which is why no one realised it was there for so long. But once they excavated it, the archaeologists realised that it had actually been used alongside the Temple of Seti during his reign, and that its function during the New Kingdom was to simulate the journey to the underworld after death. But the really strange thing is that its architectural style, as well as the way it has been constructed, is completely different from the Temple of Seti.'

'How so?' said Ethan.

'Well,' said Sophia, 'The Temple of Seti is your typical tall, grand Egyptian structure with huge columns and square geometric shapes towering over large plazas. The Osireion is compact, low and underground, but the most striking difference is the masonry. Unlike the Temple of Seti, the massive irregularly shaped stones making up the walls of the Osireion are often smooth and rounded, and they are shaped so that they interlock perfectly in ways that are virtually identical to some ancient temples found in places like Cuzco in Peru.'

'What?' said Ethan. 'You mean it looks like the masonry of the Incas? That's wild.'

'I know,' said Sophia with a small chuckle. 'I think the technique is called polygonal cyclopean masonry, and it is so precise that no mortar was needed. Nothing else like it exists anywhere else in Egypt, and it has led some people to speculate that the Osireion was not built by Seti I, but that it was from a much, much earlier time period. Maybe a different culture altogether.'

'Could it have been built by the Naqada culture?' said Ethan. 'Or maybe even before that?'

'It's really hard to say,' said Sophia. 'Some scholars have even suggested that there is some sort of connection from the Osireion to other ancient civilisations in completely different parts of the world. This is obviously a pretty controversial view among Egyptologists because it doesn't align with the current dogma. But like Goodwin always said. Keep an open mind, and the evidence will show you the truth.'

'That definitely sounds like him,' said Ethan with a pensive smile.

'One thing is for certain,' said Sophia. 'There's a lot of stuff we still don't know and understand about ancient Egypt, and there are things out there still to be found. Just as an example, it is pretty well established from many hieroglyphic records that there once existed a city by the name of Thinis. It was located somewhere near Abydos, but it is now lost, and it was supposedly the capital of predynastic Upper Egypt. But we simply don't know where it was. People have been looking for Thinis for a couple of centuries now. No sign of it has ever been found, but we know for a fact that it is definitely out there somewhere under the sands of the desert. Fascinating, isn't it?'

She looked at Ethan with her wide smile and her clear blue eyes, and there was no denying that her enthusiasm was infectious.

'Definitely,' he said, returning her smile. 'Imagine finding that place. That would be incredible. Could it be that Thinis was what Templeton was looking for?'

'I guess it's possible.' Sophia shrugged. 'Although I get the feeling that Templeton's theory revolved around an entirely different civilisation that existed long before the Naqada. But like I said, Templeton's theories were seen as pretty eccentric, even back then. And he was apparently a bit of a strange character who never communicated much with his colleagues here at Yale. He tended to keep his findings to himself, maybe because he knew that they would be challenged and opposed by his peers. But there's another reason why his work has faded into obscurity.'

'What's that?' said Ethan.

'After coming back from his expedition in late 1906,' said Sophia, 'he withdrew even more into his own world and barely talked to anyone. Then, less than a year later, without notifying the university of his purpose, he set out on a second expedition to Egypt. He left in March 1907, travelling alone and telling no one exactly where he was going, and he was never seen again. Later on, there were rumours from Egypt that he had returned to Abydos and then travelled on camel from there into the western desert. But he never came back out. No one knows what happened to him.'

'That's really fascinating,' said Ethan. 'Did he bring anything back to Yale after his first expedition?'

'Not as far as I know,' said Sophia. 'I think Goodwin

mentioned that a number of his finds from Abydos were handed over to the Egyptian Museum in Cairo, but I don't think he brought anything back here.'

'So, all we have is his journal?' said Ethan.

'Well, yes,' said Sophia. 'Except now it's missing.'

At that moment, Ethan's phone chirped, and after extracting it from his pocket and looking at its display, he glanced up at Sophia.

'It's from Detective Callahan,' he said. 'It's the security camera footage.'

* * *

Ethan led them into his office, which was a separate room overlooking Midtown towards the east. It was decorated in a minimalist style with white plaster walls, a cream-coloured carpet, and a few pieces of dark wood furniture, including a large desk by the floor-to-ceiling window. On top of it sat a wide PC monitor, a keyboard and a mouse, and Ethan stepped over to sit down in the office chair in front of it. As Sophia joined him, she looked around the room, which bore all the hallmarks of a bachelor. Not a single trace of a woman in sight. She spotted a hefty, grey gun safe in the corner and also noticed the large, thin display cabinet mounted on a wall containing a collection of military insignia, medals and ribbons. She stopped and stood next to Ethan, her arms crossed tightly over her chest, her face a tight mask of apprehension.

'Let's see what's here,' said Ethan, firing up the PC and opening his email app. 'Callahan left no comment in his email except to say that this file contains all the footage from the Council of Archaeology building and the Peabody Museum from last night that includes Professor Goodwin. So, we'll have to go through it all to try to find out what actually happened.'

'I should watch it too,' said Sophia with a steely determination that surprised Ethan.

'Are you sure?' he asked.

'Yes.' Sophia nodded sombrely. 'I know we agreed that you should watch it first, but I've changed my mind. Two pairs of eyes are always better than one, and I feel like I would be copping out if I didn't watch all of it, you know?'

'Yeah,' said Ethan grimly. 'I know what you mean. Just prepare yourself. This might get rough.'

'I know,' said Sophia. 'I'm ready.'

Ethan double-clicked on the video file, and the media player instantly popped up in the centre of his screen with a black-and-white recording of a corridor. The timestamp in the top right corner read 01:12:32.

'That's my corridor,' Sophia breathed as she leaned forward slightly while hugging herself. 'About a quarter past one in the morning. I can't believe he was working so late.'

On the screen, Goodwin – wearing dark slacks, a rumpled, light-coloured shirt and a chequered tweed vest – emerged from his office and crossed the corridor to disappear out of sight again.

'He went into the kitchen,' she said. 'Probably to make some coffee.'

As it turned out, she had guessed correctly, because Ethan ran the recording forward, and a few seconds later, Goodwin appeared with a coffee mug in his hand. He was about to go back inside his office when he stopped and turned his head as if he had heard a sound. He stepped over to the stairwell at the bottom of the frame and leaned out to look down. Then, a few seconds later, he took a sudden step back, spoke to someone out of frame, and then took another step. At that moment, a tall, muscular figure wearing black jeans and a dark grey long-sleeved T-shirt stepped into the frame. His face was covered by a black balaclava, and in his gloved hand was a menacing-looking black, slightly curved blade that was about twenty centimetres long. As the man walked up onto the landing and proceeded towards a visibly frightened Professor Goodwin, Ethan noticed that he moved with the smooth economy of motion that instantly betrayed some level of specialised military training, possibly covert operations.

'Who the hell is that?' whispered Sophia, her eyes wide with fright as her right hand moved up to cover her mouth.

Ethan paused the video and turned to look at her.

'Are you absolutely sure you want to continue?' he said.

Sophia said nothing and didn't take her eyes off the screen, but instead she gave a quick nod. Ethan then allowed the recording to continue playing. The tall man gestured towards the door to Goodwin's office and spoke again.

'I wish this thing had audio,' said Ethan tightly. 'Then we might have a better chance of identifying him.'

On the screen, a clearly terrified Goodwin complied with the order and shuffled hurriedly towards the door to his office with his hands slightly raised. He stepped inside, and the tall man followed, leaving the corridor empty again.

'I guess there are no cameras in the offices,' Ethan observed.

'No,' said Sophia, giving a quick shake of the head. 'It's not allowed.'

Once again, Ethan sped up the replay, and soon, Goodwin reappeared, followed closely by the man in the black balaclava.

'He's got the Templeton journal,' Sophia exclaimed, pointing at the screen where the tall man was carrying a leather-bound journal under his arm.

The two men proceeded out of view, and the recording then switched to a different camera mounted outside the Council of Archaeology building, where the streetlights on Sachem Street were switched on, but the street was completely deserted.

'Looks like Callahan edited the whole thing together for us,' said Ethan. 'That'll save us some time.'

The two men crossed the street to the opposite corner and headed for the entrance to the Peabody Museum. As they walked, the knife-wielding man was one step behind Goodwin with the knife still in his hand, occasionally glancing left and right to make sure no one else was around. They disappeared inside the museum building, and then the image on Ethan's monitor changed once again to show the foyer of the museum. It was built like a small Gothic cathedral with exposed bricks and tall, pointed arches reaching up to an apex high above, and the camera appeared to be mounted several metres above the floor. The duo moved straight to the stairs leading down and then disappeared from view. Then the image changed again to show a wide, windowless corridor with a painted, grey floor. Within a couple of seconds, Goodwin and the masked stranger walked into frame, and the two of them proceeded along the corridor.

'Where the hell are they going?' Ethan asked no one in particular as his eyes bored into the screen, watching the tall man holding the blade intently.

'That's the access to the storage vaults,' said Sophia, pointing at the screen. 'It looks like this man knew exactly where he wanted to go.'

She and Ethan continued watching as the two men walked about halfway along the corridor and stopped outside one of the identical doors along one side.

'Where's that?' said Ethan, peering at the slightly grainy recording.

'That's Vault 8,' said Sophia. 'That's where Yale keeps its Upper Egypt collections.'

The image changed again to show the interior of the storage vault. The room was roughly six by eight metres in size with brick walls painted white. Several banks of fluorescent light tubes hung under the ceiling, bathing the room in white light, and in the centre were three rows of tall, open, wooden shelving units with dozens of boxes, large and small, arranged across five levels.

The door opened, and Goodwin and the man in black appeared. The professor led them straight to the second aisle and proceeded about five metres along it before stopping and turning left. He then reached for a storage container sitting at around chest height and pulled it slightly towards himself before taking off its lid. He glanced at the man who gestured to the box and appeared to say something, and then Goodwin rummaged around carefully inside the box for a few moments before finally producing a small wooden box that was about the size of a cigar case. He glanced nervously at the tall man who spoke again. Goodwin fumbled with the box for a few seconds but finally managed to open it. Turning it towards the man, he flipped the lid all the way back to reveal an object that glinted under the strong, white ceiling lights.

'What is that?' said Ethan, pausing the video again.

'I'm not sure,' said Sophia. 'Can we zoom in?'

With a few keystrokes and clicks of the mouse, Ethan selected a smaller section of the screen around Goodwin's hands and zoomed in on the box.

'What the...' Sophia began, falling silent for a few seconds before speaking again. 'Is that what I think it is?'

'It looks like a sphinx,' said Ethan, astonished. 'Like the one at Giza. But it looks like it's made of gold.'

'Yes, but it has a lion's head instead of that of a pharaoh,' said Sophia, narrowing her eyes as she gazed at the small gold figurine sitting inside the wooden box. 'This is amazing.'

'What does it mean?' said Ethan. 'Do you know where it is from?'

'No,' said Sophia. 'Obviously somewhere in Egypt, but I don't know where.'

'How did it end up here at Yale?' said Ethan. 'Could it have been brought back by Templeton in 1906?'

'Well,' she said. 'As far as I know, he brought nothing back from Abydos, but perhaps that isn't true at all. This is really strange. Could he have placed it there without logging it with the university? And why does it have a lion's head?'

'Let's keep watching,' said Ethan, unpausing the replay once more.

On the screen, the tall man nodded, and Goodwin then closed the small wooden box and handed it to the man, who unslung a small backpack from his shoulder, unzipped it, and put the box inside. Then he began zipping the bag back up, and as he did so, he had evidently taken his eyes off Goodwin, because the professor turned his head ever so slightly towards the opposite shelf where a stone statue depicting one of the many Egyptian gods stood. Ethan and Sophia watched in horror as Goodwin reached for the statue, grabbed it, and swung it at the tall man's head. In one fluid movement that was almost too quick to see, the man bent his knees slightly while shifting his head to one side to evade the strike, and then his knife came up and around in a wide scything movement that cut across Goodwin's throat with terrifying speed.

Sophia gasped as the scene unfolded on the screen in front of them, and tears immediately began welling up in her eyes, but she refused to take her eyes off the monitor. In the Yale of the night before, the stone statue fell onto the floor, and for a brief moment, Goodwin just stood there looking stunned. Then his hands flew up to his throat, where dark blood suddenly began flowing copiously out between his fingers and onto his tweed vest. His eyes went wide as he fell to his knees, and with a sudden viciousness that surprised even Ethan, the tall man stepped forward and stabbed Goodwin forcefully three times in the chest in quick succession. The professor teetered for a moment and then toppled onto his back, where his body spasmed for a short while before it stopped moving altogether, amid an expanding pool of blood spreading out over the painted floor.

'Oh my God,' Sophia whimpered, tears now making their way down her cheeks. 'This is awful.'

She turned around, and Ethan then watched as the tall man on the screen stood there for several long seconds, looking down at his dying victim bleeding out on the floor. He then slung the backpack over his shoulder and headed back towards the door, where he disappeared, and the remaining thirty seconds of the camera footage showed him walking briskly up and out of the building, where he then disappeared into the night. However, during the final couple of seconds of the recording, as he was walking away from the museum across one of the campus lawns, he appeared to reach up and pull off his balaclava. The image was murky and grainy, but when Ethan paused the replay and zoomed in, he was just about able to discern the rough outline of a face. The man's hair was short and black, and he wore a neatly trimmed beard. He appeared to have a swarthy complexion and a slightly hooked nose, and if Ethan had to guess, he would have said that the man was from somewhere in the Middle East.

Upon seeing the face of Goodwin's killer, Ethan felt barely contained rage welling up inside him. As a Delta operator, he had been trained to remain emotionally detached no matter what ended up happening during a mission, either to the enemy, innocent bystanders, or even his teammates. But this was different. Tobias Goodwin had been no threat to anyone, and he never deserved this. Not in a million years. At that moment, Ethan swore to himself that he would find this man and make him pay with his life for what he had done.

The recording ended, and as Ethan rubbed his temples and let out a long sigh, he realised that he had been holding his breath for about half a minute as he had watched the murder of his friend.

'Are you OK?' he said, swivelling in his office chair and looking at Sophia as she turned back to face him.

She shook her head faintly, and her teary eyes met his as her lip trembled and she clasped her hands in front of herself.

'No,' she said weakly, suddenly looking vulnerable and overwhelmed. 'I shouldn't have watched that. I don't know what I was thinking.'

'You're probably right,' said Ethan, getting to his feet and taking her trembling hands in his. 'But what's done is done. What we have to do now is put all of our efforts into finding out who killed Tobias and why.'

'But how?' said Sophia, snivelling. 'It's like looking for a needle in a haystack.'

'I think I might have an idea for how to do this,' said Ethan broodingly. 'But first, I'll need to find someone I haven't spoken to in a long time.'

4

After having watched the harrowing footage of Professor Goodwin's murder, Ethan and Sophia spoke little as they sat in his living room, each holding a mug of coffee. After a while, Sophia appeared to regain most of her composure and announced that she would like to go home to her apartment in New Haven and spend some time alone. Ethan grabbed his phone and placed a call to Mitch, and fifteen minutes later, the former SOAR pilot took off from the helipad on top of Frost Tower with Sophia in the plush passenger cabin of a corporate helicopter. The flight to New Haven would take about twenty-five minutes, and Mitch would be able to deliver her to the wide-open cricket ground called Kimberley Field near the city's main marina. From there, she could walk to her apartment in less than ten minutes.

After giving Sophia a final wave, Ethan returned to his penthouse and stood for a while with his hands clasped behind his back by one of the huge windows overlooking the city. Thinking about the grainy image of Goodwin's killer, he pondered his options. During his time with Delta, Ethan had spent hours inside mission briefing rooms at FOBs in a handful of faraway countries. Many of those briefings had related to high-value targets that Delta was about to go in and either capture or kill, and in each of those cases, he and his fellow teammates from the Unit had sat in their foldable chairs and been presented with the most recent photos of the target. This information was often presented by a CIA liaison officer who had been involved in acquiring it through covert means, and Ethan knew that the Agency had developed a highly advanced facial recognition AI that was able to pin down the exact identity of almost anyone in the world with near certainty. The exact design of the AI was a closely guarded secret, and so was the provenance of its massive cache of training data, much of which had been compiled without the knowledge of its legal owners. It was, without question, the most powerful facial recognition tool in the world, but only senior CIA officers were able to request its use. Ethan now needed to gain access to it somehow, but this was easier said than done. Driving down to Langley, Virginia, and asking nicely was out of the question, and trying to run it through the Unit was also a no-go. He might have been one of the country's most elite soldiers, trusted with the nation's most valuable intel, but now, as a civilian, all of that was over. What he needed instead was a more unconventional approach.

His phone pinged with a message from a contact at Frost Communications who was involved in developing state-of-the-art tools for agencies such as the NSA and the FBI. Ethan had pulled a favour, and the message contained nothing but an address for a coffee house on the other side of the Hudson River, as well as a timestamp from just under two minutes earlier. As soon as he received it, he took the elevator down to street level and walked outside. It was time to say hello to an old acquaintance.

'Going on a date, Mr Frost?' said Tom with a casual grin as Ethan walked out of Frost Tower's main entrance and headed for the bike still parked nearby.

'No such luck, Tom,' said Ethan, returning his grin. 'Not today.'

'Well,' said Tom with a cheerful smile. 'There's always tomorrow.'

'You know, you're a real sage, Tom,' said Ethan, and then he mounted the Harley, put on his helmet, and started the engine. 'Take it easy. I'll see you later.'

'Later, Mr Frost,' said Tom, giving a quick wave as Ethan sped off. 'Drive safely.'

About twenty-five minutes later, after driving through the Lincoln Tunnel under the Hudson into New Jersey and beating most of the stationary traffic on the way, he pulled up near Mojo Coffee on Newark Avenue in Downtown Jersey City. The pedestrianised street was a vibrant and colourful haven for ethnic restaurants and quirky shops, and there were groups of people walking along the wide avenue or sitting at the outside tables of eateries and bars. The atmosphere was relaxed and somewhat bohemian, and Ethan felt comfortable simply leaving his helmet on the Harley's seat and walking away. He crossed to the other side of the avenue and entered the coffee house, where the fragrant smell of the brews immediately hit him, and it only took him a few seconds to spot who he had come to meet.

Her name was Scarlett Fox, and she was a slightly built woman in her early thirties sporting straight, black hair with a severe undercut on the left side. The right side almost reached down to her shoulder. Her pale, angular face was attractive, and her high cheekbones, thin lips and green eyes gave her an intense and somewhat brooding appearance as she sat there staring at the laptop screen in front of her. She was wearing jeans and a dark burgundy leather jacket over a black T-shirt, which gave her an edgy look. But she was also wearing a lipstick matching her jacket, and in her left ear was a dainty silver earring that injected a more feminine touch into the ensemble.

Scarlett was a former CIA analyst, and Ethan had come to know her through multiple deployments where she had been part of the Agency's intelligence team responsible for identifying and locating HVTs for Delta to hit during night raids. He had liaised directly with her on two occasions during covert anti-Hezbollah operations in Beirut, and he remembered her as being bright, proactive, and resourceful. She had been recruited to the Agency straight out of college, where she studied computer science, and then moved on to a fast-track intake program for highly gifted hackers. Her aptitude test scores at the Agency had been off the charts, and her IQ was in the top two per cent of the population.

However, her promising career had been cut short when a covert operation in Saudi Arabia had gone bad. The aim of the operation had been to snatch and interrogate a high-ranking Saudi official who was secretly working for a fundamentalist group planning an attack on a US military base in that country. The official's bodyguards had drawn their weapons, and a fire-fight had ensued in which a plain-clothed CIA agent had lost his life. It was a disaster that threatened to destabilise the normally cosy relationship between Washington, DC, and Riyadh, so in order to save face and retain good relations with the Saudi royal family, the director of the CIA had demanded that heads roll.

Someone had to take the fall, and so a story was invented about trigger-happy staff going rogue and causing the debacle. Scarlett was on the record as having recommended an abort, which her section chief had then overruled. However, she had been found not to follow procedure when she tried to go over the head of the section chief and pull the team out before things went bad, and this had proven enough for the higher-ups to make her take the fall for the bungled operation. Being the most junior analyst on the mission team, she had been sacrificed by her superiors and forced out of the Agency.

Ethan and a small team of Delta operators happened to also be in Riyadh at the time, and when he found out that Scarlett had been fired, he remembered being both shocked and angry with what he regarded as the premier intelligence service in the world. He had always known that large power structures such as the Army and the CIA were full of individuals who were happy to disregard all notions of morals when it came to furthering their own careers. In fact, he was sure that if tested by trained professionals, the army brass would almost certainly be shown to be crawling with psychopaths, and the same would turn out to be true about the entire corporate sector and the political class. However, even he had been disgusted by the way Scarlett had been treated. But as a mid-ranked non-commissioned officer in a completely different branch of the government apparatus, there was nothing he could do about it. He had gone to the CIA section chief and offered to provide a statement as a character witness, but by then it was all over. The last time he had seen Scarlett, she had been carrying her few personal possessions out of the aircraft hangar that had been used as an FOB and then walked across the tarmac to board the C-17 that would take her and the rest of the CIA team back to the States. That was her last day with the Agency.

When Ethan walked into the coffee shop, Scarlett was sitting by a small table for two next to the wall, but the chair opposite her was empty, and she appeared to be by herself. Next to her was a single coffee cup, and her eyes were locked firmly on the screen in front of her as her fingers, painted with moss green nail varnish, danced swiftly and effortlessly across the keyboard. As he walked towards her, he thought she looked exactly as cool and sharp as he remembered her, yet at the same time, there was a hint of fragility about her. Like a beautiful glass dagger. He walked over, pulled out the chair across from her and sat down with a faint smile on his lips.

'Hello, Scarlett,' he said as her eyes snapped up and locked onto those of the uninvited stranger.

'Hey, what the...?' she began, before falling silent as she studied his face for a moment. 'Ethan. Is that you?'

'In the flesh.' He nodded and gave a thin smile. 'It's good to see you again. Can I join you?'

'Sure,' said Scarlett. 'Wait, how did you find me?'

'I know a guy,' said Ethan with a quick wink. 'You'd be surprised by how many pies Frost Industries has its long fingers in.'

'Actually, I wouldn't,' she said without taking her eyes off him. 'I remember reading your file. In fact, I read the unredacted parts of the CIA files on all of you Delta boys, and yours was hard to forget. Somehow, being born with a silver spoon in your mouth doesn't quite cover it with you.'

'Hey, you never doubted me as an operator when you were at the Agency,' said Ethan good-naturedly. 'That's all that matters, right?'

'True,' Scarlett conceded with a small sigh. 'But those days are long gone now. I haven't spoken to any of my former colleagues since it all went to hell. They don't want anything to do with me. It's like I've died.'

'Listen,' said Ethan, leaning forward with a small shake of the head. 'As far as I'm concerned, what happened to you was a goddamn disgrace. You never deserved any of what happened.'

'Thanks,' Scarlett said with a faint shrug. 'That's nice of you to say. But there's no point in clinging to the past. It played out the way it did, and I've got to focus on the future.'

Ethan nodded, suddenly realising that the two of them were more alike than he had ever thought. Both were high achievers who had been given a raw deal like a bolt out of the blue, and both of them would rather look forward than spend time in the rear-view mirror.

'You got any work?' he said, nodding to the laptop.

'Some,' said Scarlett, looking mildly uncomfortable. 'Free-lance cybersecurity services. A lot of white hat hacking. Mostly small businesses here in Jersey, but sometimes nationwide. Dude, you'd be surprised how vulnerable a lot of these guys are. It's shocking, really. Most of them are wide open to data theft and extortion.'

'So, you live around here now?' said Ethan, glancing outside to the pedestrian street.

'I live over on Barrow Street,' she said. 'Nice tree-lined place. I have a small apartment there. But I like coming down here for some coffee every few days. Anyway, Ethan. I'm sure this isn't a social call, right? Level with me.'

'No, you're right.' Ethan nodded as his face took on a pensive look. 'It's not.'

'So, what's going on?' she said. 'You had me tracked down, so it must be important.'

'Alright,' said Ethan. 'I need to talk to you about the facial recognition AI the Agency uses to identify high-value targets. It's called Argus, right?'

'That's right,' said Scarlett. 'After the mythical Greek watch-man. What about it?'

'I need access to it?' said Ethan deadpan.

Scarlett just stared at him for a few seconds, and the beginnings of a grin flashed across her face until she realised that Ethan wasn't joking. He really meant it.

'You're shitting me, right?' she said, her voice suddenly slightly hushed as she leaned closer. 'That thing lives inside a hardened network at Langley. It has to be one of the most secure systems in the Agency. And getting caught hacking into that thing would put you away for years. In fact, they'd put you in a supermax prison, throw away the key and tell your family that you'd been abducted by aliens.'

'So, you're saying it would be difficult,' observed Ethan drily, a smile playing on his lips.

'Try almost impossible,' said Scarlett.

'Right.' Ethan nodded. 'But not actually impossible, right?'

Scarlett studied his face for a moment. 'You're really serious about this, aren't you?' she said. 'Ethan, what's going on here?'

'A friend of mine was killed,' said Ethan bitterly after a long pause. 'Did you read about the murder at Yale?'

'That old guy on the news?' she said. 'Sure.'

'That was him,' said Ethan. 'Tobias Goodwin. My former professor. One of the nicest people you'll ever meet.'

'Fuck,' Scarlett whispered. 'And I'm guessing you have an image of the killer?'

'Bingo,' said Ethan. 'I really need your help, Scarlett. Will you do it?'

Scarlett looked him straight in the eye with a serious, pensive gaze as the cogs inside her mind whirred and she wrestled with the decision. If she helped him, she would be opening herself up to serious prosecution if she were ever caught. But if she walked away, she would be turning her back on one of the few people who had tried to have her back when the shit hit the fan. In the end, the choice was simple.

'If this were anybody but you,' she said, 'I'd say no. You know that, right?'

'I know,' said Ethan, the importance of the favour he was asking etched on his face. 'I would really appreciate this.'

'You'd better,' said Scarlett as her fingertips began moving across the keyboard and she prepped her laptop for the hack.

'Alright,' she finally said, giving a small, determined nod. 'I'll do it.'

'Great,' said Ethan, breathing a small sigh of relief. 'How long do you need?'

'Shouldn't take long,' said Scarlett. 'Maybe twenty minutes if I can make a clean entry. Half an hour, tops.'

'Do you want to go somewhere else?' said Ethan, subconsciously glancing around the coffee shop. 'This is kind of a public place.'

'Doesn't matter,' said Scarlett, seemingly unfazed. 'I can mask my connection with multiple VPNs. Each node bounces around the world independently from server to server every few seconds, so even if they could pin down one of the IP addresses, I would appear to relocate almost immediately. It effectively makes it impossible for them to run a trace. And that's if they even spot me. We're secure.'

'Alright,' said Ethan, extracting a small, black flash drive from his pocket and giving her a brief nod of respect. 'You're amazing.'

'Sure am,' she said with a quick wink.

He placed the memory stick on the table in front of himself, placed his right hand flat on top of it, and slid it across to the hacker.

'There's a single photo on this,' he said, removing his hand. 'That's all I have. But this is important, Scarlett. I'm counting on you.'

'I know,' she said as she picked up the flash drive and slotted it into her laptop. 'I'll do what I can.'

She opened the image file and looked at the grainy black-and-white photo.

'Alright,' she said. 'Let's do this.'

Firing up her chain of VPNs, she quickly established a connection to a small part of Langley's computer networks that she knew was relatively unsecure. It was the procurement centre for the giant organisation's stationery supply systems. She soon found an outdated server connected to the Agency's main network and discovered that it had been left unpatched for years. She smiled. This was the back door she needed. Her fingertips were now flying across the keyboard, and the deeper into the hack she got, the faster they moved. Using a known bug in the logistics server's operating system, she slipped inside and masked her entry as a legitimate data query. She had now gained access to the network, but that access was limited, like managing to sneak into the lobby of a bank after closing. She ran a tool that scanned the system for sloppy mistakes by its developers, and it didn't take her long to identify an automated script that ran with administrator privileges but which didn't check the files it loaded. She quickly replaced one of the files with her own. Almost immediately, the script ran the file, and she suddenly had full control over that server.

Now, moving unseen like a digital ghost through the Agency's network, she searched for other connected networks, and she soon found one that she knew to be associated with the Argus system. It was a feeder network that covertly hoovered up footage from tens of thousands of security cameras all around the world, as well as the contents of personnel databases belonging to both public and private entities in about two hundred countries. All of this data was then processed by enhancement algorithms and fed into Argus, whose neural networks churned away at it day and night in an effort to perfect the process of providing near real-time facial recognition capabilities to the CIA across the globe. This was the Agency's all-seeing eye.

'I'm in,' Scarlett whispered without taking her eyes off the screen as she fed the image into the Argus AI while masking her own ID using someone else's login credentials. 'Uploading the image file now.'

Ethan watched her but said nothing. She was focused like a laser beam, and the last thing he wanted to do now was distract her. She was in the zone, and from the intense look on her face, it was as if she had momentarily let go of this world and been swallowed up by the digital world that she was now bending to her will.

'Got him,' she said, a hint of satisfaction in her voice. 'Pulling the data out now. Three more seconds. Alright. Done.'

Scarlett yanked the flash drive out of the port on the side of the laptop and handed it back to Ethan with a thin smile and eyes that were vaguely glazed over as if she was still emerging from a trancelike state.

'Who is he?' said Ethan.

'His name is Nadeem Rashad,' Scarlett said, reading off her laptop's screen. 'He appears to be a former captain in Egypt's Central Security Force, the CSF.'

Ethan remembered this unit from his time in Delta. The CSF was a paramilitary entity controlled by the Egyptian government and used for a range of different tasks, from riot control to intelligence gathering to high-risk SWAT operations. They were the well-trained muscle behind the president and the government in cases where the regular police forces were either too ill-equipped or too squeamish to become involved.

'What does "former" mean?' said Ethan.

'He retired at thirty-five and disappeared off the radar several years ago,' said Scarlett. 'But there are money trails indicating that he is active and affiliated with a man named Zosar Al-Masry.'

'Who is he?' said Ethan.

'He appears to be some big-shot businessman with connections to the Egyptian government,' said Scarlett. 'Looks like his family owns a stake in some of Egypt's oil exploration ventures.'

'Right,' said Ethan with a pensive look. 'I've got to say, I'm struggling to see how someone like that could be connected to a murder at Yale.'

'Was anything stolen?' said Scarlett.

'A journal,' said Ethan. 'More than a century old. And a small gold figurine.'

'Weird,' said Scarlett, her smooth forehead creasing slightly as she pondered the information.

'Any other detail on this Nadeem Rashad?' said Ethan.

'Nothing about his whereabouts or activities for the past few years,' said Scarlett. 'There's no record of him entering the United States, so he may have been travelling on a private plane using a fake passport.'

'OK,' said Ethan. 'Well, I guess it's a start. Is this all on the flash drive?'

'Yup.' Scarlett nodded. 'Do you want me to do anything else? I might be able to find out more if I dig a little deeper.'

'Not right now,' said Ethan. 'Maybe later. I need to think about this whole thing first. And I don't want you to get in any trouble.'

'Hey, it's too late for that,' Scarlett said with a quick smile as she fished out a business card from her jacket. 'Anyway, let me know if you change your mind. Here's my number. Just call me.'

'Thanks,' said Ethan, taking the card. 'I might do that.'

5

After arriving back at Frost Tower, Ethan returned to the penthouse, entered his living room, and sank down into a sofa for several minutes without moving. His mind was clouded by dark thoughts, and his gaze was fixed on the framed picture of his parents. The realisation that, like his parents, Tobias Goodwin was now also no longer among the living was hard to accept, and seeing the murder with his own eyes had been harrowing. He had experienced plenty of death in his life, and he had been responsible for a lot of it himself. But Goodwin's murder was different. Things like that weren't supposed to happen, least of all to people like Goodwin. The fact that Nadeem Rashad was a trained Egyptian police operative was strange and unsettling in equal measure. And the connection to the enigmatic Zosar Al-Masry only deepened the mystery. One thing was clear, though. It hinted at the fact that Goodwin's murder and the theft of the mysterious golden figurine and Templeton's journal were part of a carefully orchestrated plan whose purpose he was currently unable to gauge.

Gazing at his mother's face in the photo, he suddenly felt

the urge to talk to her again and ask her for advice. Maybe she would have been able to make sense of it all, or at least point him in the right direction. She had spent weeks and months in Egypt throughout her career as an archaeologist, so perhaps she would have been able to connect the dots. But that would never happen now. If he wanted to solve this mystery and bring the people behind Goodwin's death to justice, he was going to have to do it himself. Or was he? Sophia had already proven both capable and highly knowledgeable, and she was no doubt his best option for finding out more about the Templeton journal and Goodwin's secret work. On top of that, he realised that he simply liked spending time with her, and not just because she was easy on the eye. His meeting with Scarlett had also made it clear to him that there were certain things he would never be able to do himself, but that could become crucial in the days ahead. Perhaps throwing himself into this whole thing alone was the wrong approach. Perhaps what he needed to do was assemble a small team to help him.

It was now late-afternoon, and he got up from the sofa and wandered over to the floor-to-ceiling window, where he stood for a moment looking out over New York City. He would never get tired of that view. He walked to the fridge and made himself a ham and cheese sandwich, which he consumed at the kitchen island along with a glass of cold water. When he was done, he was about to reach for his phone to check the weather forecast when it suddenly chimed and burred on the white marble kitchen top. It was Sophia.

'Ethan?' she said as he picked up, her excited voice sounding nothing like the subdued and distressed research assistant he had met earlier.

'Yup,' he responded. 'What's up?'

'You're not going to believe this,' she said. 'Something amazing has happened.'

'What's going on?' he said.

'Howard Templeton's journal,' she said. 'I found some of it in Professor Goodwin's desk drawer.'

'What?' he said. 'We both watched the killer take it from his office.'

'Yes,' said Sophia, 'but it turns out Goodwin made digital scans of some of the pages. I guess he was worried that something would happen to the original. I found a printout of the document in his desk drawer.'

'That's great,' said Ethan, feeling Sophia's enthusiasm beginning to rub off on him. 'Have you had time to look at it yet?'

'Some,' she said. 'It's fascinating. But I called you as soon as I realised what it was. I think this could really help us.'

'Do you want to come down and show me?' said Ethan. 'I also have something I need to tell you.'

'Well,' Sophia said hesitantly. 'OK, but I don't have a car.'

'Don't worry,' said Ethan. 'I can have Mitch pick you up in about twenty minutes. He can take you straight here.'

'Uhm, sure,' she said, evidently somewhat taken aback by the prospect of more VIP treatment.

'Same place as before?' said Ethan. 'The cricket ground.'

'Kimberley Field?' said Sophia. 'Alright. Sounds good. I can be there in about half an hour.'

'Perfect,' said Ethan. 'See you soon.'

* * *

When the corporate chopper touched down on the edge of the cricket ground just to the east of New Haven's characterful town centre, onlookers stopped to watch as the young woman ran slightly hunched over to the side of the aircraft and then climbed up next to the pilot.

'All strapped in?' said Mitch, leaning over to check that she was sitting securely in her seat.

'Yup,' said Sophia. 'Ready to go.'

'Alright, just... don't touch anything.' Mitch grinned, and then he gestured to the controls and the alternate stick and rudder pedals in front of Sophia's seat.

'Not a chance,' said Sophia, raising both hands. 'I value my life too highly for that.'

'OK,' Mitch said. 'Let's go then.'

He took the chopper smoothly up to around three hundred feet, and then he pitched the nose down and the aircraft began accelerating south towards New York City.

'So, you were a military pilot?' said Sophia pleasantly, glancing at Mitch.

'That's right,' said Mitch. 'SOAR. It's a special ops unit. We used to fly the pipe hitters in and out of trouble.'

'Pipe hitters?' said Sophia.

'The operators,' said Mitch. 'The door kickers. The guys who you never hear about on the news but who kill the bad guys and keep you safe.'

'Right,' said Sophia. 'Did you enjoy it?'

'Absolutely,' said Mitch. 'Best time of my life. But all good things have to end sometime, and I figured I needed a civilian job before I got too old. Ethan hooked me up working for Frost Industries. Just like that. How do you know Ethan?'

Sophia proceeded to tell Mitch about her working relationship with Tobias Goodwin and how she and Ethan had stumbled upon what now looked like some sort of conspiracy.

'It's a damn shame,' said Mitch. 'I know he and Ethan were close. I hope they find the fucker who did it.'

For the next few minutes, there was silence in the cockpit as they both pondered the horrific events at Yale. After a while, however, Sophia was keen to lighten the mood a bit.

'So what about Ethan?' she said casually as she looked out of the window at the undulating forests passing underneath the chopper. 'You guys go back, right? What can you tell me about him?'

'Ethan Frost,' said Mitch pensively, but with a small glint in his eye. 'International man of mystery. What is there to say? The man is stupidly handsome but single. He's got more money than everyone else put together, but you'd never know it if someone didn't tell you. He's really humble. He's also kind of reserved at times, and he can be difficult to read.'

'Yes,' said Sophia. 'I got that feeling.'

'But don't let that fool you,' said Mitch. 'He's also strong and single-minded when he needs to be. A hell of a soldier, and a great leader. It was a real pleasure serving with him. But I gotta tell you. In the beginning, I really hated the guy.'

'What?' said Sophia with surprise and a faint smile as she turned her head to look at Mitch. 'Why?'

'Listen,' said Mitch with a sidelong grin as he glanced at her. 'Imagine being out drinking with the boys, and every time you walk into a bar, every hot female in the joint turns her head to look at him. Not anybody else. Just him. I mean, it was soul-destroying.'

Sophia laughed. 'Really?' she said. 'You're not a bad-looking guy yourself. Was it actually like that?'

'Every damn time,' said Mitch. 'The guys used to try to persuade him not to come. It was the only way. Anyway, thanks for saying that. I like to think that I'm reasonably attractive, but next to that guy? Forget it.'

Sophia smiled and shook her head. 'I had no idea guys were like that, too,' she said.

'Well,' said Mitch. 'That was then, and this is now. I like to think we've maybe moved on a little. The truth is, I think Ethan's a really solid dude who will always try to help you out if he can. I mean, like I said, he's the reason I got this job, so I owe him a lot. But he'd never acknowledge it that way. He's just very decent, you know? A good friend. You can trust him to do the right thing.'

'Yes, I get that feeling,' said Sophia pensively. 'How about you? Do you have a girlfriend?'

'Hell yeah,' Mitch grinned as he gestured to the cockpit around them. 'You're looking at her. Ain't she a beauty?'

* * *

Just under an hour after talking to Sophia on the phone, Ethan watched from the top of Frost Tower as the corporate chopper went from a small dot above the city on the northern horizon to a sleek, dark shape that flared out as it approached the top of the tower and came in to land on the helipad. After the down-draught had abated and Mitch had jumped out of the cockpit to open the door for his single passenger, Ethan watched Sophia disembark and give him a brief wave and a smile as she approached. She was wearing light blue jeans, white running shoes and a pink T-shirt, and her auburn hair was done up in a simple ponytail that bounced as she walked. Under her arm was a worn, light brown leather satchel.

As she came over to him, he realised that he was happy to see her again, and not just because of what she had found in Good-win's desk. Despite initially having seen her so distraught and fearful, he sensed that underneath it, she possessed a strong and self-confident character. She also had a pretty smile, intelligent eyes, and an attractive figure, and there was just something about her that made him want to spend time with her. He gave a small shake of the head and kicked himself for allowing his thoughts to drift in that direction. He had bigger fish to fry right now.

'Hi!' she said, flashing him a perfect smile as she reached him and glanced briefly over her shoulder at the helicopter. 'Do you always travel like this? I wish I had one of those.'

'I prefer my bike,' he said, returning her smile. 'Was the flight OK?'

'Yeah,' she said. 'Great views over the city. I also got to know Mitch a little bit. He's a really nice guy.'

'Yeah, he's solid,' said Ethan, glancing towards the chopper and giving Mitch a quick, informal salute, which the pilot returned.

'I told him about Goodwin,' said Sophia. 'I hope that's alright.'

'Yes, of course,' said Ethan. 'I trust him. Let's go downstairs. Follow me.'

They took the elevator down to the penthouse, where they sat down on Ethan's sofa.

'Before we talk about the journal,' said Ethan with a serious expression. 'I need to tell you something first.'

'Sure,' said Sophia, looking at him with a hint of concern. 'What's on your mind?'

Ethan proceeded to relay the results of his meetup with Scarlett Fox, including the positive ID on Nadeem Rashad, his paramilitary background, and his apparent connection to the mysterious Zosar Al-Masry. After he had finished speaking, Sophia looked concerned and perhaps even a bit confused.

'What does all this mean?' she said. 'Why would some

Egyptian big-shot businessman be involved in Goodwin's murder? That seems crazy.'

'I don't know yet,' said Ethan. 'But I intend to find out. I'm not sure how, though. I might have to go to Egypt myself.'

'Is that wise?' said Sophia sceptically. 'Can't the police handle this?'

'Not going to happen,' said Ethan flatly. 'Callahan is a good guy, but there is no way he could make anything happen inside that country. They would probably just ignore him or even complain to the US embassy. That angle is DOA.'

Sophia reached into her leather satchel and extracted a small stack of paper, which she placed on the coffee table in front of them.

'Well, here are the printouts of Goodwin's scans,' she said. 'Look.'

She slid the stack slightly sideways to allow them both to see, and then she leafed through the first few pages. They appeared to be high-quality scans of a number of pages from Templeton's old, leather-bound journal, and they showed short lines of neat handwriting, some with additional notes written in the margins. They also included sketches and drawings of structures and landscapes, and what appeared to be several ancient Egyptian artefacts.

'See these?' said Sophia, pointing to one of the brief notes scribbled in the margin of one of the pages. 'These are Goodwin's notes. I think he was going through the whole journal page by page to try to glean as much from it as possible. And he clearly thought these pages were particularly important.'

'So, what do they say?' said Ethan, leaning forward to peer at the pages.

'Well, it's obviously incomplete,' said Sophia. 'But it's a bit like a diary crossed with a notebook of random thoughts.

Templeton appears to have written in it whenever something interesting happened or when something occurred to him that he wanted to look into later. He also drew sketches of some of his finds, and it includes sections covering some fascinating legends spoken of by the Bedouin tribes in the far south whose ancestors have travelled the deserts for millennia. But the bottom line, as Goodwin found out, is that Templeton was developing a theory that the ancient Egyptian civilisation that we think of today was nothing more than the tail end of a much longer course of history that stretches far into the distant past. Thousands of years beyond what the current dogma tells us. And he appeared to have found several items during his digs in Egypt that back up this idea.'

'Such as?' said Ethan.

'Such as the golden lion that was taken from the museum,' said Sophia. 'Templeton wrote that he found it inside a tomb near one of the largest oases in the western desert, about a hundred miles west of Luxor. But it didn't fit with some of the other items he found there, mainly because it appeared to have been cast from molten gold. Yet, mining and smelting of gold isn't supposed to have happened in Egypt for another several thousand years. It is thought to have begun there around 3600 BCE, but Templeton, based on other finds inside the tomb, was convinced that the lion had to be much older than that.'

'What sort of finds?' said Ethan.

'Well, obviously fired pottery,' said Sophia, 'which archaeologists always find because once it's been in a kiln, it virtually lasts forever if it isn't broken. But also other much more sophisticated things like proto-hieroglyphic writings.'

'Couldn't this just be a case of Templeton misreading the contents of the tomb?' said Ethan. 'The dating of those things can be notoriously difficult.'

'Yes,' Sophia conceded, 'except for one thing. The pottery there was dated to at least 5400 BCE.'

'Wow,' said Ethan. 'That's a huge gap. Almost two thousand years.'

'And there's more,' said Sophia. 'Goodwin was so convinced that Templeton was onto something that he had a tiny shaving from the gold lion tested in a lab at Yale's geology department. He didn't tell the researcher where it came from but simply asked her to determine roughly when it might have been cast.'

'How does that work?' said Ethan. 'I didn't think gold could be dated. It is an element in the periodic table, right? And whatever gold exists here on this planet was created by exploding stars and has been around for billions of years, ever since the Earth formed.'

'That's correct,' said Sophia. 'But there are always impurities in the gold from when the raw ore was mined and then melted down. And these impurities can be dated using something called lead isotope analysis, where the tiny particles of lead isotopes in the gold are analysed, and relative ratios are determined. This allows researchers to map out the radioactive decay process in the lead and thereby estimate how long it has been since the gold containing these trace elements was melted and then cast in a mould. In this case, in the shape of a lion.'

'That's interesting,' said Ethan. 'How accurate is this method?'

'It varies,' said Sophia, 'but it is usually accurate to within a couple of centuries, which means that it is good enough for our purposes.'

'And what were the results?' said Ethan, keen to understand what Professor Goodwin had discovered.

'Well, this is where it gets wild,' said Sophia, raising her eyebrows as she looked at him. 'Because according to the results provided by the lab, the lion was cast from high-purity molten gold around the year 10,500 BCE.'

Ethan looked straight at her, momentarily unable to think of anything to say.

'That can't be right,' he finally said, sceptically.

'That's exactly what Goodwin thought,' said Sophia. 'It's right here in the notes he wrote in the margin of these pages. And that's also why Templeton was shunned by his peers during his lifetime and why his journal and the lion figurine were locked away and almost forgotten under the Peabody Museum. They just don't fit with the accepted Egyptological dogma. Or to be more precise, they only fit if you're prepared to take the leap and assume that there really was some ancient precursor civilisation that existed thousands of years before the pharaohs.'

'I can see why Goodwin was so quiet about it,' said Ethan. 'It's a pretty big leap.'

'That's right.' Sophia nodded. 'And I can see here from Goodwin's notes that some of Templeton's peers at the time even suggested that the artefacts he claimed to have found in the Egyptian desert were forgeries made either by Templeton himself or by unscrupulous Egyptian crooks who successfully tricked the professor into believing they were real. Either way, Templeton stood to gain nothing from talking openly about his theory. At least not until he could find definitive proof. And Goodwin was caught in the same trap.'

'What do you think about it?' said Ethan. 'This idea of a precursor civilisation. Do you believe it could be true?'

'I believe that if Goodwin was won over,' she replied earnestly, 'then who am I to doubt it? Not only was he one of the most knowledgeable experts in this field. He spent years looking into it, and it is pretty clear from this journal and from his own notes that he had become as convinced about it as Templeton was. But of course, Templeton disappeared and was never able to prove his theory. At least not as far as anyone knows. And now Goodwin is gone too, along with the journal.'

As Sophia finished speaking, a somewhat pained and despondent look swept briefly across her face. But then she appeared to recompose herself as she sat up straight again, seemingly keen not to let her emotions derail their conversation.

'You mentioned legends told by desert Bedouins,' said Ethan. 'What do these legends say?'

'According to Templeton, who talked to these people back in 1906,' said Sophia, 'legends had been passed down through generations of an ancient but now lost city somewhere in the desert far to the west.'

'But there's nothing there but arid desert,' said Ethan. 'What sort of city could exist out there?'

'The Bedouins claimed that it was a city that existed thousands of years before the pharaohs,' she said. 'And it was surrounded by green and fertile lands. It was also supposed to be immeasurably rich in gold, and it contained a mausoleum for a great ruler. A place called the Hall of Lions.'

'The Hall of Lions,' Ethan repeated, thinking of the golden lion figurine.

'According to these legends,' Sophia continued, 'this hall contained life-sized lions made of solid gold in numbers beyond counting.'

'It all sounds a bit far-fetched,' said Ethan slightly sceptically. 'Lions don't live anywhere near the Egyptian desert. And you just told me that smelting and casting of gold first occurred about five and a half thousand years ago.'

'I know,' said Sophia. 'And yet, the isotope analysis from the lab determined that the gold figurine was cast more than twelve thousand years ago. I agree, it sounds crazy. But I feel like there's enough here to justify digging deeper. And clearly, so did Goodwin.'

'Something just occurred to me,' said Ethan, glancing at her. 'If the lion figurine was made in a cast using molten gold, then you would think that there would be many more of them, right? The whole point of a cast is to be able to produce large numbers quickly.'

'Good point.' Sophia nodded. 'But as far as I know, the one Templeton appears to have found is the only one of its kind to ever be discovered.'

'Precisely where do you suppose he found it?' said Ethan.

'A place called Kharga Oasis,' said Sophia. 'It's deep in the western desert, and even today it's not easy to get to. Templeton travelled there on a camel from Abydos, which would have been quite a journey in 1906.'

Ethan reached forward and began leafing through the pages in the small stack one by one to reveal page after page of hand-written notes, brief scribbles, sketches and diagrams, most of which also included Goodwin's own annotations.

'There's a whole bunch here,' he said. 'It will take a while to go through it all.'

'There's literally nothing I would rather spend my time on right now,' said Sophia with a faint smile.

Ethan turned over another page to reveal a large shaded sketch of a dark, three-dimensional geometric shape that was roughly spherical. However, it appeared to have twelve flat, identical sides, each one shaped like a perfect pentagon.

'What's this?' he said, peering at it.

'I believe it's called a dodecahedron,' said Sophia.

'Right,' said Ethan, 'but what is it actually? What did Templeton draw here? There are no notes on the page to describe it. Have you ever seen this shape in the context of ancient Egypt?'

'No,' Sophia said with a small shake of the head. 'Never. It's strange. I wonder what it could be.'

Ethan turned over another page, and they found themselves looking at a rough sketch of what appeared to be a stone stele that was missing a large piece of its lower left corner. It seemed to depict some sort of map. On the far right-hand side was a thin, meandering shape that was unmistakably the Nile of Upper Egypt in the south near the border with present-day Sudan. Next to it was a diamond-shaped marker, and in the centre near the stele's broken edge was a circular symbol that Ethan didn't recognise, but Sophia immediately pointed to it and spoke.

'That's an oasis,' she said. 'It must be Kharga Oasis.'

'And this marker?' said Ethan, pointing at the diamond shape near the Nile.

'I think that's Abydos,' said Sophia. 'The location seems to fit.'

'This suggests that Templeton visited both of those places,' said Ethan.

'He wrote here that he found this broken stele in a small temple somewhere near Abydos,' Sophia said as her fingertips moved along the handwritten notes underneath the sketch. 'It says that it depicts trade routes across the desert during ancient times.'

'Look at these lines,' said Ethan, tracing a thin, barely visible line from Abydos and west to the Kharga Oasis, and then another from Abydos due north, and another reaching towards the south-east. 'These must be the routes that trading caravans used to take across the desert. It looks like there are more here, but the details are really faint. I would love to see the original stele.'

'This is interesting,' said Sophia, leaning forward to read the final handwritten paragraph on the page. 'Templeton wrote that the oasis was marked on the map by a black, finely cut stone with pentagonal faces that was about two inches across.'

'It must be this one,' said Ethan, finding the sketch showing the black dodecahedron. 'Two inches. That's about the size of a golf ball.'

'I guess so,' said Sophia as her fingertips moved along the journal's handwritten text. 'It says here that it was as hard as a diamond, and it appeared to have been embedded in a hole drilled into the stele before then falling out at some point over the intervening millennia. It says that he simply picked it up from the temple floor.'

'Where is it now?' said Ethan. 'Did he bring it back to Yale?'

'No,' replied Sophia. 'It was apparently confiscated from him by the Egyptian authorities when he returned to Abydos.'

'That must mean they still have it, right?' said Ethan.

'Let me just check something,' said Sophia, gesturing to Ethan's laptop, which was sitting on the coffee table. 'Can I use this for a second?'

'Sure,' he said, pulling it towards himself and sliding it over in front of Sophia. 'Knock yourself out.'

She opened a browser, and with a few quick taps, using her Yale credentials to log in, she swiftly accessed a faculty database containing a list of all archaeological artefacts found by Yale's Council of Archaeology going all the way back to the founding of the university in 1701. The entries were basic and brief, but when she searched for artefacts found by Howard Templeton, a short list came up. It included pottery, some copper fishing harpoons and a few items of jewellery. It also included the lion figurine, but with a note added later indicating the possibility of it being a forgery. However, at the bottom of the list was an entry for a black, geometrically cut gemstone. The entry included a brief note written in brackets.

'It says here,' said Sophia, 'that a black, cut gemstone measuring 1.94 inches across was found by Templeton near Abydos, and that it is currently held by the Egyptian Museum in Cairo.'

'Is it on display?' said Ethan.

'Not a chance,' said Sophia with a shake of the head. 'Howard Templeton and his theories are like kryptonite to the Egyptian scholars, even today. What he suggested threatened to upend the entire narrative of ancient pharaonic Egypt, so anything associated with him will be locked away out of view. It's probably just gathering dust in a vault somewhere. But let me try something.'

Her fingers moved across the laptop's keyboard, and a few seconds later, she stopped and stared at the screen, which displayed a recent news story.

'Hey, look at this,' she said, sounding intrigued and surprised as she turned to face Ethan. 'There was a burglary at the Egyptian Museum just a few weeks ago, and the only thing stolen was this gemstone.'

She placed a hand on the sketch of the black, angular orb and tapped her index finger.

'You're kidding me,' said Ethan. 'That can't possibly be a coincidence. Two burglaries on two different continents, and the only things taken both relate to Howard Templeton. Was it valuable?'

'I don't know,' said Sophia, looking unsettled. 'I don't know if it was ever determined precisely what type of stone it was. Either way, there's something really strange going on here. Do you think it was this Al-Masry guy?'

'It's not a bad guess,' said Ethan pensively. 'There's a real mystery here, and I think it goes beyond Goodwin's murder. For some reason, certain people have taken an interest in Howard Templeton's work, and they are prepared to kill to get their hands on it. What do you suppose they are after?'

'I'm not sure,' said Sophia. 'But I keep coming back to the golden lion. I can't shake the feeling that it is somehow connected to the Bedouin legends about the lost city and the Hall of Lions. Imagine if that were actually true.'

'Well, it would be a hell of a lot of gold,' said Ethan.

'That's for sure.' Sophia nodded. 'And gold has made people do terrible things for as long as we've been able to get our hands on it. Maybe it's really that simple. Or maybe there's something bigger at play here.'

The two of them sat quietly for a moment, both contemplating what they had discovered so far.

'If we could solve the mystery of those Bedouin legends,' reflected Ethan, 'then maybe that would help us find the people responsible for Goodwin's murder, whoever they are. But we can't do it from here. I think we need to go to Egypt.'

'Really?' said Sophia, looking puzzled.

'Well, what good is it for us to sit around here in New York?' he said. 'And if Nadeem Rashad has returned to Egypt with the journal and the golden lion, then that's where we need to be.'

Sophia appeared to chew that over for a moment before nodding and speaking again.

'Well, listen,' she said. 'As crazy as Templeton's theories might seem, and as bizarre as the timeline going back twelve thousand years sounds, there are elements of it that actually tie in perfectly with what has been found in Egypt, including things on the Giza Plateau where the Pyramids and the Sphinx are located. Things that have to do with the Sphinx and the stars.

But it's pretty complicated to explain, and it would be a lot easier just to show you.'

'So, does that mean you're in?' said Ethan with a hopeful smile.

'Yes,' she said, meeting his gaze. 'I'm in.'

* * *

Ethan and Sophia decided to aim for a departure to Egypt the next day. While Mitch flew Sophia back to New Haven on the corporate chopper so that she could pack a travel bag, Ethan placed a call to Scarlett Fox.

'Scarlett, it's me. Ethan,' he said when she picked up. 'How's it going?'

'Yeah, not bad,' she said. 'You?'

'I think I made a mistake,' said Ethan.

'What do you mean?' she said, sounding puzzled.

'When I turned down your offer to dig deeper into Zosar Al-Masry,' said Ethan. 'Professor Goodwin's assistant and I have discovered that he might be connected to another burglary that happened in Cairo a few weeks ago. A burglary that looks like it might also be related to what was stolen from Yale.'

He proceeded to tell Scarlett about Sophia and what the two of them had discovered. He also told her about Howard Templeton and his expeditions to Upper Egypt more than a century ago.

'Something dark is definitely going on,' she said by the end of it. 'This Al-Masry dude sounds like really bad news.'

'Listen, Scarlett,' said Ethan. 'We're going to Egypt tomorrow, and I have a feeling that we'll end up having to go to places that may be off limits to the public. We're also poking our noses into the affairs of a powerful business tycoon with serious political connections, so that could get messy. On top of that, we're looking for evidence that much of Egypt's history needs to be rewritten, and that usually never goes down well with anyone. Bottom line, I'd like you to join us. We could use your skills with a keyboard to help monitor police and intelligence service activity while we're there, and given what you've discovered about Al-Masry, I think it's likely that we will end up ruffling some feathers.'

'Alright,' said Scarlett, seemingly unfazed. 'Count me in.'

'Just like that?' said Ethan, surprised by how willing she was to jump in the deep end.

'Sure,' she said. 'I've got nothing better to do. And I'm happy to help you out. Plus, it's been a while since I had the opportunity to chase down a bad guy. You can count on me.'

'Great,' said Ethan. 'I'll send someone to pick you up tomorrow. Say 11 a.m.?'

'I'll be ready,' she said.

'Thanks, Scarlett,' said Ethan. 'I'll see you tomorrow.'

Ethan ended the call, and then he looked into flight options to the North African country the next day. As well as different helicopters, Frost Industries owned and operated a fleet of corporate jets, and he knew that Mitch, as well as being among the best helicopter pilots the US military had ever produced, was also certified for fixed-wing jets and would be able to join them as a pilot. Ethan was about to call the company's internal travel desk to arrange for a jet to be made available when a memory from years earlier suddenly flashed through his mind.

He was reminded of something he had overheard one day, sitting in his father's office, when the company's chief science officer and head of R&D, Marcus Becker, had updated Robert

Frost on the progress of an advanced Frost Aerospace project. It was a top-secret experimental development program that had been authorised and funded by the US Department of Defense. Codenamed Firefly, its aim was to develop the world's first super-sonic vertical take-off and landing aircraft to replace the older VTOL models that were soon to be phased out from active service. Having been inserted into war zones on numerous missions on board similar birds, Ethan remembered being impressed with the proposed performance specs of the new aircraft. The Firefly program had gone ahead and made good progress, but in the end, it had been cancelled by Congress due to cost overruns and the high price tag of each aircraft, but not before two prototype units had been produced.

Ethan pondered his idea for a moment, and then he picked up the phone and placed a call to the R&D division on the nineteenth floor. A few minutes later, he entered Marcus Becker's corner office, which looked out over the East River and Lower Manhattan towards the south. Becker was a tall man with broad shoulders and a strong physique under his mid-blue suit and tie. His greying hair was swept back from a high forehead, and his short grey beard and strong jaw gave him the impression of having a mild underbite. His thin mouth was slightly turned down, which might have given him a slightly grumpy look, but the smile lines around his narrow blue eyes betrayed an affable character who had always been a loyal friend and colleague to the late Robert Frost.

'Ethan,' he said in his Georgia accent, getting up from behind his desk as he saw the younger man walk in. 'It's been a while.'

'Marcus,' said Ethan, giving a smile and a nod as the two men shook hands. 'Good to see you. Got a minute?'

'Sure,' said Becker, gesturing to a sofa near his desk.

The two men sat down, and Becker leaned forward with his hands clasped and his elbows resting on his knees.

'What can I do for you?' he said, now all business.

'Remember that Firefly program we were developing a couple of years ago?' said Ethan.

'The VTOL.' Becker nodded. 'Sure. Damn shame about that. We were ready to go. Best aircraft we ever made. Next-generation avionics. Supersonic capability. Silent hover. Very advanced. Expensive, though. It was all in the engine design. Truly next level. But in the end, it was too costly for the DOD, so the program was canned.'

'But didn't we make working prototypes?' said Ethan.

'Of course,' said Becker. 'Two of them. Mothballed, though. We've been hoping that Congress would appropriate the funds to revive the program, but so far, no luck.'

'Where are they?' said Ethan.

'Oh, I believe they're parked in a hangar at our test facility in Arizona,' said Becker. 'But they both flew, and they performed exactly as expected. I tell you, you guys in the special ops community would have loved those things.'

'Right,' said Ethan, nodding slowly before glancing at Becker with a roguish smile. 'I don't suppose you could have one of those things flown up here to New York?'

Holding Ethan's gaze for a moment, Marcus Becker briefly looked puzzled, but then a good-natured smile began to spread across his face.

'I'm sure we can swing that,' he said. 'I'll have one of our test pilots fly it up here ASAP.'

'Thanks,' said Ethan. 'It's better if I don't tell you what I need it for, except to say that we'll be going on a bit of an archaeological excursion. So, I'm wondering if there's anything else that any of the Frost Industries subsidiaries have been developing that you think might come in handy? Call it... field testing. And also, let's just say that we might not be welcomed with open arms.'

Becker tilted his head and nodded slowly with a thin, knowing smile.

'I see,' he said as he pondered the question for a moment. 'There might be a few things that could be of use. Come with me.'

Three hours later, Ethan was standing by the side of the helipad on top of Frost Tower. The sun had set beyond the flat western horizon about an hour earlier, and all that was left of its presence was the faintly orange glow in an otherwise pale blue sky that was rapidly shifting towards black. Next to him was Mitch Kazinsky, wearing a charcoal flight suit and holding a helmet in one hand.

'So, what are we doing here?' he said.

'You're getting a new aircraft,' said Ethan. 'A prototype. I want you to test it out.'

'Alright.' Mitch nodded. 'Is this a new kind of chopper?'

'Better,' said Ethan. 'A lot better.'

'What is it then?' said Mitch.

'Just wait a moment,' said Ethan, glancing down at his wristwatch. 'It's almost here.'

Mitch looked out over the city and slowly turned his head left and right. He could see the lights from planes landing and taking off from LaGuardia Airport in the distance towards the north-east, and others coming out of JFK Airport far to the east. But there was no sign of a helicopter.

'I don't hear anything,' he said.

'There it is,' said Ethan, pointing south towards the skyscrapers of Lower Manhattan and Wall Street.

A small black shape moved against the pale blue sky, and

had it not been for its flashing navigation lights, it would have been almost impossible to spot. It came closer at speeds far in excess of a regular chopper, but neither of the two men was able to hear it. As it raced low over Midtown and rapidly closed the distance to Frost Tower and Central Park, it pitched up slightly and rapidly gained altitude to come to a complete stop some fifty metres from the side of the tower and about thirty metres above it. It hovered there for a moment, seemingly fixed in place as it slowly rotated and orientated itself towards the helipad, and Mitch's mouth began to fall open. Not only was its sleek, black, and slightly angular fuselage like something out of a sci-fi movie and of a kind Mitch had never seen before, but the aircraft was almost perfectly silent. All he could hear was the faint whisper and almost imperceptible whine of the two large next-generation jet engines mounted on half-length winglets that were slightly swept back and attached vaguely forward from the midpoint of the fuselage, giving the aircraft a muscular yet aerodynamic look. At the back were two slanted, almost vertical stabilisers that extended from the tapering rear of the aircraft, and at the front was an angular glass cockpit whose windows were heavily tinted, and they protruded slightly up and out on both sides, giving the aircraft a vaguely insectoid appearance.

'What the hell is that thing?' said Mitch, unable to hold back a boyish grin from spreading across his face.

'This is the AVX-1 Firefly,' said Ethan. 'Advanced Vertical Experimental. It was designed as a VTOL for the military, but it never went into mass production. This is one of only two proto-types, so don't break it.'

'I'm flying this thing?' said Mitch, looking like a kid in a candy store.

'Well, I sure as hell ain't doing it,' said Ethan with a wink.

As they watched, the aircraft manoeuvred itself over the

helipad and descended with a level of control and stability that impressed even Mitch. As it did so, he noticed that the fuselage was covered in a bluish-black material, which he suspected might be highly radar absorbent, probably making the aircraft appear about the size of a large bird on radar screens, despite being some twenty metres long with a wingspan of about fifteen metres. As they watched, the strange-looking engines suddenly began to change shape, becoming sleeker and smaller as panels shifted, ducts repositioned, and air intakes narrowed, and Mitch realised that they had a configurable engine housing.

'That right there is why they are so expensive,' said Ethan, pointing at the nearest of the two engines. 'The design allows for in-flight morphing of engine topology and seamless transition from hover to subsonic and then supersonic flight. It's one hell of a feat of engineering.'

'It looks like something out of a Transformer movie,' said Mitch. 'And it's just about the coolest thing I've ever seen.'

As the two engines rotated and altered their shape, narrowing the air intake and extruding a short jet exhaust nozzle cone from the rear, the noise changed from a whisper to something approaching an angry and slightly louder hiss, but it was still only barely audible.

'This thing is amazing,' he said, giving a small, slow shake of the head.

At that moment, the glass canopy suddenly went from opaque to transparent, and sitting inside in the pilot's seat was a lone figure wearing a flight suit.

'That's one of our test pilots from the Arizona testing facility,' said Ethan, pointing at the helmeted pilot who gave them a brief salute. 'He's going to show you the ropes. It flies like a helicopter, but it can go a lot faster when it needs to. I want you to take it up tonight and get comfortable with the controls and the handling, as well as the transition to supersonic. We're going to need it tomorrow.'

'Where are we going?' said Mitch, glancing at Ethan.

'We're going to Egypt,' he said. 'Pack up and get yourself ready. We're leaving in the morning.'

proven all as the acquisition is successful. We're going to need it for our...

Where are we going? said Mike, beginning to smile.

We're going to Egypt, she said. Back up and get yourself ready. We're leaving in the morning.

6

It was just after sunrise on a clear day in Cairo when Zosar Al-Masry stood on his wide, spacious balcony with his hands clasped behind his back as he looked out from his twelfth-floor luxury apartment at the top of an exclusive mansion block in the western part of the city. From his vantage point in front of a set of sliding doors to the opulent living room that dominated the huge apartment, he had an unobstructed view out across a sprawling golf course to the Great Pyramid some four hundred metres away. Behind it, he could just glimpse the smaller Pyramids of Khafre and Menkaure in the distance.

In his mid-seventies, he had a round, slightly squat face with lined, olive skin and a wide Nubian nose. His hair was short and grey with fine curls, and he sported a greying and closely trimmed goatee. His heavy brow was folded in seemingly permanent creases as he looked out through dark brown eyes under heavy, black eyebrows. Just under five and a half feet tall, he was of short stature with a slight build and narrow shoulders under his expensive, dark pinstriped suit, and he was slightly hunched forward as he stood there by the chrome balcony railing looking out. However, despite his diminutive physical appearance, he was not to be underestimated. A few people had made that mistake throughout the years, and they were no longer around to warn others.

Gazing out at the enormous structures in front of him, he reflected on recent events and allowed himself a moment to ponder what lay ahead, if the gods were willing. Watching the sun's first rays kiss the top of the Great Pyramid always filled him with a sense of awe, and it allowed him to imagine what it had been like when these monuments had first been built near the Nile in the virtually empty desert more than four thousand years ago. The pure splendour and glory of it. And the contrast to how things looked now was both shocking and disturbing. It was one thing for them to have been left to decay rather than being restored to their former glory. But worse than that, instead of being rightfully elevated to a position of veneration and respect purely for the people of his country, whose magnificent ancestors had built them, the Pyramids were now treated like a tawdry tourist trap full of mercenary tour guides and pushy street vendors looking to pounce on the latest batch of ignorant white-skinned foreigners with their expensive cameras and empty minds. It was truly pitiful.

As much as he took pride in his heritage and in his people, he had to admit to a certain sense of disappointment and perhaps even disdain for his fellow countrymen. They appeared to have lost their sense of pride in themselves and their history. The very fact that the city of Cairo had been allowed to encroach so haphazardly onto the Giza Plateau, where the Pyramids and the Great Sphinx stood, was proof of this. The city planners appeared to be in the pocket of shady real estate developers, and it showed. There were ugly and often ramshackle and badly maintained buildings everywhere, and even the streets themselves were dirty and full of unwashed rabble.

To him, Egypt was quite clearly losing its way and losing its identity, torn between the decadent, vacuous West on one side and the rabid, violent Islamists of the Middle East on the other. And all this while being governed by a profoundly corrupt and abysmally incompetent political class who existed mainly to enrich themselves and maintain their and the military's iron grip on the country and its natural resources. Sure, he and his family had benefitted handsomely from the drilling rights to the oil fields in the western desert, but political change as profound as what he was envisaging required serious funding. Irrespective of those things, the bottom line for him was simple. Egypt needed a new path for the future, but one that was rooted in its ancient and glorious past.

For years now, he had been quietly working away at this grand project, secretly preparing the ground and developing a small but powerful network of like-minded and loyal associates. He had even gone as far as to change his own name to something more suitable for what lay ahead. Something that could carry the weight of what he was planning to take on. Something for the masses to rally around.

It had all started a number of years earlier when the grand idea had first entered his mind, and the plan for its execution had then gradually begun to form. Having lived a careless and mindless life of wealth and privilege, he had eventually realised, after much study of his country's history, and after having sought out advice, insights, and guidance from respected scholars of the past, that Egypt had become sick, and that he was destined to become its remedy. And as he had transformed himself, so was Egypt going to be transformed into something pure, strong, and respected once more. Free of the influence of Western ideas, introduced first by the arrogant and deviant Greeks, who, beginning with Alexander the Great, had usurped the ancient dynasties and played at being pharaohs for centuries, pretending that Ptolemy I and his descendant Cleopatra had been rightful rulers of this ancient land. And then came the warlord Mohammed and his fanatical upstart religion of Islam, whose goal had only ever been endless conquest and subjugation of all others for the glory of a single derivative god. And across the most recent centuries, the modern West had returned through the Ottomans, the French, the British, the Soviets, and now the Americans, each one more degenerate and morally lost than the next. This was nothing short of an intolerable desecration of this ancient civilisation, and it simply had to be brought to an end before the nation entirely ceased to exist.

What Egypt needed was a revolution and a return to its glory days. What was required was for it to turn its back on the recent past, not least the rabid Islamism that now ran through every aspect of society, and a return to what once was. A return to the true greatness of the first predynastic civilisation, now long forgotten by the modern world. A glorious empire, even older than the pharaonic dynasties that he had been searching for evidence of for more than a decade. Evidence that now finally seemed to be within his grasp. And if he could find such tangible proof of this much more ancient history, this magnificent origin story that became the seed of everything that followed, including these very Pyramids in front of him, then the superiority of his culture would become undeniable to the world.

Having received his epiphany from the gods of old many years ago, everything had suddenly become clear to him. The path ahead now lay open. All he had to do now was walk it, and the greatness of Egypt would be restored. The people of these ancient lands would then finally see the light of the old gods once again and be compelled to rally around him and follow him into the future.

He turned to face the sumptuous living room with its hardwood flooring, cream-coloured walls, coffered ceiling, and plush sofas and armchairs. There was even a wide marble fireplace, which was never used, but it gave the space an elegant focal point around which the furniture was arranged. Then he stepped across the room and entered a study full of books where he spent much of his time. Here, he pored over old accounts of the first European explorers of Egypt during the eighteenth and nineteenth centuries, when much of the ancient past was being rediscovered. Many of these accounts were wrapped in florid nonsense conjured up by people almost entirely ignorant of the distant past. However, every so often, he would come across a reference or a mention of something significant. Something that would inch his research forward and move him towards the ultimate goal of finding the lost city. And discovering Howard Templeton's secretive expeditions had proven his most valuable lead yet.

He stepped past the mahogany desk and slid aside a false wall to reveal an alcove, inside which was a small stone table. Sitting on top of it were four items, the largest of which was the lower half of a stone stele that his experts estimated was from around 2700 BCE. He had uncovered it about eight years ago during initial geological sampling ahead of the establishment of a new oil well in the Abu Gharadig Basin in the western desert. The stele had been cut neatly from a block of sandstone, and it bore engravings on its front that were clearly some sort of map.

Unfortunately, the top half of the stele had broken off along a slanting angle at some indeterminate time in the distant past, and so only part of the map was discernible. However, it included the oasis near the drill site about 230 kilometres due west of Cairo, as well as several lines indicating ancient trade routes. One meandered north-east towards the Nile Delta and the Mediterranean, while another went due east towards the ancient capital of Memphis, some twenty kilometres south of modern Cairo. But there was also a third route, which appeared to go almost due south, possibly towards the large life-giving oases of Farafra, Dakhla and Kharga. All of them were located deep in the inhospitable and unforgiving southern desert, and he knew that they had been used as rest stops and trading hubs for large caravans of merchants and camels for thousands of years.

Two of the other items in the alcove were more recent acquisitions, and they might just turn out to be the key to finding what he had been seeking for so long. He picked up the golden lion figurine from the Peabody Museum and inspected it once more. It was beautiful beyond words, and its very shape hinted at the hidden truth behind the ancient legends. It was also unnaturally heavy for an object of its size, and there was something magical about the weight and feel of solid gold against the skin. Putting it down, he then picked up the other item from a small silver stand and held it in the palm of his hand. He was only just able to close his fingers around the perfectly black, roughly spherical object, and he could feel the faint corners and edges of its complex geometric shape digging into his palm.

'What are you?' he muttered as he slowly turned the item over to inspect it. 'What are your secrets?'

He had found two references to this type of object in ancient accounts, both of which related to the moon, although he did not yet understand what its purpose was. But he was convinced that it was somehow connected to what he was looking for. And the life of Tobias Goodwin had been a small price to pay for its acquisition.

He placed the black, intricately cut orb back onto its stand and picked up the final item. It was an old, leather-bound journal, and on its pages were Howard Templeton's handwriting and his sketches. The man might well have been mad, but that didn't mean he was wrong about the lost civilisation. After turning it over in his hands, enjoying the feel of the older leather, Al-Masry put the journal back onto the table and took a step back. These four items were the best evidence he had found so far that what he was searching for was real. It was somewhere out there in the desert. And he was going to find it.

* * *

Several hours later in New York City, the AVX-1 Firefly, with Mitch at the controls, lifted off vertically from the top of Frost Tower and banked slightly to take up a north-easterly heading. As it pitched down and swooped over Central Park, its engines gradually swivelled to their level flight positions, and then it rose and began accelerating out past LaGuardia Airport and the East River, before then rapidly climbing towards its cruising altitude of 37,000 feet somewhere over Long Island Sound. Once there, Mitch initiated engine reconfiguration, and a few seconds later, the aircraft accelerated further as the next-generation turbojet engines opened up with all their power and pushed the Firefly past the speed of sound, quickly reaching its cruising speed of Mach 1.4, or just over 1,700 kilometres per hour.

'How are we looking?' said Ethan after undoing his seatbelt and poking his head into the futuristic cockpit.

'Everything's looking good,' said Mitch, who was wearing a dark gunmetal flight helmet with advanced avionics displays and integrated night vision. 'Engines at eighty-five per cent power and happy as can be. She handles like a dream. Flight time to Cairo is currently estimated at five hours and forty minutes. We should be touching down at around 5 p.m. local time.'

'Great,' said Ethan, placing a hand on the pilot's shoulder. 'Keep me posted if anything changes.'

'Will do.' Mitch nodded, returning his attention to the navigational displays.

Ethan walked back into the passenger cabin, which at four metres wide was the width of the aircraft. It stretched back another six metres and had comfortable seating for six people around two small tables, and despite the Firefly tearing through the air at supersonic speed, the cabin was virtually quiet except for the muffled hum of the engines and the faint hiss of the air-conditioning system. At the rear, behind a bulkhead with a sturdy, pressurised door, was the aircraft's cargo compartment, which was just large enough to fit a small car or a couple of motorcycles. Today, however, it contained something different. Before their departure, Ethan had spoken to Marcus Becker again, and without asking what the purpose was, the CSO had then agreed to Ethan's request and arranged for Mitch to pick up one of the new advanced desert quad bikes that Frost Industries was producing for the military. It was relatively large but fast and extremely durable, and Ethan had first-hand experience with this type of vehicle from several deployments with Delta to North Africa. In a dune-covered desert environment such as that of the Egyptian Sahara, there was no other vehicle he would rather be driving.

Before leaving New York, Sophia and Scarlett had spent the past hour inside Frost Tower getting to know each other, and although the two women were very different in almost every respect, they immediately seemed to hit it off. Both were highly intelligent, and an easy sense of friendliness and mutual respect had quickly developed. Scarlett told Sophia about how she had ended up helping Ethan, briefly mentioning her time at the CIA, and Sophia relayed how she had come to know Tobias Goodwin. She also gave Scarlett an overview of his work, including his efforts to make sense of Templeton's wild theories.

Ethan, wearing jeans and a loose, light blue shirt with the top two buttons undone, slid onto a seat across from Scarlett. She was wearing blue jeans and a black, long-sleeved top, and she was sitting by the window and had flipped open her laptop. Her fingers were moving quietly across the keyboard, and her eyes were focused on the screen.

'Anything yet?' said Ethan, referring to his earlier request for her to now dig deeper into Zosar Al-Masry.

'Some.' She nodded, looking up. 'He comes from the very well-off Fayek family that has been closely connected to the highest echelons of Egyptian society for generations. They were granted drilling rights to several oil fields in Abu Gharadig in the 1920s, and this has made the family extremely wealthy. I managed to access several public records in Cairo to look into his past, but information is unusually sparse. In fact, it is almost as if most of his former life has been wiped.'

'Former life?' Ethan asked.

'Well, he seems to have undergone something of a transformation,' said Scarlett. 'It looks like he may even have changed his name. He was born Darius Galal Fayek, but about ten years ago, he changed it to Zosar Al-Masry, and most of the details of his past disappeared from public records.'

'Why would anyone do this?' said Ethan, rubbing his chin.

'Your guess is as good as mine.' Scarlett shrugged. 'Why do people change their names? To make a fresh start somehow, right? To break with their past.'

'Zosar Al-Masry,' said Sophia from the seat by the table on the other side of the centre aisle. 'That's an interesting name.'

'Why is that?' said Ethan, turning his head to look at her.

'Because,' said Sophia, 'Zosar is the modern version of the ancient name Djoser. He was the ruler of the Third Dynasty during the Old Kingdom, and he was supposedly the first pharaoh to build a pyramid. And Al-Masry literally means "from Egypt". So if this guy changed his name to Zosar Al-Masry, then it is pretty much the most Egyptian name you could possibly come up with.'

'Interesting.' Ethan nodded pensively.

'Well,' said Scarlett. 'There's more. I decided to probe the security systems at the Egyptian Museum, and boy, do they need some upgrades. I was able to bypass the main firewall with barely any effort, and I accessed the security camera footage from the night of the burglary there. Have a look.'

Sophia, who wore black trousers and a white shirt, left her seat and joined the two others as Scarlett swivelled her laptop to allow them to see its screen.

'This is where the thief enters,' she said, playing a recording of a man wearing dark clothes and a face cover emerging from a stairwell up into the foyer of the museum. 'He came up from the parking basement, so he would have found a way in from down there. But there are no alarms going off, so either the system was disabled, or he had access to the correct codes.'

'Hey, I've been there,' said Sophia, gesturing. 'I love that place. Thousands of years of amazing Egyptian history all in one place.'

On Scarlett's screen, the man walked up the steps and stood in the lobby for a moment before moving deeper into the museum. In the top left corner was a timestamp showing 3:26 a.m. Ethan's eyes narrowed as he watched, and a faint tingling sensation crept up the sides of his temples. He studied the man closely.

'It's the same fucking guy,' he said icily. 'I swear, that's the guy who killed Professor Goodwin. Same physique. The way he moves. There's no doubt in my mind. It's Nadeem Rashad.'

'Holy crap,' Sophia whispered as she leaned closer, her forehead creased. 'What the hell is going on here?'

'Well, whatever it is,' said Scarlett, switching to a different recording, 'the plot thickens, because he then heads back down into the basement level.'

'That's the access to the underground storage units,' said Sophia, pointing at the screen. 'That's where they keep all the stuff that isn't on display in the museum.'

'Watch this,' said Scarlett, jerking her head at the screen. 'He knows exactly where he's going. Like a homing pigeon. And he touches nothing until he gets to this spot.'

On the screen, the masked Nadeem Rashad stopped by a door halfway along a corridor and punched an access code into the panel on the wall next to it.

'Damn,' said Sophia in hushed tones. 'He's got all the codes.'

'Someone inside that museum got paid off,' said Ethan, watching Goodwin's killer open the door and step inside.

'And here it comes,' said Scarlett as the recording switched to a camera inside the storage unit.

As they watched, Nadeem moved across the floor of the small room, opened a metal locker, and went down on one knee while he pulled out a box from the bottom shelf. He placed it on the floor, briefly rummaged around inside it, before pulling out a labelled cardboard box with a lid. He opened the lid and extracted a cloth, and he then allowed its contents to roll out into his palm. It was pitch-black and somewhat larger than a golf ball, and as it rolled, its angular geometric shape caught the light from the ceiling and glinted briefly.

'That's the orb,' Sophia said. 'The one Templeton found. It has been down there in that museum for over a century.'

'And now Al-Masry has it,' said Ethan, as Nadeem closed the locker, rose and left the room, after which the recording ended. 'No doubt about it. He's behind all of it.'

'But why?' said Sophia.

'That's what we need to find out,' said Ethan. 'Have you had time to look at the copies of the journal?'

'Yes,' said Sophia. 'I was up most of the night.'

'So, what did you find?' said Ethan.

'Well, first of all,' she replied, nodding towards the frozen image of the storage unit on the screen, 'as I said, that orb is a dodecahedron. It's one of the five so-called Platonic solids. A perfect shape where all the faces, edges and angles are the same on all sides. In this case, twelve pentagons.'

'Why pentagons?' said Ethan. 'Any ideas?'

'Well...' Sophia nodded. 'To the ancient Egyptians, the number five was associated with the underworld called the Duat.'

'Ruled over by Osiris,' said Ethan. 'The god of the afterlife.'

'Exactly,' said Sophia. 'But precisely how this orb relates to those concepts, I am not sure yet. Anyway, I found some notes written by Goodwin in the margin of Templeton's journal, and they might have a bearing on this.'

'How so?' said Ethan.

'Well, as I am sure you already know,' said Sophia, 'for millennia, life in the Nile Valley was completely dictated by the annual floods. If the Nile didn't swell and inundate the floodplains, crops wouldn't grow, and the harvest would almost certainly fail, and this could have catastrophic consequences for these large communities, who were suddenly without sufficient food. So it is no surprise that the floods became central to the lives of the ancient Egyptians. But what they couldn't have known was that the flood of the Nile was caused by the monsoon rains much further south in Central Africa. This pattern has been repeated for tens of thousands of years, but the ancient Egyptians had no idea what the monsoons actually were or why they might fail to materialise. So, it was natural for them to connect their appearance with the whims of the gods, as has been the case the world over for millennia. And this is where Goodwin began to develop a theory, and it all had to do with the movements of the stars across the night sky.'

As Sophia continued her story and became visibly captivated by what it might mean for their search, the others remained silent.

'As you'll see when we get to Cairo,' she continued, 'the Great Sphinx sitting at the foot of the Pyramids on the Giza Plateau faces east. In fact, at exactly the date of the spring equinox, when the day and the night are the same length, the sun rises in the east directly in front of the Sphinx. And not only that, but it rises inside the constellation of Orion, which the ancient Egyptians associated with Osiris.'

'That's really fascinating,' said Ethan. 'I never realised that. I guess it explains why Osiris became such an important god during the Middle Kingdom.'

'Exactly.' Sophia nodded. 'Now, if you enter the Great Pyramid of Khufu, you will find slanted shafts extending out from inside its large chambers, and one of them happens to point south, directly at Orion at its highest point in the sky. Another points north to the star Alpha Draconis in the constellation Draco, which was the pole star when the Pyramids were built 4,500 years ago. The ancient Egyptians called these stars

"Imperishable", and they connected them with the idea of the afterlife of their pharaohs, believing that their kings would go there after death.'

'How do we know all this?' said Scarlett.

'We know this from something called the Pyramid Texts,' said Sophia. 'They are inscriptions found inside a pyramid near Memphis, and there is a quote there relating to this. It says, "I, the king, will cross to that side on which are the Imperishable Stars, that I may be among them".'

'So, it was thought that the pharaohs joined the stars after death?' said Scarlett. 'That's a nice thought.'

'Yes.' Sophia nodded. 'In the afterlife, a pharaoh was perceived to have become an illuminated spirit, or, as some have suggested, a "star soul".'

'Hence the Pyramid shafts pointing to the sacred constellations,' said Ethan.

'That's right,' said Sophia. 'In that sense, for the pharaohs, the Pyramids were a gateway to the stars. And note that this is tied to the underworld, the Duat, which was often written as a star inside a circle. That star being Orion, which was the celestial manifestation of Osiris. And what's more, the placement of the three Pyramids at Giza corresponds precisely to the three stars in Orion's belt when seen directly from above, with the smaller Pyramid of Menkaure being slightly offset from a straight line going through the Pyramids of Khafre and Khufu, exactly the way the smaller star Mintaka is slightly offset from the two other stars Alnitak and Alnilam.'

'No kidding,' said Scarlett. 'And these positions match?'

'Almost perfectly,' said Sophia. 'Of course, the relative positions of those stars have shifted marginally since the Pyramids were built, but it is hardly noticeable. So, it is still an almost perfect match, and there's no way this is just a coincidence. It is obviously intentional.'

'In other words,' added Ethan, 'it is clear that the ancient Egyptians were a hell of a lot more advanced astronomers than most people give them credit for.'

'Bingo,' said Sophia. 'And just think about it for a second. It is inconceivable that the ancient Egyptians didn't observe the night sky closely. And they would naturally have connected everything they saw up there to their gods. For example, the Milky Way in the night sky was a celestial manifestation of the Nile, on which all life in their world depended. So, of course, they would have looked up at night and thought of it as a profound and integral element to their existence.'

'Makes sense.' Ethan nodded.

'The celestial bodies,' continued Sophia, 'and the way they mysteriously and, to them, inexplicably, moved across the night sky would have been at the centre of their lives, and it would naturally have been attributed to the actions of the gods. Archaeologists have found structures in southern Egypt, at a site called Nabta Playa near the border with Sudan, that are clearly built according to astronomical alignments. And those are from around 7500 BCE. So this embrace of the celestial world has existed in Egypt for about ten thousand years.'

'That's a really long time,' said Scarlett.

'Well, back then,' said Sophia, 'the stars in the night sky were just about the most amazing thing a human could look at. Just go and stand in a barren desert at night and look up, and you will immediately understand why this majestic spectacle became the most important element in their existence, except maybe for the annual floods. And even those were observably connected to the stars through the rising of Osiris at the spring equinox, just before the floods came.'

'It's true.' Ethan nodded, casting his mind back to desert deployments where the night sky seemed to be bursting with billions of stars. 'You can't take your eyes off the sky at night if there is no other light around.'

'And if you go to places like the temples of Karnak near the ancient city of Thebes,' said Sophia, 'which we now call Luxor, you can see how this perception of the universe played out in both life and death at that time. It is well known that the ancient Egyptians perceived the west as the land of the dead and the east as the land of the living. So, Thebes and Karnak were on the eastern bank of the Nile, and the royal tombs of the necropolis were on the western bank. And the Milky Way was likely seen as a celestial representation of the Nile, which had to be crossed on the final journey to the necropolis, just like the river that had to be crossed to get to the Duat, the underworld where Osiris ruled.'

'It's kind of beautiful,' said Scarlett with a faintly dreamy expression. 'I never knew any of this.'

'Well, it's pretty nerdy stuff—' Sophia smiled '—but I just love it.'

'But what does this have to do with Goodwin and Templeton's theory?' said Ethan.

'Well,' said Sophia, 'I already told you about the annual floods and how they had returned every year, almost like clockwork, for thousands of years. But that's only partly true, and this is where Goodwin comes in, because roughly ten thousand years ago, this regular monsoon pattern was disturbed, and it essentially shifted the annual rains much further south, which then caused droughts in Egypt that might have lasted decades or even centuries. This turned previously fertile lands into arid desert. Now, this obviously had a devastating effect on whatever civilisation existed back then, and Goodwin was trying to connect this with the existence of a precursor civilisation that existed long before the droughts eventually ended and the monsoon flooding returned, which then allowed the so-called predynastic period to begin.'

'That's fascinating,' said Ethan.

'Yes,' said Sophia, 'and also pretty speculative because there obviously isn't a lot of tangible evidence left of precisely when and how this all played out.'

'Well, I'm certainly sold on the whole celestial world thing,' said Scarlett. 'It's amazing.'

'You're in good company.' Sophia smiled. 'This was what everyone in ancient Egypt believed for thousands of years. Anyway, you'll be able to see all of this with your own eyes once we get to Cairo. And there's a lot more to this story that I think will blow your socks off.'

'Can't wait.' Scarlett smiled, looking intrigued.

'Me neither,' said Ethan. 'If all of this turns out to be true, then I feel like I was only ever taught half of ancient Egyptian history. It's as if all the things that didn't fit the standard narrative were cut out and ignored.'

'Yes, my feeling exactly,' said Sophia. 'A bit like how the Bible only contains a small and carefully curated selection of all the gospels that were ever written. But that's what happens when dogma takes over and real research gets trampled on. Everyone loses out.'

'Alright,' said Ethan, glancing at his wristwatch. 'I think we should all try to get some sleep. We need to be well rested when we get there. The seats recline, so you should be comfortable.'

'What about Mitch?' said Scarlett, jerking her head towards the cockpit with a wry smile. 'Doesn't he ever sleep, or is he actually a military robot?'

'Nah, we're on autopilot.' Ethan smiled. 'I'll join him in the cockpit in a second. He and I can take turns napping. See you guys in a few hours.'

* * *

Ahead of the final approach into Cairo International Airport, Mitch brought the Firefly in low over the western part of the city, allowing for a spectacular view of the Giza Plateau and the Pyramids.

'Wow,' said Scarlett as she peered out of the window. 'Even from up here, they look massive.'

'That's because they are,' said Sophia, unable to keep a faint smile off her lips as she gazed down at the enormous, ancient structures below. 'The Great Pyramid of Khufu is almost 150 metres tall and about 230 metres at the base. It weighs in at six million tonnes, and if you took all the stone from it and built a wall one metre high and one metre wide, it would be long enough to enclose the entire country of France. It's just massive.'

'How on earth did they do this?' Scarlett said in awe. 'This was 4,500 years ago, right?'

'That's what they tell us,' Ethan said, giving her a wink.

'One stone block at a time, I guess,' said Sophia, as the plateau disappeared behind them and the aircraft banked slightly towards the Nile and the airport on the other side. 'But there is a lot of debate about this. Some of the blocks weigh fifteen tonnes. Other temples were built with blocks weighing two hundred tonnes. A lot of people are convinced that they simply couldn't have done it with the technology that existed at that time. And yet, here they are.'

As Sophia and Scarlett secured their seatbelts for landing, Ethan walked forward to the cockpit, strapped himself into the copilot's seat, and listened in as Mitch contacted the tower for landing clearance. Shortly thereafter, they passed over the Nile in the middle of downtown Cairo, and a couple of minutes later, the Firefly swooped over the rooftops to land at a designated helipad near the VIP terminal in the north-western corner of the airport complex. The engines spun down, and Mitch hit the button for the door release. Moments later, the four of them descended the metal steps that folded out from a hidden compartment under the door.

'Maybe don't leave the key in the ignition,' said Scarlett with a grin as they stepped out into the baking heat, and she glanced over her shoulder at the Firefly. 'This thing looks expensive.'

'Don't worry.' Ethan smiled as the steps folded back up automatically and the door slid shut and locked. 'It comes with biometric security features. Fingerprint or retinal scan. Right now, it only recognises Mitch and me. It also comes with tamper-proof doors. Anyone tries to open it, they get electrocuted.'

'Holy shit.' Scarlett laughed. 'Now I want one myself.'

'And good luck trying to break in through this nanofibre fuselage,' said Mitch. 'That stuff is designed to eat small arms fire. So, it's secure.'

Passing through the border check inside the terminal took only a few minutes, and the four of them then emerged outside on the concourse.

'Alright, I'll see you guys later,' said Mitch, exchanging a quick fist bump with Ethan.

'Where's he going?' said Scarlett as Mitch peeled off towards a separate building.

'We need to have the Firefly on standby,' said Ethan. 'Just in case we need quick transport. The three of us are heading for a different hotel.'

Having called ahead, Ethan had arranged for them to be picked up from the airport by a chauffeur-driven car, and about thirty minutes later, the trio walked into the lobby of the Four Seasons Hotel on the western bank of the Nile, carrying their light travel bags. Ethan had booked one of the diplomatic suites near the top of the building since it could easily accommodate all of them, and as they walked into the plush suite with views out to the west over the Cairo Zoo and the sprawling city beyond, they could glimpse the tops of the three famous Pyramids in the distance.

'What a view,' said Scarlett as she dropped her bag on the soft carpet and walked over to the large windows through which the orange afternoon sun was now shining. 'I could get used to this.'

'Let's all find a room and get comfortable,' said Ethan, glancing around the suite. 'There's plenty of space here. And then I think we should head down and get some dinner. I'd like to get up nice and early tomorrow. It could be a long day. Sophia, do you have a plan for how you want to do this?'

'I do,' said Sophia, taking off her light jacket, tossing it over the back of an armchair, and loosening her hair, which had been held up with a hairclip. 'I want to show you the Giza Plateau. Everything Goodwin talked about will make sense once we're out there.'

'Alright,' said Ethan. 'Scarlett, I'd like you to set up station here in this suite. If you could try to dig into Al-Masry's financial affairs, that might give us a clue to what is going on. Find out how a man spends his money, and you'll find out what he's trying to achieve.'

'Got it,' said Scarlett with a firm nod, now suddenly serious and businesslike as she went to get her laptop and its ancillary hacking and security devices.

While Scarlett connected her various pieces of computer hardware and prepared a place to work at the long, white marble dining table, Ethan walked through the entire place, checking all the doors and windows and assessing the suite's layout and security in case of a breach. He hadn't realised it before, but there was a part of him that suddenly felt slightly uneasy about what they were doing. Whoever Al-Masry really was, and whatever he was up to, he had proven himself willing to kill in order to get what he wanted. Ethan wasn't worried about himself. There was very little that was capable of instilling fear into him, especially when carrying the small but highly versatile modular 9mm Sig Sauer P320 Compact pistol that he had concealed under his shirt. However, he now realised that on this trip, he was responsible not just for himself but for the safety of the two women he had persuaded to join him. He was used to having a large team of highly capable operators and intelligence people around him, but now, it was all on him to keep everyone safe.

Walking back into the main living area after his sweep, he glanced towards Scarlett, who was tossing her black, undercut hair to one side as she connected a cable to her laptop. Watching her finalise the set-up, he suddenly thought that she looked small and vulnerable. In an altercation with someone like Nadeem Rashad, despite her CIA background, which would no doubt have involved basic firearms training, she wouldn't stand much of a chance. This was a potential problem that he would have to do something about.

7

Nadeem Rashad sat reclined inside a car a few houses down from the nondescript building in a deceptively neat and respectable-looking street on the outskirts of one of Cairo's newest neighbourhoods. The houses were whitewashed with pale yellow tiled roofs, and each one was set back from the road behind a similarly painted brick wall a couple of metres tall. Nadeem, who was wearing a tailored charcoal suit and tie, now looked very different from several days ago when he had triggered the bomb that had blown up a local shopping centre. It had been utter carnage, but Nadeem knew that it was a necessary evil, and it had been a powerful and glorious explosion. He had the window rolled down and was smoking a cigarette as he sat there waiting for what he had been told was a regular occurrence on this particular day of the week.

He was stocky and powerful with broad shoulders, large hands, a trimmed black beard and short curly hair, and he had a wide jaw and a heavy brow that gave him a slight Neanderthal look. But he was anything but stupid. His worst flaw was his temper, and it had landed him in trouble on more than one occasion. In fact, it was partly the reason why he was sitting here in this car instead of in some air-conditioned office inside the headquarters of the Central Security Force in central Cairo. Until a few years ago, he'd had a promising career as a special agent inside the CSF, and he was on track for a management position. However, he had been demoted to guard duty after punching an obnoxious superior officer after an altercation at a restaurant, and at that point, he had decided that his cards were marked forever and that playing by the rules would get him nowhere. He then got himself transferred to the Tourism and Antiquities Police, which is a specialised branch of the Egyptian Ministry of Interior in charge of securing the many hundreds of museums, temples and archaeological sites throughout the enormous country.

As soon as he was able, he then used the opportunity to steal relics from active dig sites, bribing the low-level site managers and selling the relics on the black market. With the fascination with ancient Egypt being near-universal across the world, it had proven a lucrative affair, and eventually, through a fence he had been using, he had come into contact with a man named Zosar Al-Masry, who asked him to come and work for him personally. Offered a significant amount of money, Nadeem had agreed, and Al-Masry had then used his connections inside the government bureaucracy to facilitate Nadeem's virtual disappearance from public view. He was now effectively a ghost, moving unseen and using a number of fake identities for travel and the various tasks that Al-Masry would set him on a regular basis. In return, he offered Al-Masry his complete and unquestioning loyalty.

This balmy evening, Nadeem was waiting for a very special person to arrive at the house about a hundred metres further along the pretty tree-lined street from where he was parked. The man was called Ahmed Nour, and he was a local, mid-level Cairo prosecutor who had been looking into Al-Masry's finances and that of the wider Fayek family. This was an unwelcome irritant for Al-Masry, who liked to be able to wield his financial influence out of view of the public and the country's legal system. However, Ahmed Nour had become much more than a nuisance after he went on the record as saying that he was very sympathetic to the idea of giving more legal powers to both the military and the religious courts. Not only did this threaten the ability of Al-Masry's businesses to operate freely, but it would make it much more difficult for someone like him to acquire and develop political power and eventually be able to take over the governance of the country. Al-Masry had explained this to Rashad in basic terms, and the former soldier had no compunctions about doing whatever needed to be done to remove any obstacles to his master's political rise. Not only was Al-Masry's vision a noble one, but if successful, it would allow Nadeem to acquire wealth and power beyond what he could otherwise ever have achieved.

When he spotted Ahmed Nour's car approach, he double-checked the licence plate and watched as the black vehicle stopped briefly in front of the gates to the house. After a short wait, the gates opened, and it was allowed in. Then the gates closed behind it again. Nadeem waited a couple of minutes, and then he started the engine, pulled out, and drove the short distance to the gate where he waited. The guard watching him through a camera inside the building had been bribed to let this particular car in, despite it not being on the list of approved vehicles for the evening. The gates soon opened, and shortly thereafter, Nadeem parked and stepped out. Although smartly dressed, he hated every minute of it. However, for this occasion, he had to make sure that he would fit in.

He stepped up to the front door, and after a short wait, it was opened by a burly man in a light grey suit. When Nadeem stepped inside, he could immediately hear the thumping music from one of the bar areas, and it was mixed with the laughter and giggling of young women. Some of them also appeared to be speaking loudly over the noise, and, as well as sounding intoxicated, it was clear to him that they were the foreign prostitutes that he knew worked here.

Stopping in the middle of the empty lobby, he took a moment to orientate himself inside the large house. Instead of moving into the adjacent bar, he immediately walked calmly but purposefully up the sweeping staircase to the first floor. As expected, he found himself in a corridor with a heavy purple carpet and dark grey walls, and on either side were three doors. As he moved along the corridor, he could hear the sounds of people having sex behind them, and as he reached the last door on the left, he stopped and listened. From inside came the sound of club music mixed with voices. One male and at least one female. He reached inside his jacket for his suppressed Glock 17, racked the slide and gripped the door handle with his meaty left hand. In one swift movement, he twisted the door handle, pushed the door open and stepped inside with the weapon raised in front of him.

On a large, circular bed with red silk sheets lay two voluptuous blonde women, each holding a glass of champagne and wearing next to nothing. Between them, propped up against some pillows with his legs slightly apart, lay Ahmed Nour, the married prosecutor who publicly pushed for more conservative values and railed against the increasing moral decay of the nation. He was wearing only his white underwear, and when he saw Nadeem walk in, he froze, and his face turned as white as the three lines of cocaine that lay on a small mirror next to him.

Without hesitation, Nadeem took two quick steps forward

and shot one of the young women in the head. The bullet drilled a neat hole in the centre of her forehead, and she slumped onto the bed an instant after the wall behind her had been sprayed red with blood and brain matter. Before her colleague could scream, Nadeem shifted the weapon and shot her once in the head. With the two women lying dead on either side of him, a panicked Ahmed Nour began to stammer something incomprehensible, and suddenly his underwear turned an unpleasant yellow.

Still aiming at the pitiful man on the bed, Nadeem brought his left index finger up to his lips, and the petrified prosecutor immediately clamped his mouth shut and sat immobile as tears of terror welled up in his eyes. Nadeem reached inside his suit jacket and extracted a phone. He held it up and took two pictures of the scene. Then he shot Ahmed Nour between the eyes. The prosecutor's head snapped back as part of his brain left his skull, and then his body went limp like a rag doll, and he slumped onto the bed next to his two companions for the evening. Nadeem took another couple of pictures, which would be added to the set that would be released online in a few hours. It would no doubt shock the public, but more importantly, it would serve as an unmistakable warning to other ambitious prosecutors to steer clear of investigating certain powerful people. The pictures would also be sent in an encrypted format to Al-Masry as proof that the job had been completed.

He slid the Glock back inside his jacket, left the room and closed the door. Less than a minute later, he drove out of the handsome neighbourhood and disappeared.

* * *

Inside the suite at the Four Seasons Hotel next to the Nile, Ethan, Sophia, and Scarlett had returned from a quick dinner in one of the hotel's restaurants. The sun had only just descended below the horizon beyond the Pyramids, leaving only a golden sky as evidence of its presence, when Sophia slumped onto a sofa and continued her research and her preparation for the next morning. Ethan sat down next to her and used his phone to look into ways of providing protection for Scarlett, who would be by herself much of the next day. He began by building a list of former Delta operators whom he trusted and who had left the Unit at some point during the past five years. The list included twelve of the best and most reliable operators he had worked with, and he sent it to a friend who was a commissioned officer at Fort Bragg, asking for a favour. The friend came good, and within half an hour, Ethan had the locations and workplaces of ten out of the twelve men. When he scanned the results, he couldn't believe his luck. One of the former operators was a man named Luke Garrett, and according to the information, he was right here in Cairo.

'Hey, Scarlett,' said Ethan, stepping over next to the hacker. 'Can you help me track down an American citizen by the name of Luke Garrett? He's here in Cairo somewhere. I need to talk to him. He's as solid as they come, and I'd like him here to protect you.'

'Protect me?' said Scarlett, looking more puzzled than worried. 'Am I in danger?'

'Well,' Ethan said, regretting his use of words. 'Not any more than the rest of us. But the reality is that we're messing with people who have no scruples about using violence, so I'd rather be safe than sorry.'

'Alright.' Scarlett nodded thoughtfully. 'If you say so. Give me what you have, and I'll see if I can find him.'

In just a few minutes, she had pinned down Luke's address in a modern apartment block in the suburbs of Cairo, and with a bit of additional sleuthing, she was able to pull his mobile phone number from the computer systems of the local dry cleaner whose firewall software was fifteen years old and had been left unpatched since then.

'Walk in the park,' said Scarlett as she handed him a note with the number.

'Thanks,' said Ethan. 'I'll try to get hold of him.'

Fifteen minutes later, Ethan was in a taxi heading north through the dusk along the Nile's western bank towards a bar and restaurant in central Cairo that styled itself as a Texas steakhouse. It was apparently a favourite haunt of the city's foreigners, especially those hailing from across the Atlantic, and upon receiving a call from Ethan, Luke Garrett had immediately agreed to meet him there.

Just like Ethan, Luke had been part of B Squadron at the Unit, and their careers in Delta had overlapped by two years, during which time they had become friendly. Luke grew up as the son of a cattle rancher in Butler County, Kentucky. After high school, he decided to go to Ranger School, after which he joined the 82nd Airborne. He was then prompted by a superior to join the elite 75th Ranger Regiment at Fort Benning in Georgia, and after a couple of years there, he passed selection to Delta. Like Ethan, he had never been interested in becoming an officer despite it being offered to him several times. He did, however, end up as team leader of his troop, and the two of them had worked closely together on several overseas operations.

Eventually, however, despite loving the job at the Unit, Luke had looked for a way out, not because he no longer wanted to be part of Delta, but because he was looking for a way to help pay off the debt on his father's struggling ranch back in

Kentucky. The last Ethan had heard of him, he had entered the State Department's Diplomatic Security Service, where he worked as a close protection officer for ambassadors and their families.

When Ethan walked into what was probably the most Texan establishment anywhere in Egypt, he was greeted by melancholy country music, reruns of NFL games being shown on a large TV behind the bar, and American accents emanating from the various tables around which sat small groups of foreigners and a couple of local Egyptians.

It only took him a moment to spot Luke, who was sitting by himself at a small table at the back of the place, holding a Bud in his right hand and leaning on the table with his elbow. He was well built, slightly taller than average with broad shoulders and tanned skin, and his mid-brown hair was straight, slightly ruffled and somewhat longer than Ethan remembered from their time in the Unit. Wearing blue jeans, leather boots and a grey and white chequered flannel shirt, his face was lean with a square jaw and a straight nose, and his pale green eyes looked out from under dark eyebrows. When he spotted Ethan, he gave a small nod as a smile spread across his face, and he lifted his beer in greeting.

'Garrett,' said Ethan, breaking into a smile as he reached him and stuck out a hand. 'Great to see you, man. Thanks for coming.'

'No problem, dude,' said Luke, giving Ethan's hand a firm squeeze. 'How have you been? Hey, I heard about your parents. I'm real sorry, man.'

'Thanks. But it's alright,' said Ethan, keen to move the conversation along. 'I can't believe you're here in Cairo.'

'How did you find out?' said Luke, seemingly relaxed with having been located so easily. 'Someone back at Bragg?'

'Got it in one.' Ethan nodded. 'What about you? How did you end up here?'

'Well,' said Luke, taking another swig of his beer. 'I joined the DSS over at State, but it didn't work out. I was pretty disappointed with the pay prospects, and the whole point of becoming a civilian was to help out my old man so he wouldn't lose the ranch. So, I decided to quit and join a PMC.'

Ethan knew of several of his former colleagues who had left the service to join private military companies. Some of those enterprises were little more than cowboys fighting other people's wars in failed states around the world, but others were more respectable and tended to focus on diplomatic and corporate protection services and firearms training for local staff.

'Yeah, I hear they pay better,' said Ethan.

'They do,' said Luke. 'I realised that I could be making more money doing more or less the same thing. So I figured that would help give my dad a shot at keeping the ranch going.'

'Sounds like the right choice,' said Ethan as the waiter came over, and he ordered a Bud for himself and another for Luke.

'What about you, man?' said Luke with a grin. 'What the hell is a gold-plated academic like you doing in a dump like this?'

'Yeah.' Ethan shrugged and smiled as the waiter came over with the drinks. 'Laugh it up. It was the right time for me to leave the Unit, and I'm happy I took that degree. I've always been interested in history.'

'I know, dude,' said Luke, giving Ethan a friendly punch on the shoulder. 'I'm just yanking your chain. Anyway, why are you in Cairo?'

Ethan proceeded to explain the situation surrounding Tobias Goodwin's murder, the theft of Templeton's journal, and the involvement of Sophia Lockwood and Scarlett Fox, the latter of whom Luke remembered from past operations with the Unit.

Trusting his old buddy, Ethan left out no details when painting the picture of why he had come, and he relayed everything he had learned about Zosar Al-Masry and Nadeem Rashad. Luke grew sombre for a moment and nodded thoughtfully as he pondered what he had been told.

'Sounds serious,' he said.

'Yeah, it is,' said Ethan. 'Which is why I need to do something about it myself. And I'd really appreciate it if you'd lend a hand. I trust you, buddy. Anyway, remember Mitch Kazinsky?'

'Sure,' said Luke.

'He got us over here on a new plane,' said Ethan.

'Mitch is here too?' said Luke. 'I always liked that guy. Hell of a pilot.'

'Yeah,' said Ethan. 'One of the best. But listen, I want to ask you a favour. We're screwing with some powerful people here, and Scarlett is going to be on her own tomorrow. She has had some firearms training, but I'm a little worried about her safety. If I asked you to come over to our hotel and look out for her, would you do it?'

'Of course, man.' Luke nodded firmly without hesitation. 'Anything you need.'

'And I'll pay you for your time,' said Ethan.

'Hell no,' said Luke with a small grimace. 'I'm not taking your money for a favour like this. It ain't right. I'm just happy to help.'

'Thanks, buddy,' said Ethan. 'I really appreciate it. So, how's life here in Cairo?'

'Damn hot.' Luke grinned. 'Thank the Lord for air conditioning.'

'Are you planning on staying?' said Ethan.

'I don't know.' Luke shrugged. 'I'm just taking things one day at a time here. I'm sure I'll get tired of it eventually, and then I'll probably move on to something else.'

'Well,' said Ethan, taking another swig. 'I sure am glad to find you here.'

'Always good to see a friendly face,' said Luke with a smile and a nod.

'Anyway,' said Ethan. 'I'd like you to meet Scarlett and Sophia. We're at the Four Seasons. About ten minutes away.'

'Sure,' said Luke, emptying his beer. 'No problem. Lead the way.'

* * *

When Ethan returned to the hotel room with Luke by his side, Scarlett was at her computer, and Sophia was lying on the sofa reading a book on her tablet.

'Ladies,' he said as he entered. 'This is Luke Garrett.'

As Luke stepped in, he nodded politely at both of them in turn and gave a quick smile. Sophia swung her legs off the sofa and got to her feet, while Scarlett remained at the table, giving the new arrival a quick salute in greeting.

'He's former Delta,' said Ethan. 'He'll be joining us for a bit to make sure everybody's safe. Especially Scarlett, who is going to be here by herself tomorrow.'

'A knight in shining armour?' said Scarlett with a sardonic wink.

'I'm just here to help,' said Luke with a disarming smile.

'Nice to meet you,' said Sophia as she came over to shake his hand. 'I'm glad to have you here.'

'Yeah, me too,' said Scarlett, now less flippant. 'I can usually take care of myself, but Ethan insisted.'

'It's just a precaution,' said Ethan, glancing amicably at Scarlett. 'I'm not expecting any trouble, but you just never know.'

'Are you from the Midwest?' asked Sophia.

'Kentucky farm boy.' Luke nodded. 'Anyway, Ethan told me about your professor. I'm sorry. I hope you guys will be able to nail the guys who did it.'

'We'll damn sure try,' said Ethan.

'Hey, Ethan,' said Scarlett, gesturing at her laptop. 'Have a look at this.'

While Luke and Sophia engaged in small talk, Ethan came over to stand next to Scarlett, leaning forward and placing a hand on the table as he looked at her computer screen.

'What's up?' he said.

'I think I found something big,' she said, glancing at the two others. 'Hey, Sophia. Luke. I think you should both see this too.'

Luke and Sophia joined the other two around the laptop, and then Scarlett began to explain.

'I did some more detective work on Zosar Al-Masry,' she said, gesturing at the screen where a grid with brief lines of text was being displayed. 'I've been able to track his movements over the past few weeks by accessing his secretary's schedule at the offices of his oil exploration company.'

'Right,' said Ethan, peering at the data.

'And look here,' she said, pointing at a cell in the grid. 'I found an entry for a private meeting inside his office with a Mr Rashad the day after Tobias Goodwin was murdered.'

'Nadeem,' said Ethan, his eyes narrowing as he recalled the harrowing footage of the former Egyptian CSF operative slitting the professor's throat.

'And then,' said Scarlett, 'I was able to access local flight data and find the flight records and manifests for Al-Masry's private jet. It touched down at Tweed New Haven Airport seven hours before Goodwin's murder, and it then took off for Cairo just four hours later.'

'Shit. That's the smoking gun,' said Ethan. 'Nadeem Rashad was the killer, but it was Al-Masry who ordered the burglary.'

'Yes,' said Scarlett, 'but I can prove it now.'

'How?' said Sophia with a look of discomfort on her face. 'Was there some sort of written instruction or a money trail?'

'Better than that,' said Scarlett, as she brought up a still image on the screen.

'What's this?' said Ethan, looking at what appeared to be a security camera shot from inside a home office where an elderly bearded man was sitting at a desk.

'That's Zosar Al-Masry,' said Scarlett, pointing at the man in the image, 'and this is his study. I worked out where he lives. It's on the top floor of a luxury apartment block right on the edge of the Giza suburb with a view up towards the plateau and the Pyramids. Now, check this out.'

She gripped the mouse, selected a small, square area near the back of the image, and then enlarged it to fill the whole screen. Running a rapid image enhancement algorithm, the somewhat pixelated image sharpened up, and both Ethan's and Sophia's eyes widened as they saw what was lying on a small stone table inside an alcove set into the wall.

'I'll be damned,' Ethan said in a husky voice. 'The golden lion.'

'And the dodecahedron,' said Sophia, pointing. 'The black orb that was stolen from the museum here in Cairo.'

'And now have a look at what he's reading,' said Scarlett, zooming in on the book in front of Al-Masry.

'Templeton's journal,' Sophia breathed. 'It's there too.'

'We need to get it back,' said Ethan resolutely as his eyes bored into the still image of Al-Masry. 'The journal, the lion, and that orb. None of those things belong to this murderous arsehole.'

'Damn right,' Sophia said without taking her eyes off the screen.

'When was this image taken?' said Ethan, his mind already racing.

'Earlier this afternoon,' said Scarlett. 'But here's the kicker. His office schedule says he is out for dinner with the energy minister tonight.'

'So, you're saying he's not at home right now?' said Ethan, glancing at his wristwatch and then looking at Scarlett, whose eyes now carried a certain glint.

'Correct.' She nodded, meeting his gaze with a firm look. 'This could be our chance. We shouldn't waste it.'

Ethan took a moment to ponder what she was implying, and then he nodded firmly.

'Right,' he said. 'I agree. I need to get inside that apartment and grab those items before he gets back. And I'm going to need your help. Can you get me the schematics for Al-Masry's apartment block?'

'Absolutely,' said Scarlett, her fingers already moving swiftly across the keyboard as she prepared to locate the plans. 'Let's do this.'

'Want me to tag along?' asked Luke, who had been standing with his arms crossed, observing silently until now.

'No thanks, buddy,' said Ethan. 'I should do this alone. Keep a low profile, you know? And I'd feel better if you stayed here with Sophia and Scarlett.'

'You got it, pal,' said Luke. 'Let's get you ready then. Do you have all the gear you need for this?'

'Yup.' Ethan nodded. 'I brought a full go-bag. It's all there, plus a few gadgets.'

* * *

Ten minutes later, Ethan got into a yellow taxi in front of the Four Seasons Hotel, told the driver to take him to Giza, and leaned back in the cracked leather seat to look out of the window. It was a still, humid evening, and the air smelled of dust, car exhaust, and exotic cooking. Within minutes, the taxi was weaving through a cacophony of honking horns, shouting drivers, and dozens of swarming scooters driven by young men seemingly unafraid to die. Soon, they were on the Al-Haram thoroughfare that reaches almost due west from the city centre and out to the Giza Plateau, and within a few minutes, downtown gave way to lower and older sand-coloured apartment blocks with narrow iron balconies packed with laundry and satellite dishes. Then came a long stretch of low-rise buildings in increasingly uneven clusters that were interspersed with open plots where children played football. Finally, after about twenty minutes, the driver steered the taxi past a large number of tour buses that were lined up like shining metal fish by the banks of a river. Moments later, Ethan paid the man and watched him disappear into the maelstrom of Cairo's evening traffic.

He had deliberately asked to be taken to the main tourist area in order to appear as inconspicuous as possible, and he took a moment to turn around to look at the impossibly huge Pyramids and the Sphinx, all of which were lit up by bright spotlights. For a moment, he found it difficult to resist the urge to walk towards them. However, he then consulted his mental map of the area and headed down along a wide avenue towards an exclusive-looking estate near a golf course where a number of apartment blocks rose up. On his back was a small, black nylon backpack with a few tools, and he swiftly made his way along the sidewalk towards the estate. Before reaching the entrance where a gatehouse manned by uniformed staff was located, he cut across a narrow stretch of lush lawn and pushed through a hedge into the estate. Keeping to the shadows, he approached the parking basement where the occasional car would come out or drive in. He pushed a small earbud into his right ear and tapped it.

'Alright, Scarlett,' he said. 'Do you read me?'

'Loud and clear,' came Scarlett's voice, her tone professional and calm as she sat in front of her laptop wearing a headset. 'Let's get eyes on.'

'Roger that,' said Ethan, unslinging his backpack and reaching inside it to extract a black quadcopter drone roughly the size of a phone but twice as thick.

He switched it on, unfolded the four rotor arms, and placed it on his palm. A second later, the small rotors spun up and lifted the mini-UAV almost silently into the air to hover a couple of metres above his head.

'Good signal,' said Scarlett. 'I have control.'

Glancing up, Ethan watched as the drone did a quick 360-degree spin, and then it zoomed up into the darkness and disappeared from view.

'Roger that,' said Ethan. 'Ready to go in.'

'OK,' said Scarlett. 'I've already patched into the parking level security cameras. There's no one down there right now. You're cleared to enter.'

'Got it,' said Ethan. 'Moving.'

He moved from behind a tree and slipped down the concrete ramp to the large parking space under one of the apartment blocks, where a dozen black limos and a handful of brightly coloured sports cars were parked.

'All the main elevators up into the building require keycards,' said Scarlett as he pushed inside. 'But there's a service elevator at the back, and I can take it over if you step inside and tell me the name of the manufacturer and the serial number on the control panel.'

Moving swiftly towards the other end of the parking level, Ethan did as she asked and stepped inside the elevator, where he read Scarlett the engraved serial number off the metal panel. Seconds later, she had pulled the override codes from the manufacturer's maintenance server and injected them into the apartment block's management system, and the elevator then began its journey up towards the top of the building.

'Good work,' said Ethan, reaching behind him to double-check that the Sig Sauer P320 was loaded and ready.

'Alright, listen,' came Scarlett's voice as he ascended inside the cab. 'The drone is currently hovering outside Al-Masry's window, and I have eyes on his study. There's no one there, but I am sure the apartment's alarm system is active. I'm going to need a moment to access it. Stand by.'

When the elevator reached the top floor, its doors opened just around the corner from the main corridor that provided access to Al-Masry's apartment. However, Ethan stayed inside the elevator cab waiting for Scarlett to come back to him.

'Am I clear?' he whispered, sensing that Scarlett was hesitating.

'Negative,' said Scarlett. 'I'm watching the security camera feed, and there's a guy in a suit pacing slowly at the other end of the corridor by the main elevator. Looks bored as all hell. He might be one of the building's security team assigned to this floor. I can't see if he's armed.'

'Or maybe he's part of Al-Masry's personal security detail,' said Ethan quietly. 'I'm sure he has his own guys. Are you sure he's by himself?'

'It looks like it,' said Scarlett. 'We can't get inside as long as he's there. But listen, I think I have an idea.'

About a minute later, Ethan walked out of the service elevator and rounded a corner to step out into the corridor. He then began walking casually along it towards the wide, oiled mahogany front door to Al-Masry's apartment. Within seconds, the guard noticed him approaching and turned to face him.

'Hello!' he called in a heavy accent, wagging an index finger in front of himself as he began approaching. 'No access here. Private.'

Most likely, the man had been made familiar with the people living on this floor, and Ethan clearly wasn't one of them. As he came nearer, Ethan now felt sure that this was a security guard working for the apartment block and not one of Al-Masry's personal protection team. He was big and broad with a hard look on his face, but he carried himself in a lazy and somewhat heavy fashion, unwittingly signalling to the former Delta operator that he was badly trained and used to relying on intimidation and size rather than any real skill.

Ethan continued walking and arrived at Al-Masry's door, where he reached inside his pocket, pretending to extract a keycard. As the guard came closer, Ethan moved his hand across the scanner next to the door a couple of times, feigning puzzlement as to why the door wasn't opening.

'Sir,' said the guard, now less than five metres away. 'I think you are on the wrong floor. What is your apartment number?'

'Damn this thing,' muttered Ethan, making a show of seeming distracted and irritated as he glared at the scanner. 'What? Uh, I'm in 1304.'

'In 1304?' the guard repeated as deep creases formed on his broad forehead, and he reached out to place a hand on Ethan's arm. 'There are only twelve floors in this building. Sir, I need you to come with...'

At that moment, Scarlett, who had been watching the show

via the dome camera mounted on the ceiling a few metres away, killed all the lights in the corridor, plunging it into complete darkness. However, Ethan had been tracking the precise movements of the guard right up until that point, and when the lights went out, he was ready and knew exactly how his opponent's body was positioned. In the blink of an eye, he twisted around and landed a hard strike through the darkness with the side of his hand where the guard's neck was, overwhelming the man's vagus nerve near his carotid artery and jugular vein. The force of the powerful blow caused a sudden change in blood pressure, and the effect was instant as the large man's legs buckled under him and he collapsed unconscious onto the floor.

'Good job, Scarlett,' said Ethan. 'Perfect timing. Lights?'

Almost instantly, the corridor's ceiling lights came back on, and Ethan looked down at the large man by his feet. His mouth was partly open, and there was a red bruise forming on the side of his neck just above the shirt collar, but he was otherwise unhurt.

'Holy shit,' said Scarlett. 'That was badass. How long is he going to be out?'

'A couple of minutes at least,' said Ethan. 'Can you open the door?'

'On it,' said Scarlett. 'Overriding floor security now. Disabling internal motion sensors. And... done.'

The lock on the door to Al-Masry's luxury apartment clicked as it unlocked, and Ethan then gripped the handle and pushed it open. He grabbed the unconscious guard, dragged him inside and propped him up against a wall. Then he closed the door. Seconds later, he was standing silently inside the entrance hall, which was about the size of a standard living room. The floor was veined marble, the walls were clad with dark wood panels, and above him was a ceiling with intricate cornicing and soft downlights. He pushed the door shut behind him and was about to move further into the apartment when Scarlett's voice came back in his ear.

'What the...?' she said, sounding puzzled. 'I've been locked out of the system. The apartment's security circuits have reset. There must be some kind of hidden tamper protection that I can't see from here.'

'That's not good,' Ethan responded calmly.

'Fuck,' Scarlett said tensely as a countdown timer popped up on the cloned security system's interface being displayed on her laptop screen. 'Listen, you have ten seconds to disable the terminal on the wall next to you, or the alarm goes off. We need to abort. Get out of there, Ethan.'

Standing in the entrance hall, Ethan hesitated for a second, but then he glanced to his side at the alarm unit mounted on the wall next to the door.

'Let's try this the old-fashioned way,' he said, and then he smashed his elbow hard into the unit's control panel.

There was a loud crack as pieces of moulded plastic casing and LCD panel exploded from the unit and rained onto the floor. The wiring produced a few electrical sparks, and then the panel winked out and went dark. He waited a few seconds, fully expecting alarms to start blaring loudly, but nothing happened.

'Well, I guess that works too,' said Scarlett evenly, watching Ethan through the electronic eyes of the drone that was still hovering in the darkness outside the living room window. 'But Ethan, the apartment's alarm system is now showing a malfunction down in the security station on the ground floor. I'm guessing you have a couple of minutes before someone shows up.'

'Got it,' said Ethan. 'Moving to the study.'

Scarlett, Sophia, and Luke watched on the screen as Ethan

moved swiftly and purposefully through the entrance hall and into the large living room from which there were sliding double doors to the study. The doors had been left pulled open, and Ethan entered the study and immediately saw that there was a false wall in front of the alcove where they had seen the artefacts. He quickly found a way to slide the wooden wall section aside, and looking down onto the stone table, he spoke to the rest of the team.

'Bingo,' he said. 'It's all here. The journal, the lion and the orb.'

'Grab them and get out,' came Sophia's voice through Scarlett's headset. 'Before more guards show up.'

'Alright,' said Ethan as he unslung the backpack and zipped it open.

He placed each item carefully inside and zipped up the backpack, and then he headed for the door. Without wasting time, he crossed the living room floor and stepped up to the front door, where he placed a hand on the doorknob.

'Please confirm the corridor is empty,' he said quietly.

'It's empty,' said Scarlett. 'You're good to go.'

At that moment, a strong hand gripped Ethan's left ankle, and an angry groan came from the formerly unconscious guard who had suddenly come to. His furious eyes glared up at Ethan as he clawed his way to his feet with surprising speed for a man of his size, while Ethan attempted to wrestle his leg free. However, the man's grip was powerful considering he had been passed out just moments earlier. He grunted again through gritted teeth, and then he was up and reaching inside his suit jacket to produce a compact pistol that Ethan immediately recognised as a semi-automatic CZ-10, often used by police forces. He could tell from the furious look in the man's eyes that he was fully intent on using it, and his reaction was purely instinctual. Stepping swiftly inside the guard's reach, he pushed the man's gun arm out and away from himself while at the same time reaching for his P320 at the small of his back. The guard's weapon went off uncomfortably close to Ethan's head, causing pain to immediately lance through his ear, followed by a loud ringing noise, but by then, he had brought his own weapon around and angled it up slightly towards the guard's chest. He fired twice in quick succession, and the two 9mm bullets slammed up into the man's torso, punched through his heart and lungs, and exited out of his back to smack into the wood panels behind his head, taking a spray of blood with them. The whole thing took no more than a couple of seconds, and then it was over.

The guard seemed to suddenly freeze, and his face went from anger to shock in a split second. His eyes went wide, and his mouth fell open, and then, while gripping Ethan's shirt, he sagged onto his knees with a liquid gurgle emanating from his mouth, and he keeled over onto the floor, where a pool of red soon began to spread around him on the white marble floor.

'Shit,' Ethan muttered.

He grimaced at the sudden, violent turn of events. This was not what he had been planning, and things were now about to get a whole lot more complicated.

'You stupid bastard,' he whispered, looking down at the dead man at his feet.

'Ethan, get out,' said Scarlett urgently. 'There's an elevator coming up to your floor right now.'

'Got it,' said Ethan, pulling the front door open and stepping out into the corridor.

Suddenly, he heard Scarlett's voice in his earpiece once more, and now, for the first time, she sounded anxious.

'Shit,' she said. 'Ethan, wait!'

But it was too late. Another two guards emerged from the elevator just as he stepped out into the corridor, and they had both pulled their weapons. Without hesitation, Ethan raised his pistol and fired two rounds that smacked into the metal panels next to the elevator. He then sprinted for the service elevator at the other end of the corridor while firing another three badly aimed shots behind him. When he reached the corner beyond which the service elevator was located, two shots rang out from behind him, and while one bullet sounded like it ripped through the plaster in the ceiling above his head, the other zipped unnervingly close to his head and punched into the wall behind him. Finally clear of the corridor, he barged into the open elevator and hit the button for the parking garage.

At that moment, Scarlett activated the fire alarm systems on that floor, and heavy sprays of water immediately burst from sprinklers above the heads of the two guards. Shocked and temporarily thrown off by the deluge, they staggered forward through the artificial downpour with their weapons up and their hands shielding their eyes. By the time they reached the corner by the service elevator, the doors had slid shut, and Ethan was on his way down the shaft.

When they opened again, Ethan sprinted out and headed not for the exit but for a section of the parking level where a handful of fast-looking motorcycles were parked. Since it was a gated and ostensibly secure apartment complex, they all had the keys in the ignition, so Ethan jumped on the nearest one and fired up the engine. It sprang to life with a vicious, high-pitched roar, and then he engaged the clutch and flicked it into gear with his foot. He twisted the throttle on the handlebar and the machine leapt forward enthusiastically, and seconds later, Ethan shot out at speed from the parking level and roared up the ramp towards the exit to the main road. At the gate, a hapless, lanky guard in a light brown uniform attempted to flag him down and make him stop, but when he saw that the driver of the bike was only accelerating further, he was forced to leap out of the way and flatten himself against the guardhouse.

With his hands gripping the handlebars firmly, Ethan punched out onto the road and accelerated away from the apartment complex with the warm evening air making his eyes water as it tore at his clothes. He soon joined the Al-Haram thoroughfare back towards the centre of Cairo, where he accelerated further, and after about thirty seconds, he turned around to look behind him, but there was no sign of any pursuer. Slowing down slightly, he continued to weave in and out through the surprisingly dense late evening traffic.

After about fifteen minutes, he turned onto the road on the Nile's western bank, which would take him south to the Four Seasons Hotel. When he was about three hundred metres away from it, he pulled over, rolled to a stop in a narrow alley next to a pair of stinking garbage containers, killed the engine and dismounted. A few minutes later, he walked through the door to the hotel suite, where three pairs of eyes greeted him with a mixture of incredulity and amazement, although Luke also gave him a brief, respectful nod for a job well done.

* * *

When Zosar Al-Masry returned to his apartment block from his dinner with the energy minister, he was puzzled to see two police cars and an ambulance parked in front of the main entrance. His driver was about to take them down into the parking garage when one of the building's front desk staff rushed over and waved them down.

'I'm sorry, sir,' said the man obsequiously. 'No one is allowed down there. The police are working there.'

Bemused and not a little irritated, Al-Masry opened the passenger-side door and stepped out just in time to see a person covered by a white sheet being wheeled out of the building and loaded into a waiting ambulance.

'Who is that?' said Al-Masry, maintaining a calm exterior, yet beginning to feel deep unease building inside him. 'What happened here?'

'There was an intruder, sir,' said the man, fidgeting nervously with his hands. 'I believe it was on your floor.'

'Was he apprehended?' said Al-Masry, straining to keep his voice under control.

'I don't think so,' said the man nervously. 'It's better if you speak to the police.'

As Al-Masry looked on, he noticed that the dead man's arm was dangling limply off the gurney, giving him a glimpse of his wristwatch. He immediately recognised it as that of one of three specially vetted and selected armed guards who he had agreed to be stationed on a permanent basis on his floor. His name was Mohsen, and he was now clearly no longer among the living.

Shit, Al-Masry thought to himself as he watched the body being loaded into the ambulance.

He was now beginning to grow seriously concerned, and when a uniformed police officer approached him, he knew that something very bad had happened. For a brief moment, he feared that it might be related to the death of local prosecutor Ahmed Nour, but from the body language of the officer, it soon became clear that this had to do with something else.

Twenty minutes later, having had the evening's dramatic events explained to him in as much detail as was available, Al-Masry was inside his apartment, studiously ignoring the staff who were busy cleaning Mohsen's blood from the white marble in the entrance hall. His face was grim, but not because a man had been killed mere metres from where he stood. Inside him, barely contained fury and a significant amount of unease were roiling after realising what had been taken from him. And he had an uncomfortable feeling about who might have been responsible for the break-in.

They were right here, he seethed silently. *Those bastards were here inside my home.*

He knew that he would be unable to involve the police, since he could hardly ask them to investigate the theft of an item that he himself had stolen from the Egyptian Museum in central Cairo. And the last thing he needed right now was for them to be snooping around his private affairs, especially in light of the recent untimely death of Ahmed Nour. The only thing he could do was allow the police to interview him concerning the death of Mohsen during what he would need to claim was a failed attempt at burglary. And then he would have to hunt down the thief himself without making waves that would be noticed or interfered with by the authorities. And as always, Nadeem Rashad would be the man for the job.

8

Early the next morning, Ethan awoke, quickly threw on a pair of jeans and a shirt, and walked out into the suite's living area to find Sophia sitting by the dining table poring over Templeton's journal. Next to it were the golden lion and the black orb. It reflected the light from inside the suite, but it did not appear to allow any light to pass through it. Sophia looked completely engrossed and was busy alternately reading and taking notes with a pen in a small notebook. The sun was lighting up the Pyramids in the distance, and a thin, pale haze of heat and smog was already draped across downtown Cairo.

'Good morning,' he said, giving a small yawn and shaking his head. 'Trouble sleeping?'

'Yeah,' she said, lifting her head to glance at him with a tired look. 'Knowing that we have this journal, I found it difficult to go to sleep. I've been dying to know what it says, so I've been up since before dawn. And as for this orb, I have no clue where it's from or what it's for.'

'Anything interesting in the journal so far?' said Ethan,

walking over to the dining table, where he picked up the unnaturally heavy golden lion figurine and inspected it again.

'Yes,' said Sophia. 'Some. But I'm still just making sense of it. It relates to Templeton's trip to Abydos in 1906. Anyway, we should get ready to leave. There's so much to show you at the Pyramids.'

She glanced out of the window, where the morning sun was bathing the Giza Plateau in its golden light.

'Hey, Scarlett,' said Ethan when he noticed the hacker and former CIA analyst emerge from her bedroom.

'Yo!' she said groggily as she rubbed her eyes. 'Last night was quite a thing. Are we OK to stay here? Al-Masry is going to be pissed off when he realises what has happened.'

'I think we're alright,' said Ethan. 'Unless he has Egypt's entire intelligence apparatus working for him, it's going to be very difficult for him to identify and locate us. Sophia, how long do you think we need at the Pyramids?'

'A couple of hours.' She shrugged. 'If we're going to have a shot at solving this whole thing, I need to explain that complex to you and how it relates to Templeton's and Goodwin's theories. And now that I have had a chance to read the whole journal, including Goodwin's notes, I have a much better sense of it all.'

'Right.' Ethan nodded. 'We should get moving soon, then. No time like the present.'

'And I'm on chaperone duty?' said Luke with a wink and a grin as he emerged from his bedroom wearing jeans and an unbuttoned shirt. 'I'm glad I'm not going out in that heat. Apparently, it's going to be another scorcher today.'

'I'm not expecting any trouble,' said Ethan. 'But better safe than sorry.'

'Well, ain't you two just a pair of gentlemen?' Scarlett said in a wildly exaggerated but good-natured southern drawl. 'Much obliged.'

Ethan shot her a glance and a grin.

'Sophia, can you be ready to go in about half an hour?' he then said.

'Yup,' she replied, closing the leather-bound journal and packing up her notebook. 'Let's get moving.'

When the two of them left the hotel in a taxi, the sun was climbing in the sky, and there was something in the air telling Ethan that Luke was going to be proven right. It was going to be another baking hot day in Cairo, especially up on the open Giza Plateau. The drive to the Pyramids took half an hour, roughly double the time it had taken Ethan to return the previous evening. When they arrived and stepped out of the taxi, the tourist conveyor belt was already in full swing with dozens of buses and taxis unloading hundreds of visitors. Ethan soon found himself scanning the area and glancing down towards Al-Masry's apartment block about five hundred metres away. He thought it was very unlikely that anyone would be able to identify him, but nevertheless, he felt happier disappearing into the throngs of tourists moving from the bus parking areas towards the ancient monuments.

'I've been here a couple of times before,' said Sophia, gazing up towards the top of the Great Pyramid some 150 metres above the plateau as they approached. 'One of them was with Professor Goodwin.'

'It's pretty spectacular,' said Ethan, noticing for the first time that behind the almost impossibly huge Pyramids and past some distant houses was the open Sahara Desert.

'Awe-inspiring,' said Sophia, donning the wide-brimmed straw sun hat she had brought. 'That's the best word I can find. As you know, the current dogma put forward by archaeologists states that these Pyramids were built by the pharaohs Khufu, Khafre and Menkaure. But I'm going to show you something that puts a question mark next to that idea.'

'Alright.' Ethan nodded. 'I'm intrigued already.'

'When I was here with Goodwin,' Sophia continued, 'I was helping him investigate the layout of what's called the Valley Temple over there near the Sphinx. And he said something that I thought was really profound. He said that if you spend enough time here, you end up looking up at these things, and you just can't make sense of them. And you end up thinking to yourself. They shouldn't be there. They're unnatural. They're too big and too perfect. It doesn't make any sense.'

'That's really profound.' Ethan smiled as he let that observation sink in.

'This whole place is like a giant question mark looking for someone to find the answers,' said Sophia. 'When you're here, you just can't help thinking that there is so much more to this story than meets the eye.'

'And also,' Ethan said, gazing up at the enormous Pyramids, 'how the hell did they actually do it? I mean, look at them. These things are so huge it's difficult to wrap your head around them.'

'And more importantly,' Sophia said, 'why? Why build these monuments?'

'So what's the answer?' said Ethan as they neared the base of the Great Pyramid.

'Well,' said Sophia, 'before I can show you, it's important to understand the ancient Egyptian creation myth.'

'Alright,' said Ethan, casting his mind back to a lecture series he had attended at Yale several years ago. 'I think I remember the basics, but feel free.'

'Right.' Sophia nodded as the two of them stopped and gazed out across the plateau. 'According to the myths, in the beginning, in a time called Zep Tepi, which literally means "The First Time", there was nothing but a watery chaos called Nun. And from this chaos rose Atum, the creator god. Atum created the first divine pair. Shu, who was the air, and Tefnut, who was moisture. They then created Geb, who was earth, and Nut, who was sky. Geb and Nut came together to create the first main deities of ancient Egypt, namely Osiris, Isis, Set, and Nephthys. Those four siblings were the first gods to be sent down to Earth, and they arguably became the most important deities in ancient Egyptian mythology. And their stories set the scene for this ancient civilisation's obsession with death and resurrection, as well as themes of justice and kingship.'

Ethan nodded as the now-faint memories of Goodwin standing behind a lectern at Yale while explaining these myths formed in his mind. But he said nothing and allowed Sophia to continue.

'After the world had been created,' she went on, 'Osiris ruled Egypt with justice and brought civilisation to the land. He taught agriculture, laws, and religious practices, and he was a much-loved ruler. However, his brother Set became jealous of Osiris's popularity and power, and he began plotting against him. Eventually, Set tricked Osiris into lying in a beautifully decorated coffin, claiming that it would be a gift to whoever could fit inside. Once Osiris lay down, Set slammed the lid shut and locked it. He then threw the coffin into the Nile, where it floated away and ended up lodged in tree roots in Byblos, which is in present-day Lebanon. Isis, who was devoted to her brother, travelled far and wide in search of him and finally found the coffin and brought Osiris's body back to Egypt. Set discovered this, and in a fury, he dismembered the body and cut it into fourteen pieces, which he scattered across Egypt.'

'A real stand-up guy,' said Ethan, sarcastically.

'Yeah, no kidding,' said Sophia before continuing. 'Isis, helped by her sister Nephthys, then retrieved and reassembled all the body parts, and using her powerful magic, she revived Osiris long enough to have sex with him and conceive their son, Horus.'

'Oh yeah, I remember that part,' said Ethan, raising an eyebrow dubiously. 'I didn't see that coming when I first read it.'

'Yeah, it's weird, I know,' said Sophia with a small shake of the head. 'Anyway, although he had been brought back to life, Osiris was unable to remain among the living, so he became king of the underworld, the Duat, where he ruled over the dead and judged the souls of the deceased. Isis then raised her son Horus in secret to protect him from Set, but when Horus came of age, he challenged Set to reclaim his father's throne. And after a long and dramatic struggle, Horus was eventually victorious and became king of Egypt, thereby fulfilling his father's legacy. And Set was exiled and banished to the desert.'

'It's a pretty cool story,' said Ethan.

'It sure is.' Sophia nodded. 'And it became the basis for the entire theology of this place for thousands of years, and it is literally built into these Pyramids.'

'Remind me how we know all this?' said Ethan.

'It's inscribed in those Pyramid Texts I told you about,' she replied. 'The oldest religious writings in the world. Anyway, let's head inside for a closer look.'

She led them up to the entrance to the enormous structure, and they soon found themselves in a narrow and claustrophobic space just under two metres tall and not much more than a metre wide. Its rough edges and irregular shape told the story of how it had been hacked and blasted into being more than a century ago. The air was warm and humid, and the floor was worn smooth by the countless number of people who had taken those same steps over thousands of years since its construction. After about twenty-five metres, they reached one of the original tunnels, which sloped up at a roughly thirty-degree angle.

The ceiling was now even lower, forcing Ethan to stoop and hinting at the fact that the ancient Egyptians were significantly smaller than modern people. However, after some thirty metres of climbing, the tunnel opened up into a large space where the floor continued its upward slope, but which was more than two metres wide, and whose ceiling was more than eight metres above them, sloping up at the same angle as the floor.

'This is called the Grand Gallery,' said Sophia, gesturing up through the sloping space. 'It's almost fifty metres long and quite a place, but no one knows for sure what it was for. It was most likely some type of ceremonial space leading up to where we're going.'

She led them onwards and up to the end of the Grand Gallery, where a small passage led into a chamber with smooth stone walls that was roughly five metres wide and ten metres long, and the ceiling was some five metres above them. Near the opposite end was a simple granite coffin that was missing part of one of its top corners.

'This is the so-called King's Chamber,' she said, turning slowly with her hands on her hips to take in the space. 'And there's a similar but smaller chamber about twenty metres below us called the Queen's Chamber. But there is no evidence that anyone was ever buried inside this Pyramid. The terms "King's Chamber" and "Queen's Chamber" only became common in the eighteenth and nineteenth centuries during the rise of European Egyptology, and they seem pretty arbitrary now, since no evidence of the Pyramids being tombs has ever been found. Archaeologists have found nothing. No king. No queen. No sign whatsoever of a burial, and no inscriptions anywhere, despite those being all over the tombs that we know for sure contained deceased pharaohs and their queens.'

'But isn't that a sarcophagus?' said Ethan, pointing at the coffin-like object.

'Yes,' said Sophia. 'But there is every chance that this place could be similar to what was found in the Osireion down south in Abydos. Namely, a structure designed to simulate something. In the case of the Osireion, the Duat. In the case of the Great Pyramid and this sarcophagus, the tomb of Osiris after he had been killed by his brother Set. What is much more likely, and this is what Professor Goodwin believed, is that the Pyramid, as well as the Sphinx, was part of a terrestrial complex whose purpose was the worship of celestial powers. And Goodwin thought that the Pyramids were actually astronomical structures with functions similar to Stonehenge and hundreds of similar structures found all over the world.'

'Where are those shafts pointing up to the stars?' said Ethan, looking around as a small group of tourists led by a bearded local guide entered the chamber.

'Here and here,' said Sophia, pointing alternately to two dark, square holes in the walls just big enough to put one's arm into. 'And here's the interesting thing. The south shaft here in the King's Chamber pointed directly to Orion at the winter solstice around the year 2500 BCE. And this fits with the idea that the pharaoh, as stated in the Pyramid Texts, is the living embodiment of Horus, who then leaves this Earth for the stars after his death and joins his father, Osiris, in the constellation Orion. So in a way, this Pyramid is a pathway for the soul of the dead pharaoh as he travels into the stars to be at the side of Osiris in the constellation of Orion. The shafts are essentially launchpads to the stars.'

'Right,' said Ethan pensively. 'Makes sense.'

'Now, the south shaft down in the Queen's Chamber pointed directly at the star Sirius, and it is associated with the womb of Isis. So consider this. The two south shafts pointing at the celestial versions of Osiris and Isis meet deep inside this Pyramid, implying a coming together of those two deities, which is precisely what happened in the creation myth when Isis made herself pregnant using the corpse of Osiris to then give birth to their son Horus. In this way, the theology of the ancient Egyptians is literally built into the Great Pyramid.'

'How about that,' said Ethan, raising his eyebrows as he tried to take it all in. 'That's incredible.'

'Well, believe it or not,' said Sophia, 'it gets even more amazing, because if you wind back the clock thousands of years, the dome of stars that we see above us changes in a very slow circular fashion because of Earth's precession, which I guess you're familiar with?'

'The wobble of the Earth's axis as it spins over time.' Ethan nodded. 'Yes, I'm familiar with the idea.'

'Well, basically,' said Sophia, 'it takes twenty-six thousand years for that wobble to finish one complete circular path through all the constellations above the planet's north pole. And if you go back in time, you'll find that at exactly 10,500 BCE, the two south-facing shafts inside this Pyramid pointed straight to Orion and Sirius at exactly the spring equinox, signalling the start of the crucial inundation season.'

'Really?' said Ethan, intrigued. 'I had no idea.'

'And not only that,' Sophia went on, 'but at that precise time in history, the positioning and orientation of the three Pyramids, one being slightly offset from the other two, were a perfect mirror of the three stars in Orion's Belt. All the angles fit at that point in time. And to top it off, at 10,500 BCE, if you stood here on the Giza Plateau and looked south, not only would you see the

Pyramids mirrored perfectly directly overhead, but the Milky Way would have rotated relative to today so that it would appear to flow directly down into the Nile in the far south. That isn't the case today, and it wasn't the case in 2500 BCE when these things were supposedly built.'

'Hang on,' said Ethan, his brow creasing. 'You're suggesting that the Pyramids are more than twelve thousand years old?'

'Well, that's what Goodwin seemed to think,' said Sophia. 'I know it seems crazy at first, but it all lines up perfectly. And there's more evidence for this at the Sphinx. Come on. Let me show you.'

As they moved towards the exit inside the dark and oppressive chamber, the bearded tour guide suddenly came up close to Sophia and gave her an angry scowl.

'Young lady, how dare you besmirch our great Egyptian heritage?' said the leather-faced man with a heavy accent and an ill-tempered snarl. 'Especially inside this sacred chamber.'

He then shot them both daggers and walked back to his group of tourists as he muttered the word 'Khawaga', which Sophia was aware was a derogatory term for foreigners.

'Besmirched?' said Ethan with a raised eyebrow as the man retreated while mumbling in Arabic. 'I haven't heard that one in a while.'

'Rude,' said Sophia, wrinkling her nose as he left, before then shrugging and glancing at Ethan. 'Well, I told you that the dogma around the history of this place is pretty much set in stone. Despite new revelations turning up every few years. It's like a religion, and anyone who dares to question it is accused of heresy. It's pretty much the opposite of what the scientific method should be.'

'I agree,' said Ethan and shrugged. 'But never mind about

him. He's just trying to make a living. Come on. I want to see the Sphinx up close.'

Twenty minutes later, they had navigated the steep steps and the throngs of tourists to emerge outside in the light and the welcome fresh but dry desert air. They then walked past the Pyramid that was supposedly built by Pharaoh Khafre and turned left along the long causeway leading roughly east and slightly downhill towards the Sphinx and the two temples near it.

'When it comes to this thing,' said Sophia, gesturing up towards the enormous figure, 'it is not at all clear that the current archaeology and Egyptology dogma is correct. Even the name doesn't really make any sense.'

'What do you mean?' said Ethan.

'The name Sphinx comes from Greek mythology,' said Sophia. 'It was a creature with the body of a lion and the head of a woman. However, this was thousands of years after the ancient Egyptian civilisations peaked, and the name has just stuck ever since the Greeks described it this way. But it was known in ancient Egypt as "*Hor-em-akhtet*", which means "Horus in the Horizon".'

'How do we know this?' said Ethan, peering up at it.

'From a stele,' said Sophia. 'The first written record of the Sphinx is on a stele erected by the pharaoh Thutmose IV around 1400 BCE, so over a thousand years after pharaohs Khufu and Khafre. It is called the Dream Stele because its text describes how Thutmose IV found it with only the head sticking up out of the sand. He then fell asleep under it and dreamt that it promised him that he would become king if he cleared it of sand. He did this, and he then ended up as pharaoh. And since then, it has been cleared of sand, covered by sandstorms, and then cleared again multiple times by archaeologists.'

Stopping near its front with the head towering over them, Sophia continued.

'Now,' she said. 'Conventional wisdom has it that it was built by Pharaoh Khafre in the twenty-sixth century BCE, based largely on it being near temples known to have been built by him. But archaeologists have found what is known as the Inventory Stele, which says that Khafre merely re-carved it, and not a single inscription has been found to suggest that it was originally built by Khafre.'

She took a few steps around to its front and stood between its two enormous paws.

'Remind you of anything?' she said, gesturing towards the huge limestone sculpture. 'Look at the feet. They are lion paws. And their design is exactly like that of the golden figurine stolen from Yale. Now look at the head. Notice anything?'

'Well, it's a pharaoh, obviously,' said Ethan. 'It looks feminine for some reason.'

'Yes, you're not the first person to notice that.' Sophia smiled. 'But what else do you notice? It's really obvious once you notice it.'

'It's small,' said Ethan, tilting his head slightly to one side as he looked up. 'It's really small.'

'Exactly,' said Sophia as she turned and glanced briefly up at the huge figure before facing Ethan again. 'The head, carved in the shape of a pharaoh, is way too small for the body. In fact, it is tiny, and once you notice it, the difference between the way it is and the way it should be if the proportions were correct becomes so jarring that you are forced to wonder if the body was carved out first and the head then placed onto it later. But we know from geological studies of the rock that this is not the case. The whole of the Sphinx was carved from one large piece of bedrock.'

'So, what does that mean?' said Ethan.

'According to Goodwin,' said Sophia. 'It means that the head was re-carved into the shape of a pharaoh by Khafre during dynastic times, and that the original and much larger head was almost certainly that of a lion.'

'I see,' said Ethan, trying to picture the Sphinx with a much larger lion-shaped head.

'Interestingly,' Sophia went on, 'archaeologists have found smaller sphinxes made to look like this one but created much later during the Middle and New Kingdoms. They are essentially smaller replicas of this one, but their heads are significantly larger in proportion to their bodies. In other words, even the ancient Egyptian artists who were working for the pharaohs looked at this original and felt that the head was much too small. I mean, what more proof do you need? The Sphinx was obviously not built during the reign of any pharaoh that we are familiar with. They simply appropriated it for their own uses. The original builders created it thousands of years before Khafre or Khufu.'

'But is there any real evidence for this idea?' said Ethan.

'Sure,' said Sophia, moving back towards the rear of the Sphinx and gesturing up towards it. 'Weathering by wind and water. We have found lots of obvious wind weathering of structures that we know were built during the Old Kingdom, after which Egypt has only ever been an arid desert, except very close to the Nile. But the weathering of the Sphinx is of an entirely different nature, namely water weathering.'

She stepped closer and pointed to deep, almost vertical, rolling fissures in the body of the Sphinx.

'Look,' she said, pointing. 'Wind erosion creates neat, angular horizontal lines into the side of a rock, like with the walls of the Sphinx's enclosure. It was formed when stones were taken out of the bedrock for the creation of the Sphinx. But water erosion results in these deep, near-vertical, undulating fissures in the rock. That's where the water found a weak point and carved out channels over millennia. Just like what we see on a huge scale in places like the Grand Canyon, where rivers have carved deep canyons over millions of years.'

'But you just said Egypt has been a desert for millennia,' said Ethan.

'That's right,' said Sophia. 'But only for the past eight to ten thousand years. If you go back far enough in time, that wasn't always the case. Remember, towards the end of the last ice age, Egypt experienced intense rainfall for centuries as the monsoons pushed much further north than they do today. This rainfall and runoff caused the erosion you can see here. And this is likely to have occurred roughly twelve thousand years ago, so very close to 10,500 BCE.'

'Damn,' said Ethan, gazing up at the statue and struggling with the sheer timescales involved.

'After that,' said Sophia. 'Goodwin theorised that the climate changed rapidly from fertile to arid over the subsequent centuries, or perhaps even just decades. This would have all but destroyed the local civilisation, and it was only restored many millennia later, and that was when Khafre re-carved the Sphinx. It was then all but forgotten after the final collapse of ancient Egyptian civilisation during the rise of Islam from the seventh century, only to be rediscovered by European explorers who dug it out of the sand again in the nineteenth century.'

'Amazing,' said Ethan. 'That's enough to make your head spin.'

'And one final thing,' said Sophia. 'The Sphinx faces exactly due east down to a fraction of a degree. This means that it faces straight towards the rising sun at the spring equinox, and in

10,500 BCE, the sun rose inside the constellation Leo, otherwise known as the Lion.'

'Holy crap,' said Ethan, briefly gazing around at their surroundings as if to find something there to make sense of what Sophia was saying. 'But if all this is true, then everything we think we know about ancient Egypt is wrong.'

'Exactly,' said Sophia. 'In fact, the entire history of the evolution of human civilisation would need to be rewritten. Something not even someone as intelligent and eloquent as Tobias Goodwin was prepared to stand up and say publicly. At least not yet. Not before he had undeniable evidence.'

'And that's what he was looking for in Templeton's journal,' said Ethan.

'I think so,' said Sophia. 'Or at least some clues to help him. But the bottom line here is that there are too many things that just happen to line up perfectly for it all to be a coincidence. What we see here at Giza was all built by design, and it was built to be integrated into the celestial spectacle overhead, which in turn was tied closely to the creation myth. It all fits, and if Templeton and Goodwin are correct, then the ancient Egyptians that we all know didn't so much develop their culture and civilisation as inherit it from those who came before, whoever they were.'

'Wow,' said Ethan. 'It's no wonder Goodwin kept all this under wraps. It's pretty mind-blowing.'

'Well,' said Sophia with a small shake of the head. 'I'm not sure what is more fascinating. The fact that this thing is about twelve thousand years old, or the fact that it lay almost forgotten and open to massive water erosion over thousands of years. Because the latter implies that the civilisation that built it was, for all intents and purposes, wiped out at some point, leaving these lands empty of advanced cultures for several thousand years until the first predynastic rulers emerged near Abydos. A sort of reboot of advanced civilisation here in Egypt after a long hiatus. Either way, that's where we need to go next.'

'To Abydos?' said Ethan.

'Yes,' said Sophia. 'That's where Howard Templeton found the golden lion. And now that we have his journal, we can follow in his footsteps.'

'Good plan,' said Ethan. 'Let's head back.'

As the two of them began leaving the Sphinx and walking back along the dusty footpaths towards the main entrance to the complex, Ethan turned to Sophia with a look betraying just how impressed he had been with her knowledge and insights.

'I've got to say—' he smiled '—you really blew my mind here. We all know that there are a bunch of speculative theories about ancient Egypt, but this actually makes a lot of sense. It's really difficult to argue with.'

'I know.' Sophia nodded, returning his smile. 'It can be a lot to take in at first, and you sort of feel the ground shifting underneath your feet a bit. Everything you thought you knew is suddenly up in the air. But that's also what's so exciting about it.'

'I totally agree,' said Ethan, sensing in Sophia a kindred spirit. 'When you think about it, almost all of the major advances in human knowledge and understanding of this world have started with one eccentric guy coming up with a seemingly crazy idea. And then a couple of centuries later, everyone knows it to be true. Think about people like Galileo and Copernicus or Tesla and Einstein. Most people thought they had gone off the deep end when they first presented their theories. Maybe this will turn out to be like that one day.'

'I think it might.' Sophia nodded. 'Something about this whole thing tells me that history is much deeper than we thought, and that we haven't even scratched the surface yet.'

'Well,' said Ethan, shooting her a wink. 'That should keep demand for people like you high then.'

Sophia smiled and was about to open her mouth to say something when a young man in jeans and a red T-shirt suddenly ran past her from behind, grabbing the strap on her leather satchel and ripping the bag from her shoulder. As he did so, he shunted her violently aside, causing her to yelp and lose her balance and almost fall over into Ethan. His instinctive reaction was to grab her and prevent her from falling onto the rocky ground, but his head was already turned to track the thief who was rapidly running away through the crowds of tourists.

'Are you alright?' he asked quickly, helping Sophia steady herself as his eyes tracked the runner.

'The bag!' she exclaimed as she looked up in near panic, gripping her left knee and wincing. 'He took the journal!'

'On it,' Ethan said with a steely look, and then he took off like a rocket.

Sprinting through the crowds of people meandering slowly along the footpath, he was just able to see flashes of the red T-shirt up ahead. The thief, who had probably been loitering, waiting for a chance to strike at an unwary victim, was not slowing down. He was clearly keen to make a clean escape and get out of the Giza complex with his loot, and Ethan caught him glancing over his shoulder a couple of times to see if he was being followed. Whether he spotted Ethan or not was unclear, but he kept up a blistering pace as if he thought a team of hounds was close on his heels.

Ethan's arms and legs were pumping, and his lungs were working overtime as he ran through the throngs of people, barely missing an elderly couple and clipping a young, smartly dressed man who then remonstrated loudly behind him. But Ethan had no time for anything other than making sure the thief didn't get away. If they lost Templeton's journal now, they might lose the ability to solve the mystery that he and Goodwin had been pursuing across more than a century. And possibly also the chance of bringing down Al-Masry and Nadeem Rashad.

Up ahead, the thief jumped the low metal fence into the huge parking lot where dozens of taxis and colourful tour buses were parked. He still had the leather satchel under his arm, and he was now running across the parking lot towards a set of steps that led up into a nearby built-up area consisting of blocky, two- and three-storey houses lumped haphazardly together along narrow streets and alleyways. As he did so, he cast his eyes back over his shoulder, and as Ethan followed suit and jumped over the fence, the two of them locked eyes for a brief moment.

'You're not getting away from me, you little shit,' Ethan muttered through gritted teeth as he cleared the fence and continued his pursuit. 'Not a fucking chance.'

After the thief had spotted the man coming after him, a look of surprise and panic seemed to flash across his face, and then he resumed his attempt at getting away, running up a short concrete footpath and disappearing into a narrow alley between two sets of houses. But before he did so, Ethan spotted him producing a phone and bringing it up to his mouth. Ethan was now gaining on him, and he sprinted up the footpath and followed the man into the somewhat drab-looking residential area where rusty drainpipes lined the exterior walls and laundry hung from narrow balconies. It was surprisingly dark and cool inside the cramped alley whose walls reached up about ten or twelve metres on either side. His eyes quickly adjusted to the gloom after the bright sunlight of the plateau, and he was just in time to spot the man in the red T-shirt disappear around a corner to his left, where the alley ended and met another.

Without slowing down, Ethan reached behind him and drew

his Sig Sauer from the small of his back, racking the slide as he ran to chamber the first round. The last thing he wanted to do was to have to shoot someone, and he really didn't want anything to do with Egyptian police if it could be avoided. But a loaded gun was a powerful and highly persuasive weapon, even if it was never fired.

Rounding the corner, he found himself in another alley that curved slightly to the right and continued up an incline with tiered houses built close together on what appeared to be a hillside. He could see the thief up ahead, and he now looked to be flagging. His arms were flailing, and his legs seemed increasingly uncoordinated, and Ethan felt sure that he was running out of steam. All he had to do was close the distance, bring the guy down and get the satchel back, and no one needed to get hurt.

Once again, the runner disappeared from view around a corner, and when Ethan reached it and rounded in at full pelt, he suddenly came face to face with the thief and what appeared to be four of his friends standing in a small courtyard. Hard and mean-looking despite seemingly being only in their early twenties, they were arranged in a crescent shape blocking his way, and each one was holding an improvised weapon such as a heavy metal pipe or a long kitchen knife. Ethan immediately skidded to a halt but then made a show of taking another couple of steps forward.

Even if he now felt that the tables had turned somewhat, there was no way he was going to let any of these goons see that. He was still panting as he approached them, and he glared at them from under his brow. Some of them were clearly very physically fit, and from the cold look in their eyes, it was clear that these young men were used to a rough and probably often violent life. No doubt, they made most of their money stealing from tourists near the Pyramids, and they most likely wouldn't shy away from violence. In the middle of the pack was the guy in the red T-shirt, and he scowled at Ethan while still clutching Sophia's leather satchel.

'Oh look,' said Ethan with a small shake of the head, doing his best to sound breezy as he took a moment to size them all up. 'Five of you against one of me. But I'm impressed. I've only been in town for about a day, and I already have my very own fan club.'

It suddenly struck him that perhaps none of them spoke English, but that was soon disproven when the thief grinned and snorted derisively before speaking up.

'Americans,' he said with a scowl and a heavy accent. 'You think you're so funny.'

'Alright,' Ethan said coolly as he brandished his pistol. 'You've got the numbers, but I have this. No one has to get hurt here. Just hand me the bag, and we'll forget all about this.'

'We're not scared of you, *Ferengi*,' said the thief with a lopsided leer. 'Go home, or we will hurt you.'

'That's not going to happen,' said Ethan evenly. 'Either you give me back what's mine, or this is going to get ugly. I'm not fucking around here.'

The thief regarded him for a moment, glanced down at the pistol and then briefly eyed his comrades, clearly evaluating the situation carefully behind his dark eyes before speaking again.

'You can never get all of us,' he said as an ugly smile spread across his lips. 'We are too many.'

As he spoke, the others in the group slowly began fanning out and moving around to Ethan's sides, and they were shifting their weapons in their hands, seemingly eager to use them and clearly getting ready to strike.

'If you fight us,' said the thief, 'we kill you.'

'And I'll take a couple of you with me,' said Ethan coldly,

genuinely hoping that it wouldn't come to that, and that the thief and his mates would think better of it.

'We're not afraid,' the thief said mockingly, slowly shaking his head, his cold eyes locked on Ethan's. 'You should go now. And leave your gun here.'

Ethan's heart sank. This was suddenly spinning out of control. He simply couldn't back down now. Not with the journal still in the bag. And even if he were to leave, there was no way in hell he could let them have his weapon. Not least because they might turn it against him, but also because it would then almost certainly end up being used to inflict untold damage on many dozens of innocent people in the months and years to come.

'Guys,' he said reasonably, loosening his shoulders and readying himself for a fight. 'I don't want to hurt you, but I will if you keep this up. Last chance. Give me the damn bag or this will turn really ugly.'

As he spoke, he noticed that one of the other young men – a lean, suntanned youth with a tattoo on his neck and a rusty metal pipe in his hand – was moving slowly towards his right side, clearly attempting to flank him. At that very moment, Ethan also caught the thief giving the lean bruiser an almost imperceptible nod, and that was when he knew. Things were about to tip over the edge and turn bad.

Oh shit, was all he had time to think before the lean youth suddenly launched himself at him.

With his pipe raised high and wide, he then swung the weapon horizontally, aiming for Ethan's head. Ethan ducked under it, feeling the pipe cut through the air above his head. As the thug overextended, Ethan allowed his pistol to drop to the ground, pivoted on his heel and then rose up with a brutal uppercut elbow to the man's jaw. The rusty pipe clattered to the ground as the thug hit the ground hard, out cold.

The second and third man immediately attacked in tandem, wielding long knives. The shorter of the two came in hard, slicing wildly from the right side while the other tried to move around to Ethan's back. The short man's blade managed to cut through his shirt, just nicking the skin on the side of his torso and drawing blood. Ethan spun free and moved towards the other man, who was now coming in low from behind. Taking his attacker by surprise, Ethan stepped forward into the man's space, catching his wrist mid-stab with both hands. With a powerful grip, he twisted sharply, causing bones to break and crunch audibly. In the same movement, he drove the blade down into the man's thigh, eliciting a cry of pain and shock. With lightning speed, Ethan then slammed an elbow into the side of the man's head with all his might, and the youth immediately sprawled onto the ground, unconscious.

As the shorter man recommitted and lunged forward, Ethan once more allowed for the swing to complete before he deftly moved in, gripped the man's wrist, pulled him towards himself, rotated under his arm and rammed the heel of his right hand up into the man's elbow with a powerful strike. The elbow crunched and bent up at a disturbing and unnatural angle as the man screamed in pain. Ethan then slammed a fist viciously into his kidneys, causing him to drop to his knees, his mouth opening and closing like a fish as the pain took him over and left him gasping for air. Then Ethan, with precise control of how much force he employed, snapped a lightning palm strike into the man's throat, just enough to stun but not kill. The thug gagged noisily and curled up on the ground, and Ethan then kicked the knife from his hand, and it skittered away. Three down, two to go.

With the thief in the red T-shirt still wavering, his last companion, a wide-shouldered brute with a shaved head and yellow teeth, moved in holding a long metal pipe with a sharp, jagged end. Holding it in two hands, he swung it in front of himself, seemingly trying to intimidate Ethan, but every time he did so, it caused him to end up off balance for a brief moment. Ethan waited for him to do it again, allowing the end of the pipe to slash past his face, and then he sprang forward, gripped the man's arm with one hand and used the other to shove him to the ground. As he went down, Ethan twisted the arm of his would-be attacker back and around with such force that his shoulder dislocated, and he let out a pained yelp as the head of his right humerus slipped visibly out of its socket. An instant after Ethan had forced him face-down onto the ground, he gripped the youth by the hair at the back of his head and slammed it into the ground, his nose crunching as it broke, and his mind going blank as the concussion left him like a wet rag on the ground.

As Ethan got back up and turned to the man in the red T-shirt, the thief stood immobile with his eyes wide and his mouth slightly open. Silence had returned to the courtyard, broken only by the whimpers and groans of the defeated quartet of thugs. Ethan stood in the centre of the bleeding men, all moaning and groaning, but none of them dead. He rolled his shoulder once and winced slightly from the pain in his side. Glancing down, he saw that his shirt was soaked through with blood, but it was nothing that wouldn't heal up on its own in a day or two. When he looked back up, he fixed the thief with a hard stare and tilted his head to one side.

'This is over,' he snarled, panting slightly. 'Now give me the fucking bag, right now.'

Whether it was blind panic or a calculated risk was unclear, but instead of surrendering the leather satchel, the thief spun on his heels with a yelp and began sprinting away along an alley leading off from the courtyard in the opposite direction from where Ethan had entered. Ethan could have picked up his gun and hit the guy in the back one hundred out of a hundred times, but instead, he quickly bent down and picked up the long metal pipe. Gripping it like a two-handed wood-splitting axe at his homestead in upstate New York, he raised the pipe high over his head and then hurled it after the thief with all of his power. Spinning end over end as it flew, it slammed into the thief's back before he had got more than ten metres away, knocking him down and causing him to crash face-first onto the ground as the leather satchel flew from his grip and landed nearby.

Within seconds, Ethan was on him. He turned him over roughly, punched him hard in the face twice to take the fight out of him, and then he gripped his T-shirt, hauled him up and shunted him against the nearby wall, where he sank down to a sitting position, leaning back against it and looking like he was about to pass out.

Lowering himself onto one knee and bringing his face to within a couple of inches of that of the thief, Ethan clenched his jaw and exhaled slowly through his nose as his steely eyes bored into those of the trembling man in front of him.

'Not so tough now, are you?' he said icily, his eyes narrowing.

'Please,' the thief stammered as blood and saliva dribbled from his badly split lip. 'I did not...'

Ethan cut him off, uninterested in what the man had to say for himself.

'Now, you listen to me, you fucking turd,' Ethan whispered through gritted teeth. 'This was me holding back, so don't you ever try that crap again. Not with me. Not with anyone. Because I just might be watching you. Do you understand me?'

The man nodded and produced a whimper that made him sound like a scared little boy. Ethan looked at him for a moment, but then decided that there was no point in wasting any more time or energy on this guy. Hopefully, he had learned his lesson. Ethan rose, stepped over to pick up his gun and the leather satchel, and then he left without looking back.

'Oh my God,' Sophia exclaimed, rushing towards him after she had spotted him walking back across the large parking lot near the Giza complex. 'Are you alright?'

Ethan merely shrugged and flashed her a grin. He felt no need to give her the full details of what had just happened.

'Hey, you should have seen the other guys,' he said.

'The other guys?' Sophia said incredulously. 'Plural? How many were there?'

'It doesn't matter now,' he said, keen for her not to worry unnecessarily. 'We have the bag and the journal. That's all that matters.'

'Are you sure?' she said, tilting her head with an anxious expression as she inspected his bloodied shirt.

'Absolutely,' he said calmly, taking her hand gently in his and giving her a reassuring smile. 'Don't worry. It looks worse than it is.'

'Do you think this had anything to do with Zosar Al-Masry?' Sophia said, a look of concern suddenly sweeping across her face.

'No,' said Ethan. 'I'm pretty sure these were just a bunch of local lowlifes.'

'I sure hope so,' said Sophia, glancing back towards the alley from which Ethan had emerged.

'Come on,' he said, placing a hand gently on her shoulder. 'Let's head back to the hotel.'

9

Zosar Al-Masry was in a small room behind a sliding door in his study that had been painstakingly converted into a space resembling a modest ancient Egyptian temple. The door was pulled shut, it was dimly lit, and the light from candles flickered on walls that had been tiled with sandstone and decorated with hieroglyphs and reliefs of ancient deities. In each corner of the room was a richly decorated stone column painted in red, blue, and gold, and the ceiling was black with dozens of five-pointed stars painted in silver. Three of them were larger and painted in an almost straight line, except for one that was slightly offset relative to the two others. At the back was a stone altar about two metres wide and one metre deep, and in the middle of it, placed against the wall looking out, was an alabaster statue of a lion's head.

Al-Masry was wearing a long, white tunic, a shorter leopard-skin shoulder cape, and wrapped around his waist was a linen kilt that was held in place with a leather belt. On his head was a gold diadem with the Eye of Horus, symbolising protection and health, and around his neck was a wide, semicircular gold necklace that lay flat across his chest. Affixed to its centre was a black obsidian disc as a symbol of the afterlife.

He stepped up to the altar and knelt in front of it, taking a few dried henbane leaves, placing them in a mortar, and using a pestle to grind them into a rough powder. Then he added frankincense and myrrh and mixed it, after which he poured it out into a small pile on a square slab of black granite. He then picked a thin, wooden lighting taper, lit it using one of the candles, and placed it in the pile.

Almost immediately, a dancing swirl of white smoke began to rise from the powder, which in ancient times was called Shemshemet. It had been used for millennia as a ritual hallucinogen capable of inducing an altered mental state in whoever consumed it. This facilitated divination and a chance at communing with the gods, but it was highly toxic in excessive quantities, so Al-Masry was always cautious about its use. However, he was prepared to take the risk in order to reach a plane of consciousness that would allow him to feel like he was in the presence of the old gods, particularly Osiris, around whom he was planning to build Egypt's future state religion once he had gained power and rid the nation of Christianity, Islam, and all the other upstart religions that had usurped the much older and much more noble ancient deities.

He closed his eyes, leaned forward, and inhaled the white smoke, and within seconds, he felt the active psychotropic chemicals enter his bloodstream and infuse his brain with what felt like an additional layer of consciousness. Like a door once hidden that had now been opened to reveal a whole new reality, much brighter and more colourful than the one mere mortals inhabited during their brief time on Earth.

Suddenly, it was as if the walls of the room melted away like smoke, and he was rushed forward at incomprehensible speeds to stand in the desert in front of the Sphinx. In the background were the Pyramids, but when he looked around himself, there was nothing but open desert. Turning back to gaze up at the huge statue towering over him, he realised that it was not the Sphinx. It was a lion. It was *Hor-em-akhtet*, and as he watched, the giant lionhead lowered its gaze and looked straight at him with its huge black eyes. Eyes shaped like black dodecahedra. His heart was hammering in his chest, and he felt fear rippling up his spine as the stone creature gazed down upon him. And then it spoke.

When Al-Masry regained consciousness, he was lying on the floor of the small temple, and several of the candles had burned down and extinguished themselves. Moving slowly and laboriously, he pushed himself up and onto his feet, and then he staggered out of the room, closing the sliding door behind him to stand in his study. Rejoining this mortal realm was always difficult. It felt empty somehow. Devoid of true colours and meaning. As if this world were merely a temporary place to dwell before the final journey into the stars that he was sure he would one day undertake.

Half an hour later, he was at his desk staring at the empty space where Howard Templeton's journal had been just hours earlier. His brow was creased, and his dark eyes were hard as flint. He had concluded that there was only a small number of people who could possibly have come to know that he was in possession of the journal and the artefacts. People who had been close to Tobias Goodwin. Once he had realised this, he had used his connections in the Ministry of Interior to discover that Goodwin's assistant, Sophia Lockwood, had entered Egypt the day before his apartment was burgled. From there, it had been easy to locate her and the companions that she appeared to be travelling with in the Four Seasons Hotel.

He had also put in a request to a major general in the Egyptian Army, whom he was grooming to become a figurehead in his future government. The general had facilitated the collection of all available intelligence on the four other travellers, including from the United States. The American intelligence services, despite all of their money and sophisticated technology, had always been easily manipulated. As organisations, they were big and powerful, but the individuals working within were never difficult to persuade, because deep down, America worshipped only one god, and that god was money. So, most of the time, there was no information he desired that he couldn't get his hands on one way or another. With several hundred thousand people working in the US intelligence services, there was never a shortage of greedy and easily compromised targets.

In this case, however, things had been somewhat different. He had been slightly unnerved to discover that the four foreigners appeared to be former soldiers or intelligence operatives. His concern had been strengthened by the fact that it had been unusually difficult to retrieve detailed information about their military careers. This would not normally have been a problem, especially if the wheels inside the US bureaucracy were greased sufficiently, and they certainly had been this time. All in all, the dossiers he had received indicated to him that Lockwood's companions might have been part of some sort of covert or special forces organisation, which certainly didn't bode well. But either way, he had to admit to being impressed that this young woman, who had been Professor Goodwin's assistant. She had been brave enough to steal from him, but he had now decided to fight fire with fire. If it was war she wanted, then war she would get.

A few minutes later, Nadeem Rashad arrived at the apartment and joined Al-Masry in the living room. Accompanying

him were two more men, Quasim and Farouk, both of whom
were leaner than Nadeem, but each of them was muscular and
mean-looking. Quasim sported a short, cropped beard, whereas
Farouk was clean-shaven, but they both had the cold, dark eyes
of people used to acts of violence and no regrets. And like
Nadeem, they had been initiated into the movement that Al-
Masry had decided to call the Sons of Osiris. This nascent, secret
organisation would one day swell to include the majority of the
men of Egypt, not least the top cadre of the country's military,
many of whom were already tacitly supporting him and positioning themselves for what would unavoidably be a violent
takeover. And together, under Al-Masry's leadership and with
the protection of the old gods, they would rise up and complete
the revolution that Egypt so desperately needed.

'Nadeem. Quasim. Farouk,' said Al-Masry grimly, looking at
each man in turn and offering them a brief nod. 'My sons. We
are under attack. Our project is under attack, and we must
respond to ensure that nothing derails our efforts to restore the
glory of our forefathers.'

As he spoke, the three men nodded gravely as they looked at
him. However, none of them spoke, knowing full well that their
job was not to offer opinions, and that interrupting Al-Masry
was the quickest way to ruin their day.

'A group of foreigners have stolen from me,' Al-Masry said.

He then placed several documents in front of the men. They
contained names, pictures and various other information about
Ethan, Sophia and the three others, most of it extracted directly
from serving personnel inside the intelligence services of the
United States.

'These people have taken important artefacts from me that
are crucial to our success,' Al-Masry went on. 'We cannot allow
anyone to jeopardise our destiny. You must find them and take

back what is rightfully ours. And if you need to use violence, then you may do so at your own discretion. The only thing that matters is returning those artefacts to my possession. All of my assets are at your disposal in this endeavour.'

'Understood, *Sa-nesu*,' said Nadeem with a small respectful bow, using the ancient Egyptian honorary term meaning 'king's son'.

'Most importantly,' said Al-Masry, now with a hint of calm superiority. 'You need to retrieve the journal at all costs. But if that proves impossible, take the girl. Ms Lockwood. Do not hesitate to kill her companions if they stand in your way. She is the key. Either she has the answers we seek, or we can trade her for the journal. The minds of these *ferengi* are like those of children. They value a single life more than history itself, and that is their weakness. Now go.'

* * *

It was early afternoon when Ethan and Sophia returned to the hotel room. In the taxi on the way back, Ethan had called Mitch to ask him to ensure that the Firefly was prepped and ready for the roughly 450-kilometre trip almost due south to Abydos. When Ethan and Sophia entered the room, Scarlett was sitting by her laptop, and Luke was standing by the window with his feet slightly apart and his hands clasped behind his back, looking out towards the Pyramids. Tucked under his belt at the small of his back was a pistol, and when he heard the door open, he turned quickly but then gave a nod in greeting when he saw who it was.

'Everything alright?' he said. 'How'd it go?'

'Good,' said Ethan, returning his nod and glancing at Scarlett. 'Sophia talked me through what feels like three thousand pages of research, and it was quite a ride. I feel like my brain has had a complete firmware update when it comes to Egyptian history. I'll tell you about it later.'

Ethan then went on to briefly mention the attempted theft of Sophia's satchel, but did his best to downplay it since he felt confident that the incident had no connection to Al-Masry.

'Everything OK here?' he asked.

'Sure,' said Scarlett. 'I've been busy, and Luke has been doing nothing at all. Isn't that right, Luke?'

As she spoke, she flashed the former Delta operator a grin and gave him a wink.

'Hey, I'm just doing as I'm told,' Luke replied in a dry Kentucky drawl, giving her a smile back as he shook his head. 'Some jobs aren't exciting, but that doesn't mean they're not important.'

'I'm just messing with you,' said Scarlett good-naturedly. 'I really appreciate you being here.'

'Alright, guys,' said Ethan, looking around at the small team. 'We need to pack up and get ourselves back to the airport. Mitch is going to fly us down south to a place called Abydos. That's where Howard Templeton did his excavations, and Sophia says Goodwin was convinced that it held the key to this whole mystery.'

'Look here,' said Sophia, extracting the old leather-bound journal from her satchel, placing it on the table, and flicking it open on one of the pages. 'I spent the morning going over it, and I found some things. Most of the stuff in here are brief notes and sketches, but I discovered a couple of passages that read more like diary entries. I think they could be important.'

With the others huddled around the table, Sophia began reading the first handwritten section aloud.

Abydos – October 8th, 1906

It is with no small emotion that one enters the Temple of Seti here at the ancient site of Abydos. One is left in awe of the King List. Names of pharaohs stretching back into mythical times. I find myself profoundly humbled, as if standing at the gateway to history. One's sense of time collapses when reading these cartouches. For thousands of years, these men lived and died here, but it begs the question. Who came before?

The answer to that question must surely lie in the newly uncovered Osireion, located not twenty paces from the southern boundary of the Temple of Seti. From its obvious alignment with stellar bodies, as well as its design, which is of a kind not seen in dynastic Egypt, I am convinced that this complex is unfathomably older than the temples here. With every day that passes, I become more convinced than ever that somewhere here is a clue pointing to the city from which all these civilisations sprang. But the desert is as vast and hostile as it is beautiful.

'Wow,' said Scarlett. 'That's really poetic. Makes me want to go there.'

'I know, right?' Sophia smiled.

'So, he spent time in the Osireion,' said Ethan, gazing down at the text. 'Did he find any clues there to what he was looking for?'

'Not exactly,' said Sophia. 'At least, not inside the Osireion itself, but listen to this next entry.'

Abydos – October 11th, 1906

My search continues, but the sands here yield their secrets reluctantly. Yet today, I uncovered a small, ancient temple some six hundred yards to the west. I am certain that I am the first to lay eyes on this place for millennia, and I believe it to be as old as the Osireion itself. Its entrance is located in a tall, rocky escarpment and was cleverly hidden, but the Osireion pointed the way across the sands. I wonder now if Ra himself, on his way to the Duat, had guided me. Inside it, I found an astonishing map stele that points to a location far into the western desert, possibly to one of the ancient oases more than a hundred miles to the south-west. The stele is broken, but I took a pencil rubbing in the hope that it might guide my search.

Sophia turned the page and showed the others the sketch of the map stele that Templeton had produced.

'That's the one you showed me, right?' said Ethan. 'The one with the trade routes.'

'That's right,' said Sophia. 'As he mentions, it is broken, so whatever lies west of the oasis is missing. But here's the final section of this journal that takes the form of a diary entry.'

Kharga Oasis – October 27th, 1906

After two weeks of arduous travel across the dunes, I finally arrived at Kharga Oasis three days ago. It is a green gem in the endless sands of the Sahara. I have spent the past two days mapping the locations of the ancient structures here, and I have located another temple containing a map stele. This stele is complete and undamaged, and it points to a location much further to the south-west. It is too far away for me to travel there on this journey. I fear I shall have to return

to Yale before coming back to this ancient land and setting
out into the desert again. The answers are out there. I feel it in
my bones.

After she had finished reading, Sophia took a deep breath
and exhaled slowly as she pondered the text.

'No details about the location of the second map stele,' Ethan
observed.

'No,' said Sophia with a slight shake of the head that hinted
at disappointment. 'Unfortunately, not. This is the last entry we
have from him that contains any useful information. The only
thing we know after this is that he came back to Yale in late 1906
and then returned to Abydos the following year in 1907. Presumably, he then travelled back to Kharga Oasis, but then he disappeared and was never seen again. No body has ever been found.
So, he's been missing for over a century, along with whatever he
discovered on his second expedition.'

'A real mystery,' said Scarlett, looking intrigued. 'I don't
blame Professor Goodwin for pursuing it. It's fascinating.'

'But now that we have the journal,' said Ethan, 'we have a
shot at finding the temple that he mentions near Abydos. And if
we're lucky, it might point us to the next stele in the Kharga
Oasis.'

'It won't be easy,' said Sophia, gently touching her lips with
the tips of her fingers. 'But we have to give it a try.'

'What about this Al-Masry character?' said Luke. 'Are we
going to leave him here in Cairo? He's a murderer.'

'We know where to find him,' said Ethan. 'At this point, we
have no hard evidence against him being responsible for Goodwin's death. We know who wielded the knife, but there's no use
taking him down if he was simply following orders from
someone else. But perhaps if we can find what Templeton and

Goodwin were looking for, then we might be able to establish a clearer motive that can help bring down Al-Masry too.'

'Speaking of which,' said Scarlett, 'while you two were playing tourists at the Pyramids, I did some more digging into Al-Masry and his various businesses. And the results are pretty interesting.'

'Let's hear it,' said Ethan.

'Right,' said Scarlett, sitting down at her laptop and bringing up her findings. 'It turns out that six years ago, he was appointed Honorary Deputy Director for Antiquities at the National Museum of Egyptian Civilization. That's the new museum built about three miles south of the old one in Tahrir Square in central Cairo. It's not clear what he actually does there, and it looks to me like he might have been appointed as a way for the museum to curry favour with him since he is wealthy and well connected. But it probably gives him access to much of the behind-the-scenes work on artefacts at the museum.'

'So, he has clearly had a serious interest in these things for a while,' said Ethan.

'Looks like it.' Scarlett nodded. 'As you know, he is also part of the eye-wateringly wealthy Fayek family, who owns rights to parts of the massive Abu Gharadig oil fields in the northern deserts of Egypt. He receives regular income from his investments there, as well as the family wealth fund that is managed by a large Wall Street firm. But it's the way he spends his money that is interesting. He has been funnelling cash from supposed charitable causes to a secret slush fund in Switzerland. Billions of dollars.'

'What's all that money for?' said Ethan. 'And why does he need to keep it a secret?'

'Well,' said Scarlett, 'this is the crucial part. I've discovered a network of shadowy companies all tied to Al-Masry that, combined, have spent huge amounts on various domestic influence campaigns. All of them seemingly designed to undermine the modern Egyptian state and sow the seeds for some sort of grassroots uprising.'

'Really?' said Ethan. 'What's the purpose?'

'Unclear,' said Scarlett. 'I have found a couple of references to an organisation calling itself the Sons of Osiris, and Al-Masry seems to be at the heart of it. But I have no idea what its purpose is.'

'If I were to take a wild guess,' Ethan said, 'then it sounds like he might be laying the groundwork for some sort of takeover.'

'Like a coup?' said Scarlett.

'Can't rule it out,' said Ethan. 'And his interest in ancient relics, along with his name change, tells me that he might be trying to fashion himself into some sort of ethno-nationalist leader.'

'That actually sounds plausible.' Sophia nodded.

'So, to sum up,' said Luke flatly. 'This guy is a real bad dude.'

'Ain't that the truth,' Scarlett observed drily.

'So, I say we take him down before he does any more harm,' Luke went on. 'But hey, that's just my personal opinion.'

'I hear you,' said Ethan. 'But like I said, we need real evidence first. We can't just go vigilante on him. At least not yet. For now, we should focus on the work of Templeton and Goodwin and see where that takes us.'

'Alright.' Luke shrugged. 'Just let me know if you change your mind. I'd be happy to oblige.'

'I'll keep that in mind,' said Ethan. 'Anyway, Luke, listen. I think we'd all appreciate it if you could come with us to Abydos. Knowing what we know now about Al-Masry, it's possible that we've stirred up a bit of a hornet's nest. What do you guys think?'

He glanced at Sophia and Scarlett, who both nodded their agreement.

'Yes,' said Sophia. 'I'd like that.'

'Absolutely,' said Scarlett. 'Four is thirty-three per cent better than three.'

'Well, since you're all asking so nicely,' said Luke, 'how can I say no? I'm in.'

'Great,' said Ethan with a nod as he placed a hand on his former colleague's shoulder. 'Thanks, buddy. Right, listen up, guys. We should pack up and get ready to leave in about ten minutes. Mitch is waiting for us at the airport.'

* * *

When Ethan and the three others joined Mitch on the tarmac at Cairo International's VIP terminal, the baking sun had passed its zenith for the day. The Firefly sat silently on the apron, and its dull, bluish-black outer coating seemingly absorbed almost all light and showed no hard reflections. As they arrived, Mitch was performing a standard preflight walkaround, inspecting control surfaces and the landing gear and checking engine inlets and fan blades.

'How's the bird?' Ethan called ahead as they approached across the tarmac carrying their bags.

'Everything's looking good,' said Mitch. 'We're ready to go. I estimate our flight time to be around thirty-five minutes.'

'Alright,' said Ethan. 'Let's light those engines.'

A couple of minutes later, they were all strapped in, and the engines were spinning up towards take-off revolutions. Then the Firefly lifted off vertically from the tarmac and rose into the air with only a muffled whisper and a faint high-pitched whine coming from its engines. As it continued to rise, it then pitched down and began to accelerate west towards the centre of Cairo in order to skirt the airport's flight restriction zone. As soon as they had cleared it, Mitch banked left and took the aircraft on a southerly heading as it continued to gain both speed and altitude. A few minutes later, Cairo was little more than a hazy desert mirage behind them, and ahead lay the fertile Nile Valley on their right and the open desert on their left. Ethan was seated next to Luke in the cockpit, while in the passenger cabin, Sophia, Scarlett, and Luke were discussing the day's events so far.

'So let me get this straight,' said Scarlett after Sophia had relayed in broad strokes what she had shown to Ethan on the Giza Plateau. 'The original Sphinx was carved from large bedrock poking up out of the desert. Initially, it was a lion, made by some previous civilisation, and then it was re-carved into the image of Pharaoh Khafre during the Old Kingdom.'

'That's right,' said Sophia. 'The people living here would obviously have known about the lionhead for generations, possibly even thousands of years. But because of some catastrophic natural event, most likely tied to climate change and the last ice age, they would have had no records of what it was or who built it. They simply found it, and by the time the ancient Egyptians grew powerful again, their leader at the time decided to expropriate it and fashion it into an image of himself.'

'That's a bit like how American settlers took over the US,' said Luke. 'When they found Mount Rushmore, they decided to carve images of their own leaders onto it.'

'Yeah.' Sophia nodded. 'That's a pretty good analogy. Except this happened thousands of years ago.'

'If all of this turns out to be true,' said Scarlett, 'then this is going to set a lot of people's hair on fire.'

'Sure is,' said Sophia with a shrug. 'But the evidence is what it is, and we should go where it takes us.'

'Just as Professor Goodwin always said,' Ethan mused. 'Let's just hope we can do him proud and solve this thing.'

'Well,' said Scarlett, 'if we don't try, we'll never know.'

'That's deep,' Luke said, glancing at Scarlett with a mischievous smirk. 'Hey, you should start writing fortune cookies.'

Scarlett broke into a smile, looked up at him and then punched him good-naturedly on the shoulder.

'I'll be damned,' she said with mock delight and a wink. 'We have a stand-up comedian on the team.'

'Trust me, you ain't seen nothing yet.' Ethan grinned at her, glad to see the team beginning to meld together.

By the time they received landing clearance and touched down at the small Sohag International Airport, some twenty-five kilometres north-east of Abydos, it was around 3 p.m., and the sun was beginning to curve down towards the western desert horizon. From the air, sitting in the copilot's seat next to Mitch, Ethan could see that approximately three kilometres west of the airport, a low, rounded and pale brown mountain range ran roughly north to south, more or less mirroring the path of the Nile. Beyond it was endless desert. As the wheels of the Firefly touched down on the designated apron, he also noticed the airport was significantly less busy than the one they had just left. This part of Egypt was nowhere near as densely populated as Cairo, and he had noticed only small settlements dotted along the Nile amongst the green fields of its fertile floodplains.

Using the credentials that came with his association with the US embassy in the capital, Luke had arranged for a car to be waiting for them at the airport. With Luke at the wheel, Ethan next to him, and Sophia and Scarlett engaged in conversation in the back, the four of them set off for Abydos while Mitch remained with the aircraft. They were soon underway along dusty roads next to fields of wheat, maize and sorghum. The roads were lined with date palm trees, and there were large vegetable patches near narrow canals that had been dug out to divert the water from the Nile further inland.

When they arrived at the Temple of Seti I, Ethan was struck by how close the authorities had allowed local housing to be constructed to the temple site. In some places, the distance between the temple's outer walls and the nearest houses was as little as thirty metres. The approach from the sprawling low-rise urban area to the temple was a wide concourse. It ran through structures that were now reduced to two or three courses of large, square stone blocks after centuries of pillaging by local residents who had used the stones to build their houses. However, the path then opened up into a square roughly fifty metres across.

Immediately behind it was the impressive, wide, colonnaded temple that rose up about ten metres into the air. The huge square columns were adorned with relief carvings of ancient deities and royals, but it was nothing compared with what awaited them inside. Enormous round columns rose up to the stone ceiling above, and the walls were covered in hieroglyphs and more reliefs.

'This place is amazing,' said Luke, turning slowly to look up at the walls that were covered in ancient writings and images. 'Why are they called hieroglyphs anyway?'

'It's a Greek term,' said Sophia. 'Hiero means sacred, and a glyph is a carving. So, because the ancient Greeks couldn't read any of this and probably didn't realise that they were words and not just images, they called them "sacred carvings". Some of them are symbols, but for the most part, hieroglyphs are phonetic, so they actually represent sounds. But there are no vowels, so you sometimes have to make an educated guess.'

'Huh,' said Luke, pushing out his lower lip. 'Who knew?'

'Look over here,' said Sophia, and the other three then joined her by a huge wall with deep relief carvings of a man standing in front of a seated male figure with a woman immediately behind him. 'This is Pharaoh Seti I offering a gift to Osiris in the hope that he will ensure his passage to the afterlife, where he will live by his side. And just behind Osiris stands Isis, who brought him back to life after his brother Set had torn his body to pieces.'

'This place is absolutely huge,' said Luke, doing a full 360-degree turn as his eyes scanned the interior of the space. 'I can't believe they built this thing more than three thousand years ago.'

'It's wonderful,' said Sophia, unable to suppress a smile. 'But if you think that's impressive, then you should see what's out the back. Anyway, let's head over to the King List. That's by far the most important find in this place.'

She led the group through a number of large rooms and chambers whose walls were full of hieroglyphic inscriptions and carved relief motifs. Finally, they arrived in a long, narrow room that felt mostly like a corridor connecting two sections of the temple. However, the walls on both sides were completely covered in royal cartouches.

'Look at this,' said a visibly amazed Sophia with a sweeping motion of her hand. 'What you see here is the chronological history of almost two thousand years of ancient Egyptian rulers. There are seventy-six cartouches here, one for each of them, beginning with King Narmer, who ruled from around 3150 BCE.'

'This is an incredible place,' said Ethan, taking in the wall and gazing up at the ceiling stones above them that clearly weighed many tonnes each. 'But it makes you wonder. If they could build something as advanced as this place three millennia ago, they would have been able to do other very impressive things much earlier than that. So, maybe Templeton really was onto something.'

'I want to show you guys something interesting,' said Sophia, heading along another corridor. 'This next bit has caused a lot of debate.'

She led them to a separate chamber and pointed up to a group of carvings on a lintel high above them.

'Have a look at this,' she said with a mischievous smile and pointed at the symbols. 'What do you see?'

'What in the actual...?' said Luke, gazing up at three shapes that looked unsettlingly familiar to someone from the twenty-first century. 'That's a helicopter, or I'm the Pope.'

'One of them sure looks exactly like one of our corporate choppers,' said Ethan, noting the main rotor, the cockpit and the tail boom with a stabiliser.

'And is that a boat and an airship next to it?' said Scarlett, peering up at the bizarre reliefs. 'How could they have known about these things?'

'Well.' Sophia smiled. 'Egyptologists maintain that what you're looking at are hieroglyphs that have been filled in and then re-carved, after which some of the mortar fell out again, creating these weird shapes. But I'll let you make up your own minds.'

'This is nuts,' said Luke, gawping at the carvings. 'It might be a coincidence, but it sure doesn't look like it to me.'

'Anyway,' said Sophia. 'Now let me show you the Osireion. That's what Goodwin was most intrigued by.'

They exited the temple and crossed about twenty metres of open ground to stand on the edge of a deep, excavated structure whose floor was some fifteen metres below the sand they were standing on. It was roughly twenty metres wide and thirty metres long, and the height of the structure itself from the floor to the ceiling was in the region of eight to ten metres. Unlike the Temple of Seti, all the massive stone blocks were rectangular with no ornamentations or inscriptions at all, and some of them were fitted together with curved shapes that looked nothing like those of the temple. It appeared to have been built in an east-west alignment, and a set of wooden stairs reached down inside it from its southern flank. There were only a couple of other tourists there, and Sophia stepped out to the edge and gestured down into it.

'This thing,' she said, glancing back at the other three, 'was uncovered by an English Egyptologist named Flinders Petrie in 1902, just four years before Howard Templeton came to this place. As for its purpose, Petrie said this: "Perhaps it was intended to be a cenotaph or a symbolic tomb of Osiris, placed near the traditional burial site of the god."'

'Kind of like the so-called King's Chamber inside the Great Pyramid,' said Ethan.

'Yes.' Sophia nodded. 'Most scholars now believe that the Osireion was probably used to simulate the passage through the Duat, and historians and Egyptologists assume that it was used as part of the Temple of Seti during his reign, simply because it is right next to it. But if you look closely, you can clearly see that it was not built by him or anyone else during that time period, for that matter. As I already explained to Ethan, the style is completely different. Even Flinders Petrie wrote this about it in 1902. "The building bears no resemblance to the Temple of Seti. It is of an earlier and more archaic style." In other words, he believed that it was much older. And Templeton clearly thought so, too, and so did Professor Goodwin. Both were convinced that this place predated even the Naqada culture of around 4000 BCE. And it makes sense. In the same way that the Sphinx was re-carved and repurposed by Pharaoh Khafre thousands of years after its initial creation, so the Osireion was repurposed by Seti I.'

'In 4000 BCE,' said Ethan as he gazed down into the elongated subterranean structure. 'That would make it at least six thousand years old. But then again. If the Sphinx is twice as old as that, then even this place is a relatively recent complex.'

'It's so difficult to wrap your head around these timescales,' said Scarlett. 'I always thought the Civil War was a long time ago, but that was like yesterday compared with this place.'

'Hey, don't knock it.' Luke grinned. 'The Civil War is the reason we have the Second Amendment.'

As he spoke, he tapped the place under his loose shirt where his pistol was concealed.

'Alright, cowboy,' Scarlett said with a thin smirk. 'Don't go waving that thing around, OK? We don't want to attract any attention here.'

They headed over to the side of the complex and took the wooden stairs down into the belly of it. As they did so, the air grew cooler, and with the sunlight no longer shining into it, it was easy to imagine it serving as a venue for religious ceremonies relating to the Duat.

'This is quite the place,' said Scarlett. 'It's kind of intimidating.'

'I see that interlocking masonry technique you told me about,' said Ethan, peering up at a point where two sets of walls met at a ninety-degree angle. 'Just like in Cuzco. That's really bizarre.'

'Well,' said Sophia, 'it doesn't necessarily mean that there is any connection between the two. But you have to admit that it's a weird coincidence, and there is nothing like it anywhere else in this country.'

'There really isn't a single inscription down here,' said Ethan. 'It feels unnatural somehow.'

'I'm with Templeton on this one,' said Sophia, glancing up towards the temple. 'There's just no way this place was built by the same people who built that temple up there. Not a chance.'

After another ten minutes, they headed back up and stood on a raised platform, which allowed them to see down into the Osireion as well as out over the desert. Ethan lifted his gaze towards the west, where the increasingly orange sun was beginning to set beyond the horizon, and it was now only about a hand's breadth from touching the top of the low mountains.

'The place with the map stele that Templeton found is out there somewhere,' he said, shielding his eyes from the sun with his right hand as he gazed into the distance. 'If only he had drawn a map or something.'

'He probably wanted to keep it a secret until he came back,' said Scarlett. 'That's what I would have done.'

'Wait,' Sophia said suddenly.

'What?' said Ethan.

Sophia didn't reply but instead raised a hand to shield her eyes and stared out across the barren stretch of flat desert towards the mountains and escarpments in the distance. Suddenly, her eyes narrowed, and a light frown spread across her face.

'I just realised something,' she finally said. 'The location is in Templeton's journal. At least partly.'

'What do you mean?' said Ethan.

'As you know, in Egyptian mythology,' said Sophia, 'the sun god Ra was believed to travel across the sky during the day in a barque, and then he would descend into the Duat at night. I think that when Templeton wrote that perhaps Ra guided him to find the small temple, he was simply describing the sunset. The hidden temple is out there on the horizon exactly where he watched the sun set on the 11th of October, 1906.'

'Holy crap,' said Scarlett. 'You might be right about this. But we can check.'

'How?' said Luke. 'You got a time machine?'

'Better,' said Scarlett, pulling her phone from her back pocket and activating it with her fingerprint. 'I can use an astronomy app to simulate the night sky from this exact position at exactly that date. Hang on.'

She quickly downloaded and installed the app, and a couple of minutes later, she had entered the precise coordinates, the date and the viewing direction. Holding the phone out in front of herself so that its simulated horizon roughly matched what they could see in the distance, the group gathered around her as she ran the simulation forward from midday on October 11th, 1906.

'There!' she said, stopping the simulation just as the sun disc on her screen touched the artificial horizon, and then pointing to the corresponding spot on a large, rocky escarpment in the distance. 'That must be where it is. Sophia, you're one smart cookie.'

'She sure is,' said Ethan, genuinely impressed with both of them. 'And good thinking, Scarlett. This could give us a real shot at finding it. But we don't have a lot of time. The sun's about to go down.'

He reached into his backpack and pulled out an experimental military-grade laser rangefinder developed by Frost Industries, which Marcus Becker had supplied him with before he had left New York. Bringing it up to his right eye and using the optics to find the spot on the distant escarpment corresponding to the location on Scarlett's simulation, he then engaged the device, and it measured the distance as being just under two kilometres.

'I reckon it'll take about twenty-five minutes to walk out there,' he said, 'and at least the same to climb to the top of those foothills and the escarpment. And then who knows how long it will take to actually find the place. It could be well past nightfall by the time we get back here. Maybe we should split up. Two of us go, and two of us stay, just in case there's a problem.'

'Well, I'm not staying,' said Sophia adamantly. 'I didn't come all this way just to watch from the sidelines.'

'I don't mind sitting this one out.' Scarlett shrugged. 'Ethan and Sophia should go.'

'Yeah,' said Luke, looking at Sophia. 'This is your rodeo. I'll stay here with Scarlett.'

'Good.' Ethan nodded. 'It's settled then. We'll head out. You two remain here, but stay vigilant. Al-Masry has probably been here plenty of times himself, and he might have eyes in these parts of the country.'

'Alright, we'll wait for you here,' said Luke. 'Be careful out there.'

'Of course,' said Ethan, and then he and Luke gave each other a quick fist bump the way they had done many times before when working together in Delta. 'See you guys later.'

10

With Sophia carrying her leather satchel with its strap across her chest and Ethan bringing his small backpack with essential equipment, the two of them exited the temple complex on its western edge and began their trek across the arid, open terrain. Up ahead, the sun was still just clear of the escarpment of the tall, pale ochre-coloured plateau they were heading for, and with the hot sands under their feet radiating a full day's heat back up at them, they soon broke into a sweat. Vegetation was almost non-existent, except for tiny, desiccated-looking spiky bushes that seemed more dead than alive, and small amounts of hardy lichen surviving on the shady parts of rocks and boulders. Every once in a while, they would startle small salamanders, which would then scurry off to hide under the nearest rock, and Ethan also spotted the telltale, undulating tracks of snakes on the loose sand.

'Stop for a second,' said Ethan after they had been walking for about fifteen minutes, reaching into his backpack and extracting a water bottle, which he handed to Sophia. 'Hydrate.'

'Man, I'm glad we brought that,' said Sophia, taking a big

gulp. 'I know we're barely out of town yet, but this place is no joke.'

'Yeah,' agreed Ethan, who had spent plenty of time in similar environments in northern Mali. 'The desert is beautiful in its own way, but it will kill you if you don't respect it. Let's push on. We'll be in shade in a couple of minutes.'

When they were about five hundred metres from the temple complex, it was barely discernible against the backdrop of the town of Abydos behind it. Roughly one hundred metres away, the limestone cliffs of the escarpment were now rising up in front of them, and they suddenly seemed much taller and steeper than they had from the temple. The terrain's million-year-old geology was now also evident with dark striations many metres thick stretching horizontally across the eroded front of the wall-like rock formations. Some of the rock layers were evidently much harder than others, because they had eroded significantly less than others, creating large, rocky overhangs between deep grooves as tall as a man.

'How do we get up there?' said Sophia, stopping and looking up with her hands on her hips. 'It seems so much bigger now.'

'Over there,' said Ethan, pointing to a spot he had been eyeing on their approach, which appeared to allow them to ascend along a winding set of small terraces and rock shelves that had been carved out by the wind and the rain tens or possibly even hundreds of thousands of years ago.

'I wonder how long it has been since anyone was here,' said Sophia as she followed Ethan up the first steep section, glancing back at the town in the distance. 'I don't imagine the locals ever leave the irrigated area near the Nile. I mean, why would they? There's nothing out here but sand and heat.'

'Well,' said Ethan. 'Unless Templeton was a fantasist, there's a temple out here somewhere. But it must be hidden inside the bedrock of the escarpment somehow. Keep your eyes peeled. It's probably very easy to miss.'

With Ethan in front picking a safe route for the two of them, they kept scaling the steep escarpment, often having to move left or right by many metres to be able to continue upwards. The rocks were covered in both sand and pebbles in some places, and twice it caused Sophia to almost slip and fall. Continuing upwards required their full attention, but then suddenly they were at the top and stepped up onto a large flat area that was bathed in the golden light from the setting sun. Towards the west stretched the raised desert plateau, to the east was the Nile Valley with its cultivated fields and irrigation canals, and behind the town of Abydos was the wide, meandering Nile in the far distance.

'Wow,' said Sophia, pointing back down to the flat, sandy terrain they had crossed about half an hour earlier. 'Look down there. Those are our shadows, and they are stretching away right towards the town. We should be in the right place. Or at least, very close to it.'

Ethan peered down at the two small shadowy shapes appearing to poke up from the otherwise flat edge of the escarpment's shadow on the terrain below. He let his eye move up and back to Abydos. It was obvious that they pointed towards the Osireion in the distance, and they didn't need a simulation of the sun's movement to know that they now had to be very close to where Templeton had found the map stele.

'Hang on,' he said, turning slowly as he looked around. 'There's clearly nothing up here, but I thought I spotted something down on one of those terraces about twenty metres that way.'

He indicated down and roughly north along the edge of the escarpment, and then he began retracing his steps back over the edge and down to the terrace below. Sophia followed him, and soon they were standing on one of the narrow overhangs that stretched for several hundred metres along the face of the escarpment.

'Over there,' he said, pointing at a set of large rocks that had a few scraggy shrubs growing around them. 'Come on. Let's check it out.'

They moved along the top of the overhang until they reached the angular rocks, which were all about the size of large suitcases. Since the sun was now setting and they were in shadow down on the terrace, the light was beginning to fade, and so were the colours of the sand and the rocks. But as they drew nearer, it became obvious that the rocks hadn't simply fallen from above and landed here. They had been deliberately placed, and in time, the shrubs had done a good job of adding some natural concealment.

'It's almost as if they mark out a path to the rock face,' said Sophia, moving up close. 'But there's nothing here but some half-dead bushes.'

Ethan stepped up to the spiky shrubs, and when he pushed some of them aside, the two of them could barely believe what revealed itself.

'Holy crap,' said Sophia, astonished and intrigued in equal measure. 'Look at that.'

In front of them was a perfect, rectangular doorway, complete with two upstands and a lintel lying across the top. Each piece of stone was expertly carved into elongated cuboids, and the opening was about one and a half metres high and a little under one metre wide. The entrance to the dark space beyond was dug into the sand by a couple of steps, which was why the entire thing had been successfully hidden behind the rocks and the low shrubs.

'This is it,' said Sophia. 'One hundred per cent. This is the temple.'

'Why is it up here?' said Ethan. 'Seems like a weird place.'

'I don't know,' said Sophia. 'Maybe because caravans from Abydos heading up onto the desert plateau used to pass by this place, and they might leave offerings to the gods for protection against the elements. Don't forget, the desert was associated with death. And remember, it was also the place that Set was banished to.'

'Right.' Ethan nodded, reaching inside his backpack and pulling out a torch, which he directed towards the doorway. 'Let's see what's here.'

Stooping to enter, they passed the threshold under the lintel to the millennia-old temple and stepped inside. The roughly square space was no more than a few metres on either side, and the ceiling was barely high enough for them to stand up straight. The floor was level but partly covered in sand, and the limestone walls were relatively smooth but unadorned. However, the main feature of the temple was the small stone altar at the back, directly opposite the doorway. Set into a shallow, neatly carved alcove in the bedrock above the altar was a stele, which was missing a large piece in the lower left corner. It was instantly familiar to both of them.

'That's Templeton's map stele!' Sophia exclaimed excitedly. 'It's still here.'

'Incredible,' said Ethan as the two of them approached. 'It almost feels like no one has been in this place since he came here over a century ago.'

Suddenly, they heard the dry sound of something moving across the sandy floor behind them. Ethan spun around, and a second later, Sophia shrieked as she spotted the two large

Egyptian cobras slithering purposefully through the doorway from the outside and directly towards them.

'Get back,' said Ethan, moving between Sophia and the snakes while pulling out his Sig Sauer and racking the slide in one fluid movement.

The two snakes appeared to be unnaturally large, and as he watched them move closer with their wide heads raised, Ethan could have sworn that they were assessing him and Sophia. One began moving slightly to the left while the other moved right, evidently trying to divide the attention of their prey.

'What the fuck is going on?' Sophia stammered as she watched the two snakes exhibit this seemingly coordinated behaviour.

'Hold your ears,' said Ethan, and then he raised the pistol, aimed at the head of the first cobra, and fired.

Amid a dry, ear-splittingly loud crack inside the small stone chamber, the bullet punched through the head of the snake, shattering its entire skull and sending blood and strips of skin and muscle flying through the air behind it, where they then slapped onto the dry sand and rolled to a stop. Contrary to what any normal snake should have done, instead of turning tail and fleeing, the other cobra continued its flanking move, but it appeared to now speed up as it did so. Ethan immediately swivelled and trained the 9mm weapon on the reptile. Seemingly unafraid, it kept coming until a bullet cut through its head and left it coiling up in a death cramp on the sandy floor, where it then stopped moving after a couple of seconds.

'Jesus!' Sophia breathed as she removed her hands from her ears. 'What the hell was wrong with those things? Why were they so aggressive? That's just not normal. It's like they were possessed.'

'I don't know,' said Ethan, his breathing only slightly elevated as he lowered the weapon. 'Two of them attacking together. I've never seen anything like it. But at least they won't be bothering us again.'

'Damn,' said Sophia. 'I hope there aren't any more.'

'I have plenty of bullets,' said Ethan, glancing back over at the stele as he tucked the pistol back under his belt. 'Anyway, let's have a good look at this thing. It looks like Templeton's sketch was pretty accurate.'

'Yes,' said Sophia, recomposing herself and going down on one knee in front of the altar while looking up at the stele. 'But the lines indicating caravan routes are much clearer here.'

'I see the Nile and Abydos,' said Ethan, lowering himself onto his haunches next to her as he inspected the broken stele. 'And Kharga Oasis is clearly visible. And there's another one in the far north. I wonder what happened to the missing piece, though.'

'This altar is red granite,' said Sophia, puzzled, as she placed both hands reverentially on the altar with their palms facing down. 'That means it has been brought up here from the quarries in Aswan in the south. It's probably made from the same stone as the sarcophagus inside the Great Pyramid. This thing might be four thousand years old. Perhaps much older.'

'I wonder if this was where Templeton found the golden lion figurine,' said Ethan, looking at the altar.

'It's possible,' said Sophia. 'If the lion was part of some more ancient belief system, then perhaps it was venerated in places like this many thousands of years ago. It kind of makes sense. As the apex predator in Africa throughout human history, it was the ultimate symbol of power, so kings would have wanted to associate themselves with it.'

'Wait a minute,' said Ethan, getting off his haunches and

leaning over the altar to look down behind it. 'There's something here.'

He reached down into the narrow gap between the altar and the back wall, where something was wedged and partly covered in dust, sand and small fragments of rock. He tried to pry it loose and lift it out, but he was unable to grip it tightly.

'Move back a bit, please,' he said, and then he wrapped his arms around the altar and began dragging it clear of the wall.

The altar was heavy, and he had to use all of his strength to shift it. Panting from the effort, he then moved around to its rear and picked up a thin piece of stone with a cracked edge that was roughly triangular in shape.

'The missing map piece,' Sophia said excitedly. 'It was here all along. How did Templeton miss it?'

'He was probably bowled over by this place,' said Ethan, standing to place the piece back in its original position. 'I can't blame him. Imagine being the first to find this after thousands of years. Let's see what it looks like whole.'

He held the broken section up to the part of the shallow alcove from which it had fallen, and when he pushed it in, it slotted neatly into place and remained where it was. Then he stepped back, and the two of them gazed at the complete, ancient caravan map.

'There's another line almost due south-west from Kharga Oasis,' said Sophia, pointing. 'But it doesn't seem to go anywhere. There's no destination.'

'It must be really far to the south then,' said Ethan. 'But there's nothing down there but open desert, right?'

'Well,' said Sophia pensively. 'Not exactly. There are mountain ranges, but the whole area is completely arid. There is practically no water for hundreds of miles. Nothing can grow there.'

'Strange,' Ethan said pensively.

'I wish we had Templeton's notes from his 1907 expedition,' said Sophia, extracting her phone and taking several pictures. 'I am dying to know what he found. He must have gone to Kharga Oasis, but what clues did he uncover there?'

'Well, since he disappeared in the desert—' Ethan shrugged '—I guess we'll never know, unless we go to Kharga Oasis and look for the answers ourselves.'

Sophia lowered her phone and glanced up at him as a thin, determined smile began to spread across her lips.

'Try and stop me,' she said.

* * *

About an hour after Ethan and Sophia had set off from the Temple of Seti across the open terrain heading for the escarpment in the distance, Luke and Scarlett had moved back through the temple and were now sitting by an outside table at a small roadside café about fifty metres from the entrance to the temple complex. The sunlight was fading fast, and even though the sky was not yet completely dark, the local streetlights had come on.

'So, how long have you and Ethan known each other?' said Scarlett, sipping her fruit juice. 'You two seem pretty tight.'

'About seven years,' said Luke, popping open his can of non-alcoholic beer, taking a sip, and nodding in what appeared to be surprised approval. 'We worked together in the Unit quite a bit. Although officially, that never happened because officially, Delta doesn't exist.'

As he spoke, he glanced at her a gave her a wink.

'Yeah, tell me about it.' Scarlett nodded. 'When I was in the Agency, you boys were the go-to guys for all the high-risk stuff.

But we never could get any background info on any of you. I heard someone in my office refer to you as the Ghosts of Fort Bragg. I always thought that was pretty accurate.'

'Deniability.' Luke shrugged. 'The government needs it in order to deploy the Unit overseas. And in my experience, nobody at Delta ever came there to be famous. They just wanted to be with the best.'

'Were you always interested in the military?' said Scarlett.

As she spoke, she glanced out over the street where the last minibuses from Luxor were now leaving to transport small groups of visitors back to the main tourist hub, which was roughly a two-hour drive away.

'Heck no,' said Luke. 'I never thought about any of that. I was just a farm boy in rural Kentucky doing farm-boy stuff. I was going to take over my dad's cattle ranch. I did get in some trouble once or twice, but nothing serious.'

'With the law?' said Scarlett, seemingly surprised by his admission.

'Yeah, nothing major,' said Luke with a sly grin. 'Just redneck stuff like shooting road signs with a shotgun. That type of thing.'

Scarlett giggled as she glanced at him.

'I never would have guessed,' she said with a smile. 'But I guess you finally ended up in the right place.'

'More or less,' said Luke. 'My dad always wanted me to become a lawyer, but I'd rather hang myself. Would have made more money, though. But being chained to a desk in an office just isn't worth it. I need to be outside, preferably with a gun in my hands. That's where I belong.'

As he spoke, he noticed a white SUV rolling to a stop about fifty metres along the road. There appeared to be three people inside, but the pale blue western sky was reflected in its windscreen, so he was unable to see their faces. They had stopped in front of what looked like a laundry service, but no one exited the vehicle. Instead, its occupants remained inside, and they appeared not to move or speak to each other. For a few seconds, he felt his carefully honed internal threat detector begin to stir, but then he reminded himself that he was in the middle of a tourist hotspot, and that he was probably just watching a couple of locals hanging around. Nevertheless, his hand instinctively moved back to the pistol tucked under his shirt at the small of his back, and he glanced briefly at Scarlett, who did not appear to have registered the car arriving.

'Are you alright?' she said, tilting her head to one side and giving him a curious look.

'Sure,' said Luke casually, keen not to make her worry for no reason. 'I'm fine. Just making sure I have my gun handy.'

'Well, anyway, I'll just go to the ladies' room,' she said. 'Back in a sec.'

Luke watched her get up and head inside the café, and then he turned to look towards the parked SUV. As he eyed it, its headlights suddenly came back on, and then it did a U-turn and drove slowly along the dusty street, eventually turning left and disappearing down a side alley. A couple of minutes later, Luke's sense of unease was still lingering at the back of his mind when he heard a familiar voice calling out his name.

'Hey, Luke!' came Ethan's voice as he and Sophia approached about thirty metres away along the gloomy street from the direction of the temple. 'Where's Scarlett?'

'In the restroom,' said Luke, getting to his feet as the two others joined him at the table. 'How did it go? Find anything?'

At that moment, Scarlett returned, and Ethan and Sophia then told them about what they had found inside the small temple hidden up in the escarpment.

'We'll be heading for Kharga Oasis tomorrow,' said Sophia. 'But we need a place to sleep.'

'There's a decent-sized town not far from here,' said Ethan. 'I'll head inside and ask the owner of this place. He might know somewhere we can bed down.'

Half an hour later, they arrived at a guesthouse in the nearby town of Al-Balyana on the banks of the Nile. The café owner had arranged a taxi for them, which just happened to be driven by his brother-in-law, who assured them that he was giving them a very special price. The bedrooms at the guesthouse were basic but clean and comfortable, and after showering, the four of them headed out to eat at a local restaurant just a few houses down the street. It was a busy and lively place whose walls were draped with red and yellow woven fabrics, from which fragrant smells oozed out into the street. Local Shaabi pop music emanated from hidden speakers, and the restaurant's many wooden tables were full of locals wearing traditional, loose, flowing *galabeya* robes in various colours, some of which were adorned with gold embroidery. After a meal consisting of spiced, grilled lamb, rice and vegetables, followed by baklava drenched in syrup, they headed back to the guesthouse to sleep.

The next morning, they were awakened by the call to prayer from the local mosque just before 5 a.m. By the time they left the guesthouse and got into a waiting minibus taxi, the sun was only just beginning to creep above the horizon, and the air was cool and slightly humid. Their driver, a small and thin middle-aged and moustachioed man named Djamal, was keen to help carry their few belongings into the luggage compartment at the rear of the minibus, but he was left disappointed when it turned out that none of his four passengers that morning appeared willing to part with their bags. He muttered something under his breath and slumped down behind the wheel, which he had to strain to see above.

Instead of heading back to Abydos and driving along the edge of the desert to Sohag Airport, Djamal took them north-west along a fifty-metre-wide irrigation canal towards a small farming town. The canal road, which ran next to various culti-vated fields, was straight as an arrow except for when it occasion-ally angled slightly to one side or the other in order to more or less follow the path of the Nile roughly a kilometre away. Eventu-ally, as the sun began to creep higher in the pale blue morning sky, they arrived at the small town where Ethan spotted a sign for the airport, although there was no indication of the distance.

'How far?' he said, glancing at Djamal.

'Not far,' said Djamal, waving a hand as if wafting away a fly. 'Fifteen minutes.'

Soon, they left the semi-urban area behind and drove along a road that cut through more cultivated fields dotted with only a few houses here and there. Every few hundred metres, small dirt tracks crossed the road, allowing for farm equipment to be driven from one field to the next, but at this hour, no one appeared to be working. However, a few minutes before they reached the main road running along the edge of the desert towards the airport, Ethan spotted a white flatbed truck parked on one of the dirt tracks up ahead. Despite there now being plenty of sunlight, its headlights were on, and it was facing the road as if waiting for the minibus to pass before pulling out and driving off. At that moment, Ethan also noticed a white SUV behind them in the rear-view mirror.

'Luke,' he said calmly. 'Check six.'

As Luke turned his head to eye the vehicle coming up behind them, Djamal mumbled something in Arabic that Ethan didn't understand, and then he rolled down the window and waved at the truck driver, presumably to thank him for waiting for them to pass. Going at roughly forty kilometres per hour on the badly maintained road, they were only about ten metres from the truck when a plume of black smoke burst from its exhaust, and it then suddenly leapt forward straight out towards the road. If the driver had wanted to block them, he was too late, but Ethan instantly realised that this was not the plan. He wasn't trying to block them. He was trying to ram them.

Djamal yelped in panic with his thin hands gripping the wheel as the truck charged towards them, but he made no attempt to brake or swerve. Instinctively, Ethan reached across and yanked at the wheel to try to avoid the collision, but it was too late. With Luke calling out, 'Hang on!' and Sophia producing a panicked scream from the back, the front of the flatbed truck rammed into the side of the minibus, shunting it aside by a couple of metres, shattering all the glass on the impact side, and causing its passengers to be violently jolted sideways in their seats. Ethan felt his head slam into the inside of the cabin as glass exploded into the air inside the van's interior.

Djamal finally slammed the brakes, Ethan heard Scarlett and Sophia produce loud shrieks, and a low grunt came from Luke as the minibus screeched to a halt with smoke and steam billowing out of the engine compartment at the front. Ethan knew what was about to happen, and it seemed that Luke was also already in full combat mode.

'Everybody out!' Ethan shouted as he kicked his mangled door open while at the same time feeling something warm and wet trickling down the side of his head.

'Move! Move!' Luke shouted, shunting the door next to him open with his shoulder and drawing his pistol.

By now, the doors of the white SUV had swung open, and

out stepped two burly men carrying black assault rifles that Ethan instantly recognised as being Russian AK-12s, used both by Egypt's infantry as well as its special forces. He also recognised Nadeem Rashad.

'Get behind the bus!' he shouted as Sophia and Scarlett scrambled out of the minibus, looking shocked and dazed.

Seeing the armed men, Djamal bolted from the driver's seat with a terrified howl and began running away across the open field next to the road, but he never made it further than about fifteen metres when the staccato sound of an assault rifle burst rang out, and three bullets smacked into his back, stitching their way up his spine as they impacted. He fell forward heavily onto his front and ended up sprawled in the dust without moving, three dark red patches spreading on his back.

Moving to take cover behind the smoking minibus that now sat at an angle on the road, Ethan spun towards the sound of the shots and saw that the flatbed truck's driver had jumped down from the vehicle, holding a submachine gun, and he had cut down the fleeing minibus driver. He was tall, clean-shaven and wiry, and as he lowered his weapon slightly to inspect his handiwork, a contented scowl curled up one side of his mouth.

At that moment, just as Ethan was lining up his gun sights on Nadeem's companion as he emerged from the white sedan, he heard Nadeem bellow something in Arabic in the direction of the truck driver, and he immediately understood what it meant.

Get the girl!

Bringing his weapon back up to aim at Ethan and Luke, the driver immediately began advancing towards where Sophia and Scarlett were taking cover. Without hesitation, Ethan spun around, brought up his Sig Sauer, aimed and fired twice in quick succession. The first bullet smacked into the truck driver's shoulder, passing clean through him and sending a spray of blood shooting out behind him. The other clipped his neck and opened up a gash from which blood began to spurt. The driver spun mid-stride and fell to the ground, and as Ethan fired again, he scrabbled furiously towards his truck and managed to get behind one of the front wheels. The third bullet punched through his thigh and severed an artery, and blood was now pumping out of the wound.

A wild roar came from Nadeem, who had just stepped out of the white SUV and witnessed the driver being cut down by bullets. A hail of bullets then slammed into the minibus as he and his companion opened up with their assault rifles while they advanced towards their target. Bullets peppered the minibus, punching through the bodywork and shattering all the remaining windows into thousands of tiny cubic shards that rained onto the road surface like diamonds. While trying to remain in cover, Ethan and Luke were now returning fire, but they were outgunned by the advancing attackers.

'Cover me!' Ethan shouted to Luke, and then he sprinted for the truck.

While Luke laid down suppressing fire, Ethan covered the distance to the truck in a few seconds, and when he rounded its front with his weapon out in front of himself, he saw the driver lying almost flat on his back, his shoulders and head resting against the tyre, his weapon by his side and both of his hands clasped uselessly against the side of his neck where blood oozed out between his fingers. Ethan dropped down, put his face close to that of the driver and pushed the muzzle of his pistol hard against the side of his head.

'Who are you working for?' he hissed menacingly. 'Tell me or I blow your brains out right now.'

The man's mouth opened and closed a few times as he made

faint choking noises, but as his eyes rose to meet Ethan's, a malignant smile spread across his lips.

'You can't stop us,' he grimaced disdainfully, showing a set of square, bloodied teeth as he spoke in a heavy accent.

'What the hell are you talking about?' Ethan yelled as more shots rang out from the other side of the truck.

'When he becomes pharaoh,' the driver wheezed between breaths, 'all you *ferengi* will be kicked out, and Egypt will rise again.'

'Who?' Ethan roared. 'Al-Masry?'

The driver didn't reply, but as he leered up at Ethan, there was a look of recognition in his eyes that left Ethan in no doubt who the three attackers were working for.

'The old gods will reign once more,' the driver said weakly, and then he exhaled one final time and sagged down onto the ground, dead.

Leaving the man behind and running back to Luke's side while firing on the move, Ethan somehow made it to the minibus without being hit. Sophia and Scarlett were now huddled by the vehicle's rear with their arms over their heads, praying that its engine block, bodywork and interior would stop the torrent of lead coming towards them at supersonic speeds.

'Run to that ditch!' Ethan shouted to them, pointing to an irrigation ditch about ten metres away. 'Luke and I will cover you. On three!'

Pulling back into cover, Ethan and Luke exchanged a quick look and a nod, and then they got ready.

'One. Two. Three. Go!' shouted Ethan, and then he and Luke emerged simultaneously from either side of the minibus, firing their pistols as rapidly as they could.

If they were lucky, they might hit their attackers, who were now roughly thirty metres away, but that was not the goal. All they were hoping for was for the two men to stop firing for long enough for Sophia and Scarlett to reach safety in the irrigation ditch. As Sophia and Scarlett sprinted for the ditch, Ethan and Luke rained fire on their attackers. Ethan felt the familiar kick of the Sig Sauer's recoil in his wrist as he emptied the magazine of its remaining bullets, and less than a second after it clicked dry, he heard Luke's weapon do the same.

It had been a desperate last move, but it had the desired effect because the two attackers threw themselves to the ground near some large rocks lying on the grassy verge, one of them seemingly having taken a bullet to the chest. However, from the way it impacted, Ethan felt sure that the man was wearing a ballistic vest under his shirt, and as he and Luke pulled back into cover behind the minibus to reload, he could hear the voices of their attackers yelling to each other in Arabic, and none of them sounded seriously wounded. Of Sophia and Scarlett, there was now no sign, which was exactly what Ethan had been hoping for. He just prayed that they were both unhurt.

Suddenly, their attackers opened up again with their two assault rifles, but this time, instead of a barrage of incoming lead, the minibus was peppered with short three-round bursts. The attackers, now safely behind cover among the rocks, were clearly attempting to pick out weak points in the minibus, hoping to be able to hit Ethan or Luke through the thin metal bodywork. Bullets tore through the sheet metal uncomfortably close to them, and it was clear that it would be a question of time before one of the shooters got lucky.

'We need a way out,' said Luke as he slammed a fresh mag into his pistol's magazine well and racked the slide. 'The longer this goes on, the better it looks for them. Fuckers.'

'I know,' said Ethan tensely, reloading his weapon and then

reaching inside his backpack for a small comms unit, flicking a switch and pressing a button. 'Mitch, do you read?'

After a few seconds, Mitch's voice came over the line. 'Loud and clear,' he said. 'I can hear shooting in the distance. Tell me that ain't you.'

'It's us,' said Ethan evenly. 'We could sure use your help right about now.'

'Roger that,' said Mitch, the sound of frantic rustling coming through the comms unit's speaker. 'Location?'

'About two kilometres south-south-east of the airport,' said Ethan, providing his best guess. 'We're pinned down by two shooters. Assault rifles. We're by a white minibus and a flatbed. You can't miss us. Hostiles are by an SUV towards the east.'

As Luke returned fire once again, in the background through the speaker, Ethan could hear the sound of Mitch strapping into the Firefly's cockpit and firing up the engines.

'Two klicks,' Mitch confirmed. 'South-south-east. On my way. Get ready to evac. I'll be coming in hot.'

'The faster the better,' said Ethan. 'We're counting on you.'

He shoved the comms unit back into the backpack and racked the slide on his pistol. Then he leaned out and fired twice towards the rocks behind which the attackers were lying prone. His bullets ricocheted loudly off the rocks, but if he and Luke could keep the two shooters pinned down where they were for long enough, then they just might get out of this alive.

'Running low,' said Luke tensely, changing his mag once again and allowing the spent magazine to clatter to the tarmac.

'Same here,' said Ethan. 'Make them count. Mitch's inbound.'

'Better fucking hurry,' Luke grimaced as he squeezed off two more rounds and then ducked back into cover. 'I've had just about enough of this shit.'

Less than a minute later, they both heard the faint whisper of the Firefly approaching, and when they turned around, they couldn't believe how close it was. Swooping down from several hundred metres at seemingly reckless speed, the dark, sleek shape skimmed the fields to then pop up and quickly rotate 180 degrees in mid-air before coming down and settling less than twenty metres from the irrigation ditch where Sophia and Scarlett were taking cover. The next-generation VTOL had barely touched down before its rear hatch opened to become a ramp, and at the same time, a panel on top of the fuselage slid aside, and a turret bristling with multiple weapons systems emerged. It immediately swivelled to aim in the direction of the white SUV, and a small red targeting laser mounted on an M203 grenade launcher switched on. After less than a second, the launcher had acquired and locked onto the vehicle. It coughed once, and a 40mm high-explosive grenade flew in an arc over the heads of Ethan and Luke and slammed into the white sedan with a violent, orange burst that ripped the vehicle to shreds and sent metal and glass flying in all directions as a thick plume of black smoke roiled upwards into the air.

Wasting no time, and with debris still raining down around their attackers, Ethan and Luke sprinted for the Firefly as Mitch fired another suppressing round, this time with a smoke grenade that took only a few seconds to leave the entire scene around the mangled vehicles enveloped in a thick white veil of smoke. Sitting in the cockpit, Mitch was watching Ethan and Luke via an exterior camera, and they were barely inside the cargo hold before the rear hatch came back up and the aircraft lifted into the air with such speed that the two men were forced to their knees.

Sophia and Scarlett were already strapped into a couple of jump seats along the interior of the fuselage, and their faces looked tense and shocked by the sudden explosion of destructive violence. However, as soon as they were up and away and the Firefly was in level flight, Ethan and Luke got to their feet and sat down next to the two women, looking as if this was just another day at the office. They simply exchanged a brief nod, as they might have done after a successful mission with Delta, and then they leaned back in their seats and breathed calmly.

'Shit,' panted Scarlett with a disturbed look on her face. 'Let's not do that again. From now on, I say we take this bird absolutely everywhere we go.'

'Anybody hurt?' Ethan asked, looking at each of his three companions in turn, and as they all shook their heads, relief flooded through his body.

'Who the hell were they?' Sophia said, her eyes still wide with shock. 'I didn't see anything.'

'Nadeem,' said Ethan. 'And two of his fellow goons. The driver of the truck won't be getting back up again, but before he died, he made it clear that they were working for Al-Masry. Seems like the man is bent on overturning this country's government and becoming a new pharaoh.'

'Shit,' Sophia said. 'That's crazy.'

'And they were trying to get to you,' said Ethan, deciding to share what he had overheard.

'Me?' said Sophia, horrified. 'Why?'

'They probably want to know what you know,' said Ethan. 'You understand more about Templeton and Goodwin's work than anyone else, and it looks like Al-Masry wants the same thing we're after.'

'We're not going to let that happen,' Luke said evenly, giving Sophia a confident nod. 'No way in hell.'

'Thanks,' Sophia said with an anxious look as Scarlett reached over to give her hand a quick squeeze.

'Luke's right,' said Ethan. 'We've got your back. If they try anything like this again, they'll all end up dead. If it wasn't personal already, it sure as hell is now.'

'OK.' Sophia nodded as she seemed to compose herself. 'We should continue. We can't turn back now. The answers are still out there.'

'Alright,' Ethan said. 'I'm going to go and give Mitch an attaboy for a top-notch extraction. And then I'm going to ask him to fly us to Kharga Oasis.'

11

At a reduced speed and using only the subsonic engine configuration, the roughly 150-kilometre flight across the desert took about forty minutes. The entire southern part of Egypt had been plagued by fierce sandstorms during the previous several weeks, and Mitch was concerned about the ultra-fine dust still floating in the air being ingested into the engines and damaging them. As they travelled mile after mile across the seemingly endless and almost featureless expanse of pale yellow sand dunes stretching to the horizon in every direction, Ethan was reminded of just how vast the Sahara Desert was, and of how enormous areas of the planet remained virtually uninhabited. Sitting in the copilot's seat next to Mitch, he was observing the 3D moving map display on the control panel when Sophia joined them in the cockpit.

'How's it going?' she said, taking a sip from a water bottle.

'Almost there,' said Mitch, pointing straight out through the glass canopy towards a faint dark strip on the very edge of the horizon.

'It's big,' said Sophia. 'Much bigger than I thought.'

'The population is about a hundred thousand,' said Mitch as they continued their approach. 'It's a decent-sized town. Mostly date farming and tourism.'

While Mitch contacted the small local airport and requested permission to land, Sophia watched as the faint strip in the distance grew to a wide, dark green valley with verdant fields of crops extending out from a central area containing several small lakes.

'Wow,' said Sophia as she looked out across the green expanse of the oasis, before whispering to herself. 'The Field of Reeds.'

'The what?' said Ethan, glancing at her.

'The Field of Reeds,' she repeated. 'Remember I told you that the Duat was the underworld through which the dead had to pass to be judged by Osiris? Well, if they passed the trials and were judged to be worthy, which was all down to whether they had been a good and moral person, then they would be admitted into the Field of Reeds. Think of it as the ancient Egyptian equivalent of paradise, but it obviously predates the Abrahamic version by thousands of years.'

'Right,' said Ethan. 'I remember now. I think I read that some researchers suggest that the Jews stole the whole concept from the Egyptians.'

'That's right,' said Sophia. 'Imagine a blissful place full of green fields, rivers and abundant crops where the dead would exist in peace for eternity. That's basically it.'

'So, in that sense,' said Ethan pensively, 'Saint Peter at the Pearly Gates is a riff on Osiris.'

'You could say that,' said Sophia. 'All these ideas are connected across time and space. But there is a good argument for the notion that many of them were first invented by the ancient Egyptians, including the Ten Commandments.'

'Really?' said Ethan.

'Yup.' Sophia nodded. 'In the Egyptian Book of the Dead, there are forty-two negative confessions that would be recited in front of Osiris before his final judgement. Essentially, the dead person would pledge not to have stolen, lied, killed, slept with another man's wife, and so on. Basically, asserting their moral purity. So, you can see how the skinny version of that became the Ten Commandments a couple of millennia later.'

'Interesting,' said Ethan. 'I never knew.'

'We have landing clearance,' said Mitch, pulling back on the throttle as he adjusted the aircraft's heading towards the airport. 'On the ground in two minutes.'

'Alright,' said Ethan, glancing at Sophia. 'Let's head back and get ready to move out. Do you know where to go?'

'Yes.' Sophia nodded. 'All set.'

As they walked into the passenger cabin, Luke stood up from his seat with an uncharacteristic frown on his face, almost as if he was concerned about something.

'Guys,' he said. 'I just realised something, and I think you should all know.'

'What is it?' said Ethan as he and the two women huddled around him.

'I recognise Nadeem,' said Luke. 'And not from the pictures Scarlett showed me yesterday, but from a couple of weeks ago.'

'What?' said Ethan. 'How? That was before Goodwin was murdered.'

'I know,' said Luke. 'But there was a bombing at a shopping centre in Cairo not long ago. There was wall-to-wall coverage here on the local news.'

'I saw that too,' said Ethan.

'Right.' Luke nodded. 'And I saw some footage recorded by a bystander across the road. It showed smoke and flames coming out of the front of the shopping centre and people fleeing, but there was one guy who just didn't fit. He was looking straight at the site of the explosion moments before it happened, and then he turned and got into a car with a weird expression on his face. Almost as if he was pleased with what had happened. At the time, I thought it looked really out of place, and now I know why. That man was Nadeem Rashad. And I would bet anything that he planted that bomb.'

'Holy shit,' said Ethan, his eyes narrowing. 'It was a false flag operation.'

'False flag?' said Sophia. 'Remind me what that is, please?'

'Some spectacular violent act,' said Luke. 'Typically terrorism, but carried out by the authorities and blamed on a terrorist group or another country.'

'The aim is to sow fear and confusion,' said Ethan. 'Make people clamour for a strong leader to come forward, straighten things out and keep people safe, even if that means curtailing their freedom. And in this case, that leader is going to be Zosar Al-Masry. At least, if he gets his way.'

'What a fucking psychopath.' Scarlett frowned. 'He needs to go down.'

'Absolutely,' said Sophia. 'But one thing at a time. First, we need to investigate Kharga Oasis. It could hold the answers to this whole thing, and we need to strike while the iron is hot.'

'I agree,' said Ethan. 'We go to the oasis, and then we take it from there.'

Half an hour later, Mitch had set the Firefly down on the helipad at the single-runway Kharga Oasis Airport. While Mitch and Scarlett stayed behind with the aircraft, Ethan, Sophia and Luke were in a rental car they had picked up from outside the small terminal building. With Ethan at the wheel, they drove past a sprawling complex of multistorey newbuilds near the airport that constituted the seat of the New Valley Governorate, which had been set up in Kharga Oasis. The Egyptian government's plan was to use the water resources of the oasis to develop the area into a large city, and it looked as if it was well underway. They followed the main road south-west from the airport towards the town centre but then turned left along a smaller road, which eventually became a dirt track leading up towards a promontory some three hundred metres from the main road. At the raised top of the promontory were the ruins of an ancient structure. There were no other people in the vicinity, and as the three of them got out of the car, Sophia donned her wide-brimmed sun hat and stood with her hands on her hips as she looked out across the large oasis sitting in the shallow desert valley.

'Down there,' she said, pointing first towards the south-west, 'is the town of Kharga. You can see it's pretty big. Not what most people think of when they imagine an oasis in the desert.'

Ethan used his right hand to shield his eyes from the sun as he gazed out over the green, cultivated fields several hundred metres away towards the town in the distance.

'And over there,' said Sophia, pointing to a number of angular structures roughly a kilometre away to the north-west, 'is the Temple of Hibis. It's a famous temple built during the time of Persian dominance here in Egypt. It is very similar to the temples found at Karnak, and by Egyptian standards, it is fairly recent. Only about three thousand years old.'

'Wow,' said Luke, peering at the tall temple structures rising above the clumps of palm trees within which they were nestled. 'And the United States is only about 250 years old, give or take. It really puts things into perspective.'

'But we are here because of this,' said Sophia, turning and gesturing at what was left of the temple next to them. 'This location is called Nadura, which literally means "The Lookout", and it has been used as a stopover for desert caravans for thousands of years. The building here was used as a fortress during Ottoman rule in Egypt, but it is believed to originally have been a temple dating back to the Roman period around the second century CE. Yale has been conducting a lot of work here to try to establish precisely what this place was for.'

'But what's special about this place?' said Ethan, inspecting the exterior walls of the temple. 'It isn't much more than a ruin.'

'Let me show you,' said Sophia, and then she led the way into the temple interior, which appeared larger and taller than it had from the outside.

'We're here because of this,' said Sophia, moving towards a wall bearing several clearly visible inscriptions and images carved into the stone.

As Ethan and Luke approached and looked more closely, Ethan noticed a tall, standing figure carved in the side-on profile typical of Egyptian art. Inspecting it further, he saw that it had a falcon's head, and on top of it was a crescent and a circle.

'This is Khonsu,' said Sophia. 'The ancient Egyptian god of the moon, who is also mentioned in the Pyramid Texts from 4500 years ago. His name means "the Traveller", most likely because of the way the moon moves across the sky. Notice the falcon head? The god Horus also had a falcon head, but above Khonsu's head, you'll always find the crescent moon.'

'Right,' said Ethan, placing a hand on the stone wall.

'The point here is that this temple is generally believed to have been built during Roman times,' said Sophia, 'yet most of its images of deities depict the moon god Khonsu, who dates back thousands of years earlier than that.'

She then reached inside her satchel and extracted Templeton's leather-bound journal.

'And now, have a look at this,' she said, opening it up on a page that she had bookmarked with a sticky note. 'Somehow, Templeton had a hunch that there was a lot more to this place than meets the eye. He made a brief note here in his journal that I think points the way to what he was thinking when he was in Abydos during his first expedition. It is a bit cryptic, perhaps so that only he would know what it meant, but I think I might have figured it out. Here's what it says.'

> *I must return to these sacred lands to visit Kharga Oasis, and I must find the Temple of the Traveller. If I am correct, the entrance to the map chamber is beneath the feet of the old gods usurped by the new.*

'A map chamber,' said Ethan. 'Like the one we found near Abydos?'

'Most likely,' said Sophia.

'And the Temple of the Traveller,' said Ethan. 'That must be here. This place is dedicated to Khonsu.'

'Exactly.' Sophia nodded. 'In 1906, Templeton wrote that he was intending to come here, and he almost certainly did so during his second expedition in 1907. But we obviously have no record of that, because he never returned to Yale. Now, the key here is something that we see at almost all ancient religious sites. You might find a temple that is dedicated to a specific deity, but it is almost always the case that it has been built on top of another, much older temple dedicated to some other deity. And this is what I think Howard Templeton was thinking about this place. This is supposedly a Roman-era temple, but what if there has been a much older temple here for thousands of years before that? It fits with the idea that Kharga Oasis has been a stopover for caravans for as long as humans have travelled these deserts.

And those travellers needed protection, so they would always build temples in which to pray and give offerings to their gods. So, I think that when he mentions the old gods usurped by the new, he must be referring to the Roman gods in this temple that quite literally took the place of the old gods.'

'And Howard Templeton thought that the entrance to the map chamber was below where the statues of the gods used to be inside this place,' said Ethan, now understanding her line of thinking.

'Precisely.' Sophia nodded. 'Now, come this way. I think I know where to look.'

She moved further into what was left of the temple and soon found what would once have been the focal point for religious ceremonies.

'This temple was oriented with its main entrance facing due east,' she said, pointing towards the opening. 'This means that the sun would rise and perfectly light up the interior of this place at the spring and autumn equinoxes. And right here, where we are standing now would have been the pride of place. The location where the statues of the temple's deities would have stood.'

'So, if Templeton was right,' said Ethan, looking down and around at the partially sand-covered stone floor, 'then the chamber should be right under our feet.'

He lowered himself onto his left knee and picked up a piece of rock that appeared to have once been part of one of the walls. Gripping it tightly in his right hand, he then thumped it down firmly onto the stone slab in front of him, resulting in a brief muffled thud.

'Nothing here,' he said, shifting slightly to one side to try a different slab. 'Also nothing.'

'Try over here,' said Sophia, stepping back further towards

the back wall of the temple and pointing to a larger central slab. 'It might be in this area.'

Ethan shifted himself forward a couple of metres and brought the rock down once more. When it connected with the stone slab, it produced a sound that was subtly different, like a low reverberation that faded after about a second. He removed some sand and rocks from its surface and repeated the exercise, and this time, the result was unmistakable.

'There's a cavity under here,' he said, looking up at Sophia, whose eyes were now gleaming with excitement. 'Definitely some kind of void. We need to get this slab up.'

He unslung his backpack and reached inside for an item that Marcus Becker had supplied him with. It was a short, black composite crowbar. Unlike metal versions, it was ultra light-weight, but it was just as strong. He used his fingers to clear one of the grooves surrounding the slab of fine sand, and then he inserted the straight end of the crowbar into it. Using the weight of his body and the crowbar as a lever, the slab groaned as it came loose and began to lift free of the floor.

'Hold this down, please?' he said, and Sophia then knelt down next to him and held the crowbar in place.

'Need a hand?' said Luke.

'I think I've got it,' said Ethan.

He pushed his fingers under the slab and began to lift. It likely weighed just under a hundred kilos, and he grimaced and clenched his jaw as he put his back into it and managed to lift the slab up to a vertical position.

'Holy smokes,' Sophia breathed as she looked at what they had just uncovered. 'There are steps going down.'

Ethan secured the stone slab with a few rocks to prevent it from toppling over, and then he stood panting for a moment as he looked down into the freshly uncovered hole in the temple floor. Despite the bright sunlight, it seemed unnaturally dark down there.

'It looks like Templeton was right about this place,' said Ethan, bending down to extract a torch from his backpack.

'He might even have found it during his second expedition,' said Sophia. 'If he did, then he clearly sealed it up again.'

'Let's head down and see what's there,' said Ethan, placing a foot on the top step.

'Right behind you,' Sophia said. 'I wouldn't miss this for the world.'

'I'll hang back up here,' said Luke, giving Ethan a meaningful look as he patted the spot under his shirt where his pistol was concealed. 'Make sure no one shows up.'

'Alright.' Ethan nodded. 'Good call.'

Ethan and Sophia then descended what turned out to be a set of ten narrow stone steps until they reached a ninety-degree turn. Then followed another ten steps further down, after which they found themselves in a tunnel with smooth, featureless stone walls and a horizontal ceiling about five feet from the floor, forcing them to stoop. As Ethan pushed forward through the narrow tunnel while holding the torch, Sophia followed behind, clutching Templeton's journal.

'There's something up ahead,' said Ethan, glancing back at Sophia. 'Some sort of chamber.'

After about five metres, they emerged into a square chamber that was roughly four metres on either side, with a ceiling high enough for them to stand up under. The air was dry and much cooler than up top, and it smelled of old dust with a faint hint of something organic. On the wall directly opposite the entrance was an eerily familiar object.

'Look there,' said Sophia. 'A stone altar and another map stele.'

They stepped up to the altar and examined the stele embedded in the wall above it. It was identical in style to the one they had found near Abydos, but apart from being undamaged and intact, it showed a different set of trade routes with the Nile Valley now far to the east and Kharga Oasis at the centre, marked by a circular symbol. There were lines extending due north-north-east, and also east towards the Nile. There was also a single trade route stretching almost perfectly south-west.

'Look at this one,' said Ethan, pointing at the route extending in a south-westerly direction. 'This is much longer than the one towards Abydos. At least three times longer, so it must be far into the desert. Hundreds of kilometres.'

'And look here,' said Sophia. 'Recognise this?'

She wafted dust from an object the size of a golf ball that was set into the map stele in its lower left corner at the end of the long south-westerly trade route.

'Holy crap,' said Ethan. 'Another orb.'

The black, slightly glassy dodecahedron was half embedded into the map stele, but when Sophia's fingertip closed around it, she was able to nudge it out of its recess. She cupped it in her hand, and they both studied it as Ethan shone his torchlight onto it. Seemingly completely identical to the one Templeton had brought back from Abydos, and which they had then retrieved from Zosar Al-Masry's apartment in Cairo, it appeared almost too perfectly made.

'These are so strange,' Sophia said, letting the black, angular orb rest on her fingertips as she held it up and rotated it slowly in front of her face. 'I don't understand them. They appear to have been made from some sort of crystal or even black diamond-like material, but the way they have been cut is really confusing. Crystal and diamond cutting techniques like this aren't supposed to have been invented until around the fourteenth century in Europe. But these are undoubtedly much, much older. Millennia older.'

'But if we have managed to find two,' said Ethan, 'there's bound to have been many more of them made, right?'

'Almost certainly,' said Sophia. 'It's a real mystery. I'm just baffled by this.'

'What about that?' said Ethan, pointing to a symbol carved neatly into the stele underneath the recess where the orb had been sitting.

He directed the torchlight towards it, and as Sophia wiped the dust away, it became apparent that it was a perfect circle with an 'X' inside it.

'What the hell?' she whispered, as she immediately recognised the shape as a standard hieroglyph carrying a very specific meaning. 'This glyph means "town" or "city". It's believed to represent a convergence of four roads inside a walled enclosure, and it is pronounced "*Niwt*".'

'A city?' said Ethan, puzzled. 'Deep in the desert? That can't be right. If the proportions on this map stele are correct, then that place is more than five hundred kilometres to the southwest near the border with Libya. But there's nothing down there but sand and some mountains.'

'What's this?' Sophia said, shifting slightly closer to the stele and wiping more dust from a brief hieroglyphic inscription below the city symbol. 'There's writing here.'

As her fingertips moved gently across the four carved symbols, her lips moved as she whispered the words of the now long-dead ancient Egyptian language.

'*Niwt-Meru-Iah-Khespet*,' she said, her brow furrowing as she turned to look at Ethan, but her eyes spoke of wonder. 'City of the Crescent Moon Lake.'

'The lost city?' said Ethan, returning her gaze as the idea

began to bloom inside his mind. 'Could this be what the Bedouin legends were about?'

'Well, there is no doubt that this is the hieroglyph for city,' said Sophia.

As she spoke, she gently touched the circle with the 'X' inside it and then ran her fingertips up and to the right along the trade route to the location that could only be Kharga Oasis and the Temple of Khonsu.

'But what lake is it referring to?' said Ethan. 'There are no lakes anywhere south-west of here. It's desert dunes for thousands of miles across the entire North African continent.'

'You're right,' said Sophia. 'There aren't any lakes. At least not now. But there used to be.'

'What do you mean?' said Ethan.

'Remember when I mentioned changes to the climate around the end of the last ice age?' said Sophia.

'Sure,' Ethan replied. 'The monsoons stopped, and the Nile no longer flooded.'

'That's right.' Sophia nodded. 'It all has to do with something called Milankovitch cycles, which track several effects of the Earth's orbit around the Sun and which play out over very long time periods.'

'And Professor Goodwin thought this was the key to this mystery?' said Ethan.

'I think so,' said Sophia. 'And it makes sense. Let me explain. There are three main cycles. One has to do with the shape of Earth's orbit, which goes from roughly circular to more elliptical every 100,000 years. This is called eccentricity, and it causes variations in the distance between the Earth and the Sun, and thereby the amount of sunlight we get. The second is changes to the Earth's axial tilt. It follows a 41,000-year cycle, and it tends to affect the intensity of the seasons. The third factor is the precession that I already mentioned, which is Earth's wobble, which follows a 26,000-year cycle. When you add all of these together, they sometimes tend to cancel each other out, but at other times they amplify each other. You can end up with millennia-long periods of pretty extreme changes to the climate, such as ice ages, of which there have been a countless number through Earth's 4.5-billion-year history. And the last time one of those came to an end, some twelve thousand years ago, it likely led to a collapse of whatever civilisation had existed here at that time. Now, according to analysis of Antarctic ice core samples, the climate warmed rapidly at the end of the last ice age. In fact, this change likely unfolded over just a few decades, which is shockingly fast by geological standards, and it left this region more or less decimated by drought for centuries or even millennia, at least until the beginning of the Naqada period when a new civilisation emerged close to the Upper Nile. But before that collapse, for many thousands of years, the climate in the far south of Egypt would have been stable and much wetter than it is today. Wet enough for it to be tropical.'

'So there could have been lakes?' said Ethan.

'Yes.' Sophia nodded. 'In fact, we know that there were. In north-western Sudan, about nine hundred kilometres southwest of here, there are huge areas of desert where there used to be so-called mega lakes thousands of years ago. Massive bodies of water and fertile lands. But now, there is just a dry desert. There is an amazing place called the Cave of Swimmers near the mountain range Jebel Uweinat in the far south-west corner of Egypt, where the borders of Egypt, Libya and Sudan meet. It was discovered in 1933, and it contains art believed to be at least eight thousand years old. Most notably, it depicts people swimming in a lake.'

'Holy crap,' said Ethan. 'That's amazing.'

'And it gets better,' said Sophia, who suddenly found herself piecing together a coherent narrative. 'There are many examples of art that has been found in that area depicting lots of animals that simply shouldn't be there, such as hippos and giraffes. Animals that today only exist several thousand kilometres south of here. In other words, those cave paintings are actual records of the very different climate conditions that existed at Jebel Uweinat roughly ten thousand years ago. And interestingly, even today, the name of the mountain range literally means "Mountains of the Springs", so clearly, this place has been associated with water for a long time.'

'Right,' said Ethan pensively. 'So, if I understand this correctly, as the climate changed from wet to arid, and the deserts expanded from the west, people living in southern Egypt were driven further and further east towards the Nile.'

'That's right,' said Sophia with a nod. 'That's exactly what Goodwin theorised. He was convinced that long before the pharaohs and even the Naqada culture, there existed some sort of precursor civilisation. And I can see from his handwritten notes in Templeton's journal that he had come up with another interesting idea. You see, in ancient Egyptian theology, there was something called the Akhu, or the "Shining Ones". These were the souls of the dead pharaohs who had successfully passed through the Duat, been judged by Osiris, and entered the afterlife among the stars. They were seen as powerful spirits, linked to the so-called Imperishable Stars that never set. Supposedly, these Akhu had the power to affect the living, providing them with protection or guidance. And offerings and rituals for the dead were partly meant to appease the Akhu and ensure their favour.'

'They sound a bit like angels,' said Ethan.

'Yes,' said Sophia. 'They might even be the origin of the idea of angels. Anyway, here's where things get interesting. Spurred on by speculation by Howard Templeton, Goodwin came to believe that the Akhu were not just spirits that were part of the ancient Egyptian belief system. They were, in fact, the actual, real ancestors that both he and Templeton were trying to find evidence of. The enlightened beings of the predynastic civilisation that existed during the Zep Tepi, the First Time, and that eventually seeded the Naqada culture and then the first ancient Egyptian dynasties.'

'Wow,' said Ethan. 'That's fascinating. But it's also quite a leap of speculation.'

'Which is why they both kept their cards close to their chests,' said Sophia. 'As you said, it's highly speculative, but when you put all the different pieces of this puzzle together, the idea makes a lot of sense.'

'It does.' Ethan nodded as he pondered it. 'The water erosion of the Sphinx. The Milankovitch cycles. The changes to the climate and the monsoons. The migration away from the expanding Sahara Desert after the end of the last ice age. It all fits.'

'Exactly,' said Sophia. 'Of course, this migration would have happened over centuries as the conditions gradually deteriorated, but it raises the question. Where did those people originally migrate from?'

'A lost city,' Ethan said as the two of them locked eyes. 'Somewhere far to the south-west in what is now a barren desert.'

'*Niwt-Meru-Iah-Khespet*.' Sophia nodded, glancing at the map stele and the inscription next to them. 'The City of the Crescent Moon Lake. The city where the Akhu lived.'

'Templeton and Goodwin were definitely onto something,' said Ethan. 'We've got to try to find that city. And I think I have an idea about how to do it.'

Half an hour after leaving the map chamber under the Temple of Khonsu, the team was huddled around Scarlett's seat in the passenger cabin of the parked Firefly directly behind the cockpit. The hacker's fingertips were moving swiftly across the keyboard, typing in commands as she gained access to a super-computer at Cornell University, where a team of climate change researchers had been attempting to simulate different possible future global climate scenarios resulting from the impact of human activity. The research involved dividing Earth's atmosphere into ten-by-ten-kilometre quadrants and then calcu-lating the way in which they were likely to interact with each other as different future climatic scenarios played out. In this way, it was hoped that they would be able to simulate and predict the effects of global warming and climate conditions centuries from now, although the team had yet to publish its first paper.

The study was highly ambitious, and it involved an enor-mous amount of data processing. To this end, an immensely powerful supercomputer named GaiaSphere spent all day and all night churning over huge amounts of data, calculating thousands of different outcomes for the roughly five hundred million quadrants of the Earth's atmosphere. However, now that Scarlett was inside, she halted the simulations and set the system a very different task.

'Alright,' she said as she accessed the simulation controls. 'This should be pretty straightforward for GaiaSphere to do since we have very detailed climate data going back hundreds of thousands of years due to Antarctic ice core samples. So, let's see what happens if we dial back the clock to around 10,500 BCE.'

She typed in the final commands, adjusted a couple of sliders on the user interface, and then hit the 'Run Simulation' button. As they watched, her laptop screen showed an animated image of the familiar Earth slowly rotating in space, and the date in the top right-hand corner then began to work its way backwards. For the first several millennia, very little visible change happened, but by the time it reached roughly 8000 BCE, the white Arctic ice cover began to expand noticeably, making its way down over northern Europe and North America. At the same time, the familiar desert areas of North Africa began retreating further towards the equator, and when Scarlett zoomed in on Egypt, the green and fertile areas around the Nile began to expand westward into what is now a virtually lifeless desert.

'Look,' said Sophia, pointing to the lower left corner of the screen. 'The mega lake in Sudan is forming, and there are lush areas all the way up to the Jebel Uweinat mountain range.'

'That's where they found the Cave of Swimmers, right?' said Ethan, peering intently at the animation that was slowly resculpting the entirety of the North African continent in front of their eyes as the clock continued winding back towards 10,500 BCE.

'That's right,' said Sophia. 'The whole desert down there is becoming green and full of life, which explains the cave paintings featuring giraffes and hippos. This was the so-called African Humid Period, also known as the Green Sahara.'

'Damn,' said Luke. 'This is some amazing stuff. I had no idea.'

'Can we zoom in further down here?' said Sophia, pointing to an area at the bottom of the screen around Jebel Uweinat. 'I think I see something.'

Scarlett zoomed in on a section of the mountain range that was roughly fifty by fifty square kilometres in size.

'Look at these ridges,' she said, tracing an index finger along a curved shape. 'This whole part of the mountain range is curved, and if you follow it all the way around, you'll see that it is almost perfectly circular. And there are several of these concentric rings, one inside the other. Can you pause it for a second?'

'What is that?' said Scarlett, pausing the simulation as she peered at the screen. 'I've never seen anything like that before.'

'It's a natural phenomenon,' said Sophia. 'It's called a tectonic dome. It happens when magma pushes up from the Earth's interior and creates a bulge in the crust, but without causing an active supervolcano. Sometimes, the pressure just fades away again as the magma dissipates from that region, but the bulge on the surface remains. Then, over many millions of years, erosion takes over, and because the different layers of the Earth's crust erode at different speeds, you end up with these concentric mountainous rings of granite spanning tens of kilometres. Could you restart it, please?'

Scarlett unpaused the simulation, and as they watched, the green and fertile areas spread north from Sudan in the south and Chad and south-eastern Libya in the west until they covered the entire mountain range. And then something incredible happened.

'Look!' said Sophia excitedly, pointing to the interior of the circular mountain range, which was now covered in lush vegetation. 'Lakes are forming.'

On the screen, some of the wide valleys between the tall, curved ridges began to fill up with water, and one in particular stood out with a familiar shape.

'Well, will you look at that,' Ethan said as he watched the screen in amazement, and the clock in the top right-hand corner began to approach 10,000 BCE. 'A large curved lake.'

'The Crescent Moon Lake,' said Sophia. 'That must be it. That must be what the map stele was referring to.'

'The lost city of the Akhu,' said Ethan, his mouth partly open as he stared at the roughly five-kilometre-long, almost perfect crescent-shaped lake on the screen. 'We need to get ourselves down there. Mitch, please prep the bird and punch in the coordinates. We should get moving as soon as possible. It is almost seven hundred kilometres south-west of here, and there won't be a single airstrip or settlement for hundreds of kilometres, so make sure we're all set.'

'Roger that,' said Mitch with a quick nod, turning towards the door to the cockpit. 'I'm on it.'

* * *

The atmosphere in the car was tense as Nadeem and Quasim raced along the wide, newly laid desert highway from Abydos towards Kharga Oasis. As the enormous dunes swept past on the arrow-straight road, both of the ex-soldiers sat immobile and looked straight ahead towards the desert horizon and the mid-afternoon sun. On the back seat of the vehicle, under a large piece of cloth, were several high-powered weapons, including a sniper rifle, two assault rifles and a rocket-propelled grenade launcher that was more than capable of taking down an aircraft at close range. During their first encounter with the foreigners, the former CSF operatives had badly underestimated their opponents, but they were determined not to let that happen again.

The two men had barely spoken after they had failed at kidnapping the female American and killing her armed escort. The loss of Farouk had been painful to watch and a bitter pill for them to swallow, but with both men having served in the Egyptian Army, where they had spent months fighting armed separatists in the Sinai Peninsula, the death of a comrade was nothing new. However, the unspoken bitterness and anger were palpable as a stony-faced Nadeem steered the car west at speed through the desert. They had barely escaped the encounter near Sohag Airport alive when the insectoid-looking aircraft had arrived and turned their vehicle into a burning wreck.

After it had left, taking the four Americans with it, they had retrieved the body of their fallen comrade and left the scene. They buried Farouk in a shallow grave nearby, vowing to return and retrieve his body for a proper burial once their mission was complete. All they could do now was focus on the task at hand and then hope that a chance at revenge would come soon. Gripping the steering wheel with his large hands, Nadeem was staring straight ahead at the empty road cutting across the seemingly endless desert when his phone rang. Glancing at the display, he could see that it was Al-Masry. He swallowed hard before answering.

'*Sa-nesu*,' he said with genuine reverence as he took the call.

'Give me an update,' came Al-Masry's stern, icy voice. 'What happened to Farouk?'

Nadeem proceeded to relay what had transpired during the

failed ambush near Abydos, and by the end of it, there was a long silence before Al-Masry spoke again.

'Losses are unavoidable,' he said in an even and unemotional tone. 'We must look forward. Where are they now?'

'You were correct,' said Nadeem. 'They are in Kharga Oasis. My contact at the airport confirmed their aircraft touched down earlier today. They are following the trail, as you expected. We're on our way there now.'

'By car?' said Al-Masry, mildly puzzled. 'You have my jet.'

'The pilot refused,' said Nadeem, glancing up at the rear-view mirror where the sky behind them was hazy and light brown. 'The sandstorms at Luxor were too powerful for him to take off. The storms are moving west, and we're only just ahead of them right now.'

'I understand,' Al-Masry said. 'I will make sure my personal helicopter meets you there. It should be possible for it to approach from the north. When will you arrive?'

'In about an hour,' said Nadeem, looking briefly at the car's satnav display. 'We will ambush them at the airport.'

'Don't let them get away this time,' said Al-Masry coldly. 'Get me the girl. Kill the others.'

* * *

Almost an hour after returning to the Kharga Oasis airstrip, Mitch had arranged for the Firefly to be refuelled, and the team was now in the process of strapping into their seats.

'Flying conditions are beginning to look dicey,' he said as Ethan poked his head into the cockpit to make sure everything was alright. 'We can take off, but there is a massive sandstorm closing in from the east near Luxor and an even bigger one moving up from the Sudanese desert in the south. We might not be able to get all the way there.'

'We have to try,' said Ethan, glancing at the weather radar, which showed the storm systems as dark orange swirls overlaid onto the map. 'Give it your best shot.'

'Roger that,' said Mitch as he spun up the engines, and the aircraft's interior began to hum. 'Let's get out of here.'

The Firefly ascended effortlessly into the afternoon sky and pitched down as it began accelerating west and out across the desert to skirt around the town of Kharga. As it climbed to about five hundred feet, it then banked left to take up a south-westerly heading. Soon, the lush green of Kharga Oasis disappeared behind it to be replaced by a virtually featureless landscape of golden sand dunes. Mitch kept the speed below two hundred kilometres per hour to try to limit any damage to the engines from the fine dust in the air, and he also kept a wary eye on the telemetry in case they began to develop problems. In the passenger cabin, Ethan and Luke were both sitting silently in their seats, looking out of the window at the rolling dunes sweeping past below them. Dozens of times in the past, they had experienced similar views from Delta Force Black Hawk helicopters heading into a war zone, and it brought back memories for both of them. Some welcome, others less so.

Sophia and Scarlett were sitting across from each other, and Sophia was engrossed in Templeton's journal when Scarlett leaned forward.

'Hey, Sophia,' she said. 'There's something I don't understand about this whole thing.'

Sophia closed the journal and looked up at Scarlett as she placed it on the table between them.

'What?' she said.

'It's about the Sphinx,' said Scarlett. 'If it was built by an earlier civilisation, then where is the evidence? Why hasn't anything else been found, like buildings or pottery? And weren't people at that time supposedly hunter-gatherers?'

'That's what conventional wisdom would have you believe,' said Sophia. 'But there is now more and more evidence available to suggest that this view is incorrect. There are plenty of sites throughout the Middle East that contain very sophisticated buildings, like at a place called Göbekli Tepe in Turkey. It's a large and very impressive megalithic complex that dates back at least ten thousand years. And since we know that for millennia, Egypt was probably the most advanced culture in the world, it is likely to have been even more advanced than Göbekli Tepe at that time. But anyway, when people say that we haven't found any evidence of this much more ancient culture, then I think they are missing the point. There may well be evidence, but it is just not to be found where the pharaohs built their monuments and temples in places like Giza, Karnak and Thebes.'

'It's such a mind-boggling timescale,' said Scarlett. 'It makes me wonder about those Akhu. What if they weren't even the first? What if there was something before them? Either way, if any of what Goodwin proposed turns out to be true, then all the history books have to be rewritten.'

'Yup.' Sophia nodded. 'It's going to make a lot of people very upset, but I am really excited about it. I can't wait to get down there.'

'It might not be as easy as that,' said Ethan from across the aisle, from where he and Luke had been following the conversation. 'That crescent-shaped lake on the Gaia simulation was at least five kilometres long. That's a big area to search.'

'Well, I'm not going home until we find it,' said Sophia with a thin smile, but Ethan could see that she really meant it. 'I didn't come this far just to quit and go home.'

'Fair enough.' Ethan nodded. 'We'll give it everything we've got, as long as the weather cooperates.'

As it turned out, Ethan's wish would not be accommodated. After about two hours of flight time, they were roughly two-thirds of the way to Jebel Uweinat when Mitch's voice came over the speaker system asking Ethan to join him in the cockpit.

'What's up?' said Ethan, lowering himself into the co-pilot's seat.

'Sandstorms are getting worse,' said Mitch with a concerned look as he pointed to the weather radar display. 'The storm from the south is coming up fast now, and the one behind us moving west from Luxor has almost reached Kharga Oasis. It's pretty unprecedented, according to the meteorologists. If this keeps going, we'll never make it. The aircraft's engines won't survive a severe sandstorm. I might get a few minutes of warning, but if it gets bad enough, they'll seize up. And then we're all going to drop out of the sky and have a really bad day.'

'What do you suggest?' said Ethan.

'My advice?' said Mitch, giving a small shake of the head. 'Turn north and try to make it back to Cairo or one of the other desert oases south-west of there. At this rate, the entire south of Egypt will be smothered inside one massive sandstorm within twelve hours.'

'No way,' said Sophia, who had followed Ethan and was now standing beside him in the doorway to the cockpit. 'We can't give up now.'

'You want to end up in a burning wreck on the ground?' said Mitch, glancing back at her. 'This is serious stuff. If we go down in this area in these conditions, none of us will be walking out alive.'

'I understand,' said Sophia. 'But I have an idea, and I think it could work.'

* * *

It had taken some effort, but eventually, Sophia had managed to convince Ethan and Mitch to go along with her plan. Following the waypoints that she had fed into the navigation system, Mitch guided the Firefly away from its original heading and now took it almost due west. After about half an hour, they arrived at the eastern edge of a huge mountainous granite plateau called Gilf Kebir near the Libyan border, some 160 kilometres north of Jebel Uweinat. It was rugged and dark against the light-coloured sand, and the enormous massif of bedrock that protruded up from the desert had been rounded and made smooth by millennia of sand scouring and shaping it as the wind blew across the terrain. When they approached the final waypoint at the juncture of a flat, sandy area to the south and a dark, rocky escarpment adjacent to the plateau to the north, Sophia pointed ahead out of the glass canopy.

'There!' she said excitedly, indicating a dark opening at the foot of the tall escarpment several hundred metres away. 'That's it. The Cave of Swimmers. I've seen so many pictures of this place, but I never thought I'd be able to make it here myself.'

'Alright,' said Ethan, pointing at a level landing spot nearby. 'Set her down over there.'

The air was now increasingly hazy and pale yellow from the fine sand particles in the leading edge of the sandstorm, and Mitch was relieved when he was able to set the Firefly down on a flat area of smooth, dark brown granite bedrock that had been sanded down by the winds over thousands of years. Small clouds of dust were whirled up into the air as the aircraft touched down, but then Mitch immediately brought the engines back to idle as he touched down.

'You've got two minutes,' he said, glancing at the ominous image on the weather radar and then back at Ethan.

'Got it,' said Ethan, who could sense the pilot's genuine concern. 'Let's hustle.'

Moving back through the passenger cabin, Luke joined him, and the two men then opened the door to the rear cargo compartment, where they released the metal clamps holding the military quad bike in place. It had large, black tyres designed to move smoothly across the sand, and it was painted in desert camo and came with weapon racks and a spare tyre strapped to the back. It also included an inbuilt communications and GPS unit that connected to satellites flying overhead. After Mitch had opened the Firefly's rear hatch and lowered the wide metal ramp, Ethan swung a leg over the seat, hit the button to fire up the engine and then drove the quad bike carefully out and down onto the hot sand outside. Its engine purred happily as he got off and did a quick walkaround to check that everything was as it should be.

'I wish I could join you,' said Luke with a hint of disappointment.

'I appreciate that,' said Ethan, glancing up at Sophia, who was standing at the top of the ramp with her leather satchel slung over her shoulder. 'But this thing only has seats for two people, and Sophia's the only one who has a chance of finding what we're looking for. The rest of you guys need to get back to safety before the storm hits. I've never seen Mitch this worried. We're really pushing it.'

'I know,' said Luke, handing Ethan a black leather go-bag with weapons and equipment and placing a hand on his shoulder. 'Take care, buddy.'

'You too,' Ethan responded with a firm nod as he looked at

his former Delta comrade. 'You just look after Mitch and Scarlett, alright? Don't let anything happen to them.'

'Not a chance,' said Luke with a stony, determined smile as he placed his right hand on the pistol sitting in the holster attached to his belt. 'I'll see you soon.'

At that moment, Luke's face suddenly changed into a wild grimace as he lunged forward.

'RPG!' he shouted, and then he barged into Ethan and dragged him to the ground.

Less than a second later, a rocket-propelled grenade fired from the top of the escarpment some fifty metres away and ten metres above them streaked loudly over their heads with its all-too-familiar hiss. It narrowly missed the Firefly's right engine and then slammed into a nearby rocky area just twenty metres away, where it exploded with a deafening boom.

'Who the fuck is that?' Luke yelled as he scrambled back onto his feet.

'Never mind who,' Ethan shouted, ripping open the go-bag and pulling out a Heckler & Koch HK416 assault rifle. 'Return fire!'

Luke reached for his sidearm, pulled it from its holster and brought it up to fire at the shooter on the ridge above them. The 9mm pistol produced rapid pops as Luke sent round after round downrange in quick succession, but with the RPG gunner partly in cover behind rocks, none of the bullets connected. They merely pinged off the sandstone and ricocheted noisily off in different directions. However, Luke's barrage provided momentary cover fire, which allowed Ethan to ready his weapon. When he brought up the HK416 and looked through the scope, he saw several figures moving crouched between boulders and rocks above them, but his attention was on the man with the RPG. He was by far the most serious threat, and his weapon had the potential to cripple the Firefly and leave them stranded in the inhospitable terrain. Even if they survived the firefight and eliminated all their attackers, they would then soon succumb to the elements of the unforgiving desert.

With bullets smacking into the ground nearby and dry rifle reports ringing out over the rocky plateau, Ethan got up on one knee and acquired the RPG gunner in his sights. The man was wearing the flowing, light-coloured clothes of desert Bedouins, but something told Ethan that these were not local Egyptians. Most likely, they were Islamist militants or roaming Tuareg tribesmen from neighbouring Libya who had spotted the Firefly land and had decided that this was a chance at a big score. Ethan understood better than most that the south of the Libyan Desert had been more or less lawless ever since the fall of that country's dictator. Now, people and weapons smuggling were big business, and it was controlled by tribal gangs who had a history of committing atrocities against the local population and generally refusing to acknowledge the governments trying to establish themselves in the coastal cities hundreds of kilometres to the north.

'Five shooters!' Luke yelled, still firing single shots at short intervals, trying to pick off individual assailants one by one. 'They have the high ground. We're in a real bad spot here.'

Ignoring the bullets hitting the sand uncomfortably close to him, Ethan lined up the reflex sight on the RPG gunner just as he brought the launcher back up onto his right shoulder and aimed at the aircraft once more. He was unlikely to miss again, so Ethan knew that he had to make it count. Holding his breath, he steadied the assault rifle and squeezed the trigger. When it broke, the rifle kicked into his shoulder, and a dry crack rang out over the desert. Leaving the muzzle at more than three thousand kilometres per hour, the 5.56 bullet covered the distance to the

RPG gunner in the blink of an eye and slammed into the man's left cheek, ripping through his skull and gouging out a huge cavity at the back of his head. As brain matter exploded out into a mist of red behind him, his legs buckled, and he collapsed into a jumbled heap as the RPG clattered to the rocks by his side.

'RPG down,' Ethan called out as he shifted his aim to another assailant roughly ten metres further along the ridgeline, pulled the trigger, and watched the man go down.

'Oh fuck,' Luke spat. 'More incoming. Ten o'clock. Technical.'

Ethan glanced left and saw a flatbed pickup truck with a machine gun mounted behind the cab. These so-called technicals were a common sight all over North Africa as well as other conflict zones around the world. They provided a cheap, mobile fire support option for insurgent forces, and they could cause serious problems for even the best-trained operators in the absence of close air support or the ability to flank around, neither of which was an option for Ethan and Luke.

At that moment, the grenade launcher on top of the Firefly's cockpit suddenly emerged from its housing and instantly swivelled to aim towards their attackers. The M203 launcher coughed twice, and a couple of seconds later, the two grenades exploded mere feet from the vehicle. This would have sent most attackers scrambling for cover, but somehow the gunner on the flatbed was unfazed. As the dust settled, he got up behind the machine gun and trained it at Ethan and Luke, who were still out in the open. Just as he racked the slide on the huge weapon, the Firefly's engines suddenly revved up, and it seemed to leap from the ground and up into the air. Within seconds, it had risen some fifty metres up into the increasingly dusty sky and rotated to face the attackers head-on. As it hovered, a weapons pod underneath its fuselage rapidly swung open, and an air-to-ground missile mounted on a rack instantly emerged. The Firefly's automated targeting system locked on, and almost as soon as the missile had appeared, it leapt off its rail, streaked across to the small group of fighters on the escarpment, and vaporised the pickup truck in a bright, orange ball of flame and metal shrapnel.

The sound of the explosion was ear-splitting, and as debris was ejected up and out in all directions, a black cloud of smoke roiled upwards into the murky, late afternoon sky. At that point, the remaining attackers appeared to have had enough because Ethan could see them scrambling for cover and disappearing from view. A few seconds later, Mitch's voice came over his headset.

'You boys OK?' he said, sounding surprisingly calm but all business.

'We're secure,' Ethan said, glancing at Luke standing by his side, his weapon now lowered. 'Thanks for the assist. It looks like you got most of them. I don't think they're coming back.'

'Yeah,' said Mitch through the static as the ever more severe sandstorm began to break up the connection. 'They are hauling ass out of here on their remaining two pickups. Heading due west back to Libya. I reckon they'll be swallowed up by the sand-storm soon enough. Anyway, I think you're safe for now. Coming back down to pick up Luke and drop off Sophia.'

'Is she alright?' said Ethan.

'Yeah,' said Mitch. 'Good to go.'

'And the bird?' said Ethan.

'All systems nominal,' said Mitch. 'I think we got lucky there.'

Moments later, the Firefly touched down from where it had taken off just a few minutes earlier, and as the rear ramp was lowered once again, Scarlett and Sophia emerged at the top of it. Giving Scarlett a quick hug, Sophia then jogged down the ramp towards Ethan and Luke.

'Everything alright?' said Ethan as she joined them. 'Anybody hurt?'

'No,' said Sophia, looking somewhat shaken. 'We're all fine. Those bastards got what they deserved. I never imagined we'd see anyone all the way out here. Who the hell were they?'

'Opportunists,' said Ethan with a grimace. 'Militants from Libya, most likely. They don't tend to care about things like laws and international borders. They saw a chance to grab some expensive hardware and went for it.'

'Well, my money is on them not coming back for a while,' said Luke as he moved towards the ramp. 'Anyway, you guys take care now. Nothing stupid from now on, you hear me?'

'We'll do our best,' said Ethan, giving his former comrade in arms a grin and then offering a wave to Scarlett. 'See you guys soon.'

'Ethan,' came Mitch's voice over the comms relay as Luke made his way up and into the Firefly. 'The weather is getting bad quickly. We need to leave now. This bird won't be able to take these conditions much longer. A couple more minutes and we'll be here for the duration. And then we might not be able to take off again.'

'I understand,' said Ethan as the ramp was retracted and the rear hatch closed. 'You just get the hell out of here before those engines die. We'll stay in touch via comms.'

'Roger that,' said Mitch.

The Firefly's engines revved up again, and the aircraft then lifted from the ground and rose rapidly into the air, immediately pitching down and accelerating north and away from the approaching sandstorm that had now turned the southern horizon into a dark, orange wall.

'See you soon,' said Ethan as the aircraft disappeared into the orange haze towards the north.

Mitch's voice came through one final time amid increasing static and noise on the line as the effects of the sandstorm continued to degrade communications. 'Good luck. We will... storm... contact...'

Then the connection died, and the small speaker in Ethan's comms unit went quiet, and the display showed a message saying 'Connection Lost'. He looked up and glanced at Sophia, who had been listening in.

'We're on our own,' he said, the wind now ruffling his hair as small grains of sand went in his eyes. 'At least until the storm clears.'

'Right,' she said, squinting as she looked up towards the entrance to the Cave of Swimmers, some fifty metres away up a small, sandy incline. 'Let's get inside and wait it out.'

13

By the time Ethan had extracted a thin but strong tarpaulin from one of the quad bike's saddlebags and covered the vehicle to protect it from the worst of the sandstorm, the gusty winds had picked up significantly, and he had to squint to try to prevent sand from blowing into his eyes. He looked towards the south, and he was now able to see clearly the ominous-looking natural beast that was approaching. Moving inexorably north and stretching almost perfectly from east to west, from horizon to horizon, it looked like a giant cresting wave about a hundred metres tall. But this was a wave made not of water but of fine sand and dust, and as it closed in on them like a powerful weather front, so did the darkness that it brought with it. The sky was now pale orange and noticeably gloomier as it approached, and even though sunset was several hours away, the light was fading fast.

Confident that his efforts would secure the quad bike through the storm, Ethan left it where it was and jogged up the incline to the roughly eight-metre-wide and four-metre-tall cave mouth where Sophia was waiting for him. She had tied a small, white cloth around her mouth to use as a mask, and as he entered the cave and got out of the wind, she helped him brush the sand from his clothes.

'I can't believe how quickly that thing arrived,' she said, wafting some of the last bits of sand from his chest and shoulders. 'Are you alright?'

'I'm fine,' said Ethan with a faint smile, wiping his face as the two of them moved deeper into the murky, elongated cave where the wind could no longer reach them. 'We'll be safe inside here until the storm blows over. But without a shelter like this, you'd be in serious trouble out there.'

'I'm hoping those militants get sandblasted to hell and back,' she said with a small shake of the head. 'I never thought this place would be so lawless.'

'It's about five hundred kilometres to the nearest police station or military base,' said Ethan. 'Out here, the only thing that matters is who has the biggest guns. Speaking of which...'

He lowered himself onto one knee and pulled open the go-bag. Reaching inside, he pulled out another magazine for the HK416 and then produced a small 9mm semi-automatic Glock 17 pistol, which he swivelled in his hand and offered to Sophia.

'Take this,' he said, glancing up at her. 'You never know when you might need it.'

'Uhm,' Sophia said, staring down at the pistol. 'I've never shot one of those before.'

'Don't worry,' said Ethan, getting to his feet again and pressing the mag release button. 'This releases the magazine. You take it out like this and slide a fresh one in. It clicks in place like this.'

He then gripped the top of the pistol and pulled back.

'You rack it like this to chamber the first round,' he said, 'and then you simply hold it firmly in your hand, aim, and squeeze the trigger gently until it breaks. Like this.'

He turned towards the cave mouth, out of which only a maelstrom of rapidly swirling sand could now be seen, raised the pistol, and fired a single round. The dry report reverberated inside the confined space, and when he lowered the weapon again and glanced at Sophia, she winced and rubbed her ears.

'Damn, that's loud,' she said.

'Give it a try,' he said, stepping over next to and slightly behind her and allowing her to grip the weapon in her right hand. 'That's it. Good grip. Now aim and fire.'

Sophia raised the weapon, aimed out through the cave mouth, and squeezed the trigger. The Glock spat another round out through the sandstorm, and once again, the report rang out through the large cave. As it fired, the recoil made her hand jerk and kick back slightly, but then she steadied her arm, aimed, and fired again, this time with much better control.

'Very good,' said Ethan, genuinely impressed with how quickly she took to it. 'You're a natural. Maybe you'd like to join me at the range when we get back to New York.'

'I don't know,' said Sophia, lowering the weapon and turning to hand it back to Ethan. 'I'm not sure I'm that kind of girl.'

'Keep it,' Ethan said, showing the palm of his right hand and then reaching inside the bag for another magazine, which he handed to her. 'It's better if we're both armed at all times.'

'Fine,' said Sophia with a nod, and then she slipped the pistol and the spare mag inside her leather satchel. 'I just hope I won't have to use it.'

'Me too.' Ethan nodded. 'But better safe than sorry.'

Sophia then extracted a torch from the bag and began moving deeper into the cave.

'This way,' she said. 'I want to show you the paintings.'

Outside, the sandstorm was now raging at full speed with winds approaching eighty kilometres per hour, and the light inside the cave had reduced to what could best be described as dusk. Sophia's torchlight moved across the cave's walls as she walked, and after about a dozen more paces, she stopped and allowed the cone of light to pan across a smooth, almost vertical wall that extended about four metres up to where it began to curve over towards the cave's ceiling.

'Look at those,' she said. 'Aren't they amazing?'

With his assault rifle slung over one shoulder and his own torch in his hand, Ethan came over to stand next to her as the two of them gazed up at the ancient artwork. There were dozens of individual shapes, most of which were of people seemingly engaged in various daily activities, but an entire section was covered in animals that belonged nowhere near the type of arid desert terrain in which they now found themselves.

'Damn,' he said, marvelling at the paintings in front of them. 'I see hippos, elephants and giraffes. This is amazing. When you see it for yourself, you get a real sense of how strange it seems out here in the desert.'

'And look here,' said Sophia, stepping closer to the wall and pointing at another creature. 'See this? Remind you of anything?'

'A lion,' Ethan said, joining her as he inspected the beautifully drawn image.

'A perfect recumbent lion.' Sophia nodded. 'Lying down with its head held high. Just like the Sphinx at Giza used to look. And now check this out.'

She moved along a few metres and pointed up at a different section of the wall.

'Here they are,' she said, her eyes gleaming with excitement. 'The swimmers.'

'Wow,' said Ethan as his eyes found the human shapes and

his brain instantly recognised them for what they were. 'Human beings swimming. It's so obvious.'

'I think so too,' said Sophia. 'Some researchers have suggested that these figures are not actually meant to be seen as literally swimming in a lake, but that they are depictions of the dead swimming in the watery chaos of Nun before the beginning of time. But I think that's pretty spurious. Especially since, according to the Egyptian creation myth, no people existed at that time. And on top of that, we now know for a fact that there were these mega lakes right here in central North Africa at the time of the African Humid Period. So, I am convinced that what we're looking at are depictions of people simply enjoying a swim in the lakes that used to be here in this area thousands of years ago.'

'This place is something else,' said Ethan, taking a step back and looking across the entire thing to try to take it all in. 'And these have been dated?'

'As far as possible,' said Sophia. 'It's very difficult to do with any precision, but most estimates say they were created roughly around 8000 BCE. I think they could be a couple of millennia older than that, and it would fit with the Green Sahara period.'

'It's strange to think,' said Ethan pensively as he glanced back outside, 'that there was a time when you could walk through that cave mouth and find yourself surrounded by trees, rivers, and animals.'

'I know,' said Sophia. 'It's mind-boggling. But that's the way it really was about twelve thousand years ago. At this spot, we're no more than a couple of hundred kilometres north of where the ancient Mega Lake Darfur used to be. A lake that once covered more than 30,000 square kilometres. It's difficult to wrap your head around it, but it makes it clear that even places like this would have been very fertile.'

'Let's see what's back here,' said Ethan, moving deeper into the cave whose wall began narrowing quickly as he moved forward. 'Any artwork?'

'Not as far as I know,' said Sophia, turning to follow him. 'But I think the cave extends a bit further into the bedrock.'

Ethan pushed further towards the back of the cave, which was much deeper than it had first appeared, and he ended up having to crouch to make headway.

'Man, it's dark back here,' Sophia said. 'Spooky. It's like a metaphor for our search. The deeper we go, the scarier it gets. Especially with that lunatic Al-Masry.'

'Well, you know what they say,' Ethan said, giving her a wink. 'It's always darkest before everything goes completely black.'

'Funny,' Sophia said, deadpan.

They continued on, and eventually, they came to a low, narrow passage that appeared to extend even further back, but it was almost completely filled with sand.

'Help me out,' Ethan said, placing his torch and his weapon on the sand so that he could use both hands. 'Let's see what's in here.'

The two of them spent about ten minutes digging loose sand out of the passage until Ethan was able to lie prone and crab his way forward through the small gap.

'If you get stuck in there,' said Sophia, 'don't say I didn't warn you.'

'It's alright,' said Ethan, his voice partially muffled inside the cramped space. 'There's a chamber back here. Big enough to stand up in.'

He inched his way through the passage, and Sophia soon found herself unable to resist the urge to follow him. She got onto her front and crawled through the claustrophobic space until he was able to help her back onto her feet. The two of them stood with their torches switched on, turning slowly to examine the small space they now found themselves in.

'This place isn't documented in any of the research I've ever seen,' she said. 'We could be the first to lay eyes on it for... who knows how long.'

The chamber was only about three metres on either side and about two metres high. The walls were featureless rock, except for a section directly opposite the entrance where a small alcove appeared to have been chiselled out.

'Look,' said Sophia, stepping up and shining her torch onto it. 'What is this thing?'

'Somewhere to put a light?' said Ethan. 'There's something at the back of it.'

He joined her and blew fine dust from the back of the alcove to reveal a faint yet perfectly visible image that had been painted onto the smooth bedrock.

'What the hell?' Sophia breathed as she took in the image. 'A pentagon. Like one side of the black orb.'

She ran her fingers over it and noticed two hieroglyphs carved into the stone.

'There's writing here,' she said. 'It says something like, "The Eye of Khonsu".'

'Is that what the orbs were called?' said Ethan.

'Seems like it,' Sophia said as she began clearing the bottom of the alcove of sand and dust.

'I feel something here,' she said excitedly. 'It's... It's a pentagonal space carved into the stone. And it feels like...'

She hurriedly flipped open her leather satchel and extracted one of the mysterious black dodecahedra. Holding it in her hand, she then carefully placed it inside the carved-out pentagonal shape in the stone.

'A perfect fit,' she breathed as her eyes went wide. 'That can't be a coincidence. This alcove was made to accommodate one of these orbs.'

'But for what purpose?' said Ethan, his brow creasing as he looked at the black orb glinting in the light from their torches. 'What do these things do?'

'I don't know,' said Sophia, moving her head slightly from one side to the other to inspect the orb as it sat neatly inside its pentagonal carved-out indent. 'Man, I really wish I could talk to Tobias. I'm sure he would have an idea.'

'I hear you,' said Ethan, placing a hand gently on her shoulder. 'But it's up to us to finish his work now.'

'Yeah.' Sophia nodded, pressing her lips together. 'You're right. And I feel like we're really close now. The answers must lie somewhere near the Crescent Moon Lake in Jebel Uweinat. When do you think the sandstorm will clear?'

'It's anyone's guess,' said Ethan with a shrug. 'Certainly hours. Perhaps a lot longer. We'll just have to wait it out. We have food and water, so we'll be OK.'

A couple of hours later, Ethan and Sophia lay down on the soft sand that covered much of the inside of the cave. They needed sleep, and now that the sandstorm was raging outside, this was as good an opportunity as any. They picked a spot near a wall to the rear of the cave, and then they huddled where they would be completely out of the wind. With the temperature dropping as night closed in outside, Sophia backed up and pushed herself up against Ethan, and he, in turn, wrapped an arm gently around her to help keep her warm.

Lying there and feeling her gradually drift off to sleep as the sounds of the violent winds made their way deep into the small inner chamber, he realised that he had come to feel protective of her and that he enjoyed the feeling of her relying on him for safety and warmth. Eventually, however, he too fell asleep.

* * *

When Sophia awoke, it was almost pitch-black inside the cave, and she realised that the noise of the storm appeared to have gone completely. Squeezing her eyes shut and then blinking a few times, she looked towards the cave exit but could see nothing but perfect darkness. Deciding to have a look outside, she gently lifted Ethan's arm and slipped out from under it without waking him. She got to her feet and walked quietly across the soft sand to the exit, and when she stepped outside under the starry night sky, it was as if she had been transported to a different time and place. In front of her was a wide concourse lined with burning torches and leading straight up to the three Pyramids of Giza, a couple of hundred metres away. The Pyramids were lit up in gold and purple light from huge floodlights, and at the foot of the Great Pyramid was a large, raised podium at the centre of which was an ornate gold lectern. Behind the lectern stood a small, elderly, bearded man wearing a white, embroidered tunic and a plethora of golden, royal regalia harking back to the time of the pharaohs. She instantly recognised him as Zosar Al-Masry, and he was flanked on both sides by military generals with severe expressions who stood to attention as Al-Masry delivered a booming speech, not in Arabic, but in the forgotten tongue of his ancient forefathers.

As she kept walking closer, she realised that on both sides of the long concourse were neat grid formations of tens of thousands of soldiers wearing black uniforms, boots and berets with gold accents. Standing completely immobile like menacing statues primed for action, they were all carrying modern assault rifles, and there was a strange sense of latent violence permeating the air as Al-Masry addressed his army. Projecting his voice out across the plateau that was packed with soldiers, he gesticulated and twisted his face angrily into fearsome contortions as he delivered his thundering speech. Sophia could not understand the words, yet the message was clear. He was railing against his enemies and preparing his army to crush any dissent and opposition to his rise.

Suddenly, Al-Masry peered down, looking straight at her, and she felt as if she was suddenly rushing forward to stand directly below him as he pointed an accusing finger at her and bellowed furiously at the top of his voice, his eyes flashing with venom and his teeth glinting in the torchlight. In the next instant, she felt two large hands grip her shoulders and pull her backwards, and with a yelp, she woke up.

'Hey,' she heard Ethan's quiet, groggy voice coming from behind her. 'Are you alright?'

She breathed in and out a few times, filled with relief at having escaped the nightmare and finding herself safe back in the cave with Ethan.

'Yes,' she finally said. 'I'm OK. Just a bad dream.'

She felt his strong arm give her a gentle squeeze and pull her close. Outside, the wind was still howling, and when she looked at her wristwatch, she realised that she had only been asleep for about an hour.

'Try to go back to sleep,' he whispered. 'We're going to need a good rest.'

'OK,' she replied, closing her eyes once more, and within a few minutes she drifted peacefully off to sleep again.

* * *

When Ethan woke up, the first thing he registered was the delicate, flowery scent of Sophia's perfume. The next thing he noticed was that the sound of the ferocious sandstorm appeared to have died down.

'Sophia,' he whispered, and she produced a small moan as she stirred and opened her eyes. 'The storm's over. We should get moving. It's better to travel during cool nights than blazing hot days.'

'Right,' she mumbled, still groggy from her sleep. 'What time is it?'

'Just before midnight,' said Ethan. 'It's the perfect time for crossing a desert. And with no wind, we should make good progress.'

'How far?' she said as she sat up, stretched, and rubbed her eyes.

'About 120 kilometres as the crow flies,' said Ethan. 'The desert is fairly flat and featureless, so we have a straight shot at Jebel Uweinat from here. With a bit of luck, it should take no more than three hours. The quad bike is literally built for this terrain, so it should be pretty straightforward.'

'Alright,' said Sophia. 'Let's get going.'

The two of them crawled back out into the main cave, gathered their few possessions, and walked outside. Standing in the cave mouth, which was facing due south, they realised that the almost flat desert that stretched away in front of them was bathed in clear, silver moonlight, giving the sand and the rock formations a faintly bluish tint.

'Wow,' Sophia said as she stepped outside. 'It's so beautiful.'

'Look at the stars,' said Ethan, craning his neck to look straight up at the bright Milky Way, which stretched across the starry sky.

'Oh my,' Sophia breathed as she gazed awestruck up at the spectacle above them, where billions of tiny lights had now revealed themselves. 'It's amazing. So many stars.'

'And every single one of them has planets,' said Ethan. 'According to our best estimates. It boggles the mind.'

'I know,' said Sophia dreamily. 'Don't try to tell me there's no other life out there. I'm just not buying it.'

'You'll get no argument from me there,' said Ethan, gazing at the dense, bright centre of the galaxy where tens of billions of stars were located. 'I'm right there with you.'

'I could stand here for hours and just look at it,' said Sophia. 'It really makes you understand the ancient Egyptians and their fascination with the night sky.'

'It's pretty awesome.' Ethan smiled.

'Hey, I just realised something,' said Sophia. 'I'm pretty sure that in this spot, this far south, we're virtually on the Tropic of Cancer. The latitude is approximately 23.5 degrees north of the equator, which is the northernmost point where the sun can be seen directly overhead. And this happens at the summer solstice.'

'Really?' said Ethan. 'That's interesting.'

'Yes.' Sophia nodded as she continued to gaze upward. 'And it can't have escaped the ancient Egyptians either. Or the Akhu, for that matter. It might well be a coincidence, but it must have felt significant to them.'

'It's mesmerising,' said Ethan, trying and failing to wrap his head around the fact that his eyes were seeing in the region of one hundred billion pinpricks of light from distant suns.

'The sandstorm is completely gone now,' Sophia said. 'Not a trace.'

'It is most likely still raging,' said Ethan. 'Only, it's now much further north.'

'I hope Mitch managed to get them all back safely to Cairo,' said Sophia.

'I'm sure they're OK,' said Ethan, glancing down the incline to where he had parked the quad bike. 'Right. Come on. Let's saddle up and get moving.'

'Hopefully that thing will start,' said Sophia as she followed him down to the vehicle. 'It's partly covered in sand.'

'It'll start,' said Ethan confidently. 'It was practically made for this place.'

He peeled off the tarpaulin, unlocked the saddlebags and placed their kit inside them, and then he swung a leg over the four-wheeled beast and pressed the starter button. The engine immediately spun up and settled into a contented purr as Ethan turned on the inbuilt navigation system and waited a couple of seconds for it to establish contact with the satellites overhead. Its display soon flashed up and showed a detailed map of the area, and as Ethan used the buttons to zoom out, the Jebel Uweinat mountain range became visible almost due south of their position across the desert.

As he sat there on the quad bike, whose engine was now purring expectantly, Sophia regarded him from a few metres away, and for the first time, she realised that she thought he was very attractive. He definitely had a sharp edge to him, but he also had a sensitive side. She knew that now. And he also shared her fascination with ancient history, cultures and civilisations. Perhaps the two of them... She pushed the thought from her mind and rejoined him by his side.

'I say we head for this spot here,' Ethan said as the two of them looked at the map, and he pointed at the north-eastern section of the vaguely circular mountain range with its concentric valleys. 'There are several valleys here that look crescent-shaped. If there was ever a lake down there, it should be in one of those.'

'It's a pretty big area,' said Sophia as she studied the map display. 'There's a lot of ground to cover.'

'I know,' said Ethan. 'So, we should get moving. Hop on.'

Sophia mounted the quad bike behind Ethan and wrapped her arms around him, and then he depressed the clutch, switched into first gear, and twisted the throttle on the handlebars. The quad bike's engine revved up, and the partly sand-covered vehicle moved swiftly from its position and accelerated smoothly further down the incline and out across the flat desert terrain at the foot of the tall, dark Gilf Kebir plateau, which then quickly began to recede behind them. The dry, pleasant desert air made their clothes flap and caused Sophia's auburn hair to billow out behind her as they rode. After about twenty minutes, she turned in her seat to look behind them, and by then, the plateau was little more than a thin dark strip of granite on the distant horizon.

The virtually flat landscape ahead consisted of dunes and the occasional dark, rounded, rocky outcropping that the desert sands had yet to grind down to fine dust. Ethan kept the vehicle on a virtually straight line as they cut across the terrain towards their destination, and the map display allowed him to more or less plan his route ahead in order to avoid major obstacles and pick the easiest and shortest path. The quad bike appeared to be in its element, and its engine growled contentedly as its large tyres flew across the terrain, producing a plume of dust behind them as they drove. After about two hours, Ethan could see on the moving map display that they were now only a few kilometres from the Libyan border, and he turned his head slightly to one side.

'Look up ahead,' he said over the engine noise. 'We're close.'

When Sophia tilted her head and squinted her eyes to look ahead, she could see the Jebel Uweinat mountains rising up perhaps ten kilometres away. Looming in the distance, the huge granite formation appeared dark and ominous from their perspective, and as the two of them drew nearer, the range rose up appreciably into the starry night sky. Had it not been for the moon, Ethan and Sophia might not have been able to see it in the distance, but the silver light of Earth's companion bathed the entire southern desert in its pale light, and since their eyes had now become accustomed to the relative darkness, they were able to clearly make out peaks and gorges of the massive mountain range as they approached.

Eventually, they came to a wadi from which water would once have flowed off the mountain, and it soon turned into a gorge that appeared to lead up into a valley high above the desert floor. Ethan slowed down and began to pick his way carefully between huge boulders, rocks and crevices as the terrain under the quad bike's tyres gradually turned from flat, soft sand to rocky, uneven ground. As they proceeded, the walls of the gorge rose ever higher on both sides, and soon they had climbed several hundred meandering metres up into the mountains. With small rocks, pebbles and sand crunching under the quad bike's tyres, they continued slowly upward until they came to a saddle pass from which they had an unobstructed view of the centre of the almost circular mountain range beyond. Ethan stopped the quad bike and killed the engine.

'We're here,' he said, pointing to the centre of the moving map on the navigation display. 'I reckon that our best bet is this large valley just west of here. The shape is almost a perfect crescent. We just need to cross this section here, and then we can drive down into it. The whole valley floor looks to be covered with sand dunes, so it should be easy going once we're down there.'

'Sounds good.' Sophia nodded, excitement building inside her as they approached their destination. 'Let's go.'

Continuing along the top of a wide, flat ridge for another

couple of kilometres, they were eventually able to make their way down a steep but somewhat even slope into the crescent-shaped valley. Once they were down onto the sandy and almost perfectly level valley floor, Ethan stopped and turned off the engine again. The two of them dismounted the quad bike and stepped away from it, turning slowly as they took in the vista and attempted to get a sense of their surroundings. The valley floor was surprisingly flat, and the even, sandy terrain reminded Ethan of the expansive salt flats in places like Utah and Nevada back in the US. They were now at one end of the roughly one-kilometre-wide, gently curving valley that appeared to stretch perhaps as much as five or six kilometres from one end to the other.

'So this whole place used to be a lake,' said Ethan, casting his gaze around the valley. 'Incredible. It's just a sea of sand now.'

As he stood there taking in the sandy expanse that was bathed in bright moonlight, Ethan felt transported back to the countless night missions in desert areas with Delta Force. The deathly quiet. The sense of anticipation. The large, bright moon overhead casting its pale blue light over the arid terrain. At one point, as he stood there with his hands on his hips, gazing out to the mountaintops on the far side of the valley, he even thought he heard the distant sound of a helicopter. He tilted his head to one side and turned it slightly in an attempt to locate the noise. As he listened intently and gazed out across the flat, sand-covered valley with the peaks and ridges of Jebel Uweinat in the distance, he could have sworn that he heard the distant, rapid thudding of rotor blades, but a moment later, there was suddenly nothing, and he wondered if his mind was playing tricks on him.

'Are you alright?' Sophia asked quietly.

'Yeah,' Ethan said haltingly. 'I just thought I heard something. A chopper.'

'All the way out here?' said Sophia, instinctively turning her head to follow Ethan's gaze.

'I don't know,' he said, giving a small shake of the head. 'Maybe it was nothing. Anyway, let's have a look at the map and see if we can find some likely locations for the lost city, if it's actually here.'

They huddled around the quad bike's map display, and Ethan then used the controls to switch to satellite photos and zoom in further so that the crescent-shaped lake filled the entire screen.

'Where would it have been placed?' he said, as Sophia leaned in and studied the high-resolution map. 'What's your hunch?'

'Well,' said Sophia, pursing her lips for a moment as she studied the display. 'Given that alignment with celestial objects seems to have been at the centre of all ancient cultures, especially this one, I would say that it should be on the far western side of the lake so that it faces the sunrise.'

She looked up and out across the huge lakebed that stretched away towards the valley sides in the distance. Then she tilted her head back and looked up at the stars to get her bearings.

'So, roughly over in that direction,' she said, pointing to the side of the valley a couple of kilometres away across the sand.

'Makes sense.' Ethan nodded, zooming in further on the map. 'That would mean roughly in this area here.'

The screen now displayed a section of the valley that was about two by two kilometres, and it showed every gorge, plateau, and crevice in resolution down to about thirty centimetres, which was detailed enough for them to make out individual boulders as well as dried-up creeks and riverbeds.

'We also need to consider that we're standing on what would have been the bottom of the lake right here,' said Sophia as she gazed towards the area they were examining. 'So the edge of the lake would have been quite a bit further up the slope in that direction.'

'Alright,' said Ethan, following her gaze. 'Let's head over there and take a closer look.'

They mounted the quad bike again and drove the roughly two and a half kilometres diagonally across the flat lakebed to the western side of the crescent-shaped valley. When they arrived at the foot of it, the sandy terrain sloped gently upwards for another seventy metres or so until it became more rocky. High above them was a tall ridge that partially blocked out the starry night sky towards the west, but further down from there was a wide, flat plateau several hundred metres deep that was partly sandy but also strewn with rocks and boulders that had fallen from the peaks above during the past many millennia.

'Over there,' said Sophia, pointing ahead to the area nearby where the sandy lakebed rose slightly and became more rocky. 'That's where the lake's shoreline used to be.'

Ethan drove the quad bike to where she had indicated and then stopped and killed the engine.

'We should proceed on foot from here,' he said. 'Otherwise, we might miss something. We need to have a really good look around this place.'

They dismounted again and began moving along the ancient lake's shoreline, looking around the vicinity as well as further up towards the ridge on the opposite side of the plateau.

'I could definitely picture a town or a city having been built here,' said Sophia, gesturing towards the flat expanse between them and the sheer side of the valley. 'It would have been right on the lakeshore facing east. And back then, this plateau would have been fertile and probably irrigated by streams coming down from the side of this valley. Perfect for agriculture.'

'Yeah,' said Ethan, scouting across the plateau for any signs of the remains of a past civilisation. 'But there's nothing here. Would any of their buildings have survived? Wouldn't they have been eroded by rain and wind?'

'Maybe,' said Sophia thoughtfully as she surveyed the rocky plateau. 'If their houses were built of stone, then probably not. If they were mudbrick houses, then almost certainly. My hunch would be that they used stone blocks, but I might be wrong. Either way, there's nothing here now.'

'Let's move closer to the cliff face,' said Ethan, gesturing across the plateau towards the sheer rise of a tall escarpment that rose at least fifty metres straight up towards the top of the ridge high above. 'It might give us a better sense of this whole area.'

They left the ancient, dried-up lake and shoreline behind and began walking towards the steep cliff a couple of hundred metres away. As they went, they examined the plateau's sand-strewn ground that was made of smooth granite bedrock and bathed in pale moonlight. After a couple of minutes, during which they drifted slightly towards the centre of the plateau, Sophia spotted something about fifty metres away. At first, she thought she was looking at an elongated boulder sticking up from the ground, but as she moved closer, it became clear that this was something very different.

'Hey, Ethan. Over here,' she called over her shoulder. 'I found something.'

Ethan jogged over to catch up with her, and when he arrived, he found her standing over an object that could not possibly be natural. It had to be man-made.

'What the hell is that?' he said as he stepped around Sophia, who now knelt next to the roughly one-metre-tall and thirty-centimetre-wide object.

'Some sort of pedestal or marker,' said Sophia, moving her head slightly as she ran her finger across one of its flat sides. 'It's a perfect rectangular shape. Smooth surfaces. Edges as sharp as anything. This is amazing. It looks as if it was machined with incredible precision by modern high-tech equipment. But that isn't possible.'

'What's it made of?' Ethan said as he went down on one knee next to her and carefully touched the neat corners and perfect edges of the pedestal. 'Some sort of stone. It looks almost black.'

'I'm guessing it's basalt,' said Sophia as she examined the object, which was black as onyx and glistening slightly in the moonlit night as if covered by a thin film of oil. 'Volcanic. But I'm not sure where it's from. I don't think there has ever been any volcanic activity in this mountain range. Everything you see around you is the result of tectonic activity over millions of years.'

She stood back up and looked around, and suddenly, standing in this exact location, she began to notice that the pedestal appeared to have been placed dead centre in the middle of what she could only think of describing as some sort of long concourse or causeway. Due to erosion, sand and small rocks strewn across it, it had been impossible to make out from where they had left the quad bike, but now that she was here next to the pedestal, its presence became obvious, along with the fact that it could only have been made by humans. The causeway was roughly twenty metres wide, straight as an arrow, and it stretched from what used to be the shoreline across the plateau to the sheer cliff face at the base of the mountain.

'Wow,' she said, turning her head to look from one end of it to the other. 'Check this out. A causeway. Maybe for religious processions? Or perhaps we're standing on what used to be the main street of this town.'

Ethan rose and followed her gaze, now also realising that this was more evidence of some sort of human presence, a very long time ago. Getting to his feet, he placed a hand on top of the pedestal, which was partly covered by a thin smattering of loose sand. As he did so, he felt the presence of some sort of indent under his palm. Turning to face the pedestal and wiping away the loose sand, he could hardly believe his eyes.

'Wow,' he muttered. 'Get a load of this.'

Sophia turned her head and looked down at the top of the pedestal, and then her mouth fell open. Now that Ethan had cleared the shallow indent of sand, she immediately recognised the shape as something all too familiar. It was a perfect pentagonal indent only a few millimetres deep that had been cut into the otherwise perfectly flat top of the pedestal, and the proportions were unmistakable.

'Holy crap,' she breathed, barely able to believe her eyes. 'I'll bet you everything I own that one of those orbs fits perfectly in there. The Eye of Khonsu.'

'Let's try it,' said Ethan.

14

With trembling hands, Sophia flipped open her leather satchel and extracted one of the two orbs she was carrying. As she did so, Ethan wiped most of the remaining sand from the indent and then blew the rest of it away, leaving it completely clear.

'Let's see,' he said, standing aside.

Standing over the pedestal with the moon at her back and the pedestal in its shade, Sophia shifted the twelve-sided orb from one hand to the other as she prepared to place it. She then carefully brought it out in front of herself and lowered it gently onto the top of the pedestal, where one of its flat, pentagonal sides fit perfectly into the indent.

'This is no coincidence,' she said, as she retracted her hands and marvelled at the union of the two black objects. 'This orb was made to fit into a pedestal like this.'

'But why?' said Ethan, gazing intently at the perfect, black geometric object. 'What's the purpose?'

'I don't know,' she said with a faint, pensive frown, lowering herself onto her haunches next to Ethan as she ran a fingertip across her lower lip. 'What could it be for?'

The silver moonlight was now shining directly onto the orb, reflecting faintly off its black, perfectly smooth sides. However, as the two of them were gazing at it, a remarkable change began to occur.

'Look,' Sophia said, breathlessly. 'Something's happening.'

Right in front of their eyes, the black orb gradually seemed to change. Somehow, the mysterious material from which it had been made began to become translucent, and over the course of just a handful of seconds, it transitioned completely from being entirely black to looking more than anything like a clear, perfectly cut crystal.

'What the hell is going on?' Sophia muttered as she gazed dumbfounded at the orb. 'It's changing.'

As they continued watching, the moonlight appeared to play and move and intensify inside the twelve-sided orb for a brief moment, but then a beam of focused silver light suddenly shot out of one of its sides like a white laser beam, instantly connecting with the smooth, sheer cliff face at the end of the causeway a little less than a hundred metres away. Both Ethan and Sophia turned their heads to follow the beam, and where it made contact with the cliff face, a small, bright spot about the size of a large coin now shone pale white.

'Look at that!' said Sophia, pointing. 'It works like a prism. It's focusing the moonlight onto the cliff.'

'I'll be damned,' said Ethan, his eyes narrowing as he peered perplexed at the now glass-like orb, which now emitted something between a faint hum and a barely audible warble. 'Somehow, the moonlight is affecting the spectroscopic properties of the orb's material. I have no idea what this thing is made of, but I've never seen anything like it.'

'Is there anything special about moonlight?' said Sophia, her brow furrowing as she tilted her head to study the orb.

'Not really,' said Ethan. 'It's just sunlight bouncing off the moon's surface. And when it passes through our atmosphere, it undergoes Rayleigh scattering, which is the reason why the sky is blue. But all of that is pretty well understood.'

'Right.' Sophia nodded. 'So, the moon does have a unique spectroscopic profile.'

'Well, yes,' said Ethan, 'but the Akhu couldn't possibly have known about that, right?'

'Who knows?' Sophia said. 'If there's one thing I have learned, it is to never underestimate how advanced the ancient civilisations were.'

'Are you suggesting that this orb was designed to have these properties?' said Ethan. 'Made to react like this and calibrated exactly to the spectroscopic profile of moonlight?'

'Maybe,' Sophia said. 'Or maybe not. Maybe the Akhu simply found the material and realised what it could do. I don't know. But I am keeping an open mind.'

'Either way, this is amazing,' said Ethan, getting back onto his feet and looking towards the cliff face. 'Come on. Let's take a closer look.'

The two of them hurried to the cliff face where the light beam from the orb touched the vertical rock face. As they stepped closer, it soon became apparent that the rock was unnaturally smooth and flat. Sophia began examining the stone, and she then discovered what appeared to be a seam between two enormous slabs of granite.

'I think this is some sort of door,' she said, taking a step back and looking up to try to get a sense of its size. 'It lines up perfectly with the causeway.'

'But how to open it?' said Ethan, looking along the sides of the cliff face. 'These things must weigh several tonnes each.'

'Over there,' said Sophia excitedly as she pointed to something by the side of one of the slabs roughly ten metres away. 'Another pedestal. And there's something next to it.'

They hurried over to what was a second pedestal, but as they came closer, they realised that there was something else slumped against the cliff face by its side.

'Oh God,' Sophia suddenly said as she stopped in her tracks, and one of her hands flew up to her mouth. 'It's a human skeleton.'

With Sophia beside him, Ethan moved up to the skeleton and knelt down next to it. Of its tissue, there was now nothing left. The bones were pale white, the ribcage was more or less intact, but the head had come off and had fallen onto the sand next to the base of the cliff. There were faint remnants of leather boots on its feet, and what appeared to be a silver pocket watch on a chain had fallen through the ribcage and onto the skeletal remains of the pelvis near the ground. Next to the disturbing sight was what was left of a leather backpack, but only a brass buckle, a couple of unopened tin cans, and a small canteen were recognisable. The rest had decomposed and virtually turned into dust. Ethan reached through the skeleton's ribcage and picked up the silver pocket watch. Extracting it carefully, he held it in his palm and turned it over.

'Meet Mr Howard Templeton,' he said solemnly as he studied the grim remains of the Egyptologist.

'Wow,' Sophia breathed as she knelt beside him. 'This explains why he was never seen again. But he's been right here for over a century.'

'He was able to come all the way here,' said Ethan, 'probably on a camel, but then the elements caught up with him. He must have died of thirst.'

'That's so sad,' said Sophia. 'He's the reason we were able to find this place.'

'Look here,' said Ethan, picking up a couple of small, circular metal rings from where the backpack had decomposed. 'This looks like the back of another journal. These are all that's left of what he would have written.'

'I guess we'll never know how he ended up here,' said Sophia.

'I don't see an orb,' said Ethan, looking over the jumbled remains of Templeton's possessions. 'He must have found the pedestals too, but he didn't have an orb to try to make them work.'

Sophia stepped over to the pedestal next to Templeton's remains and brushed away the loose sand on its top, soon realising that it too had an indent. However, it looked nothing like a pentagon. Elongated and some fifteen centimetres long, it was asymmetrical and had a vaguely organic, flowing shape to it. At one end, two short protrusions stuck out.

'That's odd,' said Ethan, getting to his feet. 'Do you recognise this shape?'

'I think I might,' said Sophia after a beat, and then she stuck her hand inside her satchel and pulled out the small, golden lion figurine. 'Look.'

She turned it over in her hand, and it was immediately clear that the shape of the figurine's underside appeared to match the indent in the pedestal.

'Son of a gun,' said Ethan. 'Let's try it.'

Sophia blew the last grains of sand from the indent, and then she placed the golden lion into it, where it fit snugly. They both stared at the figurine for several seconds without speaking, but then Sophia glanced at Ethan.

'Now what?' she said. 'Nothing's happening.'

She had barely finished speaking when the pedestal suddenly shifted downward by about an inch, and then a deep rumbling sound began emanating from within the enormous cliff face. After a few seconds, there was an abrupt sound as if something heavy was released inside the cliff, and then the two slabs of granite began moving aside. Within seconds, they found themselves looking at a four-metre-tall and three-metre-wide yawning opening into a completely pitch-black space beyond.

'Holy cow,' Sophia breathed. 'We found it. This must be the entrance to the lost City of the Crescent Moon Lake.'

'I think you're right,' Ethan said, unable to stop a smile from spreading across his face as he stood back and marvelled at the huge gates that until moments earlier had been virtually indistinguishable from the rest of the cliff face. 'This has to be it. Maybe it was never outside. Maybe it was dug into the solid bedrock of this mountainside. Like the ancient city of Petra in Jordan, but much, much older.'

'Look,' said Sophia, pointing to the centre of the opening. 'The beam of light from the orb is cutting right through here and into the interior. Let's head inside and follow it.'

Crossing the threshold past the two huge granite doors, which had now come to rest, affording them access to the interior of the mountain, they soon found themselves in a large space some twenty metres wide and thirty metres deep. Judging by its smooth walls and seemingly perfect ninety-degree corners, it had clearly been made by human beings, but compared with almost all of ancient Egypt's monuments and temples, it was surprisingly lacking in ornamentation or inscriptions. The only symbol they could see as they shone their torchlights across its interior was a single but very familiar glyph above a wide doorway leading to a square tunnel with smooth walls directly opposite the yawning granite gates.

'The glyph for the word "city",' said Sophia, pointing at the symbol. 'This is *Niwt-Meru-Iah-Khespet*.'

'Maybe this was the first city,' said Ethan. 'I mean, the first real city on Earth. Twelve thousand years ago.'

'Look,' Sophia said as she pointed at the tunnel opposite the granite gates. 'The beam of moonlight goes through that tunnel. Let's see where it goes.'

Using their torches to light the way, they left the large ante-room and moved through the tunnel. Its walls were perfectly smooth, and they appeared to be almost indistinguishable from the way in which the Osireion at Abydos had been constructed. They pushed on, and after about ten metres, they emerged into a new and much larger space. In fact, it was so large that their torches were unable to light it up, and they struggled to get a sense of its true size as they allowed their torch beams to sweep around its interior. It was as if the darkness absorbed the light mere metres from their torches, and the only clue to its scale was the way in which the echoes of their footsteps reverberated off the unseen walls around them in the pitch-darkness.

'What the hell is this place?' whispered Sophia, the echoes of her voice sounding like the fluttering wings of small birds around them. 'It must be gigantic.'

'Look at the beam,' said Ethan, pointing ahead and further into the seemingly endless, gloomy space. 'There's another pedestal up there, and the beam passes directly over it.'

They moved up along the slender, shimmering beam of moonlight to the next pedestal, which had been placed about thirty metres inside the huge dark space. Here, they discovered that it too had a perfect pentagonal indent in its otherwise smooth top. The beam passed directly over it to impact a strangely shiny point some thirty metres further into the dark-ness. Sophia reached inside her satchel and extracted the second of the two orbs.

'I think I understand these now,' she said as she knelt beside

the pedestal with the orb in her hand. 'They are all about manip-
ulating light.'

Carefully, and with Ethan standing by her side, she placed
the second black orb into the pentagonal indent so that one of its
flat sides faced the incoming beam of moonlight. As soon as the
orb slotted into place, the previously solid, onyx-coloured orb
turned completely translucent, and seemingly functioning as a
prism, it split the incoming moonlight into eight shimmering,
laser-like beams of white light. One went straight up through its
pentagonal top, and the remaining beams shot out in different
directions from the seven pentagons that faced upward at
varying angles.

With Ethan and Sophia marvelling open-mouthed at what
they were witnessing, the eight beams instantly connected with
what appeared to be gold reflectors attached to the ceiling high
above them. Here, the beams then bounced off the reflectors and
through huge crystals into a myriad of different directions,
creating a web of light beams above and around them. That was
when Ethan and Sophia realised what type of space they were
standing inside. The huge void inside the mountain had been
carved out in the shape of a perfect pyramid with its apex high
above them, its four sloping walls smooth as new concrete, and
all of them richly decorated with motifs whose colours appeared
to have faded only slightly over the millennia. Some of the
beams disappeared through holes in the sloping walls of the
gigantic space that they could now see was at least one hundred
metres on all sides and as much as sixty-five metres high, seemingly matching the proportions of the Pyramids of Giza perfectly.

From one instant to the next, the entire cavernous interior of
the mountain was lit up by pale moonlight tinged with the
golden hue of the reflectors. The floor was perfectly flat and

smoothly tiled by huge flagstones, and along the walls were placed dozens of roughly two-metre-thick sandstone columns that were adorned with hieroglyphs and various elaborate motifs reminiscent of those found at the extravagant temples of Karnak near Luxor. And as the enormous space was illuminated, they saw rows of what had to be hundreds of life-sized golden lions placed in several rows in front of the columns. It was an overwhelming sight, but as if that realisation wasn't enough, Ethan and Sophia then spotted something else.

At the far end of the pyramidal space, directly opposite the entrance, was a statue of a giant recumbent lion sculpted in incredible detail with a full mane, feline eyes, large teeth, pointy ears, and huge paws. At least ten metres tall and twenty metres long, the imposing figure was facing directly towards them, and now that the huge space was filled with light, it was clear that it appeared to be made of solid gold. Light glinted richly off multiple smooth, curving surfaces, and they both stood dumb-founded for a moment before Sophia finally spoke.

'Oh my God,' she breathed with a trembling voice. 'I can't believe it. Look at this thing. It's like the Sphinx, but it's a perfectly shaped lion.'

'And its head has the right proportions,' Ethan observed.

'The Hall of Lions,' Sophia said with a soft, dreamy voice. 'This is where it all began. This is proof that the monuments on the Giza Plateau are just faint echoes of this much more ancient place.'

'This is incredible,' said Ethan, turning slowly to look up and take it all in.

'And no one has laid eyes on it for as much as ten millennia,' said Sophia. 'I can barely wrap my head around it.'

'Look,' said Ethan, pointing straight ahead to a slightly

elevated spot between the enormous paws of the golden lion. 'Is that a throne? The seat of the kings of the Akhu?'

'I think so,' said Sophia as the two of them moved closer. 'The throne of the first rulers, before the end of the last ice age laid waste to this valley and forced the remaining population to seek safety close to the Nile, far to the east. It all makes sense now. Templeton and Goodwin were right all along.'

'Shame about Templeton,' said Ethan, glancing back towards the tunnel leading back outside, where the explorer's skeletal remains lay collapsed in a heap. 'He was so close to solving the mystery.'

'If he had,' said Sophia, raising her gaze to the enormous head of the imposing lion statue, 'then the history books about ancient Egypt would have been very different now.'

'I'm starting to think that this whole place was just for the king,' said Ethan as he looked around. 'Like a temple or throne room. And maybe the city really was outside. There's just nothing left of it now after all this time.'

'I think you're right,' said Sophia, pointing up at the sloping sides of the vast pyramidal shape that had been cut out inside the mountain. 'Look up there. There are cartouches.'

Ethan craned his neck to peer up into the murkiness of the vast space, and following Sophia's gaze, he too spotted the oval carvings with a horizontal line at their base and several symbols inside them. Now that he was looking up, he realised that there were dozens of them.

'Can you read them?' he said, glancing at Sophia, who stood open-mouthed as she marvelled at the ornate royal names.

'I think so,' she said without taking her eyes off the huge walls above them. 'They appear to have been written in some sort of proto-hieroglyphic writing, but I can just about make sense of it. One says Asirmose II. It means "Beloved of Osiris".

Another says Merenasir I, which means "Born of Osiris". There's one that says Akhenasir IV, meaning "Beneficial to Osiris". And another one says Asirhotep III, which means "Osiris is satisfied". There are so many of them. Whatever this place used to be, it is clear that this culture was here for a very long time. And worship of Osiris was at the heart of it.'

'I see something back here,' said Ethan, gesturing past the huge paws of the golden lion along the length of the statue. 'There's another doorway back here.'

They moved to the back of the enormous pyramid-shaped, cathedral-like space, where a passage led deeper into the mountain, and at the other end was some sort of chamber that was faintly lit with a strange, warm glow. The passage was cut with a precision that seemed almost unnatural considering its apparent age, but aside from that, it was perfectly pentagonal with a flat floor, angled sides, and a sharp apex overhead running along its length.

'The skill required to create this place is staggering,' said Ethan as they passed through the passage. 'Not to mention the tools. I have no idea how they did this. Even the ancient Egyptians only had bronze tools that would have been of no use against this granite. So what on Earth did the Akhu use?'

Moving through the passage, they emerged into a chamber that was roughly spherical and about six metres on all sides. It was lit up by one of the beams of white moonlight coming in from the large pyramidal throne room. It entered through a hole in the wall and was guided through a set of clear crystals to come down vertically onto what appeared to be an ornate stone altar directly opposite the entrance. The walls of the chamber were cut from the bedrock in a precise and very specific geometric shape, and it didn't take Sophia long to realise what it was.

'Oh, wow!' said Sophia. 'This whole place is clad in gold. And look at the shape. Do you recognise it?'

Ethan turned to take in the precise geometry of the chamber, whose walls appeared to be adorned with what looked almost like star charts.

'Holy crap,' he muttered, looking at the small, perfectly formed indents and the delicate lines connecting them. 'It's like the orbs.'

'That's right,' said Sophia, turning to marvel at the interior. 'We're standing inside a large dodecahedron. And it is absolutely perfect. It's as if it had been cut with a modern diamond drill and then covered with polished gold plates.'

'These look like depictions of star constellations,' said Ethan, gesturing to the symbols, lines, and small star shapes engraved into the gold plates.

'How is this place even possible?' said Sophia.

'Look at this,' said Ethan, stepping to the opposite side of the chamber, where he pointed at the top of the altar-like object. 'The light beam comes straight down into a pentagonal indent. And there's a whole set of black orbs here.'

When Sophia joined him, she saw that three black orbs, seemingly identical to the two they had already acquired, sat lined up in what appeared to be pre-designated spots at the back of the altar. Underneath them was a strange but precise, undulating carving of two ornate lines that appeared to cross each other at regular intervals, almost like a double helix. In the exact centre of the altar was another pentagonal indent where the beam of moonlight came down, and the implication was clear.

'These orbs are meant to be placed here,' said Sophia, gesturing to the indent. 'Right below where the beam of moon-light comes down. I wonder what it does.'

'There's only one way to find out,' said Ethan, picking up one of the three black orbs. 'Let's see what happens.'

Blowing small amounts of dust from the top of the orb in his hand, he placed it gently inside the indent. It instantly turned translucent, and then a beam of clear blue light shot out almost vertically from one of the small pentagonal sides facing up and away from them. The beam was shimmering faintly, and as they looked up and followed its path, it disappeared into a neat hole in the sloping wall directly in front of and above them.

'Holy crap,' said Sophia. 'It turned the moonlight blue and deflected it upwards. Where does it go?'

'No idea,' said Ethan. 'But doesn't it remind you of something?'

'Oh yes,' said Sophia as she suddenly realised the connection to something they had seen before. 'Of course. The shafts inside the Great Pyramid.'

'Pointing to Orion's Belt in the night sky.' Ethan nodded. 'I'd bet you anything that this beam points exactly in the same direction.'

'Wow,' said Sophia, gazing at the shimmering beam. 'That's incredible.'

'Let's try the next one,' said Ethan, picking up the second of the three orbs.

He removed the first orb from the indent, and as soon as he had replaced it with the second, an identical shimmering beam of light punched out through the top of the orb and disappeared into the shaft. However, this beam was red.

'Alright,' said Sophia. 'Let's try the last one. I think I can guess what will happen.'

She replaced the second orb with the third, and a beam of green light immediately shot out of it and up through the shaft.

'Primary colours,' she said, smiling at the beauty and

simplicity of it. 'Red, green, and blue. You can make any colour from those by combining them correctly.'

'But what's the purpose?' said Ethan, leaning down to gaze at the formerly black dodecahedron, inside which white moonlight now seemed to shimmer and swirl before exiting the orb as green light. 'Do you think this shaft actually exits the mountain somewhere?'

'It's possible,' said Sophia. 'It would make sense, I guess. Maybe it was a way for the spirits of the dead Akhu kings to reach Osiris in the constellation Orion. Maybe that whole idea is as old as this place.'

'Or perhaps,' said Ethan, 'they thought that they could communicate with their gods even while still alive.'

'You know,' Sophia said pensively as she turned slowly to look at the perfect dodecahedron inside which they now found themselves. 'This place could explain something strange about the ancient Egyptians.'

'What?' said Ethan.

'Well,' Sophia said, 'ancient Egypt, as we know it from Giza and Luxor, appears to emerge more or less fully formed very suddenly within the space of a few centuries. But perhaps they didn't develop it so much as inherit it. Perhaps it was given to them by those who came before. The people of this place. The Akhu.'

'But that leaves an even deeper mystery,' said Ethan. 'If the Akhu gave their technology to the people we call the ancient Egyptians, then who gave it to the Akhu?'

Sophia looked thoughtful for a moment, as if an answer was almost on her lips. But then she hesitated and simply shook her head slowly.

At that moment, the light beams inside the chamber suddenly flickered, momentarily cutting off the white beam coming through the wall from the throne room and the green beam being sent up through the shaft. Had it not been for their torches, Ethan and Sophia would have found themselves plunged into complete darkness. The beams were only cut for about a second, but it was enough for Ethan to realise what had happened.

'Get your gun,' he said, grabbing the HK416 assault rifle from his back and cradling it. 'We've got company.'

'What?' Sophia said, eyes wide with alarm as she fumbled for her pistol. 'Who?'

'I don't know,' Ethan said, racking the charging bolt to chamber a round. 'But something or someone just passed through the beam outside and cut it off. Stay behind me and keep your weapon ready.'

They switched off their torches, and with Ethan in the lead, the two of them moved cautiously through the strange, pentagonal passage back out to the enormous throne room. Exiting the tunnel, they stood silently behind the rear of the giant golden lion, listening for movement, but they could hear none. Sophia moved up next to Ethan and leaned in close to his ear.

'Could it have been an animal?' she whispered.

Ethan didn't reply but nodded slowly. It was possible that an animal had followed them inside and had walked in front of the beam of moonlight, momentarily cutting it off. However, he struggled to imagine what type of large animal could live out here, except perhaps for wild dogs, or perhaps the desert-dwelling gazelles living across arid North Africa.

Ethan advanced around the rear of the golden lion with his weapon low and ready, and as he pushed up along its side, he listened carefully for voices or sounds of movement, but he still picked up nothing. But then in the next instant, everything changed as a barrage of gunfire suddenly erupted from the far end of the rectangular tunnel leading back out to the entrance and the plateau outside. Registering the muzzle flashes at the same time as the rapid-fire reports from what sounded like a submachine gun, Ethan threw himself back and to one side while grabbing Sophia by the arm and dragging her down into cover behind one of the paws of the huge lion. A hail of bullets tore through the air above their heads, and some impacted on the solid gold paw, ricocheted, and spun loudly off towards the walls, where they hit the granite bedrock and clattered to the smooth stone floor. Sophia shrieked as she curled up close to the side of the lion and then began crawling back towards its rear.

'Stay down!' Ethan shouted, reaching out to prevent her from leaving the relative safety of their cover. 'Wait for me to open fire. Then move.'

As he spoke, she looked back up at him with wide, fear-stricken eyes, but she managed to produce a couple of quick nods, and then Ethan turned to face the threat. Waiting for a brief lull in the onslaught of bullets, he then rose to his full height and leaned out from behind the enormous paw just enough to be able to line up the HK416.

'Move!' he said, and Sophia immediately scrabbled on her hands and knees towards the back of the lion.

Ethan now saw that two burly men who had been firing from partial cover at the other end of the tunnel were moving swiftly through it with their weapons cradled in front of them. They were clearly hoping to get inside the large throne room, where they would then no doubt split up and attempt a flanking manoeuvre. And if that happened, he and Sophia would be in serious trouble.

He immediately opened up and fired several three-round bursts. None of them connected with their intended targets but merely peppered the granite walls just above and behind the two men. What happened next instantly told him that he was dealing with professionals and not just a couple of amateurs, and as he watched, he realised that one of the two men was definitely Nadeem Rashad. Instead of scrambling for cover, they both immediately went down onto one knee, aimed, and returned fire, forcing Ethan to retreat back into cover as projectiles from their submachine guns peppered his position. Glancing over his shoulder, he was gratified to see that Sophia was no longer there, and he was about to risk leaning out again to squeeze off another quick burst when he suddenly heard the distinct dry crack of single shots coming from the Glock 17 that he had handed to her. Filled with admiration for the guts of the young research assistant who was clearly attempting to provide her own covering fire, he leaned out and raised his own weapon once again.

When he emerged, Ethan was just in time to watch as the two shooters sprinted for the thick sandstone columns on either side of the pyramidal throne room. He quickly shifted his aim to Nadeem's companion, who was moving towards the row of stone columns closest to him. Realising that he only had about a second to react, Ethan flicked the fire selector to single shot and fired. The HK416 kicked into his shoulder as the 5.56 mm projectile left the muzzle and covered the distance to the shooter in the blink of an eye. It slammed into the man's shoulder and spun his torso around, causing him to lose his balance and stumble forward under his own momentum. He crashed heavily onto the stone floor with a grunt but then somehow managed to get back onto his feet and launch himself the final distance through the air to the nearest stone column, where he disappeared.

At that moment, Nadeem also reached cover behind a column near the far corner of the room, but he almost immediately re-emerged and opened fire. Ethan was forced to move back down behind the solid gold paw, and once again, bullets slammed into it and spun off it in all directions. However, as soon as there was a brief pause, he sprinted out from behind cover, crossed the roughly ten metres to the nearest stone column, and squeezed himself up against it as another barrage came in. Bullets chewed chunks out of the stone column, ruining the ancient inscriptions and causing dust and debris to rain down onto the floor. Amid a brief lull, Ethan heard the sound of running feet approaching, and they were coming from his side of the throne room. He leaned out slightly on the inside of the row of stone columns to spot the wounded shooter advancing straight towards him with his weapon up. Somehow, he was able to keep fighting despite a serious gunshot wound to his shoulder. Perhaps he was drugged up. Either way, he had evidently realised that Ethan was about to flank him, and he was now attempting to turn the tables.

Ethan couldn't help but feel impressed with the sheer bloody-minded determination of the man, but there was only one way this was now going to end. The wounded man had miscalculated, and Ethan stepped out, raised his weapon and aimed in one quick, fluid movement. Judging by the look on the man's face, he also knew what was about to happen. Ethan flicked the fire selector back to burst fire and squeezed the trigger. Three bullets left the assault rifle's muzzle in quick succession, slamming into the man's torso in a tight grouping. A split second later, they burst out through his back, taking sprays of blood with them, and then the man crashed face-first onto the dusty stone floor, where he skidded to a halt and lay still while his weapon spun away from him and came to rest near the base of one of the columns.

Ethan thought he heard a brief rustling noise coming from the opposite corner of the room, and about a second later, there was the unmistakable sound of a hand grenade landing on the floor nearby. It rolled for a couple of metres and continued past the column behind which Ethan was taking cover. It came to a stop just metres from him, and as soon as it came into view, he realised that he was in trouble. He launched himself away from it and only just managed to get behind the column when it detonated. The sound of the explosion was deafening inside the cavernous space, but even before the reverberations had died down, Ethan was scrambling back onto his feet, clutching his weapon and moving further along the inside of the row of columns stretching the length of this side of the throne room. He was trying to get to a position opposite Nadeem from where he hoped to be able to get a better shot, but it was a precarious plan. Every time he sprinted between columns, there was a brief window of opportunity for Nadeem to hit him. However, without grenades or flashbangs, there was no other way for him to do it.

Standing behind one of the columns, he was about to make a run for the next one when he spotted Sophia in cover behind a column on the other side of the room. He could see that she was less than twenty metres from Nadeem's position, and she was trying to signal him. As he looked on, she pointed frantically at the orb sitting on the pedestal in the centre of the room from which the eight beams of white light emanated up into the pyramidal space. After a brief moment, he suddenly realised what she was trying to say. Barely able to believe what she was suggesting, he nodded at her as she lifted her pistol and got ready to move. He then lined up his own weapon, aimed at the black orb, and fired once.

The bullet slammed into the dodecahedron, and in that instant, the giant room was plunged into complete darkness, save for the single beam of silver moonlight coming in from the outside. It now cut straight across the pedestal where the orb had been sitting, connecting with the front of the lion and producing a small golden bloom in the darkness. Seconds later, pistol shots rang out, accompanied by brief flashes of light, and then there was another short but loud burst of fire from Nadeem's submachine gun.

'Sophia!' Ethan shouted, and for the first time in about as long as he could remember, he noticed a tinge of fear in his own voice.

'I'm OK,' came Sophia's voice.

With his weapon raised, Ethan was already moving diagonally across the throne room towards where he had last seen Nadeem. Advancing swiftly with his weapon up through the near-perfect darkness, his eyes were now beginning to adjust to the gloom, and he suddenly spotted movement. Emerging from behind one of the columns, Nadeem was running for the tunnel leading back outside, but even through the darkness, Ethan could tell that he was wounded. Evidently, he was no longer confident in his chances against two shooters working together, and he likely wanted to retreat to a more advantageous firing position.

At that moment, Ethan realised that if he allowed Nadeem to get out of there, the former CSF soldier would have Sophia and him trapped inside the mountain, since there was no other exit. And for all Ethan knew, Nadeem had more companions waiting outside.

Ethan was now almost at the centre of the room near the pedestal, and it afforded him a clear line of sight out through the tunnel to the large, rectangular anteroom by the massive granite doors to the exterior. The beam of moonlight was still coming in uninterrupted from the outside, and it cut straight through the tunnel as Nadeem lumbered into it and headed for the exit. From the man's limp, Ethan could tell that he had been hit in the leg, and upon seeing it, he knew that this would buy him just enough time for what he needed to do. He went down on one knee, aimed the assault rifle at the back of Nadeem as he stumbled through the tunnel, flicked the fire selector to single shot and squeezed the trigger. The bullet smacked into the upper left side of Nadeem's back and spun him around. The big man went down onto one knee and reached out for the wall with his right hand. For a moment, it almost looked as if he was about to get back up, but then his arms slumped down along his sides, and he toppled forward, his head connecting audibly with the stone floor.

'Sophia!' Ethan shouted again. 'Are you hit?'

'No,' came her voice from somewhere in the darkness. 'I'm alright. You?'

'I'm fine,' said Ethan as he got to his feet and began moving swiftly towards the sound of her voice.

At that moment, her torch came back on, and she emerged from behind one of the columns some fifteen metres away. She appeared to be unhurt, but Ethan could tell from her wide-eyed stare that the gunfight had shaken her. However, she had still managed to show enough composure to close in on Nadeem in the darkness and fire her pistol, and Ethan was more than a little impressed.

'Good job,' he said as the two met. 'That took some guts.'

Sophia looked down at her slightly trembling right hand, which was still gripping the Glock 17.

'I've never shot one of these things before,' she said. 'And I'd rather not have to do it again.'

'You did great,' said Ethan, offering a comforting smile. 'Really great.'

Suddenly, Sophia's eyes widened as she looked straight past him towards the tunnel leading to the outside.

'Ethan,' she exclaimed, raising an arm to point. 'He's moving.'

When Ethan's head spun around, he was just in time to see Nadeem struggle to his feet and stagger towards the exit. Somehow, the big man had managed to get back up and was now attempting to make his escape. As he did so, he turned back with an outstretched arm and fired his pistol wildly in their general direction. The badly aimed shots went high and wide, but even a wounded man shooting a pistol near the edge of its effective range can get lucky, and all it would take was a single lucky shot. Ethan grabbed Sophia and hauled her with him as he moved swiftly into cover behind the nearest stone column.

'Stay here,' he said, after spinning back onto his feet and looking her straight in the eye. 'Don't move, OK? I'm going after him.'

Sophia opened her mouth to speak, but by then, Ethan was already up and running towards the tunnel. On the way there, he switched off his torch so as not to be spotted. When he arrived and looked along the tunnel, Nadeem was about fifteen metres away and just reaching the other end of it, and Ethan only caught sight of the badly wounded man silhouetted against the moonlit landscape outside the mountain for a brief moment. Then he disappeared around the corner. Ethan knew that as a well-trained soldier, Nadeem, even when badly wounded, wasn't just going to run away. He was going to try to set up an ambush. However, with only one way out of there, Ethan now had no choice but to follow. He had to push forward and confront the man who had killed Goodwin in cold blood.

Gripping the Sig Sauer with both hands and pointing it ahead of himself as he advanced, Ethan could feel his heart pounding in his chest, and all of his senses working overtime. He had been in situations like this more times than he could remember, but this was different. This wasn't just about taking out the bad guy. This was about revenge, and he felt no shame in that emotion whatsoever. The brutal murder of Tobias Goodwin was unforgivable. Nadeem Rashad was a vicious murderer who would no doubt kill again if Zosar Al-Masry ordered him to do it, so there was only one way to set things right. Nadeem Rashad had to die. Right here. Right now.

Moving slowly and carefully through the gloomy tunnel towards the anteroom and placing his feet silently on the floor as he approached the tunnel's end, Ethan clenched his jaw and leaned slightly out to one side while aiming down the pistol's iron sights, ready to fire. His eyes were now fully accustomed to the darkness, and his index finger was already applying slight tension on the trigger in anticipation of having to fire in a split second. Stepping further out and around the corner, he was expecting to eventually catch a glimpse of the big man and then put him down.

However, Nadeem had one more trick up his sleeve. Just as Ethan prepared to take a final step and clear the corner with his pistol aimed at the only place the former CSF soldier could be hiding, there was the unmistakable metallic click of the pin on a hand grenade being pulled. An instant later, Ethan saw the spherical explosive device sail through the gloom towards him. Realising then that he had only moments to react, instead of attempting to throw himself into cover, Ethan did the only thing Nadeem couldn't have anticipated, and it was an instinctual reaction more than anything else. As the grenade came towards him, he intuitively realised that its four-second fuse was only just over one second into its burn time when it reached him. He stretched out his left hand and caught the grenade mid-air, then spun and hurled it roughly fifteen metres across the anteroom to the other side, where it detonated in a corner with an ear-splitting crack and a bright flash that lit up the entire room. Almost simultaneously, he sensed tiny pieces of metal shrapnel peppering the walls all around him, but somehow none of them hit him.

An instant later, the bloodied Nadeem suddenly emerged with a roar from his hiding place and barged violently into Ethan, who was caught off guard by the speed and agility of the wounded ex-soldier. The two men crashed onto the hard stone floor in a messy heap, and only then did Ethan realise that Nadeem's pistol must have run dry, leaving him having to improvise with what appeared to be his last grenade. But now that this had also failed, the bear of a man was coming for Ethan with the only thing he had left. Brute force and the huge physical strength of his oversized, muscular body.

Amid the frenzied struggle for control of what was now a fight to the death, Ethan tried to twist his pistol around to fire directly into Nadeem's torso at close range, but the Egyptian's massive hands had already closed around his right wrist, threatening to break his bones. Ethan pulled the trigger twice in the hope of startling Nadeem into letting go, but the former CSF man was never going to fall for that trick. The shots rang out loudly in the anteroom, but the bullets did no damage and merely pinged off the ceiling.

Grimacing, Ethan instead brought back his head and slammed his forehead hard into Nadeem's nose, which broke with a wet crunch. Blood gushed out and spurted over both men, and the shock of the impact gave Ethan a small window of opportunity. Using all of his strength, as Nadeem's vice-like grip seemed to loosen slightly, he grabbed his weapon with both hands and managed to twist its muzzle towards Nadeem's head. Then he pulled the trigger. The report of the gun close to their heads sounded like an artillery round going off inside their ears, and the muzzle flash briefly blinded both of them. However, it was Nadeem who came away from it worse for wear. The bullet barely missed his skull but ripped through his right ear, tearing most of the earlobe off in a spray of tissue and blood. Ethan groaned with fury at the miss as he tried to fire again, but when he pulled the trigger once more, the pistol jammed.

With a furious, pained roar, Nadeem pushed Ethan away from himself, rolled to one side and somehow managed to get to his feet despite the bullet wound to his leg. Ethan was soon back up as well, and then the two men began circling each other. A menacing, maniacal grin was now etched across Nadeem's blood-soaked face, and with his fingers splayed out and giving the impression of his hands being huge claws, he breathed noisily like a wounded, frenzied bear preparing to launch itself at its stubborn prey. Blood was running from his mangled nose, and Ethan could see an exit wound on his left shoulder where the bullet he had fired inside the throne room appeared to have passed clean through him. Yet somehow, the massive man appeared unfazed by his injuries, and his wild eyes spoke only of an intent to inflict violence and death.

As Ethan glanced quickly around the anteroom for anything he could use as a weapon, Nadeem reached behind himself and produced a dark knife with a curved blade whose razor-sharp edge caught the moonlight for a brief moment. As soon as Ethan saw it, he recognised it immediately. This was the weapon Nadeem had used to kill Tobias Goodwin. Nadeem appeared to notice the look of recognition in Ethan's eyes, and he held it up in front of his face.

'You know this blade,' he hissed hoarsely with a mocking sneer. 'You know what it has done.'

Ethan felt cold fury flood through his veins, and just then, Nadeem suddenly extended his arm out to one side and launched himself forward, his deadly blade tracing a long curving arc towards Ethan's throat. At that moment, Ethan's mind seemed to speed up, and everything else seemed to happen in slow motion. Moving smoothly and efficiently, as if time had slowed down and the whole thing had been choreographed beforehand, Ethan ducked under the scything blade as it sliced through the air above his head.

With speed and power borne of years of experience and training, he stepped inside Nadeem's blow, reached up and gripped his wrist, and then he stepped out and away again, twisting the former soldier's wrist in an iron grip as he went. He both heard and felt bones snapping inside Nadeem's wrist, and the giant let out a howl of pain as he released the blade, which clattered to the floor. Letting go of Nadeem's wrist, Ethan then took a quick step forward and kicked Nadeem's knee from under him as hard as he could. Bones and cartilage crunched loudly as they broke and snapped, and as Nadeem fell to one knee with something between a pained groan and a crazed wheeze, Ethan picked up the curved blade and stepped calmly in front of him.

Nadeem sat immobile for a moment, gripping his wrist as his shoulders rose and fell with his laboured breathing. Then he raised his head slowly to look up at Ethan with what could only be described as pure venom and loathing. Even in the dim moonlight spilling in from the outside, Ethan could see that Nadeem's face, neck and shirt were covered in his own blood, and his broken nose was twisted unnaturally to one side.

'Tobias Goodwin was my friend,' said Ethan, his voice cold as ice, as his gaze bored into Nadeem's eyes. 'And you killed him for a fucking figurine.'

Nadeem stared up at Ethan, remaining expressionless for a moment before giving a small shake of the head.

'I just did as I was told,' he said with his thick accent as he winced from the pain. 'That's what soldiers do.'

'You're no damn soldier,' Ethan said icily as he looked down at the man in front of him. 'You're nothing but a paid thug, and I'm not letting you walk out of here alive.'

As Ethan spoke, Nadeem released the grip on his broken wrist, and his hand then began moving down towards his shattered ankle. With speed and agility that belied the man's huge size, he suddenly produced another smaller blade from a concealed pocket on the side of his boot. However, Ethan had seen the move coming a mile away, the wounded man in front of him telegraphing it through his shoulders, and just as Nadeem pulled out the knife, Ethan stepped forward.

With lightning speed, he brought the curved blade that had taken Tobias Goodwin's life around in an arc that sliced clean through Nadeem's exposed neck, severing both jugular veins and cleaving through his windpipe. Blood burst from the man's severed veins as a sickening, gurgling noise emanated from his throat. Suddenly wide-eyed with panic, Nadeem reached up to his throat with both hands in a vain attempt to stem the bleeding, but his hammering heart kept pumping his own blood up and out of his body.

With a wet, choking noise, Nadeem stared up at Ethan with a look of stunned surprise, as well as the realisation that this was how he was going to die. After a few seconds, a couple of brief convulsions seemed to ripple through his body as his heart stopped, and then he keeled over and thudded heavily onto the stone floor. After that, he moved no more. As Ethan stood over the dead man with a stony look on his face and his heart pounding in his chest, he finally felt a sense of closure, although he knew that there was no such thing. Not really. As much as this felt like justice, it wasn't going to bring Tobias back, and he knew from first-hand experience that taking another man's life never came entirely without paying some sort of price. He remembered all the people he had killed in the line of duty. They might have been bad guys, but they were also people, and they would sometimes haunt him in his sleep. And no doubt, Nadeem would do the same. But at least now, the man on the floor in front of him would never be able to hurt anyone again.

Suddenly, he heard movement from behind him, but as he spun around, he then breathed a sigh of relief as he spotted Sophia standing at the other end of the tunnel, still inside the throne room. Seeing him, she hurried towards him to stand by his side, but when she saw Nadeem lying dead on the floor, she covered her mouth with her hands and stared at the gory sight in front of her.

'Is he dead?' she whispered from behind the palms of her hands.

'Very.' Ethan nodded, glancing down at Nadeem's body that was lying in a rapidly expanding pool of blood. 'But there may be more outside.'

'What do we do?' she said.

'Nadeem was carrying a large bag,' said Ethan. 'I want to see what was inside.'

'Are you hurt?' said Sophia, now staring at Ethan's bloodied shirt.

'Nah.' He shrugged, jerking his head towards Nadeem's corpse. 'That's all his. Come on. I need to check something before we leave. Follow me.'

They made their way back into the throne room to where Nadeem had been taking cover behind a stone column, and there Ethan found a holdall full of weapons.

'Holy shit,' he said, kneeling next to it and reaching inside. 'They brought a whole damn arsenal with them.'

He pulled out an M72 LAW rocket launcher and looked to see that it was already loaded. The collapsible, single-use, light anti-tank weapon was a simple tube just over half a metre long with a foldable sight and a trigger mechanism underneath. Smaller and easier to transport than most RPG launchers, it was a mainstay of US infantry, including special forces, and it was more than capable of taking out an armoured vehicle. However, it could also easily bring down an aircraft such as the Firefly, and that was no doubt why Nadeem had brought it with him. For a brief moment, Ethan wondered how the hell the Egyptian had managed to get his hands on that weapon, but he knew that with enough money, there was barely a single weapon in the American arsenal that couldn't be acquired through shady intermediaries. However, he then also realised something else. The only way Nadeem and his companion could have shown up this quickly, spotted their quad bike, and then entered the mountain was with a chopper. This meant that out there, on the other side of the tunnel and the massive granite gates, was a helicopter waiting to pick up the two men once they had completed their mission.

'Sophia,' he said, seriously. 'I need you to stay here. There are bound to be more of them out there, and I don't want you in the line of fire again. Just let me handle this, OK?'

'OK.' Sophia nodded, clearly not keen on finding herself involved in another firefight. 'I'll wait here. Just... be careful, alright?'

'I will,' said Ethan, and then he grabbed the M72, slung it over his shoulder, and headed for the tunnel with his HK416 cradled in his hands. 'I'll be back soon.'

15

Sitting in the helicopter on the plateau outside, Zosar Al-Masry was now becoming impatient. He had sent Nadeem and Quasim inside the mountain more than twenty minutes ago, and ever since the two of them had relayed over the comms link that they were heading through a tunnel, he had heard nothing. Perhaps it was because the radio signal was unable to make it out through the granite, but he was becoming concerned that there was another, much less palatable explanation.

Having used his contact in the Egyptian military to track the strange aircraft to the far south of Egypt near the tri-border area of Egypt, Libya and Sudan, Al-Masry had realised that they might be heading for the Cave of Swimmers. He himself had visited that place in the past, and it had always been clear to him that it demonstrated beyond doubt the existence of water and an advanced culture in that area many thousands of years ago. However, there was no trace of the lost city he had been searching for, and so he had assumed that it was a dead end. But when the Americans had headed down there, he had decided to arrange for a helicopter gunship from the Egyptian Air Force to be commandeered and made available to him, his pilot, Nadeem, and Quasim.

Flying over the desert at night while using the military chopper's infrared long-range sensors, the pilot had been able to spot the heat signature of a small vehicle in the far distance. When it turned out to be a quad bike racing south across the desert, he knew that he had found them, and it had soon become clear that they were moving towards a specific location. All he had to do then was to tell the pilot to hang back and monitor them and then order Nadeem and Quasim to follow the thieving Americans inside the mountain, where the lost city had to be located.

The pilot had turned off the engine and was shifting nervously in his seat, but Al-Masry ignored him. His gaze was fixed on the yawning opening leading into the mountain roughly 120 metres away. He could see the slender beam of light emanating from some sort of pedestal in front of the entrance, and upon realising that it came from the orb that had been stolen from his apartment, he couldn't help but feel grudging respect for the resourcefulness of the American team. However, they had now served their purpose, and his orders to Nadeem and Quasim had been to eliminate them all.

Suddenly, there was a faint crackle in his ear, indicating that the microphone on Nadeem's headset had finally been reactivated.

'Nadeem?' he said. 'What's going on in there?'

There was more crackling and a rustling sound, and then an ice-cold voice came over the speaker in his headset.

'Your men are dead,' came Ethan's voice. 'And I'm coming for you next, you piece of shit.'

'Who the hell is this?' Al-Masry demanded reflexively, although he understood full well who he was talking to.

'I am the man who is going to end you,' came Ethan's voice,

cold as ice. 'You will never be pharaoh. You're not the future. You're history.'

Then there was a loud pop as Nadeem's mike appeared to have been tossed onto the ground, and Al-Masry winced, ripped off his headset, and immediately turned to look at his pilot.

'Take off!' he yelled. 'Now! Get out of here!'

Without hesitation, the pilot hit the button to start up the chopper's engines, and as it spun up with an ever-rising whine, the gunship's rotor blades started moving. As the downwash from the spinning rotors began pushing dust up and around the helicopter, Al-Masry glanced impatiently at the pilot, but when he returned his gaze to the outside, he saw a man emerge from the darkness in the middle of the entrance to the mountain. Holding his breath as a shiver ran down his spine, Al-Masry leaned forward and peered out at him. There was no doubt in his mind. This was Ethan Frost.

'Faster!' Al-Masry yelled at the pilot, pointing frantically out through the glass canopy.

The pilot looked up, and as he and Al-Masry watched, Ethan took several strides forward to stand outside, well clear of the opening behind him. There, he unslung a short tube from his shoulder and pulled its telescopic end out to elongate it slightly. Then he flipped up a gunsight and placed the weapon on his shoulder.

'Now, damn it!' Al-Masry yelled in a shrill voice, realising what he was looking at. 'Before he can fire.'

The pilot appeared to have come to the same conclusion because he used his left hand to yank the collective up, thereby tilting the rotor blades and creating lift almost instantly. The chopper virtually leapt up into the air, and as soon as it was in a hover some thirty metres above the plateau, the pilot switched to air-to-ground mode and selected unguided rockets on the heads-up display inside his helmet. Gritting his teeth while using the rudder pedals and the stick, he nudged the chopper to line up its sight with the target down below, and then he flipped the protective plastic cover up and away from the trigger on the control stick.

At that moment, a fierce plume of fire and smoke shot out from the back of Ethan's rocket launcher, and an instant later, the rocket streaked through the air towards the chopper. Seeing it coming straight at them, the pilot instinctively pulled back on the stick just as he himself pulled the trigger to release his own barrage. Six unguided rockets leapt off their rails outside the cockpit and began tearing through the air.

A split second later, Ethan watched as his M72 rocket slammed into the chopper's cockpit, where it exploded in a ferocious fireball that incinerated everything within several metres. Ethan knew immediately that there was no way Al-Masry and his pilot could have survived that, and almost immediately, the burning helicopter began spinning and falling towards the ground. Almost at the same time, the six-projectile rocket salvo from the chopper slammed into the cliff face some twenty metres above Ethan, and the concussion waves punched down into his back, knocking him over onto the ground amid a cloud of swirling dust and debris exploding out from the cliff face.

As the burning wreckage of the helicopter gunship slammed into the ground in an orange fireball that soon created a plume of black smoke overhead, a rockslide crashed down mere metres from Ethan, who rolled away as fast as he could, waves of rocks of all sizes cascading onto the ground and quickly sealing the entrance to the mountain. It was all over in seconds, and when Ethan scrambled to his feet and staggered through the roiling clouds of dust towards where the opening had been, a cold sweat sprang up onto his skin, and he felt an icy tightening in his chest at the thought of Sophia being trapped inside.

He clambered up onto the rocks and tried to make his way to the top in search of an opening, but it appeared as if the entire entrance was completely and permanently buried under tens of tonnes of rock. Then he suddenly heard Sophia's voice coming from somewhere inside.

'Ethan!' she called frantically. 'Please! Are you there? Can you hear me?'

'Sophia, I'm here,' he shouted, a wave of intense relief washing over him. 'Are you alright?'

'Yes,' came the reply. 'Help me get out.'

With trembling hands and rivulets of sweat pouring off him, Ethan manhandled boulder after heavy boulder away from a spot near the top left side of the rockslide where he thought he had heard Sophia's voice, and after several minutes, a small black opening appeared, and then he spotted her torchlight.

'Sophia,' he called out. 'Just hang on. I'll get you out of there.'

Twenty minutes later, Sophia had squeezed out through the hole, which was only just large enough for her slim body, and the two of them were sitting on two boulders about ten metres from the rockslide. Still panting from the effort, Ethan stared at what was left of the helicopter gunship. Small flames still licked up around its burnt-out husk as they consumed the remaining flammable materials, and apart from the warped and snapped rotor blades, it was no longer obvious that it had been a helicopter just a few minutes earlier.

'Al-Masry was in there,' said Ethan. 'Still is.'

Sophia regarded the smouldering wreck in silence for a moment before speaking.

'Well, good riddance,' she finally said, surprising herself with her strength of feeling. 'What an asshole.'

Ethan produced a wry smile, surprised by the matter-of-factness of her voice. He then took a deep breath, leaned his head back and raised his gaze to the starry sky overhead, the eastern part of which was beginning to turn pale orange as the sunrise slowly approached.

'There's Orion's belt,' he said, pointing at the three bright dots of light. 'It's amazing to think that this view has barely changed since the Akhu lived here all those thousands of years ago.'

They sat together in silence for a moment, simply taking in the awe-inspiring sight overhead.

'You know,' Sophia said as a thoughtful smile played on her lips. 'It's almost as if the ancient Egyptians, with their deep understanding of the night sky and their idea that the souls of the dead travel back to the stars where they originally came from, had worked out on some deeper level what we know today, namely the fact that we all come from stardust.'

'Stardust?' Ethan repeated, turning to glance at her.

'Yes,' she said. 'Our bodies and our brains are made of atoms forged inside stars. At the end of their lives, those stars exploded and spewed these elements out into the cosmos. And from those were formed new solar systems and planets, including all life on Earth. So, in a way, when you and I are sitting here gazing up at this spectacle and wondering about it all, then we are quite literally the universe contemplating itself.'

'Wow, that's deep.' Ethan smiled and winked. 'You almost sound like a hippie.'

'Hey, I'm just stating facts,' said Sophia with mock defensiveness. 'What I am saying is true.'

'I know,' said Ethan amiably, placing his hand gently on hers. 'I'm just messing with you.'

'Well, I think it's really amazing,' she said, returning his smile.

'So, anyway, what about this place?' said Ethan, jerking his head briefly back towards the rockslide where the entrance to the mountain had been. 'What do we do about it?'

'For starters, we tell no one,' said Sophia determinedly, seemingly clear in her mind about what needed to happen. 'No one else knows about this place right now. And I don't trust anyone at this point. Not after what happened to Tobias. Yes, I know this place is of huge historical significance, but we should keep it a secret until we've had a chance to examine it carefully. We just don't know who else might have been part of Al-Masry's plan.'

'Makes sense.' Ethan nodded, glancing towards the quad bike, which still sat waiting for them at the far end of the plateau. 'I'll try to raise Mitch on comms. The satellite connection should work now.'

'Good idea,' said Sophia with a thin smile. 'As much as I enjoyed crossing the desert on that thing, I think I'd prefer to get back to the US in comfort. Can we get rid of the wreckage of this helicopter somehow? I'd prefer it if there was no evidence of what happened here. At least not for a while.'

'I'm sure we can make that happen,' said Ethan. 'There are very few places on Earth where Frost Industries doesn't have at least some influence. I'll speak to Marcus Becker about it. We can trust him.'

'Good.' Sophia nodded. 'I have a feeling that what we found here is only the beginning. I don't think we've scratched the surface yet.'

Ethan turned his head to look at her, and then a fully formed view of a possible future suddenly entered his mind. It was something that had been percolating inside him ever since the team had left Abydos, and he pondered it for a moment, smiled to himself, and then got to his feet.

'I'll go fire up the quad bike,' he said. 'Make sure we're good to go. And then we should head back towards Cairo. I'll get Mitch on the horn and ask him to come and meet us a couple of hours north of here. Come on. Time to head home.'

EPILOGUE

Just over a week later, Ethan was standing in his apartment wearing blue jeans and a black shirt with its sleeves rolled up. In front of him were Sophia, Scarlett, Luke, and Mitch, all of them glad to see each other again, and there had been plenty of handshakes and hugs as they had arrived one by one and greeted each other. They were now each holding a cold drink that Ethan had offered to them as they stepped inside, and the mood was light and amicable, although none of them knew why he had asked them to come.

Ethan had also asked Marcus Becker to join them for the meeting, and the chief science officer was standing by his side, wearing his usual smart, light grey suit. Ethan had not asked Marcus to be a formal part of what he was about to propose, but he wanted to keep him in the loop in case the CSO's access to the latest advanced company tech might come in handy in the future.

'Right,' said Ethan, smiling as he looked at each of the four people standing in front of him in turn. 'Thanks for coming by. I asked you to come here because I wanted to tell you how glad I was that you all stepped up when I needed you. And it got me thinking. We're a great team, and I like working with you all. So maybe we should think about making it permanent.'

'What do you mean?' said Luke, who had taken the week off to fly over to the States and see his family.

'You mean getting shot at?' Mitch said with a grin.

'Well, if that's the plan, then I'm out,' said Sophia, giving Ethan a wink.

'Hey, I loved working with you guys,' said Scarlett, looking from Ethan to the other three. 'So, I think I'm open-minded.'

'Alright.' Ethan nodded. 'I'd like to show you guys something. Please follow me.'

The others exchanged glances and shrugged, and then they followed Ethan as he headed for the elevator. Once the small group was inside, Ethan hit the button for the floor below. Over the past week, he had arranged for teams of builders to convert the previously empty thirty-first floor to his specifications, and as the elevator doors opened, they all stepped out into a reception area that smelled faintly of new carpets and fresh paint. Ethan led them past the wide reception desk and through double doors in a floor-to-ceiling glass wall, beyond which was something vaguely resembling an expansive open-plan office, although it also sported several other uniquely designed areas.

Stepping into the tailored office space, he smiled to himself at what the decorators had achieved in such a short space of time. There were desks with computer monitors, one for each of them. There was a small galley kitchen with drink dispensers containing virtually any soft drink a person could want. There was a large TV mounted on the wall, currently showing a highly detailed animation of the Earth spinning slowly on its axis, and next to it, on the wall behind a piece of black silk, was a large sign that he was looking forward to revealing.

At the far end of the floor was a big gym packed with all manner of equipment, an open space for testing various drones and other electronic gadgets, and next to that was a fifty-metre-long firing range. It all looked exactly as he had hoped it would, and it was the result of the idea that had first come to him the previous week while still in Egypt. As he had sat there next to Sophia before mounting the quad bike and heading back north from the site of the ancient lost city, it had become clear to him that something extraordinary had happened over the past couple of weeks. He had ended up surrounded by a group of people who were all special. Each one of them was extremely talented in their own field, but they had all come together in the right place at the right time to achieve a remarkable result, and perhaps that was a sign that he had finally found what he had been looking for. It almost felt like it was meant to be.

'Right,' he said, turning to the small group who fanned out in a crescent shape facing him. 'You all know about me, my family, and Frost Industries, and you also know about my background in Delta. But I guess by now, it's probably clear to you that, in a lot of ways, my heart has always been with ancient history. For a long time, especially after my parents passed away, I've been trying to work out what to do with the rest of my life, and I finally think I know.'

As he smiled at them and paused, they glanced at each other and exchanged nods and expectant looks.

'I've decided to start a new company,' Ethan went on. 'I'm calling it Artefact Recovery Corp, or just ARC for short. The idea is to locate and retrieve ancient artefacts that have been lost to time. And right now, we're standing in its new headquarters. Now, before you ask, the whole point of this is not to find truck-loads of gold and make billions of dollars. This isn't about the money. The goal is simply to find and protect those artefacts that are still out there after hundreds or even thousands of years.'

Looking at their faces, Ethan could see that the idea appeared to resonate with at least a couple of them.

'So, here's why I asked you all to come today,' he continued. 'I'd like to hire all of you to come and work with me. And I mean with me, not for me. We're a great team. You all have unique skills and capabilities, and I'd really like to continue where we left off. The pay will be really good, ARC's resources will be almost unlimited, and excitement is pretty much guaranteed. So, who is with me?'

Ethan had expected at least one or two of them to hesitate or tell him they'd like to sleep on it, but that wasn't what happened.

'Fuck yeah,' Scarlett said, tossing her hair as she glanced at the others. 'Sounds great. I'm all in.'

'You know me, boss,' said Mitch with a nod and a casual shrug. 'I go where you go. It all sounds like a fun ride.'

'Absolutely,' Luke said with a grin. 'The past week has been a hoot. And this beats the crap out of babysitting a bunch of diplomats, so count me in.'

'Sophia?' Ethan said, looking at Tobias Goodwin's former research assistant. 'How about you? I know this would take you away from your work at Yale, but I couldn't think of anyone better for this than you.'

Sophia regarded him for a long moment, and then a warm smile slowly spread across her lips.

'Honestly?' she said. 'It sounds like my dream job. So, yes. I'm definitely in.'

'Great,' Ethan said, clapping his hands together.

He stepped over towards the sign that was covered by the black silk, realising then just how relieved he suddenly felt that all of them had decided to come on board his new venture.

'Now,' he said. 'I had this thing made for today, and I think it turned out pretty well. So, now that you're all onboard, I want to show you ARC's company motto, which I'm not ashamed to admit I stole from a personal hero of mine.'

He turned towards the wall and reached for a long, braided, golden string that was attached to a corner of the silk. When he pulled, the silk fell away, revealing a long, black metal sign engraved with gold capital lettering that read:

IT BELONGS IN A MUSEUM.

'Hell yeah!' Sophia grinned, glancing at the others, who variously nodded and smiled. 'I love it.'

As Ethan glanced across the faces of the rest of the team, he could see that they were all eager to come on board, and he realised that he now felt something he had not felt in a long while. The loss of his parents had been a devastating blow, but now, it was almost as if he had a new family. And, they were about to embark on a bunch of exciting adventures together. He was sure of it. The future was looking bright.

'Good,' he said, taking a moment to lock eyes with each one of them in turn. 'This is going to be something really special. Now, let's get to work.'

* * *

MORE FROM LEX FAULKNER

The next action-packed instalment in the Ethan Frost archaeological thriller series is available to order now here:
    https://mybook.to/EthanFrostBook2BackAd

ABOUT THE AUTHOR

Lex Faulkner is the Amazon bestselling author of the Andrew Sterling action-adventure series and the Ethan Frost archaeological thriller series. His novels have consistently ranked in the Top 10 Amazon Rankings for their individual categories, and they have been enjoyed by thousands of readers the world over. He lives in London.

Download your exclusive bonus content from Lex Faulkner here:

Follow Lex on social media here:

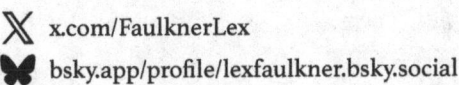

X x.com/FaulknerLex

🦋 bsky.app/profile/lexfaulkner.bsky.social

Boldwood

Boldwood Books is an award-winning fiction publishing company seeking out the best stories from around the world.

Find out more at www.boldwoodbooks.com

Join our reader community for brilliant books, competitions and offers!

Follow us
@BoldwoodBooks
@TheBoldBookClub

Sign up to our weekly deals newsletter

https://bit.ly/BoldwoodBNewsletter